The Merchant's Mark

Also by Pat McIntosh

The Harper's Quine
The Nicholas Feast

THE
MERCHANT'S MARK

Pat McIntosh

CARROLL & GRAF PUBLISHERS
New York

Carroll & Graf Publishers
An imprint of Avalon Publishing Group, Inc.
245 W. 17th Street
11th Floor
New York, NY 10011-5300
www.carrollandgraf.com

AVALON
publishing group incorporated

First published in the UK by Constable,
an imprint of Constable & Robinson Ltd 2006

First Carroll & Graf edition 2006

ISBN-13: 978-0-78671-741-5
ISBN-10: 0-7867-1741-6

Printed and bound in the EU

For Jan,
best of sisters

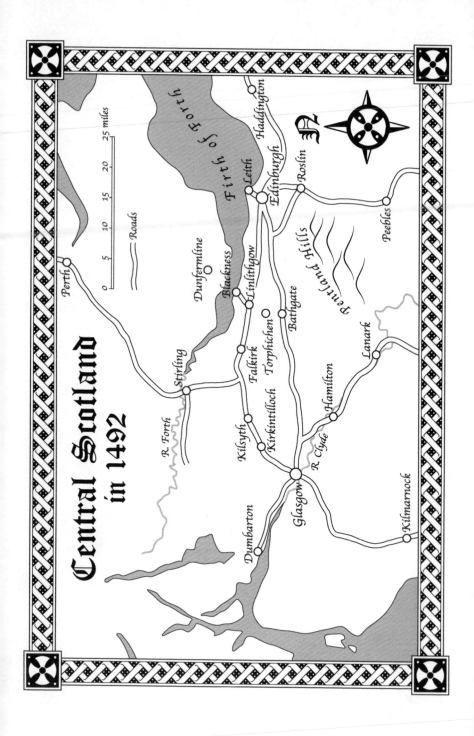

Chapter One

Gil Cunningham still maintained, after it was over, that ordering up books from the Low Countries had been a good idea.

'In spite of all that followed?' asked his sister Kate tartly.

'Oh yes,' agreed Maister Augustine Morison, merchant-burgess of Glasgow and Gil's companion in the venture. 'Though if I'd been forewarned what it would get us into, Gil, I'd maybe have thought twice that morning before I sent Andy out to look for you.'

'Indeed, aye,' said Kate, with a sardonic expression.

Gil grinned at that.

On the morning in question, his friend's steward Andy Paterson had run him to ground in the sunny courtyard of the sprawling stone house called the White Castle, not five doors up from Morison's yard, where the French master mason who owned the house was holding forth on a subject close to his heart.

'It would take little to build on a fore-stair,' he pronounced, waving a large hand at the narrow wall of the range that fronted the street. 'It is but to break a window open a little and bring the stairs down there. The door of that storeroom is not important, we may cut through from the next chamber and get access that way. What do you think, Gilbert?'

Gil Cunningham shook his head at his future father-in-law.

'There's a perfectly good newel stair in the tower,' he pointed out.

Maistre Pierre's black beard bristled. 'It has no presence! Your lodging must have an approach with some dignity.'

'I don't need that sort of dignity,' said Gil firmly, 'and I think Alys would prefer your men to be out earning money elsewhere in the burgh. I think it's an excellent idea that we should lodge here, Pierre. As you say, we'll have some privacy, Alys will be able to continue running your household, and I'll be able to set up as notary in the midst of the burgh. But we can very well go up and down a wheel stair. What accommodation is there?'

'Two good chambers,' said the mason, plunging towards the foot of the stair-tower, 'one certainly big enough to set up a great bed, and a closet near as big as mine where you may keep your books and papers. There is also a garde-robe, though I would prefer that you did not use it,' he admitted. 'We have not yet found where it drops to.'

'We can put a close-stool.' Gil, about to follow, became aware of the small bow-legged man standing patiently by the mouth of the pend, picking scraps of straw off his blue knitted cap. 'Andy? Pierre, here's Augie Morison's man. How are you, Andy?'

'It's the barrel from the Low Countries, maisters,' said Andy. He raised the cap to both men impartially, and clapped it back on his head. 'It cam hame yestreen. My maister sends to bid you come and see it broached, Maister Gil, if you will, and see what books are in it.'

'Books?' echoed the mason, swinging round sharply so that the furred hem of his red woollen gown swirled. 'What books are these?'

'It's a joint venture,' said Gil. 'Augie ordered up a batch of print through Andrew Halyburton at Middelburgh.'

'Augie Morison? I did not know you knew him. Of course, he is a Hamilton man by birth. But I thought only Thomas Webster sold books in the burgh. He's the sta-tioner, no? Maister Morison is a book-lover, I grant you, but he deals chiefly in crocks.'

'I've known him all my life. I was at school with his brother Con. We hatched this up between us to celebrate my getting my burgess ticket. Augie's idea is that we'll each take what we want from the barrel, and sell the rest to Tom Webster at cost or thereabouts, if he's willing. The market won't support two booksellers in Glasgow, more's the pity.'

'So what has Maister Halyburton sent?' wondered Maistre Pierre. 'There is some good print coming out of the Low Countries just now, but it is not easy to come by.'

'Shall we go and find out?' suggested Gil. 'The house will still be standing when we come back.'

'An excellent idea.'

Maistre Pierre set off through the pend. Andy, falling in beside Gil as he passed him, said, 'And how's yerself, Maister Gil? When's the wedding?'

'Save us, we've only now signed the contract,' said Gil. 'It's taken forever to draw up.'

'Too many lawyers at it?' said Andy knowingly. Gil laughed. 'And how's madam your mother? And Lady Kate?'

'My mother's well, thank you, and Kate's as well as can be expected. I'd forgotten you knew her,' said Gil.

'Oh, I mind her well. I'd bring our Con out to Thinacre to visit you and your brothers, and she'd be hirpling about on her two sticks. A fechtie lass, and a bonnie wee face. Does she still use the two sticks?'

'It's a pair of oxter-poles now,' said Gil, more grimly than he intended.

'So St Mungo never cam across, last nicht, then?'

'Does the whole town know?'

'I would say that, aye.' Andy paused by the yett which opened on to Maister Morison's yard, where the mason waited impatiently. 'It's one thing,' he said, peering up at Gil, 'a young lady joining the line of common pilgrims by day to ask for healing, nobody'd pay her any mind, but when the Chapter agrees to let her sleep on St Mungo's tomb, all her lone in that great kirk by night, it's to be expected that the town would take an interest.'

'She wasn't her lone,' said Gil. 'Her woman was there,

and I kept watch. And we hoped St Mungo would be present, but he never showed his favour.'

Andy threw him a sympathetic look, but leaned on one leaf of the great yett without further comment.

'Come in, maisters, come in. Ye can wait in the house, and I'll find my maister.'

The yard was quite different from the tidy courtyard of the mason's house. Behind the yett was a long open space, with a shabby timber-framed domestic range to the left, several small wooden buildings on the right, and a great barn-like structure at the far end from which there was shouting, and a desultory hammering. Barrels and boxes were stacked in lots and clusters, identified by marks in paint or chalk or branded into the wood. Several racks of pottery sagged alarmingly just beside the yett, heaps of broken crocks lay here and there, and everywhere straw blew about or lay in partly twisted ropes and pads. A cart-run of broken flagstones led the length of the yard, but the rest of the area was well-trampled earth.

Andy closed the yett and led them, picking his way, to the stone steps before the door midway along the house-range.

'In here, maisters,' he said hospitably, showing them into a chill, gloomy hall. 'There's plenty seats, you'll can wait in comfort.'

As his feet sounded on the steps outside the mason broke an uncharacteristic silence.

'I had not realized things were so bad,' he said, staring round the cold chamber.

'Nor I, till I came here to discuss this venture,' admitted Gil. 'I think trade is sound enough. He lacks the will to make things neat.'

'Or clean,' said Maistre Pierre with disapproval. 'That must be a week's ashes in the fireplace, and there is food caked on this bench. It looks bad – the business must suffer. How long since his wife died?'

'Two years, maybe.'

'So long? More than time he –'

'My mammy's deid,' said a very small voice, apparently from under their feet. The two men stared at one another, and Maistre Pierre looked about wildly. 'She dee'd two year since at Pace tide,' continued the voice.

Gil stepped round the high-backed settle which faced the empty, cheerless fireplace, and bent to peer under its seat. In the murky space, he made out two squatting children, either of a size to match the voice, with an array of broken crocks and a quantity of rags between them. They stared back at him, faces pale in the shadows.

'It's Augie's bairns,' he said.

'Bairns?' The mason came to look. 'Well, well. What are you called, my poppets?'

'Aren't your poppets,' said one in the same little voice. 'We're my da's poppets.'

'Then what are Maister Morison's poppets called?'

'Not telling.'

Gil straightened up and put a hand over his mouth to hide a grin, just as hasty feet sounded at the house door and Morison himself hurried into the room.

In appearance, Gil had always thought, Augie Morison was a middling man – of medium height, middling thin, with middling brownish hair, his face and hands neither long nor round but in-between. He had a smile of rare charm, but it was seldom seen these days, so that only his very blue eyes were at all remarkable, unless books were mentioned. Then the whole man took fire, the blue eyes sparkled, the sparse hair stood on end as he discussed authors and titles, dealers and printers, copy-houses and sources of information, until most of his colleagues on the Burgh Council found urgent business elsewhere.

'Guid day, Maister Mason! Guid day, Gil!' He flourished his round felt hat at them. 'I'm sorry not to have been here to greet you. I was called to something in the barn.'

'No trouble,' said Maistre Pierre, standing up. 'We have been attempting to make the acquaintance of your bairns here.'

'The bairns? Are they here?' Maister Morison came

round the settle to peer under it. 'Come out of that, the pair of you. Where's Mall? Why are you not with her?'

Reluctantly, the children emerged from the shadows, and were revealed as two little girls, aged perhaps six and four. The general air of neglect extended to them. Both wore bedraggled gowns of good brocade, identical in size, so that the taller child's thin bare calves showed between her sagging hem and her wood-soled shoes. She peeped at her father through the tangled curtains of her long hair, while her sister scowled at the strangers. It was evident that neither the children nor their shifts had been washed that week.

'Where's Mall?' their father asked again.

The smaller girl shrugged. 'Gone to market,' she said. 'She didny want to drag us alang.' She was clearly repeating Mall's words.

'Isn't Ursel in the kitchen?'

'No.'

'Where is she?'

The child shrugged again.

'Take your sister, Ysonde, and find Ursel. Tell her I said you were both to stay with her till Mall comes back.'

The child stared at her father in silence for a moment, then turned her head and looked at her sister, sighed, and taking her hand clopped off into the next room. After a moment they could be heard negotiating a stair.

'I'm sorry, maisters,' said Maister Morison. 'The lassie that has charge of them takes her task ower lightly.'

'Can you not hire a better?' asked the mason.

'They won't stay. Now – come look at this puncheon, and once it's broached we can sort the laidin' over a jug of something. Maister Halyburton's a good judge of print,' he added, eyes brightening. 'There was a *Blanchard and Eglantyne* last time, from Caxton's workshop ye ken, and some Italian astronomy.'

'Did you ever get *Albert on Buildings*?' asked the mason hopefully.

'Never yet, but we might be lucky,' said Morison. He led

the way out and down the steps, saying to Gil as they reached the yard, 'Andy tells me Lady Kate's petition had no success.'

'Worse than that,' said Gil.

'How so?' asked Morison, startled. 'Was she harmed by it? What came to her?'

Gil shrugged. 'Not a lot to tell. She slept the night in the arcading in the tomb, in the space that pilgrims crawl through if they're allowed the close approach.' Morison nodded, familiar with the custom. 'She woke about dawn, from a dream that she could walk like any lass in Scotland, and found there was nothing changed.'

'Oh, poor lady!' said Morison. 'Pray God the saint shows her his favour some other way.'

'Amen to that,' agreed Gil, deciding not to untangle the theology of the remark.

'She feels St Kentigern has mocked her,' said Maistre Pierre, giving the saint his other, more formal name.

'What is her trouble?' asked Maister Morison. 'I mind she went on two sticks when we were young, but I never thought to ask, at that age – is it the rheumatics, or something?'

'When she was six,' said Gil, 'and I was ten or so, there were just the three youngest ones left at home. I was at the grammar school in Hamilton, Margaret and Dorothea were with our Boyd cousins in Ayrshire, and my brothers had gone as squires to Kilmaurs. There was a fever in Hamilton –'

'Oh, I mind that. Con had it too.'

'– and the three of them took it. Their nurse always said, although they had the spots the same as the other bairns in Hamilton, it seemed like they'd some other infection as well. I wouldn't know. Anyway Tib had it light and recovered, Elsbeth died, and Kate was left with her right leg withered. It's not numb, indeed she says she feels a knock harder than in the other leg, but she has no power below the knee.'

'Poor lassie! God send her some remeid,' said Maister Morison, and crossed himself.

The mason did likewise. 'She has tried prayer and fasting and many remedies, so she tells me,' he explained, 'and made pilgrimages all over Scotland. St Mungo was her last resort. She is at her prayers just now, and my daughter with her.'

'We may yet hope for a miracle, then,' said Maister Morison, and clapped Gil awkwardly on the elbow. 'Come and look at these books. Is she still a reader? Maybe there would be one she might like.'

Across the yard, in a small shed full of racks of barrel-staves and odd timbers, the barrel had been set up on a low platform. It was not one of the huge pipes used to transport wine, which Gil was used to seeing cut in half once empty to do duty as a bath or brewing-tub. This was a small cask, less than three feet high, neatly hooped with split withies and branded with several marks, most of them cancelled by splashes of tar.

'I've the mallet and hook waiting,' said Andy from the far end of the bench as they entered the shed. 'Have you the tally, maister?'

'I have.' His master patted his chest, felt in his sleeves, and finally drew from inside his doublet a bundle of papers.

'A pipe of dishes, with the yellow glaze,' he muttered, leafing through them. 'That's what Billy and Jamesie are seeing to now, over in the barn. The sale of two sacks of wool sent by Robert Edmiston. Aye, here we are. Andrew's writing gets worse every time he sends me. To a puncheon of books, packed in Middelburgh and laid in Thomas Tod's ship. Item, cost of the puncheon, item, *pynor* fee and *schout* hire –'

'That's Low German,' Andy commented. 'Porter fee and boat hire. A *schout*'s one of their funny wee boats for getting the barrels out to the ship.'

'I've been to the Low Countries,' Gil said.

'Maister,' said Andy thoughtfully, lifting mallet and

hook from the pouch of his leather apron, 'did ye say this was laid in Thomas Tod's ship?'

'Indeed it was. I saw it hoisted out myself, while you were in Linlithgow at Riddoch's yard.'

'Because it's odd, in that case,' Andy continued, 'that there's no mark of Tod's on the wood.' He tapped with the iron hook. 'There's William Peterson's shipmark, and James Maikison, and a couple more under the tar here, and a crop o' merchant marks. There's ours. But I don't see Tod's mark.'

'This is a well-travelled barrel,' remarked the mason.

'Andy,' said Maister Morison, 'do that again, man.'

'Do what?'

'Hit the barrel. It didn't sound –'

Andy rapped the head of the barrel with the hook, and then one of the staves, and cocked his head at the resulting dull thud.

'It's no right, is it?' he agreed. He rocked the barrel, his ear close to the smooth tar-splashed planks of its head.

'You think it is the wrong barrel?' asked the mason in disappointed tones. 'But it has your mark.'

'Aye, it does.' Maister Morison went to the door and opened it wider, to let in more light. 'I'm wondering . . .'

'You're wondering if it's an old mark,' Andy prompted him.

'One never cancelled, you mean?' asked Gil. 'Does that happen?'

'Oh, it happens,' said Morison, nodding earnestly.

'So whose barrel is it?' demanded the mason. 'I suppose one of these other marks must be the right one, but I do not know them. And what is in it?'

'It's gey heavy,' said Andy, 'whatever's in it.'

'Books weigh heavy for their size,' said Gil.

'It must be the right barrel!' said Morison. 'I convoyed this shipment from Blackness myself. There was only the one puncheon. The rest was just the two big pipes out of Maikison's ship. They're in the barn now, and the men unpacking them. Go on, Andy, lift the head out of it.'

15

Andy, wielding mallet and hook expertly, began coaxing the end hoop upward off the top of the staves. It was slow work, tapping round the hoop and round again, but by the third circuit it could be seen that the withy was rising up the curve of the stave.

Maistre Pierre, peering closely at the rocking barrel, exclaimed something, at the same moment as Andy, setting mallet and hook for another blow, snatched his hands away, wiping his left hand on his doublet.

'What is it?' demanded Morison.

'Wet,' said Andy. 'My hand's wet.'

'Wet? How can it be wet? The books will be spoiled!'

'Your books canny be in here, maister,' said Andy. 'Look at it. That's a stout wet-coopered oak barrel, and the outside's dry as a tinker's throat. The wet must be inside, and right to the top. It's full of something.'

'Wine?' said the mason hopefully. He touched the trickling damp patch where two staves met, and sniffed his fingers. 'No, not wine, nor vinegar.' He tasted cautiously. 'Salt. It is brine.'

'Brine?' said Gil.

'Herrings, maybe,' said Morison. 'I never ordered anything in brine. And where are my books? I must have got the wrong barrel somehow.'

'Not herring,' said the mason, sniffing his fingers again.

'We'll have to open it now,' Andy said, 'and top up the brine, or it'll spoil, whatever it is. Will I carry on, maister?'

'Aye, carry on.'

Andy, tucking the hook in his apron, produced another implement and began screwing it into the tarry planks of the barrel head. When it was fixed to his satisfaction, he stepped on to the platform to get a better leverage, rocking and twisting expertly.

'It's like drawing a cork,' said the mason, watching him.

'It is,' said Andy. 'Could one of you steady the barrel, maisters?'

Maistre Pierre stepped forward and gripped the puncheon between his big hands. Andy, with a final heave, dragged the head from its lodging and staggered back-wards. The mason peered into the depths of liquid in the cask.

'It is mostly brine,' he reported, 'but I think there is something at the bottom.'

'Use this,' said Andy, handing him the metal hook.

Gil glanced across at Augie Morison, who was watching with a kind of puzzled dismay as Maistre Pierre trawled the puncheon with the barrel-hook. Beyond him there was movement, and Gil realized that the two little girls were staring round the door.

'Augie,' he said, and nodded towards them.

Morison turned, and tut-tutted in exasperation. 'I told you to stay with Ursel,' he said, going to the door.

'Mall's back,' said the younger one, 'so Ursel sent us away.'

'Well, go and stay with Mall now,' said Morison, making shooing motions. 'Get away, the pair of you! Take your sister to Mall and tell her I said you were both to stay with her.'

They clopped away on their wooden shoes, the younger one glancing back just before they vanished out of Gil's sight to see if her father was watching her. Morison stood at the door a little longer, apparently making sure he was obeyed, and returned to the group round the barrel.

'What is it, then?' he asked.

'A sheep's head, maybe.'

'A sheep's *head*?' Morison repeated.

'Maybe.' The mason showed hairs caught between the tines of the barrel-hook. 'I try again.' He rolled back his sleeve and stabbed the depths once more. 'Ah!'

Something came up out of the salt water and hung briefly suspended from the barrel-hook. They had a glimpse of a tangle of dark hair which floated and clung, then as the mason's free hand collided with Andy's the object evaded both of them and slid back into the dark.

'That was never a sheep's heid,' said Andy grimly.

'Then what?' said Morison, with a dawning horror.

17

Maistre Pierre exchanged a glance with Gil, crossed himself, rolled his sleeve back further, and reached into the puncheon.

'Ah, *mon Dieu, oui*,' he said as his hand made contact. 'Most certainly it is not a sheep. It's a man.'

He hauled it out with a firm grasp of the dark wet hair, and Augie Morison whimpered as the pale brow, the half-shut eyes and slack jaw emerged to view, brine pouring from between the bloodless lips.

'A man's head,' said Gil.

Maistre Pierre set the thing on the platform, where the water ran from its hair in a spreading pool. He drew out his beads, crossed himself again, and began a familiar quiet muttering.

'It was . . .' Morison began, his eyes starting. He pointed from the head to the barrel and then at the oblivious mason. 'It was in. And you. You tasted . . .'

He turned and stumbled out of the hut, and they heard him vomiting in the yard.

'Anyone you know?' said Gil to Andy over the mason's pattering prayers.

The small man, staring morosely at the head, said, 'Hard to say. Most folk I know's taller than that.'

'We need light,' said Gil, grimacing at this, 'but if we take it into the yard the bairns might see.'

'Aye,' said Andy. 'It wouldny trouble that Ysonde, but if Wynliane takes one of her screaming fits we'll have none of us any sleep the night. I'll fetch a light, Maister Gil, if you'll have a care to my maister? He'd aye a weak stomach, but he's no been himself since the mistress went,' he confided. 'Bad enough when the bairns have frichtsome dreams, without him starting and all.'

Gil followed him into the yard, where he set off for the barn, remarking to his master in passing, 'First barrel I've ever seen wi three heads, maister. You canny say Andrew Halyburton doesny give good value.'

Morison, leaning pallidly on a huge rack of tin-glazed

pots, grimaced faintly and wiped his brow with the back of his hand.

'Forgive me, Gil,' he said. 'I was just stamagasted. St Peter's bones, what a thing.'

'Aye, he's not a bonnie sight,' agreed Gil. 'Augie, we'll need to look at it closer. Andy's gone for a light. And you'll need to decide what's to be done with it.'

'Me decide?' said Morison helplessly. 'But it's not mine!'

'It was somebody's. And it's in your yard.'

'But what needs done?'

'He deserves a name, if it can be found,' said Gil, 'and his kin told. Serjeant Anderson's the man to see to that, since it's an unknown body turned up in the burgh. He'll call an inquest.'

'Not a body,' said Morison, and shivered. 'Just the head. Christ preserve us, I'm as bad as Andy. Aye, we'd best send to the serjeant. Do you suppose he'll want to keep it? I don't want it in the yard, Gil. It's one thing if someone dies in the house, you lay them out and shroud them decently, but that – I don't want the bairns to see.'

'Then send one of the men to the serjeant now.'

Morison shivered again, but nodded and shouted a couple of names at the barn. Some of the banging stopped, and a lean-faced, dark-haired head appeared round the door. Morison flinched visibly, but the gangling body followed almost immediately.

'Aye, maister?' said its owner. 'These yellow dishes has travelled fine. We've got the most of them out not even chipped.'

'Leave that a wee while, Jamesie,' said his master, 'and step down to the Tolbooth for me. Bid Serjeant Anderson bring one of the constables and come here. I need him to look at something.'

Jamesie nodded, and set off obediently, but another man, stocky and sandy-haired, appeared in the doorway in his place.

'Bit trouble, maister?' he asked casually.

'None of your mind, Billy Walker,' growled Andy, passing him with a lantern and a bundle of rags. Billy thumbed his nose at the smaller man's retreating back.

'Just go back to your task, Billy,' said Morison, ignoring this.

'Oh, aye, I'm away.' Billy hitched up his sagging hose and turned away. 'Trouble wi this place,' he muttered as he retreated into the shadows. 'A'body knows everything, except the folk that does the work.'

'I saw,' said a small familiar voice. The two children emerged from beyond the rack of yellow pots, each carrying an armful of broken crocks. 'I saw you spewing, Da.'

Seen by daylight, the younger girl had a pinched, sharp little face, and a penetrating grey scowl. The taller one, who seemed never to speak, had inherited her father's blue eyes, but gazed timidly at the stranger from behind her fall of dust-coloured hair. In both girls Gil recognized a strong likeness to their father and uncle as children.

'Not to stare!' ordered the scowling child. 'Wynliane doesny want you to stare!'

'Ysonde, where are your manners?' said her father sternly.

She shrugged. 'Don't know.'

He tightened his lips and stared at her a moment, then said, 'Go to Mall, as I bade you. Go now, Ysonde,' he added, as she opened her mouth to argue, 'before Da gets angry. Take your sister, and stay with Mall until dinnertime.'

Ysonde took a deep breath and snorted down her nose, tossed her head at her father, and clopped away across the yard towards the stone-built kitchen at the end of the domestic range, her sister drifting after her.

'I don't know. Maybe I should beat them,' said Morison doubtfully as they went.

'I'm no judge,' said Gil, 'but I think you need a better nurse for them.'

Maistre Pierre had put his beads away and was peering at

the unpleasant relic in the light from the lantern, which Andy had set down beside the pool of water.

'Did you tell the men, Andy?' asked his master from behind Gil.

'I did not. Time enough to let the word out when we canny keep it in. I fetched some rags and all, we can dry him off a bit, make him more lifelike.'

Morison threw one glance at the loose-mouthed leering face in the lantern-light and turned away, but Gil got down on one knee and looked closely as Andy performed his charitable task.

'Can we tell how long he's been in there?' he asked.

'When he died, you mean?' said the mason. 'No, I would say not. The brine, you see, would preserve all as it was at death. If he did stiffen, it has long since worn off, the jaw is quite slack –'

'I'll wait for the serjeant,' said Morison. 'Out in the yard.'

'You do that, Augie,' said Gil. 'You can keep the bairns away, if needs be.'

'Was he heidit?' Andy asked, smoothing the short wet hair.

'Is that how he died, you mean? I cannot be sure, but I think not. There is very little blood present. I think by that he was already dead, maybe from a smaller wound to the body, before his head was cut off. There is a bruise below his eye, but that would not have killed him.'

'It's more than a bruise,' said Andy, moving the lantern. 'Someone's blued his ee for him, and it's had time to fade.'

'Andy,' said Gil sharply. 'Hold the light closer.'

'What is it?' said the mason. 'Do you know him, after all?'

'I fear I do,' said Gil. 'What colour are his eyes, would you say?'

'Blue,' said Andy.

'Brown,' said the mason at the same moment.

'One blue, one brown,' said Gil from directly in front of

the blank gaze. 'Pierre, do you mind that musician that was in the burgh in May? He talked like a Leith man, but he called himself Balthasar of Liège, if I remember. He'd one blue eye and one brown like this.'

'There cannot be many such in Scotland,' said the mason doubtfully. 'I thought that man wore his hair longer. And an earring.'

'Hair can be cut.'

'This one's worn an earring at some time,' said Andy, feeling at the earlobe nearest him. 'Or is it two?'

'This is a fighting man's style of barbering,' pursued the mason, 'fit to go under a helm of some sort. I can think of reasons to kill a travelling lutenist, but why, having done so, should someone cut off his head and put it in a barrel? And that man was no fighter, I should have said.'

'Besides, his music wasn't that bad. What worries me,' said Gil, 'is when this was exchanged for our barrel of books. And where are the books?'

A small commotion at the yett proclaimed the arrival of Serjeant Anderson. His voice carried without effort across the yard.

'Aye, Maister Morison. Jamesie here says you want me.' Morison mumbled something. 'What, in the shed? Show us, then, maister.'

He proceeded into the shed, large and red-faced, thumbs tucked in the expansive belt of his official blue gown, and came to an abrupt halt as his gaze fell on the head, so that his constable collided with his broad back.

'Look where you're going, Tammas,' he said in annoyance. 'Well, well. Good day to ye, Maister Cunningham, Maister Mason. And what have you been doing here? '

The constable, catching sight of the relic over his shoulder, shut his eyes and grimaced. Behind him, the man Jamesie stood in the open doorway and stared, then suddenly turned and hurried off towards the barn.

'This was in that barrel,' said Gil.

'Instead of some books,' supplied Morison from the doorway, 'which is what we were expecting.'

'Books?' said the serjeant. 'So instead of one worthless shipment you got another, hey?' He laughed at his own humour, and bent to peer into the leering face. 'And where did the barrel come from, Maister Morison? Once we ken that we'll ken who he is, I've no doubt.'

'I don't know,' said Morison helplessly. 'I fetched the whole shipment from Linlithgow myself. It came across from Middelburgh in Thomas Tod's ship, and I saw it unloaded at Blackness shore and set on the carts. Then I convoyed it to Glasgow.'

'Ah-hah,' said the serjeant. 'And does any of you gentles recognize him?'

'I wondered if it might be Balthasar of Liège,' said Gil. 'The lutenist, you mind?'

'Oh, him. No, he left the burgh in May. I wouldny say it was him.' The serjeant considered the head. 'Would you just call your men, maister? I'll have a word with them too while I'm here.'

'I don't want –' began Morison, and got a sharp look. 'I don't want the bairns to see this.'

'Two wee lassies, isn't it no? No a sight for wee lassies,' agreed the serjeant weightily. 'So if you'll call your men, then I can get this out of your way.'

'I'll get them,' said Andy. He stepped to the door, but paused there, saying with disapproval, 'Oh, you're all here, are ye? Well, ye might as well come in. The law wants ye.'

He stood aside, and half a dozen men pushed into the shed, eyes agog for a sight of the horrors Jamesie had obviously described to them.

'St Peter's bones!' said someone. 'Did that come back on the cart, Billy?'

'How would I ken?' retorted Billy. 'I never opened any barrels!'

Slightly to Gil's surprise, the serjeant established quickly and without argument which of the men had not been near the cart or the puncheon since it came into the yard. These two he dismissed, and they went reluctantly, with sidelong glances at the head on its dais, and hovered out in the yard near the door.

'Now you, William Soutar,' the serjeant continued. 'What do you know?'

William, it seemed, had helped Andy take the puncheon off the cart this morning.

'Which we needed to do, maister,' he continued, 'since the other two big pipes needed to come off and all, and this wee one was just at the tail. But it wasny open, serjeant, for I'd have noticed that.'

'And it was this barrel?'

'Oh, aye, it was this barrel. I mind the marks on it.'

'You're certain, are you?' the serjeant pressed.

'Aye, I'm certain!' retorted William. 'I've marked enough barrels mysel, maister.'

'Aye, right,' said the serjeant, his tone combining acceptance and scepticism. 'And then what did you do?'

'Went back to my work, and the laddie helped Andy handle it over here to the shed.'

'And had you seen it afore that?'

'Just when it came into the yard last evening, serjeant. On the cart. Which it wasn't me drove it, for I was left here at the yard while Andy and Billy and Jamesie went with the maister.'

'And you, John? Had you seen it afore?'

'No, serjeant,' said the laddie, a scrawny fourteen-year-old with a strong resemblance to Andy. 'No till my uncle bid me help him with it.'

'Right,' said the serjeant, tucking his thumbs into his belt. 'Now, Blackness, I think ye said, Maister Morison?' Morison nodded, still standing by the door where he need not look at the head. 'Who was it put the barrel on the cart? Was it you, Billy Walker? Our Mall tells me you're carter here.'

'Aye, it was,' agreed Billy. He came forward reluctantly when the serjeant bade him, and eyed the head, biting his lip.

'And it's the same barrel?'

'There was only the one this size. I canny see that we'd have got it by mistake.'

Anderson grunted, but forbore to press him on this point. 'And does any of you ken who he might be?'

There was a silence, and then a general shaking of heads.

'Maybe he's from the Low Countries,' said Billy suddenly. 'Aye, that's a good thought. Wherever Tod's shipment was from.'

'Right,' said the serjeant again. 'Well, Maister Morison, if ye've a cloth handy we can wrap it in, Tammas here can carry it back to the Tolbooth –' Gil was aware of a faint sigh from the constable – 'and I'll send to the Provost. I've no doubt he'll tak an inquest the morn, find out if any in the burgh kens who he might be, then you can get the Greyfriars to bury him decent. One thing, Maister Morison, you'll can save on the cost of the grave-digging.'

'I'll get a poke,' said Andy.

'There should be some at the back of the shed here,' said Morison. Andy ferreted briefly in a corner behind one of the racks of timber, and drew a stout linen sack out from a bundle of folded cloths. 'Don't trouble to return it, serjeant.'

'I won't,' said Serjeant Anderson. He took the sack, turned towards the head, and turned back. 'Just one wee favour, maisters, and you, Andy Paterson, Billy. Would you be good enough to touch him for me?'

'Touch him?' repeated Morison in horror. 'Why? What for?'

'So I can see you touch him,' said the serjeant.

'Andy dried him off,' said Gil. He stepped forward and put his hand on the dark hair. It was beginning to curl, but felt slightly sticky under his fingers. Probably the salt, he reflected, and gave way to Maistre Pierre, who made a cross on the clammy forehead and muttered something.

'Christ save you, whoever you are,' said Andy, and touched one cheek. Billy, visibly gritting his teeth, clapped a hand on the curling crown and retreated, wiping his fingers on his jerkin. He looked round for his colleagues, found them all out in the yard, and followed them hastily.

'Maister Morison?'

'Must I?' said Morison.

Gil, seeing the serjeant's eyes narrow, said, 'Come, Augie, it's not so bad. He can't hurt you. Shut your eyes and I'll put your hand on his hair.'

'That's worse,' said Morison, shuddering, but when Gil took his elbow he allowed himself to be led forward, head averted, biting his lip. When his hand was set on the salt hair he shuddered again, but found the courage to grope about enough to sign the forehead as the mason had done. As he stepped back Gil saw tears glittering below his closed eyelids. What ails him? Gil wondered. He's an educated man, he can hardly expect the dead to accuse him by a show of blood as the superstitious believe, so what is so fearsome here?

'Well,' said the serjeant, with a faint note of disappointment in his voice, 'we'd best get this out of your way, maisters. Here, Tammas, put it in the sack. I suppose there's nothing left in the barrel? No books? None of his gear?'

'See for yourself, serjeant,' said Andy, indicating the puncheon. Serjeant Anderson peered into its depths, and grunted.

'Waste of good brine,' he commented. 'I suppose you'll no want to use it again. Is that you ready, Tammas? We'll away, then. I'll send to let you know what time the inquest's to be, Maister Morison. You'll have to compear, you ken that, and all your men that's in the barn yonder. And you, maisters.'

'Serjeant,' said Gil, 'if I can trace Balthasar the lutenist, we'll know it's not him. Do you want to ask about the burgh if anyone knows where he might be, or will I do it?'

'Oh, it's no Balthasar,' said the serjeant. 'It's some shore porter from the Low Countries as your man says, I'll wager, got on the wrong side of a packer and got his head

26

in his hands to play with. No, Maister Cunningham, I canny be aye running about asking questions. I've a burgh to watch and ward. If you want to take up your time that way, go right on and do it.'

He set off, nodding to Morison as he passed him at the doorway. His constable trailed after him holding the sack at arm's length. It was already dripping slightly. Andy bustled out and accompanied the two men to the gate, nodding and gesturing. Gil, watching, caught the words *Weak stomach*, and the serjeant's *Aye, that would explain it.*

'Is there truly nothing more in there?' wondered the mason, still in the shed leaning over the barrel.

'It's no empty,' said Andy, returning. 'I've set Billy and them to go down the back and wash the carts, maister.' He stepped up on to the platform and rocked the barrel so that the liquid swirled and splashed. They all heard something move against the inside of the staves. 'Mind your feet.'

Gil moved hastily out of the way as brine splashed on to the earth floor. Andy let most of it run off, then held up the lantern and reached into the bottom of the puncheon.

'A scrip of some kind,' he said. 'By here, it's heavy. Could it be his?'

'Should we send after the serjeant?' said Morison. 'It may tell us who the man is.'

'Is that all?' asked the mason.

Andy set the bag down on the platform with a thump and swirled the dregs of brine again. 'See for yourself, maisters.'

'It isn't a scrip,' said Gil, dragging it closer. 'It's a saddle-bag, and a well-made one. This has been good leather before it went in the brine. What is in it?'

He turned the bag over to wrestle with the buckle, and frowned as he heard a faint chink and scrape of metal from inside it.

'Coin?' he said. Finally unfastening the buckle, he lifted back the flap and drew out a dripping canvas purse the size of the mason's fist, and then another. Below them was a roll of sodden velvet. Maistre Pierre whistled.

'Coin,' he agreed. 'How much?'

'A lot.'

'Near a thousand merks in each of those, I would guess,' said Morison authoritatively, 'depending what coin it's in, of course. Forbye what's in the roll of cloth.'

Gil weighed the first purse in his hand. 'As you said, Andy, this is heavy. If I had this weight in my saddlebag, I'd make sure there was the same again in the other, though I suppose it needn't all be coin. Are you sure there's no more in the barrel?'

'We can take it out into the day,' Andy said. 'I'm certain.'

'There are a few shavings of wood,' said Maistre Pierre, exhibiting the pale soggy curls in the palm of his hand. Gil looked at him, then drew the lantern closer to the saddlebag and looked at the long strap which was intended to fasten it to the saddle.

'This has been unbuckled, rather than cut,' he said. 'You can see where the leather has stretched with the weight of the coin in the bag.'

'Does that tell us anything?' said Morison blankly.

Gil shrugged. 'No urgency about the deed, I suppose.'

'I still think it should go to the serjeant,' protested Morison.

'Yes,' said Maistre Pierre, 'but did our friend here steal this bag, or was the other stolen from him, and whose is the treasure?'

'I can hazard a guess at that,' said Gil. He unfolded the wet velvet with care. 'Aye, as I thought. Look at these.'

Pinned to the cloth, an array of elaborate goldsmith work gleamed in the lantern-light.

'*Mon Dieu!*' said the mason. 'What are these? Look at those rubies!'

'The sapphires are better,' said Morison, 'at least by this light. St Peter's bones, Gil, what have we got into here?'

'My mother had a unicorn jewel like that,' said Gil, touching one of them, 'save that hers was enamel. It was her badge of service when she was in the Queen's household. I reckon these are from the royal treasury.'

28

'D'ye mean he'd robbed Edinburgh or Stirling Castle?' said Andy.

'No. It's part of James Third's missing treasure,' said Morison with sudden confidence.

'I think you're right, Augie,' said Gil. 'And if it is, I think we should leave the serjeant out of it. This should go straight to the Provost.'

Chapter Two

'Mind you, I thought James Third's treasure had all been found,' said Maister Morison.

'Not all,' said Canon Cunningham.

They were in the garden of the stone house in Rotten-row, where Gil and his companions had called on their way to the Archbishop's castle. They had found the Official admiring a bed of brightly coloured pinks before he returned to his chamber above the Consistory Court, in the south-west tower of St Mungo's. He had listened atten-tively to Gil's account of the morning, ignoring the inter-ruptions from Maistre Pierre and Augie Morison, and inspected the contents of the still-wet saddlebag with interest.

'Robert Lyle spent most of two weeks carping on about it,' he continued, 'when the Lords of the Articles met in February there to approve the Treasurer's accounts.'

'Lord Lyle?' said Maistre Pierre quickly. 'He is one of the Auditors, no? And a friend to the old King, if I recall. One might suppose he had some idea of how much should still remain.'

'Aye,' agreed Canon Cunningham. 'I think we all assumed he was simply attacking Treasurer Knollys, and that what was recoverable was now recovered, and any still at large was spent long since. In the end we issued orders to the Sheriffs to hold secret enquiries about it, only to silence him so he would audit the accounts. In the face of a sum of this size together with these jewels, which are certainly from the King's own treasury, there can be no doubt that we were wrong and Robert was right.'

'Knollys,' said Maistre Pierre thoughtfully. 'This is the man who is also Preceptor of the Knights of St John at Torphichen –' he pronounced the name with some care – 'although he has never been either cleric or knight, or been at Rhodes to be confirmed in the post.'

'The same,' agreed Canon Cunningham without expression. 'He sits in Parliament as Lord St Johns. He is a most successful merchant.'

Morison looked from one to the other, baffled by this exchange.

'But why was all the money in a barrel with the head of an unknown man?' he asked. 'Where has it been these four years?'

'Agreed,' said Maistre Pierre. 'I do not think that poor soul had been in salt for so long, I would say no more than a few days, and nor has the coin, so the treasure must have been elsewhere in the meantime.'

'Good questions,' said David Cunningham. He clasped his hands behind his back under his rusty black gown, and paced away from them along the gravel path. Maister Morison, crushing a sprig of lavender between his fingers, watched him anxiously. Gil bent to rub the ears of the young hound Socrates, who had recovered from his initial paroxysms of welcome and was now sitting with his head firmly thrust against Gil's knee.

'Aye, good questions,' repeated the Official, turning at the far end of his traverse. 'However, since the head and the treasure both were found in the burgh, it becomes a burgh matter and it is out of my jurisdiction.'

'No harm in speculating,' Gil commented.

His uncle threw him a sharp look, and continued, pacing back towards them, 'If ye'd been a couple of hours sooner, the Provost could have sent it to Stirling with an armed escort. My lord of Angus was in Glasgow, with the Chancellor and Andrew Forman, lying at the castle overnight.

They left before Terce. Something about reporting a gathering in Ayrshire.'

'What, is Hugh Montgomery causing trouble?' said Gil.

'So it seems. Armed encounter at Irvine betwixt Cunninghams and Montgomerys.'

'If the Montgomery will not listen to the Earl of Angus,' said Maistre Pierre, 'he will surely listen to the King.'

'I think that was Angus's idea.'

'But until it's settled,' said Gil uneasily, 'I had better not go alone into Ayrshire. That's awkward – I want to go to Kilmarnock.'

'I would agree,' said his uncle severely. 'Forbye you will be required when the Provost takes an inquest into the matter. You may have an income now, Gilbert, but no need use it to pay the fines for non-compearance before the Archbishop's justice.'

'The inquest on the head is for this afternoon,' said the mason. 'The bellman was crying it as we came up the town just now.'

The Official looked down at the bright majolica dish lying on the grass, in which the saddlebag still wept salt tears, and nudged it with one well-shod foot.

'As for this,' he said, 'there may well be a reward for the finding. Maister Morison deserves some compensation.'

'Aye, for our books,' said Morison, reminded of his loss.

'You could take an inventory,' Canon Cunningham remarked, 'and count the coin. No doubt Sir Thomas would find it helpful.'

'I can do that, I suppose,' said Morison reluctantly.

'Come, come, maister,' said the mason. 'The money does not smell. We can count it together, and my son-in-law can write down the jewels.' He lifted the majolica dish on to the bench and sat down beside it.

'I must away back up to St Mungo's,' said David Cunningham with some regret. 'I believe I have a case waiting, and two sets of witnesses. What poor Fleming will have done wi them by now I canny think.' He raised his hand, blessed Gil in particular and the company in general, stooped to pat Socrates and strode away under the archway which led to the kitchen-yard and the gate to the street. Just on the other side of the archway he checked, and they heard him say, 'Aye, Kate. And Alys. Gilbert's in the garden, with a wee pickle treasure.'

He strode on and out of sight, and Gil jumped to his feet, dislodging the dog, as the mason's daughter came into the garden, a slender girl in a blue linen gown, her honey-coloured hair loose down her back. Her gaze found his immediately, and she smiled.

'Treasure?' She came to Gil's outstretched arm, and curtsied to her father's fellow burgess. 'Good day, Maister Morison. What treasure is this?'

Morison, standing to greet her, opened his mouth to reply, and looked beyond her to the archway. He stopped, staring open-mouthed. Gil turned his head, and saw only his sister Kate coming through the archway on her two crutches, her gigantic waiting-woman Babb at her back.

'Kate,' he said. 'You remember Augie Morison?'

'I do,' she said, swinging forward, the crutches crunching on the gravel. 'Good day, maister.'

'Lady Kate,' said Morison, stammering slightly. He hurried forward, holding his hand out, and suddenly realized it was full of coins. Turning to put them back in the majolica dish, he came forward again but was too late to assist her to a seat in the arbour by the wall.

'I'll do here, Babb,' she said, settling her tawny wool skirts about her. 'You go and sit with Maggie in the kitchen, I'll send when I need you.'

'Aye,' said Babb grimly. 'And don't be too long about sending, my doo.'

She propped the crutches against the wall, near to her mistress's hand, and strode off, ducking under the archway. Morison cleared his throat and said, 'I'm right sorry to see you like this, Lady Kate.'

'Not as sorry as I am to be like it,' said Kate.

'I prayed for you yestreen.'

Kate's chin went up. 'You never thought there'd be a miracle, did you?' she said challengingly.

'*Une tête*?' said Alys from beside her father. 'A head? In a barrel?'

Gil grimaced. Kate looked from one to another of them, and then at the dish of coins on the bench, and raised her eyebrows.

'It's mine,' said Morison awkwardly.

'What, the head?' said Kate, and he blushed.

'Well, it's not mine, it ought to ha been mine. The fill of the barrel, I mean.' He took a deep breath and began again, with a more coherent explanation of the circumstances. The two girls heard him out, Alys sorting coins as she listened.

'Why should you hand it to the Provost,' asked Kate when he had finished, 'and have him take the credit for finding it?'

'He's the Archbishop's depute in the burgh,' Gil pointed out. 'It must all be done with due process.'

'Hah!' she said, but Alys looked up from a stack of coins and said seriously:

'And who is the dead man? He cannot be a shore-porter from the Low Countries, can he, Gil? The serjeant must be wrong.'

'Well, he might, but I don't see how he can have died there,' Gil agreed. 'Unless the King's treasure has been out of the country and back again. We need to find out where Balthasar of Liège has gone.'

'Oh, is that why you wish to go to Kilmarnock?' said Maistre Pierre. 'To trace the musician? It is now three months ago he went there. He has surely moved on by now.'

'The McIans will know,' said Alys. 'But I think they are in Stirling.'

'The McIans?' said Morison. 'Is that that harper you were telling me about? And you're tutor to his son, you said.' Gil nodded. 'Is he not here in Glasgow?'

'He and his sister came by the house last week,' said

Alys, 'to see the bairn, and to say they were leaving the burgh for a time. They have invitations to play at one house and another, and I am sure he said they would be in Stirling by now. You could ask for them there, Gil, at least.'

'These jewels are bonnie,' said Kate. Gil looked round, and discovered that Morison had unrolled the wet velvet on the arbour bench beside her. 'Look at the goldsmith work. And is that a sapphire? What a colour it is!'

Morison mumbled something. She looked sharply at him, and said as if recalling her manners, 'I was sorry to hear of Agnes, maister. Two years past, isn't it?' He nodded, and opened his mouth, but she went on speaking. 'And you've – two bairns, I heard. How old are they?'

'Wynliane is near seven, and Ysonde is four,' said their father.

She stared at him in disbelief. '*What* are their names? Wynliane – Ysonde! Augie Morison, only you could have named two bairns like that.'

'They're bonnie names,' he protested, reddening. 'Out of the romances.'

'Oh, I ken that. *Greysteil* and *Sir Tristram*. Well, if they hope for either to come and carry them off, they'll grow old hoping,' said Kate acidly. 'There are no heroes left in Scotland, maister. If you've a set of tablets on you we can make a list of these jewels, while my good-sister counts the coin.'

Sir Thomas Stewart of Minto, the Archbishop's civil depute in Glasgow, Bailie of the Regality and Provost of the burgh, small, neat and balding in good murrey velvet furred with marten, stood on the fore-stair of his lodging in the castle, surveyed the gathering in the outer yard and scowled.

'Serjeant, ye've rounded up the scaff and raff of the town again,' he said. 'I'll likely need my own men to keep the peace before this is over. Walter,' he said to his clerk, 'gang to Andro and bid him bring five-six of the men, just to keep an eye on things.'

'It's none of my doing if the better sort never answers the bellman,' said the serjeant in righteous indignation as the clerk slipped away, his pen-case and inkhorn rattling at his waist. 'I've a burgh to watch and ward, sir, I've no time to go calling on each man by name for a case like this.'

'Aye, well,' said Sir Thomas irritably. 'Silence them, then, man.' He glanced at Gil and his companions, standing nearest him. 'These gentlemen at least have better matters to attend to than all this giff-gaff. We'll get done wi and get about our day.'

He glowered at the source of the loudest conversation and comment, the group around the head, which was exhibited on a trestle in the centre of the yard and guarded by the same reluctant constable and a colleague. The barrel stood on the ground beside the trestle, and had come in for some attention itself; one tavern-keeper from the Gallow-gait had already offered to purchase it from Maister Morison when all was done. Gil recognized Morison's carter, the stocky, sandy-haired Billy, in the thick of the group, his blue bonnet wagging as he talked to those interested. What was he telling them? wondered Gil.

The serjeant, shouldering the burgh mace, stepped up on to the mounting block and shouted for silence, his voice carrying without effort across the yard. The clerk returned, half a dozen armed men tramped after him, and the proceedings began. Gil, used to the Scottish legal process, was not surprised by the length of time it took to select fifteen respectable men to form an assize, but as the sixth name was agreed upon, he could feel Maistre Pierre becoming restive at his side.

'Is it always like this?' the mason asked as someone objected to the proposed seventh juror on the grounds of infamy, since his wife was well known to serve ale in short measure.

'We're getting on well,' said Morison at Gil's other side.

'Gil, tell me more of last night. What did they do for your sister, over yonder? Was there a Mass?'

Gil nodded, and glanced at the towers of St Mungo's where they loomed above the castle wall.

'My uncle said Mass for her,' he said, 'before the shrine.'

The saint's shrine stood in the centre of the lower church, a dim, pillared place like the undercroft of a tower-house. Last night, entering the Laigh Kirk by its south door, he had paused to look out over St Mungo's kirkyard in the evening light. Near at hand the ground was shadowed by the building site where the Archbishop's plans to add to his cathedral were going ahead in fits and starts as the funding permitted. The clumps of trees cast long fingers beyond that, and the gable-ends of the tall stone manses at the edge of the kirkyard glowed bright where the light caught them. Eastwards the sky was darkening as he watched.

'Gil?' said his sister behind him. 'You going to sleep there?'

He stepped aside quickly. 'Forgive me, Kate. I'm keeping you standing.'

'I can stand forever,' she said. 'It's getting up or down that's the difficult part. Come on, they won't wait all night for us.'

She turned on her crutches with clumsy expertise, and thumped towards the few steps down from the doorway. Gil followed watchfully as she worked her way down into the shadows. He knew better than to offer help.

Under the vaulting immediately opposite the doorway, within the wooden screens which defined the Lady chapel, candlelight flickered on the carved latticework. The Virgin herself, small and ancient with a blackened foot, presided from her pillar, her babe perched on her arm. Kate paused, leaning on her crutches, looked towards the figure briefly, crossed herself, and swung to her left, towards the ornate structure of St Mungo's tomb.

The altar to the west of the tomb was lit and furnished, and before it their uncle knelt in his Mass vestments, while the remainder of the little group waited in silence. Gil caught Alys's eye over his sister's shoulder, and smiled quickly at her. Maistre Pierre had his head bent over his beads; the two servants of the Official's household who had known Kate since childhood were present, Maggie sitting on the base of a pillar with a lantern at her feet, Matt standing beside her, and beyond them towered Babb. She was gazing at the brightly painted end of the tomb, her lips moving silently. Kate on her crutches thumped past the draped side of the altar, David Cunningham rose from his knees, Gil moved hastily into place and lifted the smoking censer, and the Mass began.

It was an experience he knew he would find it hard to forget. As the familiar, comforting phrases rolled into the vaulted roof, the light from the windows faded, and the candlelight flickered on his sister's face. Taut, intense, she stared at their uncle's back, apparently unaware that she was chewing the end of a lock of her long mouse-coloured hair. The invocation to St Kentigern, Mungo the dearly beloved founder, usually saved for his feast days, rose in the candlelight, and shadows jumped on the pillars and vaulting, on the arcading and miniature crocketed spires of the tomb on its four steps, until Gil began to think they were not in a church but in a forest.

Thump and shuffle as Kate moved forward and stood before her uncle to receive the Host, tears leaking from her closed eyes, sweat darkening the patches in the armpits of her woollen gown. Final encomium on Kentigern, praising his steadfastness in the faith and his generosity to his followers.

'Ite, missa est.'

There was a long silence, in which Babb sniffled and Maggie fidgeted but Kate stared unmoving at the candles. Finally Canon Cunningham rose from his knees, crossed himself, and turned to look at them all.

'Well,' he said. 'Attend your mistress, then, Babb. We'll wait you here.'

Babb moved forward, Maggie lifted the lantern and got stiffly to her feet. Kate wiped her eyes on her sleeve, looked from one to the other, then scowled over her shoulder and jerked her head at Alys. All four women moved off towards the chapter-house. Gil put the lid on the censer and exchanged a long look with Maistre Pierre.

'We must hope,' said his father-in-law in French, 'and pray. We can do nothing else for the poor girl. And now you stand guard for her?'

'I do.' Gil smiled wryly. 'When we were young, she liked to swim in the great pool in the burn near to where we were brought up. I used to stand guard, so nobody would catch sight of her in her shift. I'll spend this night on my knees, but it's the same thing.'

'Likely St Mungo himself knew the Linn pool,' said David Cunningham in Scots. 'He was a great man for visiting his flock, we hear. I don't doubt he knew Cadzow parish well. No harm in reminding him of the place in your petitions, Gilbert.'

'I'll do that.' Gil turned as the door of the chapter-house opened. Candlelight showed beyond the screens of the Lady chapel, and they could hear footsteps and the thump and scrape of Kate's crutches. The little procession approached between the pillars, Kate at its head now barefoot, stripped to her shift. Behind her Babb carried a bundled plaid, Alys and Maggie a candle each. Kate worked her way down the three steps to the level of the altar, and came forward to stand before her uncle again.

'Uncle David,' she said, meeting his eye, 'whatever comes of this, I'm grateful.'

'Well, well,' he said, and reached for the little flask of oil. 'You're a good lassie, Kate.'

Now, in the crowded castle yard, Maistre Pierre said, 'She feels the saint has mocked her.'

'Maister,' said Andy behind them.

'Indeed she must, poor lady!' said Morison. 'What a painful thing.'

Sir Thomas turned and scowled at them.

'Maister,' said Andy again. 'Have ye looked at the assizers?'

'Painful indeed,' agreed Maistre Pierre.

'For that's Willie Anderson the cordiner from the Gallowgait, and John Robertson, and John Douglas, and Archie Hamilton the litster,' Andy recounted, 'and there's Mattha Hog. And if ye're thinking, maister, the same as I am, ye're thinking they're all friends of Serjeant Anderson's.'

'Maybe she asked too much,' said Morison.

Gil was silent.

The waking in the dawn was inexpressibly painful to think about. Kate had sprung up out of her dream, out of the bundle of blankets, to stand upright in her shift with her face exalted in a beam of sunlight from the east window. Scrambling to his feet from knees stiffened by a night's prayer, he had not been in time to catch her when she trod forward and fell her length, barely saving herself from rolling down the steps away from the elaborate painted tomb. Heart hammering, he had helped her to sit up, and she had elbowed him aside to snatch back the hem of her shift and stare at her shrivelled foot, pale and unchanged in the growing light from the nearer windows. He thought he had never seen such an expression of disbelief. He had spoken her name, but she ignored him, still staring, for a long moment, then threw back her head and howled like a gored hound. Babb had come running, and snatched her up in brawny arms, and she had clung to her and burst into a great storm of weeping.

'None of us realized, I suppose, how certain she was that St Mungo would help,' said Maistre Pierre. Sir Thomas turned and glared at them again. 'Ah, we are near the number we require.'

'And that's Jemmy Walker,' said Andy in ominous tones as the final assizer was named.

'What, Billy's cousin?' said his master. The members of the assize made their way to the area roped off for them at the side of the courtyard, where Sir Thomas's clerk approached them, wielding a copy of the Gospels in a much-rubbed leather binding.

'Oh, ye're listening, are ye? Look at that fifteen men, maister, and tell me how many of them's a friend to you?'

'Wheesht, Andy. They're fencing the court now.'

After the long process of swearing-in, Sir Thomas addressed the assize, explaining clearly that they were there to establish who the dead man was, how he had died, and who was responsible for his death; but that if they were unable to say any of these things for certain, 'which seems the maist likely circumstance, neighbours,' he added, they were to admit it clearly rather than bring an accusation which could not be proved. Gil, watching, saw the sidelong glances some of the men exchanged, and was suddenly uneasy.

As he had proposed an hour earlier when they delivered the treasure to him, Sir Thomas began by drawing from Maister Morison an account of the opening of the barrel.

'It was well sealed before you broached it?' he prompted.

'Oh, aye,' agreed Morison. 'Sound and tight.'

'And you expected to find books in it,' the Provost went on, with faint incredulity. 'What books in particular?'

'Just what Andrew Halyburton was able to send,' said Morison, his eyes brightening. 'We were in hopes that he'd get books neither one of us owned yet.'

'Aye, well, it's an odd way of doing business,' Sir Thomas commented. 'And that's the barrel yonder, is it? Has it your mark on it, maister?'

'It has,' agreed Morison. 'And two shipmarks forbye, and some other folk's merchant marks.'

'But never Thomas Tod's shipmark,' said a voice loudly from the crowd. Sir Thomas stared round, frowning.

'Who said that?' he demanded. There was a disturbance, and the sandy-haired Billy made his way to the front.

'Me,' he said. 'Billy Walker, that's journeyman carter to

Maister Morison. See that puncheon,' he went on, without waiting for encouragement. 'It's not got Thomas Tod's shipmark, for all my maister says it's the one that cam out of Tod's ship. I just thocht it was strange, that.'

'Is that right?' Sir Thomas said to Maister Morison, who nodded.

'Both right,' he said. 'I saw it lifted from Tod's ship myself, and so did Billy here, the only puncheon in the shipment, but it's not got his mark on it. We thocht it was strange and all.'

'Did you ask Tod why it was in his ship, if it never had his shipmark?'

'No, for we only saw it was lacking his shipmark when we had it here in Glasgow and set up ready for broaching,' said Morison reasonably.

'The carter has changed his tune from this morning,' said Maistre Pierre in puzzled tones. Gil nodded absently, staring over the heads of the onlookers. At the back of the crowd was a man as tall as himself, in a black cloak and felt hat. He was watching Billy intently, his flat, big-featured face expressionless. Then, as if aware of Gil's scrutiny, he looked round, and suddenly smiled, a sneering expression that made his tuft of a beard twitch, and ducked away among the crowd. He had a long-hafted weapon in a vast leather sheath on his shoulder.

'Who was that?' Gil said. 'I've not seen him in Glasgow before.'

'Who?' asked Maistre Pierre.

'Hush,' said Morison.

Sir Thomas, frowning again, persevered with the account of the summoning of the serjeant, and finally obtained corroboration from Morison's companions by the simple method of saying rapidly, 'And you gentlemen agree with that? And you, Andy Paterson? Good. Now, has any of you ever seen this man before?'

'Never,' said Morison confidently.

'Nor I.' Maistre Pierre nodded agreement. Gil opened his mouth to speak, but Sir Thomas had already turned to the assizers. They agreed, with much mumbling and shuffling, that they thought the man was a stranger.

'I seen him afore,' said Billy Walker from the front of the crowd. Morison turned his head to stare at him, open-mouthed, and Gil was aware of some muttering among the assizers where they stood penned at Sir Thomas's right hand.

'Where have ye seen him, man?' demanded Sir Thomas. 'Who is he, then?'

'I've no notion who he is,' said Billy hastily. 'Just I've seen him somewhere.'

'That's no help,' said Sir Thomas crisply. 'Now, I've looked at the head myself, and so has Maister Mason here. He looks to us like a fighting man, and it seems possible he was heidit after he was dead, no killed by being heidit, but there's no more to be told beyond that. Does anyone present have anything more to tell the quest?'

'Aye,' said Billy. 'Just this, sir. If they've no seen him afore, how come my maister and Andy and those got Jamesie Aitken and me out of the way while they broached the puncheon, and what was it they were agreed no to tell the serjeant?'

'What are you saying?' demanded Sir Thomas. The courtyard was suddenly full of noise. Over it the serjeant shouted for silence, with little success.

'I'm saying they were for leaving Serjeant Anderson out of it,' repeated Billy in righteous tones, 'for I heard one of them say it.'

Gil, with a sinking feeling, stepped forward and caught the Provost's eye, and when Sir Thomas leaned towards him he said quietly, 'I mind saying that, sir. It was in connection with the other matter, the one we discussed the now, that's to go to the King.'

Sir Thomas nodded, and gestured again at Serjeant Anderson, who renewed his stentorian calls for silence. When he was eventually successful, the Provost said res-onantly, 'That was a matter which came straight to me, and very properly too. What about this, of getting you and the man Aitken out of the way?'

'It must ha been when they found the heid,' said Billy obligingly. Morison looked at Gil in dismay, and one or two of the assize nudged each other and pointed at this. 'Me and Jamesie was kept working in the barn, and first they never said a word to us about what was in the puncheon, just bade Jamesie go for Serjeant Anderson instead of setting up a hue and cry of murder, and then after the serjeant took the heid away Andy Paterson sent us down the back to wash carts. But I'd to go back up into the yard for cloths and a bucket,' he explained virtuously, 'since Andy never furnished us ony, as Jamesie'll bear me out, and I heard them saying this about keeping the serjeant out of it.'

'*Ah, mon Dieu,*' muttered the mason. Andy drew a long breath through his teeth.

'Keeping the serjeant out of it's no matter,' declared Sir Thomas, 'for I ken what that was for and it's none of his mind. It's already gone to the Archbishop. And Maister Morison got the serjeant to see to the head afore the other matter came to light, as you've just told us, Billy Walker. But why did you no set up a hue and cry, maister? The law's quite clear on that.'

'I was just horror-struck,' Morison protested. 'We all were. And my bairns were about the yard, I didny want them to see – that.' He nodded at the trestle with its burden.

'I never saw the bairns about the yard,' asserted Billy. Several of the assizers looked at one another and nodded significantly at this. The man Andy had identified as Billy's cousin was speaking in confidential tones to his neighbour.

'This man is destroying his own employment,' said Maistre Pierre in Gil's ear. 'What is he about?'

'I wish I knew,' said Gil. 'But I don't like the look of the assize.'

'Serjeant,' said Sir Thomas irritably, 'can you add any sense to this?'

'All I can say is, I never saw any bairns either,' said Serjeant Anderson portentously. 'What's more, sir, when I asked the gentlemen to touch the corp they all did it very willingly except –' he paused dramatically – 'for Maister Morison.'

'And did the corp bleed?' asked an assizer from behind the rope.

'How could it bleed?' asked Sir Thomas irritably. 'He's been heidit. He's no blood left.'

'No, it never bled,' admitted the serjeant regretfully.

'This is getting us nowhere,' declared the Provost. 'Has the assizers any questions they want answered? Or anything more to tell the inquest?'

'Aye. I'd like to know how long Maister Morison had the puncheon in his keeping,' said a grey-haired man in a tavern-keeper's apron.

'Not as much as a week,' said Morison nervously. 'The carts only came home yestreen. No, the day before now. I convoyed them straight from Linlithgow after the whole load was put ashore at Blackness on Monday.'

'And ye had it under your eye all that time, maister?'

'Oh, aye,' said Morison. 'Well,' he amended, 'save for when it was warded for the night, and then there was a guard on it.'

'Was there aught else in the puncheon?' asked a man with the stained hands of a working dyer. Morison looked at the Provost, who intervened.

'Aye, there was, Archie Hamilton, but it's a matter for a higher court than this one. It's all in hand, so ye've no call to speir at that.'

'And there was a deal of brine,' added Morison.

'Is he a Scot?' asked another man with a strong likeness to the dyer. 'Or is he some kind o foreigner? A Saracen, maybe? Or English, even?'

'What would a Saracen be doing in Glasgow?' demanded Sir Thomas in exasperated tones. 'And if he's

English, he's past telling us himself, I warrant you, Eckie. He could be anyone. He's been a grown man, wi one blue eye and one brown, and his hair's dark, and that's all we ken.'

'And he's no half an ell high,' said someone from the back of the crowd, to general laughter.

'It's Allan,' said someone else. 'Like the sang. *Gude Allane lies intil a barell.*'

This raised more laughter, but there seemed to be no further questions or information. Sir Thomas withdrew, and the assizers were ceremoniously released from their pen and escorted into confinement in the hall of the Provost's lodging to deliberate on what they had heard.

'How long will this take?' asked Maistre Pierre as the last man disappeared, followed by Sir Thomas's clerk.

'There's a refreshment to be served,' Morison said. 'They'll be no quicker than it takes to get that by, and maybe a lot slower.'

'A refreshment? I thought such a jury should be starved to hasten its decision.'

'How would you get anyone to serve if you starved them?' Gil asked. 'What is Andy doing there, Augie?'

'Giving Billy orders for the rest of the day, maybe.' Morison watched the two men, who were conversing in a fierce undertone. 'Tell your sister again how sorry I am, Gil, that the saint never answered her prayer. What will she do now?'

'I have wondered that,' said Maistre Pierre.

'I've not asked her. Go back to Carluke, likely, and try to accept her lot. She and Tib have no tocher,' Gil said directly, turning to look at Morison, 'and who would take her with that leg and no land to sweeten the bargain?'

'Courage and a bonnie face might make a tocher,' said Morison diffidently, 'to the right man.'

'They don't bring in rents,' said Gil. 'And Kate isn't one to take bread at a man's hand either.'

Andy was still haranguing his junior. As Gil watched over Morison's shoulder the younger man turned away with a self-righteous air; at the same moment Andy swung round and marched back to their master, every line of his small bow-legged frame expressing anger. Billy glanced after him to thumb his nose again, at which the men round him nudged one another and sniggered.

'Arrogant wee scunner,' said Andy, rejoining them. 'By here, that was quick.' He nodded towards the Provost's lodging. 'The assize is coming out.'

The fifteen men of the assize filed down the steps, preceded by the serjeant with the mace, followed by Sir Thomas's clerk, and were herded into their roped enclosure again. The serjeant went back to conduct Sir Thomas, and then climbing on the mounting-block shouted for silence and got it. Sir Thomas nodded to Gil and his friends, and in a short speech reminded the assize of the penalties for a wilful false verdict and asked them if they had selected someone to speak for them.

'Aye, maister, we have that,' said the grey-haired tavern-keeper, 'and it's me. Mattha Hog, keeper of the Hog tavern, and we've a new barrel of ale –'

'That's enough of that,' said Sir Thomas sharply. 'Well, Mattha, what has the assize found in this death? Do ye ken who he was?'

'No, maister, we do not, except maybe he was a Saracen. Ye said so yerself, that we didny ken him,' Mattha reminded the Provost.

'And were you unanimous in that decision?'

Mattha looked alarmed. 'No,' he said, 'no, indeed, it didny take long to decide at all. We were all agreed, you see.'

Sir Thomas exchanged a brief glance with his clerk, who bent his head over his notes again with a smile quirking his mouth.

'Very well,' said the Provost. 'And do ye ken how he died?'

'No, not that either,' said Mattha. 'We wereny agreed on that,' he admitted, 'for some of us thought he was heidit, and some of us not, but you tellt us yerself, maister, there's

47

no knowing now. He's too long deid, and in that brine and all.'

'Very good,' said Sir Thomas. 'The clerk of the court will write that out, and read it to you, and you will affix the seal of the assize to the record –'

'Aye, but sir,' said Mattha, 'we're not finished.'

Sir Thomas stopped to stare at him.

'You tellt us to decide on who saw to his death,' continued the tavern-keeper with the air of a man about to set off a culverin. 'So we did, and we were agreed on it. Well, nearly all of us was agreed on it,' he modified as someone growled from the back of the group. 'We reckon there's one man knows more about the whole matter than he lets on, and we say he should be held and put to the horn for the killing, and that's Maister Augustine Morison.'

'What?' Morison almost shrieked.

Uproar broke out. Several men from the crowd rushed eagerly forward to seize the merchant, who dived hurriedly towards the Provost for protection. Sir Thomas gestured angrily to his own men, who were already advancing towards the fore-stair using their mailed arms and boots, and dragged Morison on to the stair and out of the grasp of those nearest him. Andy, knife drawn, scrambled up the steps beside his master, and Maistre Pierre also stepped into the mêlée. Gil tried to address Sir Thomas, but could not make himself heard above the noise of the onlookers and the serjeant bellowing from his mounting-block for silence and order. Anxiously he worked his way towards the stair.

'Should we all withdraw, sir?' he suggested when he was close enough. 'Debate this in private?'

'Aye, come up, come up!' shouted Sir Thomas as his men formed a barrier at the foot of the stair. 'Let him through, Andro! Serjeant!' he bellowed.

The serjeant paused in his red-faced appeals for silence.

'I'm away into the house. I'll come back out when you've silenced them, man.'

One of the constables struggled through the throng, and appeared to be trying to tell Sir Thomas something. The Provost waved him away, waited until he saw that Gil was safely on to the steps, and retreated through his own door. Following him, Gil was aware of the serjeant descended from his mounting-block, laying about him with the burgh mace.

Within, Morison was saying desperately, over the noise from the yard, 'I didn't kill him, I don't even know who he is. I never saw him till we opened the barrel!'

'Augie,' said Gil.

Morison stopped to look at him, open-mouthed, and Sir Thomas said into the pause, 'It's all a muddle. I'll have to hold ye, maister, since they've brought in that verdict, and I don't believe a word of it either.'

'I think it is malice,' declared the mason from beside the empty hearth.

'And either I hold a man or I put him to the horn, one or the other, not the both at once. Where's the point in sounding the horn at the Mercat Cross and calling a search for him if he's lying in a cell in my castle?'

'But I never –'

'Augie,' said Gil again, 'if you're charged, will you deny it?'

'Of course I will –'

'Then don't say any more now,' Gil advised. Walter the clerk gave him an approving look. 'The plea is *twertnay*, and that's all you need to say.'

'Oh.' Morison stopped, and repeated the word soundlessly a couple of times.

'I still think it malice,' said Maistre Pierre. The noise from the yard had dropped.

'Aye, you could be right, maister,' agreed Sir Thomas. 'A wilful false verdict. I'm not happy about the assize, that's certain. Walter, you have all their names writ down, have you?'

'All writ down, Provost,' agreed the clerk. 'We can get them back any time we want, provided they've not run.'

'Then I'll go out and discharge them. Bide here, gentlemen. Walter, I'll need you.'

He went out, and shortly could be heard haranguing the members of the assize. The four left in the hall looked at one another.

'What do we do now?' asked Morison, whose teeth were beginning to chatter. 'Oh, Christ assoil me, what of my bairns?'

'Must he be held?' asked Maistre Pierre.

'I'm more practised in the canon law than the civil,' said Gil, 'but I'd say he must be held. It's a charge of murder, so he can't be released on recognition.'

'But –' began Morison, and stopped. 'Twertnay,' he said carefully. 'Gil, will you help me? You found out who killed those other folk – the woman in St Mungo's yard and the one at the college. Can you find out this for me?'

'I can try,' said Gil.

'I'll gie ye a hand, Maister Gil,' said Andy.

'I'll need you to see to the yard,' said his master, sinking on to a stool. 'The business, the bairns, the household – what's to come to any of them if I'm chained up here?'

'I'll have to hold ye,' said Sir Thomas in the doorway, 'since it's a charge of murder, but I'm not putting ye in chains, maister. If you'll give me your word not to run, you can bide here in the castle. I'll find a chamber.'

'I'll see to the yard, maister, if that's what's wanted,' said Andy. 'And the first thing, I'll give Billy Walker leave to go before I throttle him.'

'No, Andy,' said Morison, 'he told the truth as he saw it.'

'Aye, and as he hoped it would harm you, maister,' said Andy bluntly.

'For how long must he be held?' asked Maistre Pierre.

Sir Thomas shook his head. 'I need to send to my lord Archbishop. I wish I'd waited to report the coin, the one man could ha carried both words. Robert Blacader will decide whether to set the matter aside or to pursue it, and in what court. After that, who knows? If Maister Morison's being held at his expense,' he added shrewdly, 'he'll want to resolve it sooner than later.' Voices rose in the yard again, and he turned his head to listen. 'Walter, sort that, would ye, man?'

As the clerk went out on to the fore-stair again, Gil said formally, 'If you're sending to my lord, may I ride with the messenger? Maister Morison has asked me to make enquiry into the death of the man whose head we found in the barrel, and my first road must be to Stirling.'

'Aye, very wise.' Sir Thomas scowled at Gil. 'And let me know what ye find and all.'

'Unless there is a conflict of interests,' agreed Gil.

The Provost stared at him for a moment, then nodded grimly. 'I suppose it might happen,' he admitted. 'Aye, you may ride. You can be the messenger, indeed. If you can be ready within the hour.'

'I need to question Maister Morison.'

'Aye, and the men must eat,' admitted Sir Thomas, reconsidering. 'Two hours, then. No longer.'

'Maister,' said Walter the clerk, reappearing at the door, 'it's a messenger from my lord Archbishop.'

'What?' Sir Thomas turned to the man in dusty riding-clothes who followed Walter into the hall. 'I trust my lord's well?' he said, removing his murrey velvet hat.

'He is well,' said the messenger, bowing and holding out a letter with a dangling seal, 'and he sends to let you to know, Provost, that he will lie here at Glasgow the morn's night, together with his grace the King and my lord of Angus and others as numbered in his letter.'

Chapter Three

'We need all you can tell us,' said Gil.

'About what?' said Morison blankly.

'About this barrel,' said Maistre Pierre.

They were in the chamber which Sir Thomas, muttering curses, had allotted as a prison cell before he hurried off to see to the preparations for the arrival of the Archbishop and more particularly of the King. It was a small, pleasant room two storeys up one of the towers, with a view of the west towers of St Mungo's and a bed at least as good as Gil's own on which Morison was seated, leaving Maistre Pierre the stool while Gil hunkered down against the wall.

'You were there when we broached it,' said the merchant, 'you know as much as I do.'

'Tell us from the beginning,' Gil said patiently, 'when you saw it hoisted from Tod's ship at Blackness. You said it was the only one that size. Are you certain of that?'

'Well, it's what Tod said,' said Morison. 'I think. It's all tapsalteerie in my head, Gil.'

'You didn't look in the hold yourself?'

'I was never on Tod's deck. I stayed on the shore and had an eye to the cransman,' said Morison more confidently.

'Certainly he'd no reason to say so if it wasn't true,' said Gil. 'And then what happened? It was put on the cart?'

'Aye. Well, it stood on the shore till we saw how much there was to go on the cart.'

'And how much was that?' asked Maistre Pierre.

Morison dragged his gaze from the towers of St Mungo's and looked apologetically from one to the other.

'I canny mind,' he said. 'I canny think. It's all tap-salteerie,' he said again, demonstrating inversion with one hand. 'There's nothing left in my head but the thought of what's to come to my bairns if . . . if . . .'

'This is the best way to help your bairns,' Gil said bracingly, though sympathy gnawed at his gut. 'When you got the cart home, how much was there to be unloaded?'

'Oh. Aye.' Morison frowned at his feet. 'There was the two great pipes that came out of Maikison's vessel. One was mostly tin-glazed, with a couple steeks velvet for Clem Walkinshaw on the top, and the other was a mixed load. Aye, just the two,' he nodded. 'And the puncheon which,' he went on more certainly, 'went on at the tail of the cart, roped well in place.'

'Who roped it on?'

'One of the men, I suppose. Likely Billy, he's my carter.'

'And how many carts did you have with you?'

'Just the one. Billy and Andy saw to the driving, and Jamesie and I rode alongside.'

'And where did the cart go?' prompted Maistre Pierre.

'Why, it came home,' said Morison, the blank look appearing again.

'Straight home in one day?'

'Don't be daft, Gil!' Morison paused. 'Oh, I see what you want. We lay at Linlithgow Monday night, and Kilsyth on Tuesday.'

'And what happened to the cart each time? Did you leave it in the inn-yard?'

'No, no. I take better care of my goods than that. We've an arrangement wherever we lie, to run the cart into someone's yard where it can be secure, and Billy sleeps with it as well.'

'We'll need the names of the yards,' said Gil. 'Now, after it came home, where did the barrel lie? Where was it yesternight?'

'Last night.' Morison frowned. 'Is that right? Just last

night? I suppose it must be. We were so late back, we ran the cart into the barn and shut the doors on it. Billy had to take the mare down to stable her, but I'd not the heart to make them start on the load after.'

'So the barrel sat in the barn overnight with the rest. Was it undisturbed when you saw it this morning?'

'Oh, yes. Well, it must have been,' qualified Morison, 'for there had been nobody in the barn. Then I got Andy to roll it down and handle it into the shed, and sent him for you while the other men made a start on the pipe of tin-glazed, and . . . and . . .' He paused, staring at nothing. 'St Peter's bones, Gil, when he came up out of the water like that!'

'He was a gruesome sight, poor devil,' Gil agreed.

'Aye, but . . . aye, but . . .'

'What is it, Augie?' Gil asked. It was clear the man needed to say something, and was reluctant to form the words. 'Out with it, man!'

'It was the way the water ran from his mouth,' said Morison in a rush, his face reddening. 'When – when I saw my Agnes lifted from the milldam. She was all white like that, and she could have been asleep, only for the water running out of her mouth – oh, Gil, it minded me so strongly!'

He scrubbed at his eyes with a sleeve, turning his face away.

Orpheus, thought Gil. *Quhair art thow gone, my luve Ewridicess?* He rose and walked about the small room, overcome with embarrassment. Behind him Morison groped for his handkerchief and hiccuped, while Maistre Pierre tut-tutted in sympathy.

'I'm sorry,' Gil said at last. 'I never realized she had –'

'It was the melancholy,' Morison explained, and blew his nose resoundingly. 'After the bairn died. He only lived a week, the poor wee – and I knew she was – I'd to be away too much, but how could I leave the business? And now if my wee lassies are to be left with neither father nor mother, what's to come of them? What's to come of the

54

household?' He turned away again, ramming the damp linen against his eyes.

'It won't come to that,' Gil said firmly. 'Would you like to see a priest? I forget who's chaplain here when Robert Blacader's away, but there's plenty priests over yonder.' He waved at the towers of St Mungo's.

Morison nodded, sniffing unhappily, but said, 'Or maybe someone from the Greyfriars?'

'I can send to Greyfriars for you,' said Maistre Pierre.

'I'll have a word with Sir Thomas, and then I'll get away, Augie, for the first thing I need to do is speak to someone about the treasure.'

'Oh, aye, the treasure,' said Morison vaguely. 'I keep forgetting that.' He sniffed again, biting his lip, and Gil patted him awkwardly on the shoulder.

'I hadn't. I think it may be the key to the whole thing. Keep your spirits up, man,' he said, 'and pray for my success, and I'll see you when I get back to Glasgow.'

'I see two trails we must follow,' said Maistre Pierre as they crossed the castle yard.

'At least two,' agreed Gil.

'You must go now, to take advantage of the escort and speak to Robert Blacader,' continued the mason, 'but I could set out tomorrow, and trace Morison's cart back to Linlithgow.'

'And then I could meet you there,' said Gil. 'Pierre, if you can spare the time, I'd be glad of the help.'

'How fast will the law proceed? How long have we got?'

'The law will take time,' Gil admitted, nodding to the men on the gate. He set off right-handed along the rose-coloured outer wall of the castle, and continued, 'Even if Robert Blacader sits in judgement while he is in Glasgow, which I hope to avert, he would then have to send Augie to Edinburgh for trial, and that would have to wait while the King's Justice was sent for and the witnesses were summoned from Glasgow. But I'm concerned about Augie's business and even more about his bairns. The sooner we get this straightened out, the better.'

'Oh, indeed. But at least we are not attempting to hold the hangman's arm.'

'Not yet.'

Maistre Pierre paused by the stone cross at the Wynd-head, where the four roads of the upper town met.

'We need to give that poor soul a name,' he said, 'and find how he died. We must trace your books in their barrel, wherever they have got to.'

'And we need to find out where the coin has been these four years and how it got into the barrel we have.'

'But why must you go to Stirling?' asked Alys, turning within the circle of Gil's arm to look up at him. 'Surely if the King and the court will come to Glasgow on Saturday you can ask your questions when they arrive.'

'It will be late in the day when they get here, and I had sooner make a start today,' said Gil. 'Augie is fretting about the bairns and the business. Besides, there's no saying whether the people I want to speak to will travel with the court.'

'Leave him, Alys,' said his sister, from where she sat in bleached dignity in the arbour by the wall. 'He wants off his leash.'

Gil looked at her with sympathy, and found her looking back at him, a faint ironic smile overlying the tear stains. She was the best-looking of his four surviving sisters; according to their uncle she was bonnier than their mother in her prime. Here in the garden, weary with grief, she looked older than their mother was now. At least, Gil thought, scratching Socrates behind the ears with his free hand, she had recovered enough spirit to rake up old family jokes.

'What will you do first?' she asked. 'Who must you speak to at Stirling?'

'Treasurer Knollys,' said Gil. 'Robert Blacader, of course. The McIans, if they're in the town.'

'You should speak to Maister Morison's men before you go,' said Alys thoughtfully. 'They may have noticed something without recognizing its importance.'

'No time just now. When I get back,' said Gil. 'Unless . . .'

She looked up at him again. Unable to resist, he leaned down to kiss the high narrow blade of her nose. Her smile flickered, but she said seriously, 'I could do that. My father's man Thomas likely knows them.'

'If you have the time,' he said. She smiled, and he kissed her again, then said reluctantly, 'I must pack. If I set out as soon as I've had a bite, I should be in Stirling before Vespers.'

'I will have a word with Maggie,' said Alys. 'She always has food for you.'

She rose from the bench where they were sitting. Gil caught her hand, attempting to detain her, but she looked down, met his eye, and with a significant glance directed his attention to the arbour, then turned and left the garden. Socrates turned his long nose from Gil to her retreating back and whined.

Kate was sitting quietly, with her hands in her lap, staring out over the burgh. It was only when he went over and sat down beside her that Gil saw the small movements of fingers and thumbs, doggedly tearing at the calloused skin of her palms. He put his hand over hers, to still the movement, and she jumped convulsively and looked round at him.

'Kit-cat,' he said gently. She turned her head away sharply. 'What will you do now?'

'Babb will help me in for my dinner,' she said, 'and then I'll go to my prayers in our uncle's oratory, though what I should pray for now is anyone's guess, and then I suppose Babb will carry me up to my bed, and –'

'Kate. You know fine that's not what I meant.'

She bent her head.

'Aye,' she said after a moment, 'but it saves me answering you.'

'A life needs a direction. Like a daisy facing the sun, maybe.'

'You've found yours,' she said. 'I've not said to you before now, Gil. I like my new sister fine.'

'I'm glad of that,' he said. 'Stop changing the subject.'

'I'm not. There's nothing else to discuss, for I've no direction. My daisies are all in darkness. Maybe I'll study,' she said a little wildly, 'teach myself the Latin or the Greek or High German. That could be it. I may be tocherless and crippled, but I'll be the most learned crippled ancient maid in Scotland, and doctors of the Laws will come from Spain and Tartary to consult me –'

'Better to study the Laws themselves,' said Gil. 'You could set up your sign in Lanark and convey documents and write wills. You might earn yourself a tocher that way.' He put his arm round her. 'Kate, what was it you dreamed?'

'Oh, that.' She was silent a moment, then sighed. 'I saw the saint himself.'

'St Mungo?' he said, startled.

'Himself,' she said again. 'He wasn't robed as a bishop, he was barefoot in a brown robe like a Franciscan's, with a great checked plaid over it like mine, of all things, but I knew well it was St Mungo by the bishop's crook in his hand.'

'And?' Gil prompted.

'I was lying on the grass by the pool – the Linn pool, you mind, Gil. He bent and took my hand, and said, *Rise up, daughter*, and pulled me to my feet. And then he led me away from the pool, and I could walk on both feet. Gil, do you know, when I'm dreaming I can still walk like other people. But in this dream it was different, because I knew the walking was a gift, it was a grace, something the saint had done for me.'

'Dreams are strange things,' he said, past the lump in his throat. 'Was that it?'

'One thing more,' she said bleakly. 'The final cup of wormwood. Whoever he was, he led me forward to my wedding. I never saw my bridegroom, but I knew he waited for me. And I woke, and not a word of it was true.'

'Oh, Kate,' he said helplessly. 'Kit-cat. I'm sorry.'

'Gib-cat,' she said. She put a hand over his where it lay on her shoulder, and sighed. 'I've no doubt there's a lesson to my spirit in it, but even the old man hasn't suggested what it might be yet.'

It was some time since Gil had been out of Glasgow, and longer yet since he had the chance to ride fast on a good horse. The road to Stirling was well made, and though it was busy the sight of five well-armed riders moving in a cloud of dust caused most travellers to give them the way. Gil, with the Provost's two messengers in front of him and two of his uncle's men at his back, swept through villages scattering hens and attracting barking dogs, slowing to pick their way more carefully through the small towns such as Kirkintilloch and Kilsyth, making most speed in the open farmlands between, where the folk loading hay on to carts or hay-sleds paused to hand the leather bottle of ale and watch them pass. To begin with, Socrates bounded happily alongside, but by the time the messengers left them at Stirling town gates, to hasten up to the castle, the dog was draped wearily across Gil's saddlebow.

He clattered more slowly up Stirling's busy High Street, and his uncle's men followed him, all three horses too done to shy at the raucous cries of the market and the noise of stalls being dismantled. Gil looked about with care in the hope of catching sight of a familiar face, and preferably one who might be of some help.

'I've a cousin's a stable-hand to Robert Blacader,' said Tam helpfully behind him. 'If it's the Bishop you want, maister.'

'I know one that's servant to one of the canons at the Holy Rude,' offered Rob, not to be outdone.

'It may come to that yet,' said Gil, 'but I've no doubt there are others who could get us close to him faster. There's one, indeed. Maister Dunbar! William!'

The small rat-faced man turned, shading his eyes against the light, and a large wife with a basket of limp greenstuff collided with his back and made her way round him, commenting freely on his common sense.

'Maister Cunningham,' he said formally, ignoring her. 'Good day to you, Gil. And what brings you to Stirling, covered in dust? I thought you were chained to St Mungo's gateway.' He smiled sourly. Gil dismounted, handing his reins to Rob, and lifted Socrates down. The dog shook himself vigorously and sat down, yawning.

'I'm looking for a word with my lord Archbishop,' Gil said. 'Where can I find him?'

'Oh?' Maister William Dunbar, secretary to Archbishop Blacader, raised his eyebrows. 'Can you mean something's actually happened in Glasgow?' He considered Gil, and the acid smile appeared again. 'It's been quiet since May, and now Gil Cunningham wants a word. Another killing? Another secret murder? Who is it this time, the Provost and all the bailies? Or is it something to do with a portion of the late King's hoard found in a barrel?'

'Partly,' said Gil. 'Where is his lordship?'

'Oh, attending on the King.' Dunbar waved in the general direction of the castle, and another passer-by ducked and cursed him. 'Is that what you're after? Entry to the court?'

'Robert Blacader will do well enough,' said Gil. 'Can you get me in to him?'

'I'm bound there the now,' admitted the smaller man. 'I should be with him, only he sent me out an errand for the King's grace. Confidential, I need hardly say.'

'Oh, of course,' Gil agreed. 'And you've delivered your message? Can you get me to his lordship?'

'I can,' said Dunbar, turning to walk on up the hill. 'What's it worth?'

'I'll tell you all about it,' offered Gil, suppressing annoyance. 'After I've spoken to Robert Blacader,' he added.

Dunbar considered this, his eyes narrowed, and at length he nodded. 'See your men and your beasts settled,' he said, 'and apply for me at the gatehouse in an hour. I'll do what I can for you. Mind, it had better be a good story.'

'Oh, it's all of that,' said Gil.

'And I suppose you want a lodging this night as well?'

'I can see to that for myself. How is the court just now?'

'Right now, very unsettled,' said Dunbar morosely. 'My lord of Angus arrived before noon for a word with him.' From the emphasis on the pronoun, Gil interpreted it as referring to the young King James. 'We think he's planning to go into Ayrshire, and we're not certain how many of us are wanted. How big a house is the place at Kilmarnock?'

'Angus's place? Not big enough for the court,' Gil replied. 'You'll have to lie out in the town, as you do here.'

'Hmm.' Dunbar considered this prospect, and halted again. 'Even my lord Archbishop?'

'Better ask some of Angus's people. I'll leave you here, William. My lodgings are on Back Wynd. In an hour at the gatehouse, then.'

Following Maister Dunbar along a seemingly endless enfilade of stuffy rooms, through waves of conflicting smells of civet and moth-herbs, musk and lavender and stale furs, Gil barely had time to pick out the familiar faces. People he had been at school with, at college with, or met briefly in Glasgow were among those sitting or standing about, playing cards or dice or talking about hunting. One or two showed signs of recognizing him.

'My lord's playing at the cards with the King,' said

Dunbar, pausing in a doorway. 'Wait in this chamber, Gil. I'll see if I can get him out between games.'

Gil grimaced. A good game of Tarocco could last the best part of an hour. He nodded, and looked about him as Dunbar's tonsure disappeared past someone's green brocade shoulder into the next room.

'I know you,' said a voice beside him. 'You're a Cunningham, aren't you?' He turned, to find a big fair man at his elbow, all cherry-coloured velvet and yellow silk. Noll Sinclair of Roslin, friend of his parents and of the late King, clapped him on the shoulder and grinned at him. 'Gled Cunningham's youngest. Gilbert, is it?'

'Sir Oliver,' said Gil formally, looking into the handsome face level with his. 'My God, I haven't heard my father's by-name in years.'

'Aye, well.' Sinclair's grin vanished briefly. 'A bad business, that. And your brothers and all. Grievous. How's your mother? How does she manage?'

'My mother's well, thank you, sir. She has her dower-lands near Lanark, and wins a living.'

'Oh, aye.' The grin reappeared. 'She stayed with us at Roslin a time or two, and some of your sisters with her. I mind her then instructing me on horse-breeding. So she's running horses on her dower-lands, is she?'

'It's good enough grazing out by Carluke,' said Gil, nodding. 'And it's high enough to breed hardy beasts. She knows what she's doing.'

'I've no doubt of that where Gelis Muirhead's concerned. And what are you doing, yourself? Will you be for the Church or the Law?'

'The Law,' said Gil firmly. 'I'll take my notary's oath next month, and hang up my sign in Glasgow.'

'If I've business to do in Lanarkshire I'll remember that,' said Sinclair. He hitched at the wide sleeves of his gown, turning back the cuffs so that the yellow silk lining showed to advantage. 'So it's the secular life, is it? And a marriage in mind, so I heard.'

'Contract signed,' agreed Gil.

'My good wishes on that,' said the other affably. 'And how is Glasgow? What's this we've been hearing today? A piece of the old King's hoard turned up in the burgh? In a barrel?'

'I suppose the word would spread fast,' Gil said in some annoyance.

'This is the court,' said Sinclair. 'There's nothing to do but gossip or listen to gossip. I thank God fasting every time I come near the King that I've no need to hold office.' Gil, who knew the story of the bargain struck by a previous Stewart with a previous Sinclair, merely nodded. 'I suppose there's no doubt that it's the King's money?' Sir Oliver went on, his tone casual. 'Coin is only coin, after all, it doesn't have the owner's badge on it.'

'It isn't only money,' said Gil reluctantly. 'There are jewels as well. Some of those are the owner's badge, indeed – very obviously out of the royal treasury.'

'Oh?' Sinclair's eyebrows rose. 'And where did ye find this? Was it really in a barrel? And what's this about a head? What like was it? Do you ken whose? Is it some thief or other, or a fighting man?'

'You're well informed, sir,' said Gil. And full of questions, he thought. 'No, I've no notion whose. If I knew where the coin had been hid these four years I might be closer to giving him a name, but it won't be easy to get an answer to that.'

'I should say not,' agreed Sinclair. 'Ask at Robert Lyle, why don't you. He seems to have information the rest of us lack.'

'Gil,' said Maister Dunbar at his elbow. 'My lord will see you now.'

'I'm sure Robert Lyle will want a word,' reiterated Sinclair. Gil, with some relief, raised his hat and bowed to him before turning to follow the little poet from the chamber.

Robert Blacader, well-found, blue-jowled and tonsured, was waiting in a windowless closet between that room and the next, seated on a folding chair, a stand of newly lit candles on the chest beside him. The light gleamed on the dark brocade of his gown, the silver fittings of belt and purse at his waist. When Gil entered he held out a hand.

'I can spare you a short time, Maister Cunningham,' he said. Gil knelt to kiss the ring. 'I hope your uncle is well?' Gil murmured something. 'I believe it was you found this treasure that appeared this morning?'

'I was present when it was found, my lord,' Gil parried.

'Sir Thomas never sent me more than the bare bones of the tale to it.'

'There's more to tell now in any case, my lord.'

The Archbishop gestured, and Gil stood obediently and gave him a succinct account of the finding of the head and the treasure, and then of the inquest and its result. Blacader heard him out in growing annoyance, and finally shook his head, saying irritably, 'The Provost has acted as he must, but Christ aid me, I never heard such nonsense. It's surely been a wilful false verdict. I'll send to Sir Thomas the morn, and look into it closer when I reach Glasgow. Has this fellow – what's his name, Morison? Has he enemies in the burgh?'

'No more than any successful merchant,' said Gil. 'He's harmless enough, I'd have said. A gentle soul.'

'Hmm,' said the Archbishop. 'And he has asked you to sort it out, has he?' Gil nodded. 'Aye. After you dealt with those other two matters, it would be an obvious choice,' continued Blacader thoughtfully. He stared at Gil for a moment, the candlelight flickering on brow and padded cheeks. 'I think you must. We'll not waste the Justiciars' time with this kind of thing. William,' he said, and Maister Dunbar stirred at the door of the little room. 'Something towards Maister Cunningham's expenses, I think. Ten merks should do it. And you'll report to me, Gilbert.'

'Gladly, my lord. Thank you,' said Gil fervently, going down on one knee again. This was more than he had hoped for: Blacader had just attached him to his own retinue, however informally.

'And now,' said the Archbishop, getting to his feet, 'I must go back to the King. Come with me, Gilbert.'

The inmost chamber was crowded with bystanders and servants in the royal livery, but their gaze, direct or side-long, showed where to look. Near the empty hearth a table was set up, covered in a silk carpet, the cards still lying on it in tricks as they had been gathered in among the heaps of coin. Three people were seated round it. On the far side King James, aged nineteen, chestnut hair and long-nosed Stewart good looks set off by green velvet and blue silk, was talking to a hulking man whose cropped hair and beard showed streaks of grey: Archibald Douglas, fifth earl of Angus. On this side was a well-found blue-jowled person in furred red silk embroidered with trees of life, a match for the Archbishop save for the lack of a tonsure; plump hands studded with rings were folded on his knee as he watched the conversation with the open smiling gaze of a statesman.

'His grace will want the story of the finding of the treasure,' said Blacader, placing himself expertly to catch Angus's eye, and his counterpart turned his head sharply, his silk rustling.

'Are ye sure of that, Robert?' he asked. 'This is gey public. And is this the man that found it?' He looked closely at Gil with round pale eyes, and then cast a pointed glance at Maister Dunbar, who stared at the patterned ceiling.

'Wheesht, William,' Blacader said, intent on the King, and Gil appreciated that the other man was that chimera of his age, neither cleric nor layman, William Knollys the Treasurer of Scotland and Commendator of the Knights of St John.

The royal conversation paused, and Blacader inserted a practised word. Gil found himself kneeling again, and then somehow seated on a stool which manifested behind him, giving an account of the finding of first the head and then the bag of coin. The two men of state watched him as he talked, intent and impassive, and Angus leaned back to whisper to a servant, but the King listened closely, his mobile face expressing interest, concern, dismay as the narrative proceeded.

'And what has the inquest found?' he asked. 'Did they get a name for the man?'

'No, sir,' said Gil. 'Nobody in the burgh knew him.'

'No surprise in that, I suppose,' said the King. 'He's likely from wherever the hoard money's been hid these four years, and not from Glasgow at all. And the barrel came from Linlithgow, you say?'

'The barrel was exchanged for ours,' said Gil with care, 'somewhere between Linlithgow and Glasgow. Or so I believe, sir.'

'Aye,' said James thoughtfully. 'No saying, is there? But why? And why put the head and the coin both into brine?'

'I hope to find out,' said Gil.

'Tell me when you do. And I hope you find your books, maister,' said the King, and Gil realized this was the first person to whom he had told the tale who had expressed the wish. 'Meantime, there's the matter of a reward for finding the treasure. That's two thousand merks waiting for us in Glasgow, forbye the jewels – we're certainly grateful, man. My lord Treasurer, you'll see to that the now, will you?'

Thus dismissed, Gil retreated from the card-room, followed immediately by Knollys, who gestured to one of his own servants and bustled Gil back through the sequence of stuffy crowded rooms, asking affably after his uncle as they went, studying him with those round pale eyes. Gil, recalling Canon Cunningham's strictures on this man as one of the most litigious in Scotland, answered as non-committally as he could.

'And this barrel,' said Knollys, pausing at a door which led out into a courtyard. The servant began striking light for the torch he carried. Knollys stepped into the yard, and Gil followed. Windows glowed above them, and overhead the sky was still greenish with the last of the light. 'Naught else in it?'

'No, sir,' said Gil. 'Just the saddlebag of coin and the head.'

'Aye,' said Knollys thoughtfully. He stopped in the centre of the courtyard, tapping his teeth with a fingernail. One of his rings glittered as his hand moved. 'What made you so sure it was from the late King's hoard, then?' he asked, his tone soft.

'The only thing that's certain,' said Gil with caution, 'is that along with the coin we found a roll of jewels, including badges of the Queen's household and the like. There's no seal on the purses, but we assumed the coin went with the jewels. The saddlebag isn't marked, the barrel and the head could have come from anywhere.'

'Aye,' said Knollys again, and the ring sparked. 'What like man is it, the head I mean?'

Gil shrugged. 'He looks like a Scot,' he began.

'I never suggested he wasny,' said Knollys.

'Maybe a fighting man, by the haircut. No more than thirty year old, maybe less.'

'Aye,' said Knollys a third time, tapping his teeth again. The man in the St Johns livery approached, holding the sputtering torch high. 'I see what you mean. Could be anyone.' Ignoring his servant, he set off towards the far corner of the courtyard. 'I've no doubt you'll keep the Archbishop informed,' he added as Gil followed him.

Up two more flights of stairs they reached a tower chamber where, even at this late hour, a clerk was working at a tall desk. The servant stationed himself outside the door, torch in one hand, the other on his sword.

'Aye, Richie,' said Knollys to the clerk. 'Where are your keys? We'll have the great kist opened, if you please.' He produced a bunch of keys on a chain at his own belt, and he and the clerk went through the careful procedure of opening the great iron-bound box in the corner of the chamber, selecting and counting out twenty merks, placing them in a canvas purse, closing the box and locking it again.

'The man who found the treasure will be grateful,' Gil

said, signing the receipt presented to him and thinking of Andy. 'If it is from the late King's hoard, is that the last, do you suppose?'

The clerk paused in turning to file the paper, but did not speak; the Treasurer said blandly, 'Oh, I am certain Robert Lyle thinks there is more out there.'

'Is there no record of who held the different portions?' Gil asked.

'None that I ever saw,' said Knollys. 'Or if any was kept, it was lost at the battle. I doubt if even his grace himself knew, by the end, where he'd planted this or that portion.'

'Who do we know of, that has returned their kists?'

'Atholl the late King's uncle,' said Knollys promptly. 'My predecessor in this office. Robert Hog at Holyrood. Alan of Avery, or rather his sire.' The clerk said something. 'Aye, Richie, I'd forgot that. George Robinson the Edinburgh custumar was said to ha taken a thousand pound o' the customs money,' he explained to Gil, 'and carried it to the north to raise a host, where folk were mostly for the late King. If he did, it's never been recovered, and in any case I have my doubts. It's a suspicious kind of sum, a thousand of anything. The sort of amount folk name when they just mean a lot of coin.'

Gil nodded agreement.

'But you must understand, Maister Cunningham, this was all in my predecessor's time. I know nothing of the matter, other than what has appeared since the start of the present reign.'

The clerk flicked a glance at his master, but said nothing. Gil nodded again, and took the canvas purse from the desk and stowed it in his jerkin.

'Why this portion should have appeared now, in such circumstances,' he said, 'is beyond me.'

'Your father was out at Stirling field for the old King, was he no?' said Knollys.

'He was indeed, my lord,' said Gil politely. 'And died for him too.'

The ruby ring flashed again, but Knollys, a man who had changed sides at the moment most expedient to himself, did not respond. Instead he said, in considered tones, 'Some of his friends might be a help to you, if you want to know where the barrel came from. Ross of Montgrenan, Ross of Hawkhead, Dunbar of Cumnock, all might have ideas about it.'

'It's very possible, my lord,' Gil agreed. 'A valuable suggestion.'

'So now if you'll excuse me,' said Knollys, 'I'll get back to the cards.'

'Afore ye go, my lord,' said the clerk quietly, and his master turned to look at him. 'If you'd just sign this.'

'What is it? What is it?'

'For the coin I gave out to Wilkie and Carson at noon. Expenses.'

'To –?' Knollys bit off the question. 'Aye, right. I hope to God they catch up with Carson's brother. Why they ever let him go off his lone –' He stopped himself again. 'You never paid them for that last piece of work, I hope, Richie?' The clerk shook his head. 'Right. I don't pay for failure.'

'The word was good,' muttered the clerk, and fell silent at a burning glance from Knollys. Gil made some business of ensuring that his jerkin was laced over the purse he had been given, and Knollys signed the paper and flung the pen down on the desk, shaking his wide furred sleeve down over his rings.

'So you'll be into Ayrshire, then,' he said, making for the door. The man with the torch set off in front of him, to light the stair.

'One other thing you might be able to tell me, my lord,' said Gil, following the Treasurer down the spiral. 'I'm looking for a harper I believe might be in Stirling – the man McIan. He and his sister have played for my lord Archbishop before now. Do you know how I might find out his whereabouts?'

'Aye, I believe I've heard them,' said Knollys dismissively over his shoulder. 'If they've played before Robert

Blacader, likely Maister Secretary will ken where they're to be found. Ask at William Dunbar, Maister Cunningham.'

Having warned the household of the Precentor of Holyrude Kirk that he would likely be late, and promised to bar the door when he came in, Gil set off with Socrates towards the lodgings Dunbar had suggested as a likely place to find his friend the harper. Despite the curfew bell there were many people still about, day labourers hurrying homeward, folk going visiting for the evening. A troop of mounted men clattered past him down the hill, the eight-pointed star of the Knights Hospitallers gleaming pale on their black cloaks. The harper's lodging lay one stair up, well down a vennel off the High Street, but the dog seemed to detect no unusual threat, and Gil picked his way down the darkening alley with no more than ordinary caution.

This much of Knollys's advice was sound: the harper was clearly at home. There was light in the windows, the shutters were open, and the sound of voices and several conflicting musical instruments floated into the evening. Gil followed the sound and knocked on the door, and was admitted by a man in royal livery with a vièle under his arm and a beaker in his hand.

'Angus!' he called over his shoulder. 'Here's another singer. Christ save us, have we no enough? Have you no instrument, man?' he added to Gil.

'I'm no musician,' said Gil hastily. 'I'm the audience.'

'Oh, well,' said the doorkeeper. 'We aye need an audience.' He stood aside, and Gil stepped into a candlelit room full of people in well-worn finery. Nearest him, two more men with vièles of different sizes and another with a German flute were arguing about the pitch of a note someone had just played, but beyond them three lutenists were tuning their awkward, fragile instruments, and a mixed covey of singers beside one of the candles had their heads together over a piece of paper and were humming something.

'Who is it, Will?' The harper's sister Ealasaidh came forward. For a moment Gil did not recognize her: instead of her usual loose checked gown, the common garb of a Highland woman, she wore fine brocade and velvet, and her long dark hair was hidden under a French hood. 'It's yourself, Maister Cunningham. Come in, come in. Is the bairn safe?' she demanded urgently.

'The bairn is well,' said Gil reassuringly, annoyed with himself for not thinking of this before. Naturally, their first thought would be for the harper's motherless infant son. 'I'm in Stirling about another matter, and I thought the two of you might have the answer to one of my questions.'

'Another death, is it?' she said, staring at him from under dark brows. Socrates, uneasy in the crowded room, wagged his tail doubtfully at her and she bent to pat his head.

'Maister Cunningham?' called the harper from his chair by the hearth. 'Come in, maister, and be welcome.' He rose, clasping his harp. Gil made his way past the lutenists, two men and a woman who had now launched into a plangent setting of *I long for thy virginitie*, and as he recognized the tune he was assailed by a sudden sharp thought of Alys, and of the impossibility of setting a date for their marriage yet.

'It will be well,' said McIan, standing imposing in his blue velvet gown, his white hair and beard combed out like snow over chest and shoulders. He turned his silver eyes towards Gil. 'It will be well, and worth the wait. Where your treasure is, there will your heart be, but that is not what you have come about.'

Gil, used to enigmatic statements like this, said simply, 'No, I have a question for you, sir. And some of these others might have an answer to it as well,' he added.

'Ask it,' said McIan, as his sister put a beaker of wine into Gil's hand. Gil hesitated, wondering where to begin.

71

'The woman of the house is right, is she not, maister? It concerns a death? And more than one.'

'Only one,' said Gil. 'When did you last hear of the lutenist called Balthasar of Liège?'

'What, is it Barty that is dead?' asked Ealasaidh at Gil's elbow, and crossed herself in dismay. 'Sorrow is at me to hear the word.'

'I don't know that,' said Gil. The lutenists stopped playing and turned to stare, and the singers and the broken consort took the opportunity to start a part-song, Scots words to French music. 'Someone very like him has turned up dead in Glasgow, and I hope you can tell me it's not him.'

'Balthasar of Liège?' said one of the male lutenists. He was wearing a regrettable striped doublet of red and cream with bunches of crumpled green ribbons attached to all the seams, bright even by candlelight. 'Who's that?'

'Barty Fletcher,' said the woman beside him. 'I've seen him, but no since last week, maister.'

'When was that?' Gil asked. 'Where was he?'

'When we came through Falkirk,' the woman said, looking at the third lutenist, more soberly dressed in rubbed blue velvet. 'Would that be Thursday?'

'I never saw him,' he said suspiciously.

'You were paying for the ale. I never spoke to him, I just saw him go past.'

'Falkirk,' said Gil above the music. 'When would that have been? What day?'

'Friday,' said the man, still frowning. 'When was I paying for the ale?'

'After we ordered it,' she said. The singers finished their part-song, and without consultation started it again, the vièles coming in raggedly.

'Friday,' said Gil doubtfully, reckoning in his head. 'Friday of last week?'

'When did the man die, that was found in Glasgow?' asked McIan.

'And why should you think it might be Barty?' asked his sister.

'What do you recall about him?' countered Gil.

'Nothing that would identify a dead man,' said the harper rather harshly. 'Voice and manner do not survive.'

'His eyes,' said the lute-woman. The man in blue looked sharply at her.

'Aye, his eyes,' agreed Ealasaidh. 'They are different colours. One blue, one brown.'

'Yes,' said Gil. 'So I recalled.'

'He has an earring,' added Ealasaidh. 'Just the one.'

'And is that what you have found?' asked the harper. 'A dead man with odd-coloured eyes?'

The words fell into a silence as the singers paused again, and suddenly everyone was paying attention.

'We found,' said Gil, picking his words with care, 'the head of a man, put in a barrel of brine. The dead man had short dark hair, he had worn an earring at some time, and he had one blue eye and one brown. We think the barrel had been exchanged for one unloaded at Blackness on Monday last.'

'Barty's hair is long,' said Ealasaidh with relief. 'Down on his shoulders, it is.'

'Hair can be cut,' said McIan.

'Just his *head*?' said one of the singers, a round-eyed woman with gold curls, and a great deal of swelling flesh above her low-cut velvet bodice. 'Who is it?'

'Barty,' said the tenor beside her.

'Alissy's saying it's Barty,' qualified the bass vièle.

'Our Lady protect us!' said the plump singer, crossing herself energetically. 'And to think I saw him just yesterday.'

'Yesterday?' said Gil. 'Where was this?'

'Linlithgow, I think,' she said vaguely.

'You were here in Stirling yesterday,' the tenor reminded her.

'Well, maybe it was the day afore. When were we through Linlithgow, Georgie?'

73

'Tuesday,' said the bass vièle confidently.

'Oh, aye. I mind now. Everyone was coming from the Mass at St Michael's, and I saw Barty among them.'

'Did you speak to him?' Gil asked.

'Oh, aye.'

'Did he answer you, Marriot?' asked McIan heavily, and Gil recalled tales his nurse had told him, of people seen clearly after they were dead.

'He did,' said Marriot, nodding her head so that her gold curls bounced. 'He said he was fixed in Linlithgow a day or two. He had to meet someone, he said.'

'And that was Tuesday,' said Gil.

'Aye, it was Tuesday,' agreed the bass vièle. He propped his instrument against his shoulder, reaching round it to count on his fingers. 'We left Edinburgh on Monday, played at Linlithgow that evening and Falkirk on Tuesday evening, reached here yestreen.'

'And now he's deid,' said Marriot in round-eyed regret.

'No if you saw him on Tuesday, lass,' said the tenor next to her. The lute-woman closed her eyes and crossed herself, and the man in blue velvet, without looking at her, gripped the neck of his instrument so that his knuckles showed white in the candlelight.

'I don't see what you mean,' said Marriot, reluctant to be balked of her drama. 'He could have dee'd after I saw him.'

'The man who is dead was dead before that,' said Ealasaidh.

'The barrel that we found the head in,' Gil explained, 'left Linlithgow early Tuesday on a merchant's cart. By the time you saw Balthasar coming from Mass, both barrel and head were halfway to Castlecary.'

'Oh,' said Marriot, not fully convinced.

'I'm glad to hear you saw him,' said Gil encouragingly, 'for I liked the man. I still have to find a name for the dead man, but at least I've eliminated one.'

'Just leaves the whole of the rest of Scotland, eh?' said the flute player.

'If the dead had odd eyes like Barty,' said the man who had admitted Gil, 'was he maybe some kind of kin to him? It's no that common a feature, see.'

This was generally agreed to be a good point.

'There you are, maister,' said the lutenist with the green ribbons. 'Gang to Linlithgow, find Barty, and you'll get a name for your corp.'

'If he's still there,' said the bass vièle.

'If he wasny, he'd be here, where the pickings are,' said the tenor singer beside Marriot.

One or two of the men laughed, but McIan said, with sudden authority, 'Go to Linlithgow the morn, Maister Cunningham, and ask your questions again. There will be answers.'

'But the now,' said the bass vièle, 'he said he was the audience. We aye need an audience. Gie the man another drink, Alissy, and he can listen to this new piece for us. I still say you want to be half a tone higher there, Edward,' he went on, turning abruptly to the flute player. 'It's away too sweet like that.'

Chapter Four

Kate Cunningham, sitting in the arbour in her uncle's garden, stared out over the lower town and thought bleakly about her future.

It seemed to contain very little that was positive. St Mungo had been her last resort. Restricted though their income was, she had travelled widely in the past two or three years, following the pilgrim roads of Scotland with offerings and petitions for saints from Tain to Whithorn without success. She wondered if she had offended Mungo by turning to him the last, and found her mouth twisting in a bitter smile.

'What has changed?' said Alys in her accented Scots.

Kate looked round, and found her new relation sitting on the grass nearby. The smile softened; in the few days since they had met she had found a great liking for this slender, elegant, terrifyingly competent girl.

'Changed?' she said now.

'Since yesterday, for example,' said Alys.

Kate turned her head to look out over the burgh again, trying to decide whether she could answer that.

'All my hopes are away,' she said at last. 'The rest of my life's still the same, but now I've no hope of ever getting rid of – these.' She nodded at the crutches propped beside the arbour.

'All your hopes?'

'You sound like my brother. No, I suppose, not all. I still have my hope of salvation, but what else is there? How can I lead a useful life? How can I lead a good life, even?'

'You said,' said Alys diffidently, 'that the saint bade you *Rise up, daughter.*' Kate nodded. 'Dreams often go by image and metaphor. Do you think, perhaps, he meant you were to rise up above your difficulties? To ignore them?'

'He could have said so,' Kate said sourly. 'It's no that easy to ignore having to be carried downstairs every day.'

Alys was silent for a while. Then she said, 'I came out to ask for your help.'

'Mine? What help can I be? Did you not hear me, Alys?'

'Your brother,' said Alys, colouring slightly as she always did when she mentioned Gil, 'left me a task. Someone must speak to Maister Morison's men about the bringing home of that cart, with the barrel on it, and the sooner the better. I need a companion. Would you come with me?'

'Why not take one of your lassies?' said Kate, aware that she sounded pettish. 'Or that Catherine?'

'I'd rather have this Katherine,' said Alys, her elusive smile flickering. 'My lassies will be busy about the dinner just now, and Catherine will be asleep over her prayer-book, since she last saw me in my father's care. Will you not help me? We can have your mule brought round, and you can ride down, and Babb and I can walk. Then you may dine with us, and come home after.'

'Oh, well,' said Kate after a moment. 'I might as well, I suppose.'

The three women halted in the gateway to Morison's yard, staring at the disorder within.

'*Mon Dieu,*' said Alys after a moment, '*quelle espèce de pagaille!*'

'You've not been here before?' said Kate, as her mule pricked his long ears at a blowing wisp of straw.

'No,' admitted Alys, looking round. 'How ever could he

let his men work like this? I would be ashamed to – of course his wife is dead.'

'*Her is non hoom, her nis but wildernesse.* Where should we start?' asked Kate. 'Is there anyone here to question, or is the place deserted?'

'There's somebody down yonder,' said Babb suspiciously. 'Ye can hear voices.'

As she spoke the door of the barn at the far end of the yard was flung open and a skinny boy scurried out, making for one of the sheds. Halfway there he caught sight of the visitors, skidded to a halt staring, then turned and scurried back into the barn. The words *Three bonnie leddies* floated out.

'Hmf!' said Babb. Andy Paterson appeared in the doorway, and hurried forward, the boy beside him.

'Forgive the wait, leddies, we're a wee thing owerset here,' he said, raising his blue knitted bonnet, and stopped, a grin spreading across his face. 'Lady Kate! John, you never said it was Lady Kate!' he remonstrated, aiming a cuff at the boy, who ducked expertly.

'No reason the boy should know me,' Kate said. 'How are you, Andy? And the family?'

'All well, so far's I've heard,' said Andy. 'Madam your mother's well, then, leddy?'

'She is,' said Kate. 'Andy, this is Mistress Mason, who's to marry my brother.'

'Wish ye well, mistress,' said Andy. He raised the bonnet again to Alys, and nodded companionably to Babb. 'And what's your pleasure, Lady Kate? Mistress?'

The two girls exchanged a brief look, and Alys gave Kate one of her infinitesimal nods.

'A word with the men who brought the cart from Linlithgow,' Kate said.

Andy's eyes narrowed. 'What for?'

'In case any of them remembers something that might be useful,' said Alys. 'You want your master out of the castle and back in the yard, don't you?'

'Aye, I do, mistress,' said Andy. 'And if it's like that.' He turned to the boy. 'John, run and mak siccar Billy Walker's no left the yard yet. I've just bidden him gie us his room,' he expanded to Kate. 'You'll have heard from Maister Gil what passed at the quest, then?'

'What like a man's Billy Walker? Is that him at the back yett?' asked Babb. Andy swung round, let out a roar, and set off at a run. Babb, grinning, dropped Kate's crutches with a clatter, hitched up her skirts and pounded after him. She overtook him easily halfway down the yard, swept past him and seized Billy as he slipped through the gate.

'Let me loose!' he shouted as she dragged him triumphantly back to her mistress. 'Let me away, you fairground show! I've been turned off, it's none of my mind now, it's nought to do wi me!'

'Well, now,' said Kate thoughtfully, studying him from her perch on the back of the mule. 'Maybe if you can tell us anything useful . . .' She paused, glancing at Andy's scowling face, and changed what she had been about to say. 'One of us might put in a word for you with another master. I take it you'd liefer work than starve?'

'What if I would?' he said sulkily. 'That yin wasny for giving me the choice.'

He jerked his head at Andy, who expostulated, 'I wasny? What about yersel, Billy Walker? Ye've tried to put us all out of our work! If the maister gets hangit for murder, what will the rest of us do?'

'I tell ye, I never meant for that,' said Billy. 'And forbye, he's got the money to get off. He never done it, he'll no get –' He squirmed in Babb's grasp. 'Will you let me go, you great lump?'

Kate exchanged another glance with Alys, who said, 'Is there somewhere we can talk to Billy? And then to the rest of the men who went to Linlithgow?'

'One at a time, you mean?' said Andy, and chewed his lip briefly. 'Aye, well, ye can sit in the house, if ye can get up the stair, my leddy. Or there's the sheds. No that one,' he said in significant tones, nodding at the nearest, 'ye'll not want to sit in that one, but there's others. Only thing is, the women are a' to pieces in the kitchen, the both o them. We'll no can offer you any refreshment, you'll understand. It's a good question whether me and the men'll get any dinner.'

'I can get up the stair,' said Kate. 'We'll sit in the house.'

Established in the hall, the two girls confronted the resentful Billy still in Babb's unloving grip. Alys had flung wide all the shutters, only partly lightening the gloom and in addition revealing the thick layer of dust which lay alike on dull furnishings and the clutter of musical instruments in a corner. Kate dragged her gaze resolutely from these and said, 'Explain yourself, Billy.'

'I'm no wanted here,' he retorted, 'the auld ruddoch made that clear enough, so I don't see why I should help ye, and ye've no right to be holding me here neither. Mem,' he added reluctantly as both stared pointedly at him.

'Billy,' said Kate, 'do you know what a wilful false assize is?'

'I do not. And I'll no take lessons in the law from a lassie.'

'That's a pity,' said Kate calmly, 'for if it was proved this day's assize was wilfully false, and you had aught to do with it, you'd be up for a fine that would have you working for your keep the rest of your life.' Maybe Gil was right, she thought, and I should study the law.

'I had nothing to do wi it! It's no my doing if my cousin . . .'

'Yes?' said Alys.

Billy muttered something inaudible. Babb shook him, and he said, 'If my cousin repeated what I tellt him to the other assizers.'

'And what did you tell him?' demanded Babb in his ear. 'Tell my leddy, now.'

Billy rolled his eyes at her so that the whites showed in the dim.

'What I said at the assize,' he said, with an attempt at nonchalance. 'That it was my belief the maister kent by far mair nor he was saying about the barrel, and how he kept us out of the way while it was opened. As for him saying it was books inside it,' he added sourly, 'a likely tale that was, and so I thought from the start.'

'And what did you know about the barrel yourself?' asked Alys. 'Did you see it hoisted out of the ship?'

'Aye, I did,' he admitted reluctantly. 'And it stood on the shore while we got the two big pipes on to the cart, and then we got it on the back of the cart and tied the tail up.'

'Why load it on the back?' Alys asked curiously. 'Why not on the top, in the dip between the two great pipes?' She held up her hands to illustrate the question, and Billy gave her a sharp look.

'Because the maister was feart it might fall off the top,' he said. 'So I kenned it was worth something.'

'And there was no other barrel the same size?' Kate said.

'I never saw one. There might ha been.' He stopped, staring at Alys, who had drawn her wax tablets from her purse and opened them. 'Here, are you to write down every word I say? For that's no fair!'

'And how not, if you're speaking the truth?' Babb demanded, towering over him. 'What's to fear from your own true words?'

'And how do I ken she writes it down exact? You're on my maister's side, you're going to twist all I say against me —'

'So you admit you aren't on your maister's side?' Kate said quickly.

'I never said that,' said Billy, hunching his shoulders.

'Then answer my leddy,' said Babb, giving him a shake. He glared at her, then at Alys.

'Aye,' he said sulkily, 'but she better write it down right.'

'Be sure I will,' said Alys sweetly, her stylus poised.

'Was the cart covered?' asked Kate. 'A hood, a canvas apron?'

'Naw. No this time o year.'

'And then what happened?' asked Alys. 'That was on Monday afternoon, was it?'

Billy shrugged, as far as he might in Babb's rigorous grip. 'If you say so,' he muttered.

'Where did it go next?' Alys prodded.

'Linlithgow. To the cooper's yard,' said Billy sulkily.

Bit by bit they got the information out of him. At Linlithgow the cart had lain in a barn in Riddoch the cooper's yard; at Kilsyth the next night it had been put in the dyer's cart-shed.

'And I got logwood dust on my hose,' said Billy sourly, displaying the dark mark down one thigh.

'You slept with the cart?' said Alys. He nodded. 'So you would have seen anyone who touched it?'

'I never saw anyone near it,' said Billy.

'So it was a quiet night, both nights?' said Kate.

'Hah!' said Billy, looking faintly smug. 'That's all you ken.'

Kate considered him briefly. 'What way was it not quiet?' she asked. 'What happened, then?'

Billy wagged his head. 'No a lot.'

'Go on,' said Babb, shaking him again. 'How was it no quiet? You've said this much, you'll finish the tale or I'll beat it out of you.'

'You've no need o yir threats. It was – it was just a thief in Riddoch's yard,' revealed Billy. 'But whoever it was I never saw him near the cart,' he said again.

'A thief? Why did you not come out with this at the inquest?' Kate demanded. 'There's Maister Morison held in the castle, and –'

'I tell you, I never saw him near the cart!' Billy repeated.

'What did you see?' Alys asked.

He shrugged again. 'No much. I heard more.'

Another prolonged session of questioning got a description of sorts. Billy had been woken by shouting, and possibly by the sound of a fight. He had looked out of the barn, but the yard was dark. The cooper had leaned out of a window bellowing threats, and then come down in his shirt, roused his household and searched the yard with lanterns.

'But they never found anything,' said Billy. 'Nor anything missing,' he added. 'There was barrels overturned and that, and when I rose in the morning the shavings had all been kicked across the yard, so I sweepit them thegither for them, but they said there was nothing taken. But I did think one of them got away by the back yett.'

'One of *them*,' repeated Alys. 'You said just now you never saw *him* near the cart. Was it one man, or several?'

'I never counted them,' said Billy. 'It was all dark, see.'

Babb shook him angrily. 'Keep a civil tongue, you,' she growled.

'If there was a fight, there must have been more than one man in the yard,' said Kate.

'Oh, very clever,' said Billy. 'There you go, the both of ye, turning a man's words against him.' Babb shook him again, and he glared over his shoulder at her.

'If you are speaking the truth, you have nothing to fear,' said Alys. Billy snorted.

'You said it was dark,' said Kate. 'Would you have seen if anyone went near the cart?'

'I'd ha heard him at the barn door, would I no,' Billy pointed out. 'Or when he shifted the barrels.'

'So you still don't know when the barrel with the books in it was changed for the barrel that was opened yesterday,' said Alys.

'Maybe it was witchcraft,' suggested Billy, and crossed himself.

'That was hard work,' said Alys as Babb ejected the indignant journeyman.

'It sounds easy when my brother talks about questioning witnesses,' Kate admitted, sitting back in Morison's great chair, 'but it isn't, is it?'

'Will I ask at the kitchen, my leddy,' said Babb, returning from the house door, 'if they could manage a wee refreshment for ye, before you have in the other men?'

The two girls exchanged a glance.

'The kitchen will be busy. Perhaps call Andy in first?' Alys suggested.

Andy, turning his blue knitted cap in his hands, confirmed the initial details of Billy's account. The barrel had been hoisted out first, laid on the shore, loaded on the tail of the cart. There had certainly been no other puncheon the same size in Thomas Tod's vessel.

'And what about this tale of a thief in the cooper's yard?' Alys asked.

'A what?' Andy's open-mouthed stare and swelling indignation were answer in themselves. 'He never – In the cooper's yard? At Linlithgow? There was no a word of it in the morning, he just brought the cart round to the Blue Lion his lone when we was ready to get away. What thief's this, mistress? What was taken? Did they catch anybody?'

'So you weren't in the yard yourself?' Kate said.

He shook his head. 'No in the morning, we just set straight off for the West Port to get out afore the traffic coming in blocked the gate. See, my maister's got an agreement with Willie Riddoch,' he expanded. 'We don't pay him by the night, they settle it up at the quarter-day atween them. But what's this about a thief, my leddy?'

'It wasn't clear,' said Kate. 'I'd hoped you could give us a better story. It seems from what Billy says as if there was a fight in the yard, and someone got away by the back yett, but he claims nobody went near the cart.'

'But did the cooper hear nothing? Has Billy invented it all, maybe?'

'The cooper came down and roused his men,' Alys said, 'and they searched the yard, to no purpose. So Billy said.'

'I don't like it,' muttered Andy. 'Someone should get to Linlithgow, ask at Willie Riddoch what happened.'

'My brother –' Kate began, and was interrupted by a shrill, furious voice from the next room.

'If you think I'm staying another hour wi they unnatural brats, wi an ill-natured auld besom like you in the kitchen and your like in the yard –'

'It's none of my part to raise those bairns,' declared another, more distant voice, 'I've enough to do cooking for a dozen, and no money in my hand beyond tomorrow –'

'Well, that's no trouble o mine,' said the first voice, and a plump young woman backed into the hall from the chamber beyond it. 'If you choose to stay here, you can deal wi what comes.'

'Aye, Mall,' said Andy grimly. The maidservant swung round, plainly startled to find the hall occupied, and Babb appeared in the doorway behind her, carrying a tray.

'What ever is the matter?' said Alys, moving forward. 'Why should you not stay? Surely the bairns need you?'

'Them?' said Mall, and tossed her head. 'They never mind a word I say, why should they need me? I tell you, the wee one's possessed and the other never heeds a word I say, and I've been here long enough –'

Babb came quietly into the room to set the tray down on a convenient chest. Behind her another, older woman, spare and upright, hurried across the further chamber. Her apron was stained and scorched, though her linen coif appeared clean; the cook, Kate assumed.

'You leave now,' said Andy, 'and you'll not see a plack of what's owing for the quarter, I can tell ye that, my girl.'

'You have stayed this long,' said Alys, 'why not a little longer? Just till your maister comes back? Who will mind the bairns if you go now?'

'Who's to say he'll come back?' said the nursemaid pertly. 'That's no what I've heard at all. And what wi him locked up in the castle for murder, and this auld –' she jerked her head at Andy, apparently at a loss for a suitable term – 'turning folks away without a by-your-leave, and now Ursel telling me what I can do and I canny do, I tell you I've had more than I can stomach o Morison's yard. I'm away up to fetch my gear, and you can mind the bairns yoursels if it worries you.'

'And well rid o a bad-tempered hizzy,' said the older woman from the door, her voice rising again, 'no fit to have charge o decent folk's bairns, trollop that ye are, and filthy with it! Where were you all this noontime, tell me that, Mall Anderson, while I'd to mind they lassies?'

'And I praise all the saints that's named, Ursel Campbell, I'll not have to eat another mouthful you've burnt!' retorted Mall. She flounced away towards another doorway at the far side of the hall, but recoiled with a shriek as she reached it. 'St Anne protect us, what's that? Oh, it's the deil's get. Come off the stair, you, and let me pass.'

'No,' said a small voice from the shadows beyond the doorway.

'Come here, my wee pet,' said Ursel in gentler tones. 'Come on, the both of ye, we'll see if I've a bit gingerbread for good lassies.'

'Aren't good lassies,' said the little voice. 'She said so.'

'Get out of my way,' said Mall between her teeth, 'afore I come up to you.'

'Why?' asked the voice, with what seemed to be genuine curiosity.

Kate, who had watched the drama unfold in amazement, suddenly found her tongue.

'Mall,' she said with authority, 'stand aside from the door. Wynliane, Ysonde, come down here to me.' And thanks be to Our Lady, she thought, that I asked Augie their names.

After a moment the two children stepped into the room, moving silently, hand in hand. As soon as they were clear of the door Mall brushed past them and on to the stair, and the little girls came forward hesitantly into the lighter part of the hall. Across the room, Babb folded her arms, watching.

'Come here,' Kate said encouragingly.

'Why are you in our house?' asked the smaller one. 'My da's no here.'

'Mind your manners, Ysonde,' said Andy. 'This is Lady Kate Cunningham and that's Mistress Mason. Where's your obedience, then?'

'Don't got one.'

Ursel clicked her tongue.

'He means a curtsy, like I taught you,' she said. The child shot her a glance and stuck her bottom lip out.

'Maybe they're too little to make a curtsy,' said Alys.

'I expect you're right,' agreed Kate. Andy opened his mouth to contradict, and was silenced by a glare from Ursel as the younger child, scowling, arranged her bare feet with care, spread her tattered brocade skirts and sank into a rather wobbly salute. Her sister looked at her from behind her elf-locks and rather hesitantly copied her, and Kate clapped her hands as they straightened up.

'Very good,' she said. 'I can see you were well taught.'

The older girl stared timidly at her, but the younger was not listening. Chin up, she was glaring at the ceiling; Kate, following her gaze, realized that she too had been aware of Mall's footsteps, which had now halted.

'Now will you come and get a bit gingerbread?' said Ursel. Kate hushed her, listening, and they heard the clunk of a kist lid closing.

'That's my da's kist,' observed Ysonde.

'You don't know that,' said Ursel.

'Do.'

'It could be any of the kists up yonder,' the old woman reasoned, 'yours or your da's or –' She broke off, and the child finished for her:

'Or my mammy's. Wasn't either my mammy's, and not Wynliane's and mine neither. It was my da's in his chamber where he sleeps.'

'We'll find out,' said Andy grimly. He moved to the house door as Mall came down the stairs, wrapped in her plaid and carrying a canvas satchel. The older child shrank silently towards Kate where she sat enthroned in the oak chair, and Andy went on, 'Right, my lassie. Let's see what's in yon scrip before you take it out of here.'

'What's in my scrip's none of your mind!' retorted Mall, clutching at the bag. 'You can just get your nose out of my business, you interfering old ruddoch, and let me by!'

'Mall,' said Alys, 'what did you take out of the kist just now?'

'I never touched any kist!'

'We all heard the lid closing,' said Kate.

The girl bridled. 'Well, maybe I just bumped it a wee bit. I never touched a thing inside it,' she averred.

'So you won't mind showing us what's in your scrip?' said Alys gently.

'Aye, I do mind!' Mall looked around, but the other door was blocked by Babb's considerable bulk. 'Let me pass, Andy Paterson, since you're so eager to get me gone from here, and you'll no bother speiring into my belongings either!'

'Then may I look in your scrip? I am not of your household.' Alys came forward with her hand out, and Mall ducked sideways, clutching the satchel to her again. Her plaid slipped, and at Kate's side the older girl suddenly pointed and screamed shrilly. There was a flurry of movement, and Ysonde was beside her nurse, tugging at the plaid, shouting.

'It's mine! It's mine! It's no yours! Give it back!'

'Get it off me, the wee deil!' exclaimed Mall, swinging her free arm wildly, impeded by the need to keep hold of her satchel as well as the plaid. The other child was still screaming, and both Andy and Ursel added their voices to the mêlée, but Babb strode forward and with one large hand scooped Ysonde shouting into the air while with the other she tugged the plaid from Mall's back. As the swathe of hodden grey wool came free, several more bundles of cloth fell to the floor from its folds.

'Put me down! Put me down!' shouted Ysonde, but Wynliane's screams halted abruptly as she pounced on the bundle nearest her. Kate, leaning forward from where she sat, saw that it was a linen garment, finely embroidered. The child hugged it to her, and reached with her other hand for the next item, which seemed to be a length of tawny worsted cloth.

'Could these be from Mistress Morison's kist?' Kate asked.

'Come, Mall,' said Alys. 'Let us see what else you have there.'

Mall was inclined to go on arguing, but Babb settled the matter by putting Ysonde on the floor, removing the satchel from the nursemaid's grasp, and upending it on to the settle beside Alys. Ursel hurried forward, exclaiming in annoyance.

'That's my St Ursula, and you know it, thieving hizzy that you are, Mall Anderson.' She seized a small, brightly coloured picture from the bench, and Kate recognized the sort of cheap painted woodcut print commonly sold at fairs. 'And that's mine and all,' added Ursel, snatching up a comb, 'and I don't know why you'd bother to steal it, you've no notion of how to use it. And is this no the box Jamesie was looking for last week, Andy?'

'That's my good belt buckle, I ken that,' said Andy, coming forward from the door.

'That's my bitie,' said Ysonde from the floor, where she was helping her sister to retrieve the scattered garments. She pointed to the coral teether with its dangling ribbon. 'That's mine. She can't have that.'

'Aye, Ursel, it's Jamesie's box right enough,' said Andy. 'And how did it get in your scrip, you wee – Stop her! Get her!'

He sprang forward as Mall reached the door, but as his outstretched hand touched her sleeve Babb collided with him on the same errand and the girl eluded them both. Disentangling themselves they set off down the steps after her, pursued by Alys.

Kate, left sitting by the cold hearth, looked from the children clutching their dead mother's clothes to the old woman picking her property out of the magpie assortment on the bench, and then round the shadowy hall. With a sudden feeling of making a momentous decision, she said to Ursel, 'And who will look after the bairns now?'

'I wish she had not got away,' said Alys.

'Aye,' growled Andy. 'I'd ha had her charged wi theft, and a pleasure it'd been too.'

'She was that quick,' said Babb, handing ale to her mistress. 'She must ha jinked down one vennel or another, and out of sight.'

'Is it worth laying a complaint?' asked Kate.

'No wi John Anderson,' said Andy. 'He's her uncle.'

'We got her scrip,' said Babb, 'and what she had hid under her plaid forbye.'

'Is anything else missing?' Alys wondered. 'Anything she could have hidden about her person?'

'Down her busk, ye mean, mistress?' said Andy. 'Here, I never thought o that.' He took the beaker of ale from Babb and sat down in obedience to Kate's gesture. 'Trouble is, the maister's no here to tell us what's missing. Those bairns might ken,' he added thoughtfully. 'Where are they, anyway?'

'With Ursel for now,' said Kate. 'She had to see to the men's dinner.'

'And I must go home to see about my father's, and Kate with me,' said Alys. 'But I think we must return after it. There are things I must ask you, Andy. For one thing, do you know where the barrel has gone?'

'What barrel? That barrel, ye mean, mistress?' Andy gave the matter some thought. 'I think Mattha Hog wanted to buy it for a show, to keep in the tavern. I could find out for ye.'

'Would you send one of the men to ask before his dinner?' Alys requested.

'I could. What are ye at, mistress?'

'Billy said the cart lay at a dyer's yard on Tuesday night.' Andy nodded agreement. 'He was complaining about logwood stains on his hose. If there is logwood dust on the barrel, we can be certain it was on the cart on Tuesday night.'

'How will you tell that?' asked Andy, staring at her.

She smiled, but shook her head and drank some of her ale. 'Find where the barrel is,' she said.

'And what about the bairns, my leddy?' said Babb. 'That Ursel's right, she's enough to do seeing to the men's dinner without a pair of wee tykes like yon underfoot all day.'

'I can gie her a hand getting them to bed, maybe,' said Andy doubtfully.

'They should be washed,' said Alys.

'Aye, well, that's no happened for a while.'

'Does any of your men have a sister or a sweetheart or the like?' Kate asked. 'A lassie who'd come in to help for a few days?'

Andy looked at her, chewing his lip.

'I'll ask,' he said finally. 'I don't think they do, but. There's only Jamesie that's courting, and his leman's well placed in Andrew Hamilton's household.'

'I could spare one of my household for a day or so,' said Alys.

'Besides,' continued Andy, pursuing his own train of thought, 'who'd direct a lassie? I've no notion what's to do for a pair of bairns like that, and she'd maybe no mind Ursel.'

'She'd mind me,' said Kate confidently. 'I'll be back here after I've had my dinner. Babb and I can sleep here the night.'

'I thought there would have been more argument,' said Alys, avoiding a puddle.

'I did too,' said Kate from the back of her mule, 'both about me staying at Morison's and about this idea.'

'Where is this Hog tavern, anyway?' Alys wondered.

91

'He said the Gallowgait, but we are nearly at the port and I have not seen it.'

'Andy seems to know where he's going.' Kate nodded at the small man making his way along the busy street just ahead of them. 'Come up, Wallace,' she said as her mule balked at the sight of a towering cartload of kindling. Babb stepped up from behind them and seized his reins in her free hand. 'I can get him by, Babb, give him his head.'

'Hmf,' said Babb, getting between the mule and the cart.

'No, let him see it go past, or he'll think it's still waiting for him.' Babb let go the reins but took hold of the animal's bridle. He turned his head into her grasp, attempting to bite. 'Deil take you, Babb,' Kate exploded, 'will you let me ride my own mule?'

'Oh, I will, my doo,' said Babb innocently, 'just as soon as he's minding you.'

'Andy has gone up that vennel,' said Alys over her shoulder. Wallace flicked his ears towards her voice, then suddenly decided the cart was not a threat and moved on, tugging at Babb's grasp on his bridle, to follow Alys into the vennel. Two doors down, Andy was waiting for them under a crudely painted sign: a boar with curling white tusks.

'Will the mule be safe here?' said Kate doubtfully, as she became aware of curious neighbours appearing in doorways.

'Aye, if I stay wi him,' said Babb, helping her down. She handed over the crutches, one by one, and took hold of the bridle again. 'You go wi Andy, Lady Kate, and be sure and mind what he says. And the same for you, mistress,' she added sternly to Alys, who smiled quickly and followed Andy into the tavern. Kate adjusted her grip on her crutches and swung after her.

There was one crowded room. By the door, near the barrel of ale on its trestle, groups of people stood about or sat on stools or benches, discussing the day's work in loud voices. Beyond them some were eating at a long table, and at the far end of the room a peat fire glowed in a brazier and a woman was stirring something in a big cooking-pot hung from an iron crane. The flagstone floor had not been swept that day. As the smells and voices hit her, Kate realized with some relief that there were other women in the place apart from the cook. One of them was saying, across the noise, 'Yir tavern's fairly coming on, Mattha. There's the gentry come calling now.'

A grey-haired man in a tavern-keeper's apron bustled forward from beside the big barrel, peering intently at their faces.

'And how can I help ye, leddies?' he asked suspiciously. 'What's your will of the house, then? We've a barrel of good ale, broached just yesterday, and a wee tait o the twice-brewed from last week, and a pot of mutton broth on the cran, wi barley and onions in't,' he recited, still watching them carefully. Kate, testing the manifold odours of the place, identified all these, and wondered if there were turnips in the broth as well.

'Aye, Mattha,' said Andy. 'I sent the boy down no an hour ago to ask about the puncheon.'

'Oh, aye, Andy Paterson, so ye did,' said the other man, his suspicions obviously borne out. 'What was it ye wanted about it?'

'I'd like to look at it,' said Alys, smiling at him. He looked at her blankly. 'Was that not why you bought it? So that people would come into your tavern to see it?'

'There you are, Mattha,' said a bystander in jocular tones. 'It's fetching folk in already.'

'It's no much to see, mistress,' said a man seated near Kate. 'It's just an ordinary barrel. No even any blood-stains.'

'It's my belief it's the wrong barrel,' said the stout woman with him. 'It'd no be the first time Mattha Hog cried up wares he never had.'

'It is the right barrel an all, Eppie!' said Hog indignantly. 'I bought it off the serjeant afore ever I left the castle this morning, and fetched it home myself on Willie Sproat's donkey-cart. You tell her it's the right barrel, Andy Paterson!'

'I canny tell her that,' said Andy reasonably, 'till I set my own een on it. So where is it, Mattha?'

'Aye, bring it out, Mattha,' said the man with Eppie. 'Let's all hear what he has to say.'

Kate, standing back on her crutches, watched as the barrel was handled out from behind the trestle. The bystanders fell silent, though the noise in the room was not much diminished. Andy bent to look at the marks on the staves, muttering names to himself, and then took the barrel-head from Hog and tilted it to the light from the door.

'Well?' demanded its owner.

'Oh, aye,' said Andy sourly. 'It's the same puncheon I opened yesterday morn. Ye can see where I set the hook to the withies.'

'It was you that opened it?' said a younger woman hopefully. 'And what all was in it? Was it a Saracen's head? And is that right there was treasure?'

The last word fell into a break in the noise, and heads turned. Kate, watching, had a glimpse of a face on the edge of her vision which seemed to be familiar, but when she looked round the room she could not see it.

'What was in here,' said Andy, 'all went up to the castle. The Sheriff kens all.'

'Aye, right,' said someone else, with irony.

There was general laughter, and Hog said, 'Is that it, then? You've seen it, lassie. Can I put it by now?'

'In a moment,' said Alys. She opened her purse, at which Hog looked hopeful, but all she drew out was a white cloth, which she unwrapped to disclose a small flask.

'What's that?' demanded Hog, all his suspicion returned. 'It's no holy water, is it?'

'No, no,' said Alys soothingly, and drew the stopper. 'Only well-water.' She tilted the flask so that water ran on to the cloth, then bent over the puncheon as Andy had done.

'What are you doing now?' said Hog, alarmed, 'I'm no wanting it washed!' He tried to pull the barrel away, but Andy prevented him with a firm grip of the rim.

'What are you after, mistress?' asked the man with Eppie. 'Is it bloodstains you're looking for?'

Alys, intent on her work, did not answer him.

'Gold dust, likely,' offered the girl who had asked about treasure.

'What, on the outside?' said someone else.

Kate, looking about the room again, found the by-standers had shifted. The familiar face was still hidden, but this time she could see the back of its owner's shaggy, sandy head, the shoulders hunched uncomfortably away from her where he sat at the long table. Who, she wondered, was Billy Walker talking to in this tavern? She turned carefully, so that she could keep an unobtrusive watch in that direction, but a squat man in a patched red doublet kept getting in her way and all she could establish was that it was someone large, wrapped in a dark cloak despite being seated close to the fire.

'And may I see the head?' said Alys. Andy lifted it for her, and balanced it on the rim of the puncheon; she folded her damp cloth again and began dabbing at the planks, paying careful attention to the joints and the edges.

'What are you doing?' demanded Hog again. Alys finished, and unfolded the cloth and held it up. It was a piece of old table linen, much-mended and bleached white, and even this far from the door the dark smudges were clearly visible on the diaper weave.

'Is that blood?' said the treasure-seeker eagerly.

'No, not blood,' said Alys. 'Logwood. The cart lay one night in a dyer's barn on the way home, we are told, and the carter complained he had logwood stains on his hose.'

'So what's that tell us?'

'Tells them the barrel was on the cart,' said Eppie.

'We knew that,' said Andy.

'Billy Walker was right,' said Alys. Kate, glancing down the room again, found that the squat man had moved.

Billy's sandy head turned sharply as he picked his own name out of the conversation, and the cloaked man opposite him looked up. Kate had a glimpse of a broad, flat, big-featured face with a tuft of beard on the lower lip; then the man's eyes met hers, and he smiled. She looked away quickly, a sudden trickle of fear running down her spine.

'Have ye seen enough, mistress?' demanded Hog.

'I have, indeed,' said Alys. 'Thank you, Maister Hog.'

She opened her purse again, and this time a coin changed hands. Hog, looking less surly, twirled his property away behind the tapped barrel, and returning went so far as to say, 'And thank you, mistress. Ye'll aye be welcome in Mattha Hog's tavern, and I hope you'll tell all your gossips what's here.'

'Oh, be sure of that, Maister Hog,' said Alys with a sweet smile. Kate bit her lip appreciatively, and turned towards the door as Andy began the task of shepherding his two charges out of the tavern.

There was some disturbance behind them, movement in the press of people, and exclamations of annoyance, but intent on making her way out without setting her crutches down on any of the feet Kate did not look round. She was unprepared, therefore, for the man who pushed roughly past her, putting her off balance. Recovering herself, she was aware of Eppie's indignant shouting, and of a shaggy head against the light in the doorway; then something struck her right crutch a heavy blow. It gave way under her, and she went sideways on to an acrid lap, and then as its owner, too, overbalanced they both went sprawling. There was more shouting, an exclamation from Alys, a furious bellow from Andy.

'Are ye hurt, lassie?' said a voice nearer her ear. 'Only if my wife was to hear o this, I'll get her rock about my ears when I get home the night.'

She pushed herself up, embarrassed, then moved her hand hastily and apologized.

'Oh, never apologize for that,' said the man, grinning, and heaved himself back up on to his stool. 'Can ye rise?'

'Are ye hurt?' said someone else. 'What did he do to ye? Was that an axe he had?'

'I can't get up my lone,' she admitted furiously. 'My leg –'

'An axe?' said Andy, hauling ineffectively at Kate's shoulders. 'Did somebody say an axe? What did he do wi it? Was that Billy Walker I seen? Surely he never had an axe!'

'Has he cut her leg off?' said the treasure-seeker.

'Fetch Babb,' said Kate urgently, knocking Andy's hands away, and scrambled round into a sitting position. 'Andy, get Babb here to me.'

But Babb was already there, elbowing people aside, ranting angrily about Andy's lack of care.

'As for you, my leddy,' she said furiously, getting a capable grip as Kate reached up to link her arms round her neck, 'you've no the sense you was born wi, coming into a dirty place like this where folks has no more courtesy than knock down a lassie off her oxter-poles.'

She hoisted, with practised ease, and set her mistress upright.

'It was Billy Walker,' said Andy, dusting at Kate's sleeve. Alys appeared anxiously at the doorway, with Wallace's soft enquiring nose beside her. 'Did he hurt you, my leddy?'

'It couldny ha been one of my customers,' claimed Hog in haste. 'I never seen him afore he was in here this day.'

'It was a great big man wi an axe,' said Eppie, 'for I seen it catch the light all blue. An axe on a long haft. What did he do wi it, lassie?'

'He knocked my pole from under me,' said Kate shakily, accepting one of her crutches from Andy.

'She's complaining o her leg,' said the man she had fallen on, dusting himself down.

'And why should she no,' said Babb, still angry, 'when

it's never worked since she was six years of age? And St Mungo himself refusing to do anything for her –'

'Babb!' said Kate.

'Oh, are ye *that* lassie?' said Eppie. ' We was all hoping the saint would listen to ye, with them letting ye in for the night. I was heart sorry to hear it never worked, hen.'

'You're kind,' said Kate. Someone handed her the other crutch, and she set it to the floor. '*Oh!*'

'What now?' said Babb, and stared in astonishment with her.

The padded top of the crutch, which should lodge neatly under Kate's arm, barely reached above her waist. Kate upended the thing to look at the other end, and several people exclaimed around her. Instead of the metal-shod tip which still graced its pair, the shaft ended in raw wood, half cut, half splintered.

'Would ye look at that!' said the man she had fallen on.

'I tellt ye he had an axe,' said Eppie triumphantly.

Chapter Five

'It could have been a dear sight worse, my leddy,' said Ursel forthrightly, handing Kate a beaker of spiced ale.

They were in the kitchen at Morison's yard, a stone structure down the slope next to the timber-framed house. It was far less gloomy and better cared-for than the hall. Cooking-crocks and metal pans were ranged on a set of shelves, a small spice-chest stood on another set among crocks of dried fruit, the wooden bowls and platters the men ate off were stacked neatly in a rack near the fire. Babb had brought Kate in there, at Ursel's urgent invitation, as being the most comfortable place in the house, and the old woman had immediately set a jug of ale to warm, with spices to lift the spirits, as she said.

'So I thought too,' said Alys. 'When I saw Babb, here, carry you out of the tavern, I truly feared for you. It was a great relief to find you were not injured.'

'I should never ha taken yez,' said Andy from the doorway. He came into the kitchen, accepted ale from Ursel and sat down on a stool. 'Your mule's stabled, Lady Kate, alongside the old mare. Where are those bairns, Ursel?'

'That lassie Jennet that Mistress Mason sent down,' said Ursel, nodding at Alys, 'she's taken them away up to wash them and redd up a bit, to let me see to my kitchen. She's a good worker, mistress.'

'She is,' agreed Alys, 'and has five sisters, so she can deal with bairns.'

'We'll see if she can deal wi these bairns,' said Andy sceptically. 'And what about yersel, Lady Kate? I should never have let the pair of you into that place,' he repeated. 'I kent from the minute you asked me about the barrel, mistress, there would be trouble.'

'But nobody was hurt,' said Alys. 'Kate has sent up to Rottenrow for her spare crutches, and the broken one can be replaced. And Our Lady be praised,' she added to Kate, 'that I do not have to tell Gil you were hurt about something I started.'

'I should have gone myself,' said Andy obstinately. 'You could have tellt me what you wanted. And what were you about, anyway, mistress? What did we achieve wi that? Was there anything on your wee bit cloth?'

'Oh, yes.' Alys opened her purse and drew out the cloth, unfolding it to exhibit the blue-purple streaks on the white diaper. 'See, there was certainly logwood dust in the joints of the barrel-head, and also lodged in the hoops.'

'So that barrel was at the dyer's yard,' said Andy.

'It was at a dyer's yard,' corrected Kate.

Alys nodded. 'Yes, unfortunately, we can't be sure it was the same one.'

'It's a coincidence, if it's no the same barrel,' said Andy.

'And my father always says he does not believe in coincidence.' Alys looked thoughtfully at the stained cloth. 'But even if it's the same barrel, we are very little forward.'

'How?' said Andy.

'That barrel must have been at the dye-yard on Tuesday night,' said Alys, 'but it could have been put on the cart at any time before that.'

'Or after it reached the yard,' Kate supplied.

'We could have guessed that already,' said Andy. Alys nodded, and folded the cloth again.

'You mean all that was for nothing?' said Babb. 'And my leddy cast on the floor and her stick chopped in two, just for something we kent before?'

'There's one thing more,' said Kate. They looked at her where she sat enthroned on the kitchen settle, even Ursel turning from the cooking-pots she was scouring. 'Billy Walker was in the tavern –'

'I was that sure I saw him!' said Andy.

'Aye, and I did and all,' said Babb, 'when he pushed out of the door, just afore you came out, mistress, to tell me my leddy needed me.'

'The cheek of him!' said Ursel.

'Talking,' Kate continued over them. 'Talking to a big man in a dark cloak. Billy was trying to hide his face, but I knew him. The other one was a stranger, but I got a look at him.' She stopped, thinking of the leering smile, and bit her lip. 'I think I'd know him again,' she added. 'I never saw a weapon. I suppose he had it hidden under his cloak.'

'It was him had the axe,' said Babb, 'for he followed Billy out the tavern. A big man in a dark cloak, as my leddy says. I never paid any mind to him, since he was a stranger, but I seen the axe, for it was in his hand, and he raised it up and kissed the flat o the blade. It wasn't under his cloak then,' she added darkly.

'*Kissed* it?' repeated Alys. Babb nodded, and Kate felt a shiver down her spine again.

'But why did they knock her down?' asked Ursel. 'Was it that crowded?'

'There was room and to spare,' said Andy witheringly. 'He aye was a clumsy –'

'It was no accident,' said Alys, 'for I saw. There was room to get by, as Andy says, though maybe not to spare. Billy pushed her quite deliberately. The other man went by just after him, and I suppose struck at her crutch as he went past.'

'Out of spite,' said Babb, 'the nasty creature.'

'Not only spite,' said Kate thoughtfully, 'for if I did anything, falling on that poor man, I provided a diversion.'

'A what?'

'So they could get away unchallenged,' said Alys. Kate nodded. 'So it was important they get away!'

'But who was it Billy Walker was talking to?' asked Ursel.

'Some broken man, likely,' said Andy. 'Who else would have a weapon like that in a Gallowgait tavern?'

'Would the serjeant know him?' Kate asked.

'Him?' said Andy witheringly. 'Forbye he's a friend of Mattha Hog's.' Kate understood this to be a dismissal of her suggestion. 'No, I don't see that we can find the man, and I don't see that it's any of our worry. We can give thanks Lady Kate's taken no hurt, and put the matter by. I've enough to look to, my leddy, mistress, wi keeping this place orderly for my maister.' He tossed back the last of his ale and rose. 'And I better go and see what the men are at.'

As the door closed behind him, the four women looked at each other.

'Now,' said Alys, with an air of rolling up her sleeves, 'we have work to do. Lady Kate will stay here tonight, Ursel, and Babb and Jennet will have an eye to the bairns until Andy can find a nursemaid for them.'

'Andy find them a nourice?' repeated Ursel doubtfully. 'He found the last two, mistress. They couldny deal with the bairns. They're orra bairns,' she said lovingly. 'The wee one's so sharp she'll cut herself, and Wynliane's a poor wee thing, but I've never found them any trouble. It's my belief they want a grown woman to mind them, no some bit lassie wi no sense.'

'That's a good word,' said Babb.

'Could you no help us yoursel, mistress? Does maybe someone in your household ken a woman looking for a place?'

'I will ask,' Alys promised. 'But for now, Babb and I need to make up a bed for Kate.'

Ursel bit her lip and turned away from the pots, drying her hands on her apron.

'You'll no want to get up the stair to the sleeping chambers, my leddy,' she said, considering the matter. 'There's a truckle bed under my maister's great best bed, in the chamber next the hall, but I've no notion what the strapping's like, it's that long since either was slept in.'

'We can sort the strapping,' pronounced Babb confidently.

Ursel nodded, and turned to Alys. 'I'll show ye where the linen's kept, mistress, but it's no in very good order either. I've done my best, but I've as much to do keeping the kitchen, and none of the other women would stay, with no mistress about the place.'

'Indeed, you keep a good kitchen,' said Alys, looking about the well-ordered room. 'Come and we will see what can be done.'

Kate, left alone by the fireside, leaned back on the settle and closed her eyes.

She remembered Augie Morison as a friend of her brothers, an awkward fair boy who would wait for a struggling small girl on two sticks while the others, even Gil her favourite brother, ran ahead. He seldom spoke to her, but hovered nearby, making certain she could manage rough ground without help, or finding an easier path to take. At the time, she recalled, this had made her very angry, but curiously she had been just as angry when she heard he had married Agnes Cowan and settled in Glasgow. It was very strange now to be sitting stranded in his house in his absence.

Gil had passed on his message of sympathy before he left. That was like the boy she remembered, to think of her problems in the midst of his own. And surely he had problems enough, she thought, before ever they opened that accursed barrel. This bleak, ill-kept house, the ungoverned children, the thieving servant – he needs a housekeeper, she thought.

'The lady's sleepin',' said a little voice. She opened her eyes, and found the little girls standing in front of her hand in hand, completely naked and dripping wet. The older one peeped at her with one eye from behind the elf-locks, but the younger was surveying her with that direct

103

scowl. A trail of wet footprints led across the flagstones to the stair.

'Jennet will be looking for you to dry you. Why are you two poppets not in bed?' she asked them.

Ysonde shrugged. 'Don't know. Why are you sitting in Ursel's kitchen?'

'Because I canny walk about.'

'How not? Did the man with the axe cut off your leg?' enquired Ysonde with interest.

Kate bit back her first response. These children, like their father, had problems enough. No need to leave them with the seeds of bad dreams.

'No,' she said. 'He broke my crutch, but he never touched my leg.'

'Why can you no walk about, then?'

'My leg doesn't work.'

'How not?'

'When I was Wynliane's age,' she said patiently, 'I was sick with a fever, and after I got better my leg never worked any more.'

They both stared at her, Ysonde with a sceptical air. After a moment Kate drew up her tawny woollen skirts and displayed both legs, the left one sound and muscular in a striped stocking and stout leather shoe, the right one shrivelled and shortened below the knee, the curled foot encased in its soft slipper.

'You've got odd stockings,' said Ysonde. But Wynliane, letting go her sister's hand, leaned forward to stroke the white knitted stocking on Kate's right leg, with gentle, wet fingers. Her lips moved soundlessly. Ysonde looked at her, and then at Kate.

'Wynliane wants it to get better,' she said.

'Oh, my poppets,' said Kate, and tears sprang to her eyes. 'If anything could mend it, I think that would.'

Footsteps on the stair down from the main house made her hastily rearrange her skirts, but only heralded the arrival of a flustered Jennet.

'There you are, you wild bairns!' she exclaimed. 'Come

and be dried before you catch your deaths! I'm sorry for this, mem, I turned my back a moment to find them clean shifts and they were away. Come back up, the pair of you.'

'No,' said Ysonde.

'Do as you're bid, now,' said Jennet, trying to get hold of their hands. Wynliane allowed herself to be captured, but Ysonde squirmed out of reach.

'Talkin' to the lady,' she said indignantly.

'You can talk to Lady Kate the morn,' said Jennet, 'for she'll be here then and all.'

Ysonde looked searchingly at Kate. 'Will you?'

'Yes, I will,' said Kate. 'Go with Jennet now. Maybe she'll tell you a story, if you go to bed quickly.'

'Oh, aye,' said Jennet. 'A'body needs a story once they're in their bed.'

The child stared at Kate a moment, lower lip stuck out; then she looked consideringly at Jennet, sighed heavily and offered her hand to be led away.

'And ask Lady Kate for her blessing,' prompted Jennet, 'like good wee lassies.'

Kate, taken aback, recalled her own nurse giving her the same order before carrying her up the wheel stair to the chamber she shared with her sisters. She had a moment's panic as she tried to recall the blessing her mother had used, and then found her hand raised to make the sign of the Cross and the words coming readily to her tongue.

'Christ and His blessed mother guard your sleep, my poppets.'

'Amen,' said Jennet firmly, and led the children away.

'The linen is of the best quality,' said Alys, 'but it has been neglected. We found a pair of sheets fit for use, and good blankets, and you should be comfortable enough here.'

'I should say so,' agreed Kate. 'We've shared worse, Babb and I.'

'And I tightened the strapping,' said Babb. 'Sagging to

105

the floor, it was.' She prodded the pile of blankets on the truckle bed and it creaked in a satisfactory way.

'You would hardly have slept in the great bed,' said Alys, 'but it must be cleaned before anyone does, or they will choke on the dust.'

They were in the chamber next the hall, at the head of the short stair down into the stone kitchen wing. Maister Morison's best bed stood against one wall, imposing in a set of very dusty hangings of dark blue dornick. Two plate-cupboards, bare and equally dusty, occupied two other walls; the plate was presumably locked in the iron-strapped kist at the foot of the bed which completed the major furnishings of the chamber. Several stools had been rounded up and set aside, and the truckle bed drawn out and made up on the inmost side of the room, away from the window.

'The moon's well past the full,' continued Alys, 'but I thought best to keep you out of its light just the same. You must be very weary, and it might keep you awake.'

'At least I have my other crutches now,' said Kate.

Babb snorted. 'The laddie took his time about getting back wi them. As for that Matt, down here speiring how you were –'

'My uncle will have sent him,' said Kate.

'Aye, very likely. But coming in here, looking about him and going away with never a word,' said Babb indignantly, 'was that not just like him, my leddy?'

'I must go home,' said Alys. 'I will come back tomorrow, and we will consider what to do next.'

'About what, exactly?' asked Kate. Their eyes met, and Alys nodded.

'There are many different problems,' she acknowledged. 'Tomorrow.'

'Tomorrow,' agreed Kate.

Lying awake in the dark, listening to Ursel's snores from the upper floor and Babb's quiet breathing at her back,

106

Kate found the problems crowded in on her without waiting for the morrow. They tangled round her like ropes, and whenever she tried to pick at one, another tightened its grip. She could not bear to think about her experience this morning, of the end to her hopes of a miracle or the bitter flavour left by the words of the man in her dream, but if there was to be no miracle, what of the other things which had happened in this very long day and which somehow demanded her attention? Here in Maister Morison's own house, it seemed impossible not to help him in his difficulties, but what could she do, thumping about on two sticks or carried up stairs by her muscular servant, that could not be done faster and better by another? Would he wish to be helped, or was it simply meddling?

The house itself, neglected for two years by a dwindling succession of careless servants, cheerless and disordered, begged to be put right. It needed willing workers and someone to direct them. As for the two little girls – the older one, whatever was wrong with her, had a sweet face and seemed to have the nature to match. Her sister, on the other hand, reminded Kate of a nest of wild kittens she and Tib had once found. The mother was a house cat, not a wildcat of the woods, but she had reared the kits away from people, and they were fierce and furious, with no smatch of timidity in them, spitting and lashing out with sharp little claws at a grasping hand.

She smiled into the dark, thinking of what had happened after Alys left. Not yet ready to sleep, Kate had taken herself into the hall again, to look at the jumble of dusty instruments in the corner. A lute with five broken strings lay on top of a harp-case, two recorders had rolled against the panelling, and under all was a painted box. Babb, with much argument, had dragged this out and set it on a small table for her, and she had opened the lid. As she had suspected, it contained a set of monocords, the dark keys and brass wires dull with disuse but clean inside their case. She opened out the folding prop for the music.

'Now, my doo, that's none of yours,' Babb had protested.

Ignoring her, Kate pressed one or two of the boxwood keys. To her surprise, the little instrument was out of tune but otherwise in good order.

'It's a good set,' she said, reaching for the tuning-key in its slot at the side of the lid. 'It's not been touched for a while.'

'No, and you shouldn't be touching it,' grumbled Babb. 'It's time you were in your bed, my doo.'

'I wish we'd never sold mine.' Kate bent down to hear the faint silver notes. 'Mother never got the price we'd paid for them.' She tapped one key, tightened the string again, then tested the other keys which struck the same string. Satisfied, she moved the tuning-key to another pin. Babb snorted, and stalked away.

Once she had brought the whole instrument into agreement with itself, and confirmed the tuning with the proper broken chords and scales, she picked out a few familiar turns and trills, then moved on to such music as she could remember. The stiff keys eased as she worked on them, and the sound they struck from the wire strings was sweet and delicate.

She had no idea how long she had been playing when there was movement in the corner of her eye. Caught in the tune, her hands kept going of their own accord as she glanced sideways, to find a pale little figure almost floating at the foot of the stairs: Ysonde in her clean shift, unaware that she was observed, dancing barefoot to the music.

She kept the tune going, glancing up from time to time, noting that the small feet kept exact time with her fingers. When the dance wound to its end she took her hands from the keys and held one out to Ysonde.

'Where's Jennet?'

The child paused, staring at her across the shadowy hall. 'Asleep.'

'So should you be.'

'It was dancy. Do some more.'

'Not now,' said Kate, 'but if you go back to bed I'll play some more tomorrow.'

Ysonde considered this. 'Will you say that thing again?' she bargained.

'What thing?'

'Christ a blessed mother.' Ysonde held up her hand. Kate, keeping her face straight, delivered the blessing, and the child vanished back up the stair. A bump and a distant murmur suggested that she had returned to bed.

Above Kate, now, Ursel's distant snores stopped for a moment then started again on a different note. The bars of moonlight beyond the great bed moved slowly across the wall, and timbers creaked round her as the house settled into the night. Used to a stone tower-house, Kate found the noises unsettling, but Babb's sleeping presence was a comfort.

What did the two children need? Ysonde should be sharp enough to learn her letters and some music, young as she was. It might be possible to teach Wynliane to read, even if she never spoke. Did she hear? Kate wondered. If the child was deaf, it would explain a lot.

The house creaked again. Kate turned on her back and lay with her ears stretched, and Ursel snorted upstairs.

As for Maister Morison's most immediate problem, this charge of murder from the inquest on the head in the barrel – was there anything more she and Alys could do about that? So far, she had to admit, their meddling had only achieved the loss of two of his servants and the partial confirmation of Billy Walker's account of the bringing home of the barrel. Chaucer came to her mind: *many a servaunt have ye put out of grace.* Perhaps Gil is doing better, she thought, staring at the bars of moonlight. How did it go on? *I take my leve of your unstedfastnesse.* Would Maister Morison see it that way?

Something moved across the moonlight.

Tucked in the darkness beyond the blue dornick hangings, Kate froze, concentrating on the movement she had seen, desperately praying that she was invisible in the shadows and that Babb would make no sound in her sleep beyond her steady breathing.

For a long moment there was no further sign. Then a chink of metal sounded, followed by a small scuffle. Someone was by the kist which stood at the foot of the great bed.

Kate lay still, hardly breathing. The sounds were repeated, stealthily. There was an indrawn breath, and a muttered word too soft to make out. Another chink of metal, and then a clatter as if something had been dropped on the floor, and a muffled curse. A man's voice.

Beside her, Kate became aware that Babb was awake. The woman did not stir, but the change in her breathing and the tension in her big frame were unmistakable. As the dropped item was picked up, scraping on the boards, Kate reached out under the sheet and grasped her servant's hand. She squeezed once, twice, and Babb returned the pressure.

Ursel snorted again above-stairs, and the stealthy movements at the foot of the carved bed checked, then continued. In the truckle bed, Babb gathered herself, and slowly turned back the bedclothes, ready to swing her legs out and stand up as quietly as she might. Kate reached down on her side of the truckle bed and grasped one of the crutches laid ready as they always were.

There was a rattle and click at the bed-foot, a soft exclamation of satisfaction, and a long creak. Babb seized her chance and rose to her feet in her shift. Kate, gripping the crutch, swung it up and on to the bed to meet Babb's groping hand. Armed with a four-foot stave of stout timber, Babb stepped forward into the moonlight, and with a sweep of her free hand slammed the lid of the kist down.

The intruder cried out in pain and alarm, and there was a scuffling as he tried to rise, to escape, but Babb pounced.

'What are ye about?' she demanded, dragging him away from the kist. 'Who is it, anyway, creeping into decent folk's houses in the night? Who are ye? What are ye after?'

'Let me go, you fairground show!' said her captive

breathlessly, writhing in her grasp in the barred light. 'Let me go! Ah, you've broke my wrists!'

Kate, trying to make out the two struggling figures, saw Babb shake the intruder by the back of his shirt. Then it appeared as if he flung up his arms and ducked, almost seeming to vanish. Babb exclaimed in annoyance and plunged towards the door, but before she reached it there was a flurry of movement and a sharp agonized scream. Something large scurried across the floor towards Kate, but the yelling continued.

'I'm stabbed, I'm bit! I'm dying! What is it, get it off me!'

'What on earth –?' demanded Kate, reaching for the tinderbox under her pillow. Her hands were shaking so much it was difficult to light the tinder, but finally she set a flame to the candle on the stool by the bedhead. In its sputtering glow she saw Billy Walker, bare to the waist, one arm clutched in Babb's renewed grasp. With his free hand he was rubbing at his hindquarters, gibbering in fear and what seemed to be genuine pain. The shirt he had ducked out of lay where Babb had dropped it.

'What ails ye, fool?' demanded Babb, shaking him energetically.

He howled, and twisted to look at the seat of his hose. 'I'm bleeding! What was it? What did ye set on to me, witch? I'm bitten! Look at the blood there!'

'There's no blood,' said Babb, turning him so that the light fell on the afflicted portion. 'Well, maybe a wee drop. Nothing's bitten you, man, unless it was one o yir ain fleas. More likely ye've stabbed yersel with whatever ye were using to get into Maister Morison's big kist, you nasty wee rugger.'

'I never! It was something wi teeth, for I felt them.'

'What's wrong?' called an anxious voice on the stair. 'What's to do down there? Are ye hurt, mem? Is it a thief in the house?'

'Jennet!' answered Kate. 'Put your shoes on and come down, lassie. I need you to go out to the bothy and waken Andy.'

111

'What's bit this thievin' creature? Was it a ratton, maybe?' asked Babb nervously.

'A ratton?' exclaimed Billy. 'It was bigger than that. It was like to take my leg off!'

Kate shook her head, smiling. 'No ratton,' she said. 'A wildcat, more like.'

She turned back the bedclothes to reveal Ysonde in her clean shift, curled in a ball at her side. The child looked up, and the candlelight showed her wicked grin.

'I bited him on the bum,' she said triumphantly.

'Should we send for the Watch, Lady Kate? There's nowhere we can shut him away,' said Andy anxiously, 'except the cart-shed, and I doubt me he'd get out o that no bother.'

'Is there nowhere in the house?' Kate asked. She was seated once again in Maister Morison's great chair, uncomfortably aware of how hastily Babb had laced her gown for her. 'A larder, maybe? The coalhouse?'

'Aye, the coalhouse,' said Andy, brightening. 'And did ye say he was at the maister's big iron kist, my leddy? What did he get from it?'

'A bruising,' said Babb with satisfaction, indicating Billy's swollen wrists. Pinned between two former workmates, he glowered sullenly at her across the lit hall, but did not speak. 'I slammed the lid on him,' she added. 'It's an auld trick, but it works fine. No, he got nothing out the kist, for I stopped him.'

'But how did he open it?' wondered Andy.

'He had a key,' said Kate, holding it up. 'He woke Babb when he dropped it.'

'Well, how was I to ken a pair of meddlesome witches was sleepin' there?'demanded Billy. One of the men holding him shook his arm, and he winced visibly.

'You just keep a civil tongue in your heid, Billy Walker,' his colleague admonished. 'And where did you get the maister's key, that's what I'd like to ken.'

'None o your mind, Jamesie Aitken,' said Billy.

'Oh, but it is,' said Kate. 'How did you get a key like this one? And what were you after, anyway?'

'Money,' he said insolently, 'what do you think?'

'And that's a lee!' exclaimed the man who had spoken before. 'When all of us kens the maister keeps his coin up at the castle wi the Provost. Come on, tell the leddy. What were ye after?'

'Up at the castle!' repeated Billy, and spat. 'Believe that, you'll believe anything.'

'Watch your manners!' began Andy, but Kate leaned forward from Maister Morison's great chair.

'What does that mean, Billy?' she asked. 'Do you know something we're not privy to? What does Maister Morison keep in that kist?'

'It's just the plate-chest,' Andy said.

'Billy knows different,' said Kate, watching the man in the light of the three candles on the pricket-stand. 'Well, Billy? What were you after? Was it coin, right enough, or treasure? What did the man with the axe send you for?'

It had been a shot almost at a venture, but it struck home. Billy jerked back, gaped at her, and then said in panicky tones, 'Ye never saw me! I wasny there!'

'Oh, but I did,' she said.

'Where were you no?' said Andy. 'For if it's the Hog you mean, I saw you an all, Billy Walker. As for pushing Lady Kate off her crutches, I'll pay you for that some day.'

'I'll pay him first,' said Babb darkly.

'I never! It wasny me that couped her ower!'

'He kens a lot for one that wasny there,' said Babb.

Kate nodded. 'So the man with the axe sent you for something in the kist,' she said.

'No, he never,' said Billy wildly. 'He never had anything to do wi it. He wasny there!'

'You broke in of your own accord?'

'Aye,' said Billy in relief. 'It was my idea. To look for the . . .'

'The what?'

113

'I forget,' said Billy.

Kate looked at Andy. 'He breaks into his master's house,' she said, 'opens his iron kist with a key, and then forgets what he was looking for.'

'Aye, well,' said Andy, 'maybe the serjeant can help him remember the morn. He's got a set of thumbscrews he's a great hand at using,' he continued, without conscious humour. 'I've no doubt he'd get an answer in no time.'

'We've no need to wait to the morn,' said Babb. 'Ursel's got a pile o kindling in the kitchen. We could get wee splinters and put them under his fingernails.'

'Ye can set light to them and all,' said the man at Billy's other side unexpectedly. Billy flinched.

'What were you looking for, Billy?' asked Kate. 'You might as well tell us, for we'll have it out of you sooner or later. If we don't, the Provost will. For a start, where did you get the key to the kist?'

'Likely his lassie gied him it,' said Jamesie Aitken. 'Her that took a strunt and went off without her dinner. Mall Anderson.'

'I said she had something down her busk!' said Andy inaccurately. 'Ten to one it was the key she took from the kist upstairs that we all heard her opening.'

'What if she did?' said Billy with an attempt at bravado. 'It doesny prove I took it from her. Maybe I was bringing it back,' he added. Kate laughed aloud at this effrontery, but Andy produced a menacing growl. 'Anyway you never saw it in my hand,' he added. 'You canny prove I brocht it wi me or that I made use of it to open the kist.'

'Ah, a man of law,' said Kate. 'Billy, you were caught with your hands in your maister's iron-bound kist. I don't think arguing points of law will make it any easier for you when the Provost sets his questioner to work on you.'

'We've no need to wait for the Provost,' said Babb. 'Will I get a bit kindling, my leddy, and start splitting wee skelfs off it?'

'You've no right to be talking like that,' blustered Billy. 'It's no your house!'

'It's no yours either,' pointed out Babb.

'Billy,' said Kate patiently, 'you can help yourself by telling us now what you were after. Why, if Jamesie is right and Maister Morison keeps his store of coin out of the house, did you go straight to the iron kist ? What did you think to find there?'

Billy glowered at her. 'Will you let me go if I tell you?' he demanded in belligerent tones.

'Oh, no. But I will bid the serjeant not to put you to the question.'

Billy shrugged, as well as he might in the grip of his two fellows. 'Aye, well. He's no hid it there, anyways.'

'Hid what?' exploded Andy. 'Get to the point, man!'

Billy threw him a look of extreme dislike and said direct to Kate, 'The treasure they found in the barrel. He only took the half o it to the Provost. There should be another bag o coin and that, hid somewhere in the house.'

'Who says?' said Andy incredulously.

'Is this what the axeman told you, Billy?' asked Kate.

'No,' he said in a panic. 'No, I thocht o it mysel. Nothing to do wi any axeman.'

'You're a fool, Billy Walker,' declared Andy. 'I was present the whole time, and there was only the one bag of treasure came out of that puncheon. And that went to the Provost entire. Where did you get the notion there was more?'

'Aye there's more,' said Billy. 'Even that Cunningham said there should be more.'

'You mean my brother?' said Kate evenly.

He swallowed. 'Maister Cunningham,' he began again, 'said if there was that much in one bag there should be the same again in another.'

'I mind that,' said Andy. 'And I said there was no more in the barrel.'

'Aye,' said Billy. 'Expect me to believe that?'

'We had all the brine out of the puncheon,' said Andy,

115

'before the maister, and Maister Cunningham, and Maister Mason. There was no more treasure in it, as you'd ha heard if you'd stopped to speir a bit more, you nasty sneaking wee bauchle.'

'What's he called, the man with the axe?' said Kate.

'He's got no name,' said Billy, taken by surprise as she had hoped. 'They cry him the Axeman, just.' He realized what he had given away and stopped, gulping in alarm.

'And the Axeman sent you to fetch the treasure out of your maister's kist,' said Kate. 'What were you to do with it? Were you to take it to him at the Hog?'

'He'll kill me!' said Billy. 'I'm a deid man!' He flung himself forward, taking his warders by surprise, and fell on his knees. 'My leddy, you'll protect me, won't you? He'll get me for letting on about him!' He shuffled forward to grasp at Kate's skirts, and she drew back instinctively into the chair. The two men bent to haul him up, but he grovelled on his face, moaning in what seemed like real fear.

'What does he have to do with it?' Kate asked. 'Why did he send you for the treasure? How did he know about it?'

'I dinna ken!' wailed Billy. 'I never cheated him!'

'When did he first speak to you?'

'In the Hog this afternoon,' said Billy quickly. 'I swear it, by St Mungo's banes I swear it! I never seen him afore that in my life.'

'In the Hog this afternoon,' repeated Kate, looking down at the man with distaste. 'You said just now neither of you was there.'

'Aye we were!'

'Put him in the coalhouse,' she said to Andy. 'And never mind giving him a light. We'll see if he can tell the serjeant a straight tale in the morning.'

Chapter Six

'This is a handsome town,' said Maistre Pierre, 'though it is smaller than Glasgow.'

Gil did not reply.

He was seated on a block of stone, throwing pebbles into Linlithgow Loch. The music and the drinking had gone on in the harper's lodging well into the night, and even after the brisk two hours' ride from Stirling in the sunshine his head still felt thick. Moreover, all through the merriment, the part-songs and snatches of consort-music, the ride in the bright morning, McIan's comment had nagged at the back of his mind. *Where your treasure is, there will your heart be.* It no longer surprised him that McIan could quote Holy Writ; the surprise was that he had quoted it in Scots and not in Latin. But what did the harper mean by it? His heart, certainly, was with Alys, but there was precious little treasure involved, and until there was more he was reluctant to agree a date for their marriage. I am a Cunningham, he thought, rubbing a stone with his thumb, I won't live on my bride's money.

The mason turned to look up at Linlithgow Palace in the morning sunshine, with St Michael's Kirk wrapped in scaffolding beyond it, and added approvingly, 'And that is a well-run *chantier*. I have spoken with the master. He tells me the church has been many years rebuilding.'

Gil threw another pebble into the loch, and nodded. Socrates, loping back along the water's edge, saw the splash and leaped in.

'Where are your men?' the mason asked.

Gil pulled himself together. 'I gave them some drink-silver and sent them into the inn by the West Port.'

'The Black Bitch, I think.'

'Aye.' Gil threw another pebble for the dog, who plunged joyfully after it, biting at the ripples. 'I told them to find the whereabouts of the cooper's yard for me.'

'The *tonnellerie*? I have asked the master builder. It is the other way – along towards the East Port beside the tower, which he tells me belongs to the Knights of St John. I did not realize they were here.'

'Oh, yes,' said Gil. 'Their headquarters is a few miles away over the hill.' He waved a hand vaguely south-west.

'Is it, indeed? I had thought it much further south. That would account for the number of their servants one sees in the town,' said Maistre Pierre. 'Likely your men find my lad Luke in the Black Bitch too. Well, I got nothing of use at the dyer's yard in Kilsyth. There had been no disturbance, and no orphaned barrels left lying about. And what have you learned in Stirling?'

Gil shook his head. 'I think our dead man is not the musician, since I've a sighting of him here on Tuesday morning, but I'll be happier about that if I can get another trace of him.' The mason grunted agreement. 'And I had no useful word concerning the other matter. Nobody would admit to knowing where it might have been hid, or to knowing who would know . . .' The mason grunted again. 'Except,' Gil added thoughtfully, 'that William Knollys was very keen to send me into Ayrshire to talk to my father's friends there.'

'Into Ayrshire,' Maistre Pierre repeated, raising his eyebrows.

'Cumnock and thereabouts. So what we have to do here,' said Gil, 'is speak to the cooper, and ask after the musician.'

'Do we also go out to the shore at Blackness?' asked Maistre Pierre. 'I understand it is not far.'

'It could be worth the trip,' Gil agreed, 'but we may learn all we need here in the town.'

'I have been thinking,' said Maistre Pierre. He looked about, selected another disregarded block of stone, and seated himself. 'Why put a severed head into a barrel? How many reasons can there be?'

'Concealment,' offered Gil. Socrates bounded out of the water, shook himself copiously, and sat down at Gil's feet, staring intently at the remaining handful of pebbles. *'We dule for nae evil deed, sae it be derne haldin.'*

'Yes, but where is the body? The rest of the man?'

'Hidden somewhere else, I assume,' Gil said.

'Where?'

'Somewhere in Scotland.'

'Yes.' His friend pulled a face. 'And what is being concealed? The murder, or the fact that this man in particular is dead, or the place of his death? Or something else?'

'And why should these need to be concealed?' Gil wondered. 'Both of the bodies we dealt with in May had been left openly where they were killed. Well, fairly openly,' he qualified. 'What was this man doing, that he had to be made to disappear?'

'Presumably that is connected with the treasure.'

Gil stared unseeing at a journeyman mixing mortar in the distance.

'Yes,' he said slowly. 'So the head was hidden in the barrel to conceal an unlawful killing, or the death of this man in particular, or his death in a particular place,' he ticked the points off on his fingers, 'or perhaps to get it past a watcher.'

'Or to preserve it to accuse someone later,' suggested Maistre Pierre. 'It was put up in brine, after all.'

'Mm.' Gil thought about that. 'If that was so, it may have been put in the barrel by someone other than the killer. We must keep it in mind, but it adds a complication and the question is already sufficiently complicated.'

'Mon Dieu, oui!' agreed the mason. 'And the treasure? Why did the killer not simply take it with him, since he has apparently made his escape?'

'Yes. That puzzles me. It surely means whoever put both

in the barrel intended to keep track of it – of the barrel. I wish we had some idea of where the hoard has been.'

'So does that mean the head was hidden for some longer purpose, not simply to conceal an unlawful killing?'

'Perhaps.' Gil got to his feet, and Socrates scrambled up looking hopefully at his face. 'We need to find a name for the dead man. Once we have that, we will have something to work on, and perhaps we can discover where he was killed.' He gestured towards the little town in the sunshine. 'Shall we go find the men? They'll be a stoup or two ahead of us by now.'

As they reached the foot of the Kirkgait, Maistre Pierre paused and stared eastward past the Mercat Cross along Linlithgow's other, busier street. There was a cavalcade approaching among the bustle of women with baskets and journeymen with boards or bales of merchandise. Helmets glinted in the sunlight, bright badges and well-waxed boots collected the dust of the dry road.

'Who is this with such a retinue?' he wondered. 'Do you know the blazon?'

'Yes, and I know the leader,' said Gil a little grimly. 'Sinclair. I saw him in Stirling.' He raised his hat as Oliver Sinclair reined in his horse, the ornaments on its bridle clinking. 'Good day, sir.'

'Good day again, young Cunningham.' Sinclair grinned at him. 'So Will Knollys never persuaded you into Ayrshire, then?' Gil shook his head. 'Probably wise, man. And what brings you this way?'

'My good-father and I are tracking a murder,' said Gil.

'Oh, the man in the barrel?' Sinclair nodded to the mason, and checked his horse, which was touching noses with Socrates. 'This is you in hot pursuit, is it?'

'Say rather, in cold pursuit,' said Gil wryly. 'The trail's near a week old, and may be crossed. That's what I want to find out.'

'Good hunting, then,' said Sinclair carelessly. He nodded again and nudged his horse on, summoning his men after him with a wide gesture of one arm. They clattered away east along the curve of the High Street, scattering chickens, pigs and burgesses as they went.

'He never mentioned leaving Stirling when I spoke to him last night,' said Gil, staring after them. 'Not that I had much conversation with him,' he added, after considering the point.

'Perhaps it slipped his mind,' said Maistre Pierre. 'Come and let us drink.'

The taproom of the Black Bitch, which had probably been the hall when the sprawling building had been somebody's house, was large and smoky from an ill-drawn fire, but clearly the ale was good, for even in mid-morning the room was busy and loud with gossip. Gil's men and the mason's Luke were there; Luke and Tam were sitting at one of the long tables, and Rob was in colloquy with the man in charge of the great barrel of ale on its trestle. Seeing them enter, he broke off his conversation and returned to his seat with a jug and two more beakers.

'Talk the man in the Moon to death, that one,' he said, grinning, as Luke moved along the bench to allow his master to sit down. 'William Riddoch the cooper has his yard along near the East Port, Maister Gil, at the back of the first Cross tavern, and there's been no musicians in the place since the court moved to Stirling.'

'In the town,' Gil questioned, 'or here in the Black Bitch?'

'Now that I don't know,' admitted Rob, 'for I never thought to ask it. Will I go back and find out? Only it might take me till dinnertime, the way that fellow talks.'

'We can ask further,' said Maistre Pierre. 'But what did you mean, the first Cross tavern? Is there more than one of the same name? That must be confusing.'

'Aye, well, I asked about that,' said Rob, 'and one's the Spitallers' cross wi the eight points, and the other belongs to the Sinclairs, so it's got their badge on the board. You ken, their cross that looks as if it's been chewed all up the edges.'

'The engrailed cross,' said Gil absently. 'I suppose, if

Balthasar was here to meet someone, as that singer in Stirling said, he might not have been playing.'

'He'd be playing, maister,' said Tam. 'They'll aye take the chance to turn a penny or two. I would myself, if I could play more than *Two taps on ae tun.*'

'He'd lie at a smaller place than this,' volunteered Luke, 'like the one across the way. The Green Lion, or something. This is maybe ower dear.'

'Will I go and ask?'

'No, leave it, Rob. I don't want to make too much of it. We can ask in the town.'

'Lute strings,' said Maistre Pierre, emerging from his beaker. They looked at him. 'There is a butcher's yard,' he pointed out, 'and the court spends much time here. Some-one must make and sell strings out of all that gut. Perhaps our quarry has been sighted there.'

'And there's another thing, Maister Gil,' said Rob, help-ing himself to the last of the jug of ale. 'Drouthy work it is, talking to a man like that. When I mentioned the name, maister, he asked me was I looking for work, for it seems this cooper's a man short. His laddie hasny been seen for near two weeks.'

'Is that so?' said Gil thoughtfully.

'Our man was nobody's prentice laddie,' said Maistre Pierre. 'He was nearer thirty than twenty, I should have said.'

'Just the same,' said Gil, offering Socrates his beaker to lick, 'we should keep it in mind.'

'He was warning me off,' added Rob, 'for there was a thief in the same yard just the other night. I'd say the cooper's luck's away the now.'

The luthier's workshop was halfway along towards the Mercat Cross, well up a steep narrow vennel which seemed to lead to the hillside south of the town. Inside, at a bench by a wide-open window, Maister Cochrane him-self was working on the delicate rose of a lute, an array of small sharp carving tools by his elbow. Beyond him a journeyman was shaping the neck of another instrument with a drawknife; an apprentice in the corner was rubbing what smelled like boiled linseed oil into a finished lute. More instruments hung on pegs, lutes and vièles, a psaltery and something which might be a cittern. Neat stacks of wood were tucked into a rack at the far end.

As Gil and Maistre Pierre entered with the dog at their heels, the two younger men looked up, and the journeyman set down his knife and came forward, brushing curls of wood off his jerkin.

'What's your pleasure, my maisters?' he asked. 'A new instrument? Music, strings, a ribbon fairing for your sweetheart's lute? We've all of those.'

'Music?' said Maistre Pierre, pricking up his ears. 'You sell music?'

'We do, maister.' The journeyman turned to lift a wooden tray from a shelf. 'We're a bit low at the moment,' he admitted. 'The court cleaned us out before they left for Stirling, and the package we're looking for from Edinbro's no come in yet.'

'No matter.' The mason bent over the pages in the tray. 'There will be something I do not have. These are good copies.'

'You sell much music?' Gil asked, watching his friend leaf through the loose sheets.

The journeyman shrugged. 'When the court's here, and the musicians, aye. Other times it's a slow trade.' He grinned. 'There's many of the gentry likes to have an instrument and strum it a bit, but playing a tune ye can put a name to's another matter.'

'So you sell to the King's musicians?' Gil said. 'And how about the travelling sort, as well? Do they come here for new tunes?'

'No that often. They'll get the maist o their music in Edinbro,' said the man regretfully, 'what they don't just learn each frae the ither by ear.'

'Edinburgh,' said Gil. 'I don't want to go that far. I was hoping you might have seen Barty Fletcher lately.'

'Barty?' said the journeyman. 'Oh, we've seen him, aye. No for a week or two, right enough.'

'A week or two?' repeated Gil. 'That's a pity. I wanted a word with him.'

'I seen him,' said the apprentice, looking up. 'I seen him in the town the other day.'

'What day was that?' asked the journeyman. Their master paused in his careful work, and turned to look at them. The apprentice thought briefly, and grinned, showing a chipped tooth.

'The day we got that new barrel o lights and put them to soak. For I said to him, my maister's just started a new load, there'll be fresh strings in six weeks or so.'

'Monday, that would be,' said the journeyman. Socrates, who had been checking the smells of the place, reached his ankles, and he bent to offer the dog his hand to sniff.

'I'll just need to keep looking,' said Gil.

'Did he say aught?' asked Maister Cochrane from his bench. Gil was reminded of McIan's portentous question.

'Aye, he did,' nodded the boy. 'He said that was good to hear and he'd be sure and call by before Michaelmas.'

'Hmph,' said Maister Cochrane, and turned back to his carving.

'I take this,' said Maistre Pierre. 'See, Gil, it is a piece by that Flemish fellow, and printed too. Alys was speaking of him recently. Myself, I prefer Machaut, but she seemed to find his music worthwhile.'

'Ockeghem,' agreed the journeyman, mangling the name badly. 'A good choice, maister. The lady'll ha pleasure out of that.'

Down on the High Street the men were still gathered round a well with a stone lion perched above the basin, deep in conversation with two maidservants. Gil and Maistre Pierre left them there and set off towards the East Port, and the imposing stone tower-house and its surrounding buildings which the mason had commented on earlier. The two taverns were next to it, one clearly more of a hostel for the knights of the eight-pointed cross and their guests, the other a sprawling structure very like the Black Bitch at the western end of the town. A group of men emerged from it as they approached, to stand in the sunshine with their ale. Light glinted on helmets, and on the chewed crosses stitched to sleeve or breast of their leather jacks.

'The *tonnellerie* is up this vennel, I believe,' said the mason, gesturing up the side of the tavern. 'Do all these alleys lead on to the hillside?'

The cooper's yard, as well as being up a vennel, was full of pieces of wood, but there the resemblance to the luthier's shop ended. Looking out through the open window of the cooper's best chamber, Gil could see a sloping cobbled yard nearly as big as Maister Morison's. It held two large open sheds and a barn, and a neat kailyard climbed up the hillside beyond them. Quartered tree trunks lay drying in racks in one corner of the cobbled area, split planks were stacked in another. Finished barrels crowded along the fence opposite the gate, a scrawny journeyman with prominent ears was sweeping up shavings to add to the brazier which was putting up a thin column of blue smoke, and five or six men were working with hammer or knife.

To one side the big gates were open, and a cart laden with puncheons was being handled out to the waiting horses by several men in leather jacks. Another man was just vanishing into the barn. Clearly Maister Riddoch's business was prospering well.

'Near as noisy as a stoneyard,' commented the mason.

'What's that you say?' asked Maister Riddoch, bustling into the chamber. He was small, bald and neat-featured, his expression both anxious and wary. Over leggings and a worn leather jerkin he had put on his good stuff gown to entertain visitors. He flourished the matching hat of tawny wool in a jerky bow and went on, 'Forgive me keeping you waiting, maisters, a wee bit business wi my landlord. A boneyard? Aye, it's like a boneyard, now you say, wi the staves there and the puncheons here instead of the leg-bones and skulls. A good thought, maister!' He laughed nervously. 'A good thought. Now, Mistress Riddoch's to bring a refreshment and you can tell me what's the trouble. Something wrong with Augie Morison's last load, you say? I'm sorry to hear that, for he's a good customer. What is it, was aught damaged? Aught missing?'

'No so much missing,' said Gil, 'as changed.'

'Strange, you say?' Riddoch had put the hat on, and it slipped sideways as he tilted his bald head sharply to catch Gil's words. He pushed it straight, staring hard at Gil. 'What way, strange?'

'One barrel had been exchanged,' said Gil, pitching his voice louder.

'Never in my yard, surely!' Riddoch had obviously heard that clearly. He swallowed. 'One o the pipes o crockware, was it?'

'The small barrel. The puncheon.'

'Puncheon.' The man swallowed again, and and nodded. 'I mind it. One o my make. He had it lashed on the back o the cart. But his man aye sleeps the night in the barn,' he averred. 'How would anything get near the cart without waking him?'

'That's what we're trying to find out,' said Gil.

The door opened, to admit a comely young woman with a tray in her hands, and Riddoch turned to her. Socrates, at Gil's feet, raised his head, his nose twitching.

'Mistress, here's these gentry telling me a strange thing. One o Morison's last load was the wrong puncheon when he got it home.'

She paused in setting down the tray, to exchange a long look with her husband.

'The wrong one?' she repeated. 'Saints preserve us! What way the wrong one?'

'It was a different barrel,' said Maistre Pierre, eyeing the contents of the tray appreciatively. 'Mistress, what is this you offer us? It looks very good.'

Mistress Riddoch blushed becomingly, and laid the tray on the stool by the hearth.

'There's ale,' she said unnecessarily, indicating the jug, 'and today's bread, and a dish of potted herring. Riddoch's very partial to a bite of potted herring to his midday piece, whether it's a fish day or no.' Her eyes met her husband's again in an anxious smile. 'And some pickled neeps,' she added, moving the little dish into sight from behind the ale-jug.

'Was it marked?' asked Riddoch.

'It was well marked,' said Gil, wishing he had got a list from Andy. 'Two shipmarks at least – Peterson and Maikison, I think – and several merchants' marks including Maister Morison's.'

'But not Thomas Tod's,' contributed Maistre Pierre, 'though the barrel we expected had been lifted from Tod's ship on Monday.'

'Saints preserve us!' said Mistress Riddoch again, looking from one to another of them. She had a plump, sweet face under her white linen headdress, and now wore a serious expression as she counted on her fingers. 'Monday, you say? So it lay here on Monday night?' She turned to her husband again, biting her lip. 'Who else's cart lay here on Monday, Riddoch?'

'But how did Augie's man not notice it was the wrong puncheon?' worried Riddoch, not answering her. 'I mind the man well, he seems a sharp fellow, and helpful enough. Offered to watch the barn on his own last time he was here, let the other carters go drinking round at the tavern. Right enough I suppose that would ha been Monday.'

'Nobody noticed the exchange, until it came home and we were about to open it,' said Gil. 'I suppose they were alike in size.'

'Then it must ha been another of my puncheons,' said Maister Riddoch positively. 'Any that works wi barrels, maister, will tell ye – a barrel out of one yard's as different from a barrel out of another as kale is from neeps. It's like hand-write. I've heard Maister Abernethy the notary say he kens the hand-write in this document or that. Barrels is the same. Every man has his ain way of doing things.'

127

'So also in my craft,' said Maistre Pierre. He and the cooper exchanged glances. 'So this puncheon that came home to Glasgow must have been switched for another of your make.'

'Monday,' said Mistress Riddoch again. She faced her husband and raised her voice a little. 'It was Monday night the thief was in the yard, Riddoch. Could that be it right enough?'

'Monday?' He counted on his fingers as she had done. 'Aye, mistress, you're quite right, it was Monday night. But that canny be the answer – he was nowhere near the carts, whoever he was.'

'A thief ?' Gil repeated innocently. 'Did you take him?'

'No, we never. I heard something fall over in the yard,' said Mistress Riddoch, concentrating on pouring ale, 'so I looked out, and I thought something was moving, so I woke Riddoch, and he rose and put his boots on, but he found nothing. I've tellt you, husband, whoever it was, they were moving about near the gate.'

'There was nobody to see when I went out,' said the cooper. 'Time I got on my boots, he was away.'

'You say you saw something moving?' said Maistre Pierre to Mistress Riddoch.

'Aye,' she said, handing him a cup of ale. 'It was a clear night, and the moon near full, you ken, so the yard was well lit. There was a banging, like something going over, and a kind of shouting, and it woke me, and when I looked out I saw . . .' She faltered, and glanced at her husband.

'I tell you, you were dreaming, Jess,' he said sternly. 'Better safe than sorry, and you did right to wake me, for there had been someone in the yard, but there was nothing like what you thought you saw. There was nothing taken, and never a great roll of stuff here that night.'

'I wasny dreaming,' she said, as if she had said it often already. 'I was dreaming before I wakened, about the yard and the men working, but what I saw was never part o my dream.'

She handed Riddoch his ale, and began to cut the loaf on the tray.

'What did you think you saw?' Gil asked.

'Movement,' she said, and paused in her work. 'Like, maybe, two or three men. There was certainly two in the light, and I thought another moving in the shadows by the barn.'

'What were they doing?'

She looked at her husband, and back down at the loaf. 'I couldny see what the man by the barn was up to. If there was one,' she added, before her spouse could comment. 'But the two out in the moonlight were bent over some big thing, I couldny make it out. Almost like as if it was someone lying on the ground, it was. So then I woke Riddoch, and he woke the men, and then I had to help him wi his boots.'

'There was nothing of the sort in the yard when I got down,' said Riddoch firmly.

'Aye, for they never waited while you went down and got the door open,' she responded, and sawed another wedge off the loaf. 'I tell you, husband, I saw them go when I looked out again.'

'How many?' asked Gil. 'Did they have a puncheon with them?'

'I never saw a puncheon. One was away up the kailyard. Likely he went out the back yett. And the other – the other went by the barn.' She paused, biting her lip, and began spreading potted fish.

'Did you see what he looked like?' asked Maistre Pierre, watching her hands.

She shook her head. 'Like a big man in a black cloak,' she said, and hesitated, with another glance at her husband. 'And he was carrying something, it might ha been the same thing that was on the ground. I never saw what it was, except it was long and seemed heavy – maybe like a roll of cloth, or a side of meat, or such. Then he stepped into the shadow next the gate, and Riddoch cam back from waking the men, and wanted his boots on,' she went on with more certainty.

'This man in the cloak,' said Gil slowly, 'was he one of the two you saw earlier standing in the moonlight?'

'She never saw anything,' said Riddoch.

'N-no,' said his wife, thinking hard. 'It's hard to say, maister, but I think the two I saw first were smaller.' She shut her eyes, the better to conjure up the image she needed. 'I tell ye what, sir, one of them had a hat wi a feather, it might ha been him that was away up the kail-yard, and the other wasny in a cloak.'

'So there were three men in the yard,' said Gil. She gave him a serious look, and nodded.

'At least three. You saw only the one man at the yett?' asked Maistre Pierre.

'Aye.' She shivered. 'Just the one.'

'Augie Morison's man saw nothing of that kind, and so I said to –' said the cooper, and bit off his words. After a moment he continued, 'He tellt me – Morison's man tellt me he woke, and came to the barn door, and saw one man running for the gate. I asked, what was he wearing, and he said he thought just shirt and hose. And right enough the gate was opened.'

'Aye,' said his wife.

'Shirt and hose,' repeated Gil. Mistress Riddoch handed the platter, and he took a slice of bread smeared with a generous portion of potted herring. Maistre Pierre was already chewing. 'I'd ha thought a man would dress in darker clothing if he was planning a theft.'

'Aye, he'd left,' agreed Riddoch, helping himself as the platter went past him. 'Whoever he was. And Morison's man swore he was never near the carts. There was three carts in that night,' he recalled.

'Madame, this is excellent,' said Maistre Pierre with enthusiasm, reaching for another portion. Socrates watched the movement of his hand, nose twitching. 'Is it your own work? What do you put with the fish? I am sure my daughter would like to know.'

'The secret's in the salting,' confided Mistress Riddoch, dimpling in pleasure at the compliment. 'I salt my own, ye ken, and I put a chopped onion in the brine to every dozen fish. Will you have some more ale, maister?'

'And then nutmeg when you pound the salted fish?' said Maistre Pierre speculatively, and took another mouthful. 'And is it galangal?'

Gil took his own ale and a second wedge of bread over to the window, thinking about what he had heard. Out in the yard Maister Riddoch's men were hard at work with hammer or drawknife. In the centre of the open space a man was working with an adze. Lifting a long narrow plank from the stack beside him he trimmed one end, first one side and then the other, with quick even strokes of the adze, then tossed the stave in the air, caught it the other way up and set about shaping the other end. Gil found himself watching, fascinated.

'That's David Seaton,' said Maister Riddoch at his elbow. 'No a stave-maker his like in the country, I dare say. I'm no equal to cutting staves now, I'm too stiff for it, but I think he's as good as I ever was.'

'He's been well taught,' said his wife from across the room. Riddoch did not look round, but the corners of his mouth quirked. 'Is it time for the men's noon piece, husband?'

'Aye, call them in, lass,' he said. 'We can serve ourselves wi the rest in here.'

'May we look at the barn, once we have eaten?' Gil asked, as Mistress Riddoch bobbed to her guests and left. 'I'd like to understand how the cart was stowed on Monday night.'

'I can see you would,' said the cooper, nodding, 'but it seems to me it's most likely Augie's men loaded the wrong puncheon at Blackness. I'll show you the barn, maisters, and anything else you've a notion to see.'

Gil broke the last of his bread in half and gave a portion to Socrates, watchful at his feet. The dog took it delicately and swallowed it whole, and Gil held out the other piece.

'When you're ready, maister,' he said.

They went out through the hall, where Mistress Riddoch presided over the long board, and the men and three maidservants were addressing barley bread and stewed kale. Once in the yard, the cooper showed an inclination to explain the entire process of making a barrel, and Maistre Pierre took this up with interest. Gil listened, looking carefully about him at wood-stacks and benches, the work-space in the two open sheds, and the brazier with its smouldering fire. Nothing seemed to be amiss.

'You'll have to be wary of the fire,' he suggested.

Riddoch nodded. 'Aye, you're right, maister, particular when it's windy. The shavings blow about.' He looked at the heap of shavings waiting to be burned, and tut-tutted. 'That lad Simmie! I've tellt him and tellt him, and he aye gathers the scraps too close to the barn. Simmie!' he shouted at the house. After a moment the young journey-man who had been sweeping earlier appeared in the door-way, wiping his mouth on his sleeve. 'Simmie, get this moved, now.'

'Now?' repeated Simmie, taken aback.

'Aye, now, afore you finish your kale. If the wind were to change, and sparks blow into they scraps there, the barn would go up afore we kent what was happening, and then the whole yard, and you'd have no living, Simmie. So get it moved.'

Simmie scowled, but rolled up his sleeves and came across the yard to lift his besom.

''S none o my part to sweep the yard,' he muttered. 'If we hadny run out of withies I'd be making hoops, no sweeping the yard. When that lazy Nicol gets back, I'll black his ee for this, see if I don't.'

'What was that?' demanded his master.

'And another thing, maister,' added Simmie aloud.

'You've been on at me all week to move it, every time I sweep it here, but you put this heap here your very self the other day, so why are you –'

'I never did, you daftheid!'

'Aye, you did, maister. For it wasny me, nor any of the other men, and the lassies wouldny come out sweeping in the yard –'

'What are you talking about, man?' demanded Riddoch.

'Just the other day,' repeated Simmie. 'I cam in at the day's start, and all the shavings in the yard was swept up, but they wereny where I'd put them the night before, they were here.'

'They must have blown, you great lump. I'd never put them here. Now get them over where they belong, and stop arguing.'

'No arguing,' muttered Simmie, bending to his broom. 'I'll get that Nicol for this, so I will.'

'What day was that?' Gil asked casually. Riddoch turned to look at him. 'What day did Simmie find the chips swept over here?'

'What way?' repeated the cooper. 'It must ha been the wind.'

'What *day*, maister,' said Simmie, pausing to lean on his broom. 'What day? Well, it wasny yesterday.' He thought deeply. 'It might ha been Wednesday,' he admitted.

'Tuesday? Monday?'

'No Monday. I'd a heid like a big drum on Monday, I'd no ha noticed a deid ox in the yard.' He grinned, and mimed pounding on his skull. 'Might ha been Tuesday.'

'Tuesday or Wednesday,' said Gil, and the man nodded. 'And the chips and shavings were all swept over here?'

'Aye. Just like this. A neat job someone had made of it.'

'Well, get on with it, and make a neat job of it now,' said his master, 'or you'll no get your kale.' He marched past his henchman and pushed open one leaf of the door to the barn. 'You wanted to see this, maisters.'

The barn was a substantial building, nearly as big as Maister Riddoch's house, but without the upper floor. Gil stood while his eyes adjusted to the light which filtered under the eaves; over his head swallows darted in and out to nests of shrieking young among the rafters. The floor was packed earth, swept clean; stacks of barrels, bundled staves, folded canvas cart-aprons, spare workbenches, were ranged round the walls

'Augie's cart was here first, if I mind right,' said Riddoch, pointing with his left hand, 'so it would lie there, up this end, this corner. Now whose was next?' he wondered. 'He was bound for Leith, I mind that. It'll come to me. That lay in the other corner, side by side wi Augie's. And last in was a great pipe o clarry wine, off a ship at Blackness and bound for Irvine, though why he never brought it ashore at Irvine in the first place – that'd be down here, near the door. Last in and first out, it was, out on the road so soon as the gates was open, for my lord Montgomery must have his clarry wine it seems. There was just the great pipe on the cart.'

'I know Montgomery,' said Gil rather grimly. 'If it was just the one pipe of wine, our barrel can't have come off his cart. What about the other? What sort of load was it?'

'A big load,' said Riddoch. 'Mixed. More than a dozen puncheons and kegs, off different coopers, and a hogshead or two and all. Salt fish, the most of them, by what the man said. But how would a barrel jump from one cart to another, maister?' He led the way to the end of the barn, while the swallows whirred and twittered overhead. 'See – Augie's cart lay here, maybe this wide. Robert Henderson's – aye, I kent it would come to me. He's a Kilsyth man. Robert Henderson's lay here, there would be more than an ell between them, and a full puncheon's no light weight. It wouldny happen by chance.'

'No,' said Gil thoughtfully. 'And Augie's man said the fellow he saw never came into the barn?'

'This does not make sense,' complained Maistre Pierre. 'Three thieves who stole nothing, a barrel which vanishes, a watchman who did not see it.'

'But did it vanish?' Gil looked about him. 'Where would you hide a barrel, Pierre?'

'Maister?' Simmie's large ears were outlined against the light at the barn door. 'Could you call your dog, maybe?'

'The dog?' Gil strode towards him. 'What's he up to? Socrates!'

'It's just he'll no leave this bit alone,' explained Simmie. 'He's found a scent he likes, and I canny sweep round him.'

'Socrates!' Gil stepped out into the sunlight. Shading his eyes he found his dog sniffing intently at the newly swept cobbles by the end of the barn. 'Come here!' he said sharply. Socrates wagged his stringy tail, but gave no other sign of hearing. His head was down, his muzzle close to the stones, and the rough grey coat was standing up on his shoulders and spine. Gil seized the animal's collar to pull him away, and realized he was growling quietly.

'What have you found?' he said. 'Leave it! Leave!'

'What's drawing him?' asked the cooper. 'What's he scented? Have we emptied a load o fish there, or what?'

Gil bent to look closer at the patch which interested the dog.

'There's something caked between the stones,' he reported. He rubbed at it and sniffed his fingers.

'What is it?' said the cooper.

'Gilbert!' called Maistre Pierre sharply from inside the barn. 'I think you were right. Come look at this!'

He was poking about at the far end of the barn, near the place where Morison's cart had stood. As Gil entered the barn towing a reluctant Socrates he turned his head, and indicated a shadowy corner.

'Look here!' he said dubiously. 'It has been opened and emptied, but it is very like the barrel we had, the head here has by far less birdlime on it than on the goods beside it, and though the light is bad I think it has both Maister Morison's own mark, and also Tod's shipmark. Could this be our missing barrel?'

'Aye, very likely it is,' said Gil in Scots, 'for what the dog

135

wouldny leave out there is a great patch of blood. I'd say it's no more than a few days old.'

'Blood?' repeated Riddoch in growing dismay. 'In my yard? What's been going on?' He looked from one to the other of them. 'What was in the barrel you had home, anyway?'

'Let us get this one outside,' requested Maistre Pierre, 'and we will tell you.'

Out in the light, the puncheon he had found was indeed very like the one which had reached Morison's yard. Gil thought he recognized several of the marks, and the additional brand on head and flank seemed to be a fox's head, which was presumably Thomas Tod's mark. It was dry inside, and held a few handfuls of the chopped lint which had padded the contents. Gil shook the barrel so that the lint shifted, and something white showed under the fluffy clumps. Letting go the dog, who immediately slipped back to the interesting cobbles, he leaned in to extract a folded paper.

'Is that the docket?' said Maistre Pierre hopefully.

'It is indeed.' Gil scanned the small looped writing. 'Well! He has done us proud – Pierre, we must find this load. Look at this!' He handed the sheet to the mason, who bent to inspect it.

'What was in the barrel that went to Glasgow?' asked Riddoch again, frowning. 'You're very close about it, maisters.'

Gil looked directly at him, dragging his mind back to the matters of most concern.

'Maister,' he said, 'what like is your missing laddie?'

The frown drained from the cooper's face, leaving open-mouthed dismay.

'Nicol?' he said hoarsely, and crossed himself. 'Christ aid us, what's come to him?'

'Can you describe him?' pursued Gil. 'What colour is his hair? His eyes? What age is he?'

'Now that I can tell you,' said Riddoch, licking his lips. 'He was born the same year as the King's brother Prince

136

James. He's sixteen past at Corpus Christi. Sinclair never –
I – I beg you, maister, if you ken aught about him, tell me
now. He's my son.'

'Does he resemble you, maister?' asked the mason, looking at the neat-featured face before him.

'They tell me he does, aye.' Riddoch looked from one to
the other of them, not daring to repeat his question. 'His
een are grey. Like his mother's, God rest her soul.'

'Then all I can tell you is we ken nothing about him,'
said Gil.

Riddoch clutched at the rim of the barrel in front of him,
as if for support.

'Our Lady be thanked for that!' he muttered, crossing
himself again.

'Now can you tell us in return,' said Gil, 'who found and
emptied this barrel?'

Chapter Seven

Seated once more in the cooper's best chamber, with an offended dog at his feet, Gil repeated the question.

'Who emptied the barrel, maister?'

'I've no a notion,' said Riddoch firmly. He had found a new confidence; Gil, eyeing him, regretted reassuring the man about his son. And yet, in conscience, he thought, could I have left him in anxiety any longer?

'Where has your son gone?' he asked. 'Was he alone?'

'He went into Stirlingshire,' said Riddoch cautiously. 'He's done the journey afore, he kens the road. For withies,' he added.

'Where do you get them?' asked the mason curiously. 'I should have thought there was a supply closer to hand.'

'We get them at a good price from his lordship,' said Riddoch.

'Sinclair, you mean?' said Gil casually. Riddoch froze a moment, then nodded. 'Has the boy been away long?'

'Aye.' This appeared to be surer ground. 'We've kin there, he was to visit his uncle.'

'And you looked for him back before now,' Gil stated. Riddoch nodded with reluctance. 'When? How long overdue is he?'

'A few days now.'

'How would he carry the withies?' asked Maistre Pierre.

'He'd pack them on the old horse. Or if he got a double load,' qualified Riddoch, 'they might hire him a cart. And that's another thing. We'll need the beast shortly, to take our turn at the carts when we win the hay off the burgh muir. The laddie kens that.'

Gil turned a little to face Riddoch directly. 'The barrel which should have reached Glasgow,' he said, 'the one we found empty in your barn the now, would have held books.'

'Books?' Riddoch laughed, with little humour. 'I'd like to ha seen that!'

'Seen what?'

'When it was opened. A right laugh that would be.' He looked at Gil. 'And the one you did get? What was in it, maister?'

'Brine.'

'Brine?' repeated Riddoch. He licked his lips. 'Just brine? I mean – was there aught in the brine? Fish, maybe, or salt meat? Or –'

'Not salt meat, no,' said Gil, grimacing. 'We found a man's head. And a few shavings of wood, very like what's blowing about your yard.'

The cooper gaped at him.

'A man's head, in one of our barrels?' said Mistress Riddoch from the door. She came into the room to stand beside her husband's chair. 'What like man, maister?'she asked, her voice high and tense.

'It's no the boy, Jess,' said her husband. They crossed themselves simultaneously.

How long had she been there, Gil wondered. Long enough to govern her countenance, though not her voice.

'Past twenty but not thirty years, short dark hair, one ear pierced,' said Maistre Pierre concisely, 'and odd-coloured eyes. One blue eye, one brown.'

'Nobody we ken,' said Riddoch quickly. His wife looked down at him, opened her mouth, closed it again.

'You're sure of that?' said Gil. 'Mistress? Would you ken anyone like that?'

'N-no,' she said. 'No. Nobody like that.'

'Nobody we ken,' repeated Riddoch. 'Was there aught else with the head?'

139

'What should there be?' asked Gil, and the cooper looked wary.

'Nothing, maybe. Just I wondered if there was, well, any more of him, or any of his gear perhaps, that might tell you who he was, Christ assoil him.' He crossed himself again, and his wife and Maistre Pierre did likewise.

'Maister,' said Gil, 'consider what we have found. The barrel that was missing off Maister Morison's cart has appeared in your barn, empty.'

'And has been there for no more than a few days, it is obvious,' put in Maistre Pierre.

'There is a great patch of dried blood on the cobbles in the yard.'

'Blood?' repeated Mistress Riddoch. 'Where? What –' She looked down at her husband again, and bit her lip.

'Under the pile of shavings, at the end of the barn,' said Gil. 'Socrates, here, found it when Simmie swept it clear.' Socrates' ears twitched at the mention of his name, but he kept his head pointedly averted from his master. 'And I'd like another word with Simmie, maister,' he added to the cooper.

'He's away an errand,' said Riddoch. 'He'll be an hour or so, if ye can wait.' His wife turned her head sharply to look at him. 'Himself wanted a word carried out-bye,' he muttered, in response to the question in her eyes. She pursed her mouth, and turned to Gil again.

'A pile of shavings by the barn? But Riddoch never lets the men keep it there, for fear of fire. It's only sense.'

'Quite so,' agreed Gil. 'So who first moved the heap from its usual place?'

'It doesny have a usual place,' she said. Her husband sat silent. 'The men just sweep up where there are the most scraps.'

'And the barrel that reached Glasgow,' pursued Gil, 'contained a man's head.' He studied Mistress Riddoch for a moment. 'When did you last put up salt fish, mistress?'

She jumped as if he had struck her, and one hand rose to cover her mouth.

'Tuesday,' she said. 'It was late for the quarter-day, but himself had never sent for the rent. I had two baskets of herring off Lizzie Cowan on Tuesday morn, and just in time.' She lowered the hand, and her husband put up his own to grasp it. 'I made the brine on Monday, sirs. It stood in the vat in the storehouse overnight, to let the sand settle, and the barrels washed and waiting beside it.' She looked down at Riddoch. 'I said I was one short in the morning, Riddoch, didn't I? I kent we'd washed six.'

'You did, lass,' agreed her husband heavily.

'Was the storehouse locked?' asked the mason.

'No, no.' She laughed nervously. 'Who'd steal an empty barrel?'

'Quite so,' said Gil. 'And it was Monday night there was the disturbance in the yard.'

'But Morison's own man said the thief got away!' said Riddoch.

'He did, didn't he,' said Gil. 'I think I need to talk to Morison's man.'

'This is not the way we came,' said Maistre Pierre. He looked out over the low hills towards the Forth and waved an arm. 'We are going east.'

'That's right, it's the way to Roslin,' said Gil. Behind them rode the three men, deep in an argument about football. Socrates was ranging round the party, inspecting the scents of the neighbourhood and carefully ignoring his master.

'And why are we going to Roslin? I thought you wanted to speak to Maister Morison's carter, whatever his name is.'

'Billy. He'll keep, I hope, though we do need to question him. We're going to Roslin because Riddoch paid his rent this morning, in barrels of salt herring.'

The mason eyed him resentfully for a few strides, then continued, 'And where are your books, do you suppose?'

'They'll be at Roslin too, I hope. With Oliver *li proz e li gentil*.' Gil turned in the saddle to interrupt the discussion behind them. 'Did you learn any more in the Black Bitch, Rob?'

'No a lot, Maister Gil,' admitted Rob.

'The ale's good,' said Tam, grinning.

'It's been quiet since the court left,' volunteered Luke, 'but there's been a wheen strangers in the place just the same.'

'Would they notice strangers?' asked Maistre Pierre. 'A busy place like this?'

'Aye, but I just said it's been quiet, maister,' Luke pointed out.

'They noticed us,' said Tam. 'Brought out all the long tales. The serjeant's boar run wild and slain two chickens, three geese and a dog, they said. Show me it, I said, and they said, No, it hasny been seen for days. A likely tale. And the burgh muir's haunted, there's been a gathering of corbies over the hill behind the Whitefriars this week past, there's a black ship on the Forth if you see it you'll be deid within the year –'

'Aye, Andro Wood's *Flower*,' said Rob, to general laughter.

'The corbies,' said Gil. He shaded his eyes in his turn to peer into the light. 'I had noticed them. A week, you said? And nobody took thought to look at what they've found?'

'This close to harvest and all?' said Rob. 'Naw.'

'Surely a week is too long,' said Maistre Pierre.

'What is it, Maister Gil?' asked Tam. 'What are you thinking?'

'I'm thinking we can take that track we passed a quarter-mile back,' said Gil. 'It seems to go the right way.'

'Where is Socrates?' wondered the mason.

'He went off after a rabbit. He'll find us when he's forgiven me,' said Gil confidently.

He turned his horse and rode back the way they had come, whistling now and then for the dog. Behind him the men grew silent; at his side the mason appeared deep in thought.

The crows were clearly to be seen from the road, circling and dropping, spiralling up again, centred always round one particular patch on the hillside. Gil, following the track up through the farmlands and past the stone buildings of the Carmelite friary, was reminded of the pillar of cloud.

'So what have we learned?' demanded Maistre Pierre, giving up the contest. Gil turned to look at him. 'They denied all, the *tonnellier* and his wife, indeed he was an example of how to be hospitable but taciturn. But did they in fact know all?'

'Not all,' said Gil, 'but more than they admitted. They looked for the boy back sooner than this, they feared it might have been him in the barrel – they must be beside themselves with worry, though they concealed it.'

'But if Sinclair is involved, had he not told them what is afoot?'

'I don't think so. Or not all of it.'

'Do you think Riddoch has guessed? Could he have told us his suspicions?'

'In his place, I'd ask questions and keep my own counsel. He truly feared for his son, you noticed. And he asked what else was in the barrel, as if he expected there to be something.'

'And where has the boy been? His wife said, when I asked her, they had expected him on Monday. Where is he now? And who were the thieves?'

'We need to find that out.'

'I had a word with Maister Riddoch,' divulged Maistre Pierre, 'while you were writing down what his wife had seen.'

'And they were very reluctant to talk to me separately. What did he say to you?'

'He told me that one had arrived at his yard on Wednesday, asking about the carts that had lain there on Monday.'

'What kind of a one? And only one? What prompted him to tell you this?'

'I asked that also. He said, The Axeman, as if he expected me to know who that was. I said, What axeman, did he mean his man who was shaping staves, and he laughed as if I had uttered some piece of bravado. So I asked what this axeman looked like, and he described a big ugly man, wearing black, and carrying a poleaxe maybe,' he measured with both hands, 'five foot long. Which I suppose might mean it was four foot.'

'A Lochaber axe? That's a fighting man's weapon – a mercenary, or someone's man-at-arms. And this man was asking about the carts from Monday night,' said Gil thoughtfully. 'Did Riddoch say what he told him?'

'I understood,' said Maistre Pierre, retrieving his reins, 'that he told him what he has told us. One for Leith, one for Irvine and one for Glasgow, and the names of the owners.'

They rode on, past a small farm-town whose barley was ripening in the field.

'They'll be shearing that soon, now they have the hay in,' said Gil. He leaned down to listen to the grain, then went on in silence for a few minutes, reviewing the conversation they had had with the cooper and his wife. 'Provided Mistress Riddoch was not dreaming,' he said at length, 'we can assume that at least one man arrived at the yard and was attacked by two or three others.'

'Unless they fought among themselves.'

'I suppose so. Anyway, I think it's clear enough that one man was killed in that yard, probably by beheading, possibly by a Lochaber axe and probably not by Riddoch himself, and his head put in a barrel of brine out of Mistress Riddoch's brine-vat. I wonder who knew she had made brine that day?'

'All the household, I suppose.'

'Aye, but who else?'

'And who sealed the barrel so expertly?' asked Maistre Pierre. 'That was done by a cooper – by a craftsman. Moreover, it is a noisy process. Riddoch showed me just now, and I have seen it before. It should have woken Mistress Riddoch, if not her man.'

'She dreamed about the men working.'

'You mean she may have heard the noise, but not woken?'

'Aye. And when she did wake, she saw someone in black carrying something long and heavy towards the gate.'

'And you think that is what we seek just now.' Maistre Pierre gestured towards the spiralling crows.

'It could be.'

'Or it could be a dead sheep.'

'We still have no name for him.'

'Oh – and another thing I learned while you were making your notes. I remarked, as by chance you understand, that we were seeking the musician. I gave both his names, and Mistress Riddoch said, Oh, no, she had not seen Barty in the town for a week or two.'

'So they did know a man with odd-coloured eyes. I rather thought so.'

'She might not have been close enough to see his eyes,' admitted the mason fairly, 'but it is a very noticeable feature.'

'If she knew him well enough to use his right name,' said Gil, 'she knew him enough to see the colour of his eyes. They are not good liars, either of them.'

'Which makes it the more likely that they did not kill our man.'

'True.' Gil stopped talking while he persuaded his horse past a boulder which it seemed to find alarming. Once past, he continued, 'I hope Andy has not carried out his threat to dismiss Billy.'

'The carter, you mean? Indeed, yes. What did Riddoch say of him just now? He offered to keep watch so the other carters might go drinking,' Maistre Pierre recalled, itemizing the points on one large hand, 'he claimed to have seen only one man, improbably dressed for an evening's thieving, running towards the gate, and he said nobody went near the carts.'

'I wonder how much we can believe?'

'You said yourself, Riddoch is a poor liar.'

'I have no doubt he reported truthfully,' agreed Gil, 'but were the words he reported the truth?'

'They corbies is fair noisy,' commented Rob from behind them. Gil looked up, and checked his horse.

'They are,' he agreed. 'There's no doubt they've found something. Can you work out where it's lying?'

The crows were circling above a stand of trees, off the track and up to their right, with much cawing and croaking, but after they had all studied the movement of the birds for a time Maistre Pierre said, 'I think they come and go from behind that dyke yonder.'

'And nane do ken that he lies there,' said Gil. 'I agree. If we stay a-horseback the birds won't take fright, and we can keep the spot marked. Come on.'

'Must we?' muttered someone behind him.

Gil looked over his shoulder. 'We'll circle round,' he said, 'come down on it from upwind.'

This proved to be a necessary precaution. Even from upwind, the smell of death reached them several yards away.

'Sweet St Giles,' said Gil.

Luke gagged, and Rob said uneasily, 'Likely it's just a sheep, maister. Can we go now?'

'Then sall erth of erth raise a foul stink. You can get back out of range,' said Gil, wadding his handkerchief over his nose. The mason said nothing, but dismounted and gave his reins to Tam, who immediately led the animal away upwind. Two crows perched on the drystone wall watched with identical bright glares, and another flew up with something dangling from its long vicious beak as the two men approached across the rough grass of the field.

There was a ditch below the dyke, over which the grass grew long. The crows and other creatures had trampled a

146

narrow path through it into the ditch; something pale could just be seen in the shadows, and the grasses themselves were spotted and specked with fragments, of flesh, of bristly skin. Gil pressed his handkerchief tighter against his nose, stepped forward and parted the grasses with his boot.

They looked in silence at what lay there.

'Poor devil,' said Gil after a moment.

'How long, would you say?' asked Maistre Pierre.

'There's been a fox at his legs, would you say, as well as the crows. Four or five days would be about right.'

'He is well blown,' agreed his companion, considering the bloated belly. 'I think so too. That would account for the time the crows are said to have been here. Well, there is no more to be done.' He backed away, and called over his shoulder, 'We are both wrong, Rob. Neither a sheep nor a dead man, but a pig. A great boar, overturned in the ditch.'

They turned to tramp back across the rough grass to join the men. Rob said, 'The burgh serjeant's boar –'

'Maistre Gil!' said Tam urgently. 'Look yonder!' He gestured at the stand of trees where the crows were still circling and cawing.

Gil looked, and exclaimed sharply. He lunged forward to leap into his saddle, drawing his whinger as he found the stirrups, wheeling the horse about with his knees. His mount danced sideways, snorting, as the first of the men on foot reached them, and Gil was just in time to hack at the hand attempting to snatch his rein. The man fell back, shouting, but two more sprang past him, one armed with a sword, one with a cudgel, and joined in the fight.

Clashing metal behind him told Gil there were more attackers, but his attention was fully occupied. His horse, which was certainly not battle-trained, flattened its ears and plunged away from the swords. He collected it with seat and heels, managed to turn it, and charged down on the mêlée round Tam, who was already bleeding from a cut to the head. As Gil arrived he took another blow from

147

the cudgel which made him cry out. Beyond him someone had fallen, and Luke and Rob were holding off another swordsman, who was leaping about their plunging horses slashing wildly with his blade.

'Pierre! Over here!' Gil shouted.

'That's them right enough!' gasped one of the assailants. 'Go for the packs, Willie.' He ducked as Gil's whinger whirred past his face, and two things happened almost simultaneously. Up the hillside from the direction they had come hurtled a low grey silent form which sprang at the man with the cudgel, knocked him over, and seized him by the throat; and as Gil struck away a blow aimed at the dog's back a horn blew further up the hill, and four horsemen appeared round the curve of the track, approaching fast, light catching on their drawn swords.

'Get the packs!' shouted someone. 'Cut the straps, Willie!'

'No time!' answered the man who was fending off Gil's attack. 'Get away! Save yersels!'

As the newcomers swept down towards them the attackers broke and ran in all directions, leaving three men lying in the grass. One was Tam, who had fallen off but had somehow kept hold of both sets of reins, one was the man who had gone down first and still lay unmoving, and the third was pinned down by a triumphant Socrates. The dog had a large paw planted firmly on the high leather collar of his captive's jack. His entire set of white teeth was on display, and he was growling, very quietly, every time the man stirred.

'Good dog!' said Gil. 'Leave. Leave it.'

Beyond them, Luke and Rob were grinning at each other, and Maistre Pierre, still afoot, was sheathing his weapon in a businesslike manner.

'I apologize that I did not come to your aid, Gilbert,' he said, 'but I was somewhat distracted. How many were there? We had certainly four at this side.'

'And these two, and two more who ran,' said Gil. He looked at the approaching horsemen, who had turned off the track and were now moving purposefully towards them over the grazing-land, and did not sheath his whinger. 'Eight all told, I suppose. Tam, can you rise, man?'

'Aye, maybe,' replied Tam, making no attempt to do so. 'My head's broke, and I think I got kicked in the knee. They were after the packs, Maister Gil. What's in them, that they were so eager to get them? What did you fetch from Stirling?'

'I don't know,' said Gil absently, still watching the riders.

The newcomers slowed as they reached them; they wore black mantles over well-worn, well-maintained armour, and the fishtailed Cross of St John showed white on each man's left shoulder. Two of them separated and moved past the scene of the attack, one to each side in a practised way. They turned, and all four halted.

'Maister Gil,' said Rob uneasily, 'what'll we do?'

'Good day, *messieurs*,' said a tall man with a dark, neat beard like Maistre Pierre's. He bowed slightly over his horse's neck and his sharp eyes scanned them all, missing nothing 'Raoul de Brinay, at your service. I regret that I must ask you not to move. Except,' he added with a gleam of humour, 'perhaps to call the hound off his kill.'

Gil looked round at de Brinay's men, each with sword drawn and ready, each as relaxed and watchful as their leader. He exchanged a look with Maistre Pierre, and sheathed his whinger.

'Keep still, Rob. We are peaceful travellers, sir,' he went on in French. 'We have done no wrong. Even if we are on St Johns land, I do not think you have the right to hold us like this.'

'Probably not,' agreed the Hospitaller amiably, 'but I feel compelled to ask you what are you carrying, to attract such a band of thieves?'

'I wish I knew,' said Gil.

'We are seeking a shipment of books,' said Maistre Pierre, 'and have travelled from the west in pursuit of them, but we have not found them so far. We have nothing of value in our packs.' His right hand moved on his knee.

'Let us make sure,' suggested Sir Raoul, unbending slightly. He nodded to one of the men beyond Gil. 'Johan? And you may as well leash your dog, *monsieur*, and tend to your servant if you wish it.'

Gil dismounted, gave his reins to Rob, and dragged Socrates away from his prisoner, praising him lavishly. The man scrambled to his feet, despite the dog's threatening snarls, and would have made off, but a small movement of the bare sword of the nearest rider appeared to change his mind for him, and at a word from Sir Raoul the same rider lighted down and bound the thief's wrists.

'De Brinay,' said Maistre Pierre. 'Are you from Brinay itself, sir?'

The Hospitaller glanced curiously at him, and nodded. 'I am. You know it?'

'I have built there, before I was a master. Repairs to two columns in the church nave. You must be the brother of the present lord.'

'His cousin.'

The man addressed as Johan had removed his mailed gauntlets and was searching their packs quickly and economically, feeling each of the saddlebags and moving on to the next. The horses fidgeted, and both Luke and Rob watched him warily as he felt expertly at their scrips, but neither dared to say anything. The two purses in Gil's pack caused him some interest, but when he had ascertained their size through the heavy leather saddlebag he went on. Finally he met his leader's eye again and shook his head, the light glinting on his grey steel helm.

'*Nicht hier,*' he said. '*Nur Kleingelt.*'

There was a short exchange in a language which Gil took to be High Dutch, though he only caught one or two words. The other two St Johns men watched, bare swords unwavering, and Gil wondered what Robert Blacader would say to hear his quite generous contribution to expenses described as small change. He bent over Tam, but decided there was little wrong with him besides a sore head, and bruising on shoulder and knee. The remaining man had a lump the size of a duck egg on his skull and was just beginning to stir; Socrates eyed him suspiciously but made no comment.

'Sir Raoul,' Gil said at last. The Hospitaller turned to look at him. 'If I tell you our story, you will see that you have no reason to hold us.'

'Who said I was holding you?' said Sir Raoul very politely. 'I should be enchanted to hear this history, sir. Is it long?'

'Not long.' Gil recounted, as briefly as he might, how the wrong barrel had come home and what had happened to its contents, and how they were still searching for the books and the missing musician.

'A head and one saddlebag,' said the Hospitaller when he had finished. 'Is there any reason why I should believe you, sir?'

'Not in the immediate term,' Gil admitted, wondering if he had imagined the slight emphasis on the *one*. 'I have the papers for the barrel we're searching for, giving the contents as books, but as to the rest, you would have to send to Glasgow to catch up with my lord St Johns, assuming he travels with the King, and to get word from the Provost.'

Sir Raoul smiled, showing white teeth with one missing.

'It is an advantage of dealing with a lawyer,' he proclaimed. 'They always have a clear idea of what is proof. I think I may not trouble our noble Preceptor in this matter. Is there any more, sir? Did nothing appear along with the empty barrel?'

'One thing more,' said Maistre Pierre, who had been silent for some time. 'One told me, as to a fellow craftsman, you understand, that someone else enquired for the carts which had lain in Linlithgow on Monday night.'

'Did he give a name?'

'No name. He called him the Axeman.'

'*Was ist?*' said Johan. '*Was heisst das?*'

'The Axeman,' said Sir Raoul in Scots.

151

The standing prisoner let out an exclamation. 'What did ye say? The Axeman? Is he in this? Oh, man! Oh, man!' he moaned, and dropped to his knees. 'Just kill me now, maisters, for I canny bear to wait till he catches up wi me! Oh, man!'

'*Ma foi*,' said the Hospitaller, gazing down at the man. 'What is the matter? What is he saying?'

'It seems he fears this axeman,' said Maistre Pierre.

'And so would you, if you'd heard the half o what I've heard,' groaned the prisoner. 'He never tellt us the Axeman was in this.'

'We must hear more,' said Sir Raoul, and looked at the sky. '*Messieurs*, it is late in the day to be setting out for Glasgow, and one man injured at that. Will you come with me to the Preceptory, where we may question these two in more comfort?'

'We are still travelling,' said Maistre Pierre. 'We have come from the west, as I told you, and now I think we must go south, till we find what we seek.'

'We weren't making for Glasgow,' said Gil with reluctance. 'But I admit I would like to hear them questioned. After all,' he grinned suddenly, and switched to Scots, 'this one was taken *in fang* – caught by the dog in the very act of robbery.'

Sir Raoul grinned back at him, sharing his enjoyment of the legal play on words. 'Ah. Then we may at least be seated while we talk to them.' He looked about. 'And if we are to dispense justice, simple tact suggests we should do it off the Carmelites' land. Let us repair to the track, which is ours.'

Tam was heaved back on to his horse, and the groaning thief slung over someone's saddlebow, and they moved off the grazing-land. The conscious prisoner complained bitterly as he was herded along, on the theme of the ill-treatment of a condemned man.

'Nobody's condemned you yet,' said Gil in some amusement.

'Oh, I'm doomed. He'll get me,' sniffed the man. 'He'll

catch up wi me. I need a priest, I have to make my confession. *Ave Mary grassy plena,*' he mumbled. 'And I canny sign myself wi my hands bound like this.'

Questioned, he admitted that his name was Andrew Gray, their other captive was Jemmie Forrest, and they were both from Linlithgow. Sir Raoul seated himself on a convenient earthen dyke, inspected him sternly and asked, 'Who else was in your band?'

'I never kenned all their names, maister,' said Gray, and sniffed again. 'It was a man I met in the Green Lion, he was looking for help to get back something of his maister's so he said, and he hired four or five of us there in the tavern.' He glowered at Tam, who was being anointed and bandaged by Johan and Maistre Pierre in committee. 'He showed us him yonder, walking along the street, said he'd laid him information so you'd be sure to come up here, so we came out to wait for you, and never had any dinner, and he never tellt us the Spital was in it neither, and if the Axeman wants the same thing he'll get me, he will.'

'What was he wanting back?' Gil asked. Socrates, lying at his feet, raised his head and looked from one face to another.

'He never said.' Gray flinched away from the dog's intent gaze. 'We had to get a pack o some sort,' he added, apparently trying to be helpful.

'He ordered someone to get the packs,' Gil recalled, and the man nodded.

'And who was his master?' asked Sir Raoul.

'He never let on, maister. Never said nothing about him, nor what his own name was, nor his friend's.'

'What did his friend call him? Did he have a name for him?'

Gray looked warily at Gil while this idea penetrated his skull.

'Baldy,' he said at length. 'He cried him Baldy. He wasny bald, just the same,' he elaborated kindly, 'for ye could see his hair sticking out at the back of his coif. Likely it was short for Archibald, ye ken.'

'I ken,' said Gil. He looked at Sir Raoul. 'Does that mean anything to you, sir?'

'How should it?' parried the Hospitaller.

'Did either of them say anything else?' Gil asked Gray hopefully. 'Where they had come from, maybe, or who had sent them? Who told them we had this thing of their master's?'

Gray stared at him, and shook his head. Too many questions, thought Gil, annoyed with himself. He tried again.

'Were they from hereabouts?'

'No.' The man shook his head again. 'They wereny anybody we ever saw afore. Willie said,' he added, 'he thocht they were from Stirling, or there. Just by the way they talked, ye ken.'

'Can you describe them?' asked Sir Raoul. Gray looked blankly at him. 'What did they look like?'

'Just ordinary,' said Gray. 'One of them had a hat on,' he recalled. 'No Baldy, the other one.'

'A hat?' repeated Sir Raoul.

'Instead of a blue bonnet,' explained Gil, gesturing at the decrepit knitted object on Gray's head. 'What kind of a hat? A felt one? Did it have a brim?'

'Just ordinary,' said Gray again. 'It had a feather in it,' he added.

Further questioning produced no more details. At length the Hospitaller said, 'I ought to fine you for attempted robbery, Andrew Gray.'

'I've nothing to pay a fine wi,' muttered Gray. 'Nor I'll have no time to earn it afore he gets me.'

'Then leave Linlithgow,' said Sir Raoul impatiently. 'Go now, without returning to your home, and this man you fear will never find you.'

'Go? Where would I go, maister? Set out on a journey unshriven?'

'How would I know? Stirling, maybe, or Leith.'

'No Leith,' said Gray, shivering. 'One o them said he'd been to Leith and no found it, whatever it was they socht.

Or maybe someone else had been to Leith. Any road, I canny go there.'

'Then go to Edinburgh,' Gil said. 'It's big enough to get lost in.'

By the time the augmented party stopped, an hour or so later on the other side of the hills, to get a bite of food and rest the horses a little at a tavern in Bathgate, Gil was no clearer in his mind about the afternoon's events.

'What's going on, anyway, Maister Gil?' asked Rob, pushing Tam down on to the bench between them. 'Are the Spitallers on our side or no? We drove off the thieves, and then the Spital held us and searched us. I was feart that fellow Johan would be away wi my St Peter medal out my blanket. And now he's to ride along wi us, whether you will or no.'

'He was after bigger game than your medal,' said Maistre Pierre, sitting down opposite.

'He was, wasn't he,' agreed Gil. 'Though Sir Raoul wouldny admit it. Here he comes,' he added, as their new companion followed them into the tavern.

When the interrogation on the hillside was ended, the man Gray had been supplied with a few coins and a loaf from someone's saddlebag, and offered a sight of Tam's St Christopher medal to ward off sudden death.

'Look on St Christopher's face and you willny die unshriven,' Rob had said, borrowing the medal from his still-dazed colleague.

The man had been genuinely grateful. Gil had watched him trudge away along the track to make for Edinburgh, and then remarked to the Hospitaller, 'Now why should the Preceptory be interested in this?'

'Have I said it is?' asked Sir Raoul lightly. 'Our concern is for justice and the King's Peace on our lands.'

'So what did you hope to find in our baggage?'

'Nothing,' said Sir Raoul. 'And nothing was what we found.'

155

'Nothing,' said Gil deliberately, 'in a small heavy bundle.'

The Hospitaller turned and looked directly at him. 'You cannot expect me,' he observed, 'to discuss the Preceptory's business with chance-met travellers.'

'It was no chance,' said Maistre Pierre at Gil's shoulder.

'And we are involved in the business already,' Gil added, 'if half Linlithgow can be raised to steal our baggage. It would surely benefit both parties if we were to share information.'

'I cannot discuss the Preceptory's business,' said Sir Raoul again, on a faint note of apology. 'Excuse me.' He strode away from them towards Johan, who was inspecting the still-dazed second prisoner a little way away. Gil and the mason looked at one another, and Rob spoke up from where he and Luke were sharing a flask of something.

'Can we no get on the road, Maister Gil? We'll no be where we're going afore Prime at this rate.' He rose, and came over to his master. 'And another thing,' he said quietly. 'This lot were after us right enough.' Gil looked enquiringly at him. 'Him they cry Johan, he said something to their leader in High Dutch. I canny speak it that well, but I can understand it, from when Matt and me was away at the wars, and he was saying we was the band some laddie had tellt them was on the road.'

'Simmie,' said Gil. 'I'll wager that was his errand. But why should St Johns be interested in our barrel?'

'You said Treasurer Knollys was eager for you to ask questions in Ayrshire rather than the Lothians,' said Maistre Pierre.

'Maybe it was one of theirs that was in the barrel,' suggested Rob. 'You thocht he was a fighting man, maister.'

'Maybe,' said Gil thoughtfully. He turned as Sir Raoul approached. 'We must be on our way, sir. The day wears on.'

'True,' agreed the other. 'And you do not wish to be held up again. For that reason,' he said politely, 'I have commanded Johan to ride with you, as protection.'

Gil had attempted, civilly, to decline the man's company, but Maistre Pierre had said suddenly, 'Let him join us, Gil. Our friend is right. Another sword may be of assistance.'

Now, in Bathgate, on one of the major routes between Edinburgh and Glasgow, they had paused for food. Johan slid along the bench to sit by Maistre Pierre, and nodded at the group.

'Ve go far?' he asked, in horribly accented Scots.

'We go to Roslin,' said Gil.

'Roslin? Ver dwells Sinclair?'

'Aye,' agreed Gil. The inn-servant slapped a platter of boiled salt fish and bread in front of them, and stood with his hand out for the money. Gil opened his purse and counted out the coins, while the others helped themselves to the food. Johan, when invited, took a portion and ate moderately, casting thoughtful looks at Gil from time to time. He had removed helm and coif, revealing short fair hair and a strip of pale skin between the hairline and the weatherbeaten tan of his bony face.

'The man Gray,' said Maistre Pierre through a large mouthful, 'told us little of value.'

'You heard it, did you?'

'I did. We know, I suppose, that he was hired by this Archibald – Baldy – and another with a feathered hat, to steal from us something in a pack which had belonged to their master, and which had been sought and not found, by Baldy or another, at Leith.'

'We'd a horse we cried Baldy once,' said Tam vaguely, 'for the white spot on his broo. A good goer he was an all.'

'A fair summary,' agreed Gil, ignoring this, and took a bite of bread and fish. 'And we heard of a man with a feathered hat,' he added, switching to French. Johan frowned, watching them.

'The same, you think?'

'Or a coincidence.'

'Mm.' Maistre Pierre took another wedge of bread. 'And what have we got, or not got, that they are after? The load that went to Stirling, or something else?'

'And why is the Spital interested? They had obviously heard a lot about us,' observed Gil in Scots.

'How so?' asked the mason, annexing the last pickled onion. 'Shall we have more food?' He waved to the man at the tap of the big barrel without waiting for an answer.

'De Brinay knew I was a lawyer,' Gil said, and looked down at his dark clothing. 'I may be soberly dressed, but my inkhorn and pen-case are out of sight in my baggage. I never said to Riddoch what my calling might be, though I know you named your own, and we left these three out in the street. So the Spital never got the information from him.' He glanced at Johan, who looked enigmatically back at him. 'Either Simmie brought that word as well as the rest from Sinclair this afternoon, or they knew about us already.'

'Out in the street,' muttered Tam. 'There was something . . .'

'What is it, man?' asked Rob, looking at him in concern.

'Something I've forgot, when we were out in the street. Did someone speak to us?'

'Half the lassies o Linlithgow,' said Rob, grinning. 'You were cawin' the pump handle to them for kisses.'

'I never!' said Tam in alarm.

'No, you never,' said Luke, despite Rob's grimaces. 'He's having you on.'

'If you kick me again,' said Maistre Pierre to Rob, 'I will eat your share of the food.'

'Someone did speak to us,' said Tam, and rubbed his forehead. 'Who was it?'

The second platter of bread and fish disappeared more slowly. Gil shared a great hunk of bread with Socrates, and tore a portion of stockfish into shreds for the dog, relishing as always the contrast between the strong, sharp teeth set in the narrow, powerful jaw and the delicate, well-bred manners the animal displayed.

'Well,' he said, licking onion sauce off his fingers when the platter was empty, 'shall we ride on? Tam, are you fit, man? Maybe I should have taken you to your kin at the Wheetflett.'

'Kin,' muttered Tam, edging along the bench after Rob. 'Kin. That's it. He said kin.'

'What are you on about?' demanded Rob.

'Is it what you'd forgot?' Luke asked.

'Aye,' said Tam, and lurched to his feet. 'Aye, Maister Gil, I'll manage, never you worry. But that's it, right enough. That's what I'd forgot. When we were at the well, the three of us, waiting for you and Maister Mason,' he said earnestly, hobbling after Gil to the door, 'a man cam down the vennel from the place you were in first. The lute-maker's, was it? Well clad, he was. Might ha been the lute-maker hisself.'

'So?' said Gil, helping his servant over the doorsill.

'He said to me, Was I with those two men that were there just now. I said, Aye I was, since there wereny two other men thegither, saving us, in the street at the time,' he added, grinning. 'And he said, Tell your maister, he said, that Barty Fletcher, would that be the right name?'

'It would,' said Gil. 'Go on.'

'That Barty Fletcher has kin in Roslin.' He looked uncertainly at Gil's expression. 'That was all he said, Maister Gil. And then he turned and went back up the vennel.'

Chapter Eight

'It must have been terrifying,' said Alys, her brown eyes round. Not, Kate noted, *You must have been terrified*, but, *It must have been terrifying*.

'I'd not have forgiven myself,' said Augie Morison earnestly, 'if you'd come to any harm, Lady Kate. Whatever he was after, it could never have been worth that.'

'It's one thing about a life of pilgrimage,' Kate said lightly. 'You meet soon or late with every ragabash in Scotland. Babb and I have trapped pilferers before now – though never so redhand,' she admitted.

They were seated in the castle courtyard on a bench, which two of the Provost's men had carried out for Kate rather than have Babb heave her up and back down several turns of the tower stair to Maister Morison's lodging. About them, members of the castle household scurried back and forth carrying furniture and rolled-up tapestries, readying the Archbishop's lodging for the arrival of the King's party the next day.

'But what was he after?' Alys asked.

'The second half of the treasure. He seemed quite certain it should be there.'

Morison shook his head, biting his lip.

'I took him for an honest man,' he said sadly. 'Well, as honest as any of them.'

'Most of us are honest till we're tempted,' said Kate. 'I think maybe Billy was tempted beyond his limits.'

'By the man with the axe,' said Alys, nodding.

'Axe? What man with an axe?'

160

'We saw him in Hog's tavern,' Alys explained.

Morison looked from one to the other of them in horror.

'What have you lassies been up to?' he demanded, and then, 'I'm sorry, Lady Kate, that slipped out. But what your brother will say when he hears this I just don't know.'

'Maybe we shouldn't tell you, then,' said Kate.

'I've heard this much,' he said. 'I'd better hear the rest.'

'Oh, it gets worse,' said Kate. She recounted the episode in the Gallowgait, while Morison's mobile face reflected amazement, anxiety, concern, and finally a stern determination.

'Lady Kate,' he said when she had finished, 'I can't accept any more help if it brings you into sic danger. You could have been badly hurt there in the tavern, and as for Billy Walker breaking into the chamber where you lay sleeping, well! I can't bear to think of it. I must ask you to leave my house, my lady, and go back to your uncle's in Rottenrow.'

'What, and leave your bairns alone?' said Kate. He paused, open-mouthed. 'I'm not finished, Maister Morison.'

'Aye you are. I'll send the bairns to our Con out at Bothwell,' he said, recovering himself. 'Andy can take them. Con's got an altar at St Bride's, you know that, he can surely find a woman in the town to mind them till I can bring them home again. The Provost's men will question Billy and learn what he knows, and you can stay out of it in safety, Lady Kate. And yoursel, Mistress Mason,' he added belatedly.

Kate exchanged a glance with Alys past Morison's shoulder.

'I'm still not finished, maister,' she said. 'There's more to tell you yet. I said it gets worse, and it does.'

'Why, what's happened? Not the bairns?' exclaimed Morison in alarm.

'No, no, the bairns are well. One of Mistress Mason's lassies is with them just now,' she assured him, 'teaching them to play at merry-ma-tanzie.' She took a breath, and plunged on before he could interrupt again. 'No, maister. Last night, after all was quiet again, there was a second inbreak. Whoever it was, he never got into the house, but he found where we'd shut Billy in the coalhouse.'

'And?' He looked intently at her face, and read the news there. Appalled, he put out a hand and covered hers where they lay in her lap. 'Lady Kate, you've met a deal of trouble and pain for me. Was it you found him?' She shook her head, thinking of the moment when Andy had stumbled into the house, grey-faced with shock, blood on his boots. 'Our Lady be praised for that mercy, at least. How was he killed?'

'Cut to pieces,' said Kate carefully. 'With an axe, or something of the sort.'

'With an *axe*?' Morison looked down at his hand, retrieved it hastily, and crossed himself. 'Our Lord have mercy on him,' he muttered, and both girls said *Amen*. After a moment he continued, 'Did nobody hear anything? The other men? Ursel? No, Ursel wouldn't hear the Last Trump once she gets to snoring. How did he get in the yard, Lady Kate?'

'The same way Billy did, Andy reckons,' said Kate, 'up from the stable yett. Babb and I never heard a thing. One of the men said he thought he heard shouting, or maybe something fall, out in the yard not long before dawn, but there was nothing else so he jaloused it was maybe a cat. Andy had a word to say to him about that, but as he said, who'd have thought there would be two inbreaks in the one night?'

Morison nodded, took a deep breath, and passed a hand down across his face. 'Have you taken it to the Provost?'

'We told him first,' said Alys. 'He agreed you must be informed, maister.'

'I'm grateful.' He smiled wryly. 'At least I think so. The poor fellow. God and Our Lady have mercy on him,' he said again. 'Lady Kate, you must see – this is not safe for you. Tell me you'll go back to your uncle's house.'

'Babb's with me,' said Kate, looking across the yard at

her waiting-woman, who was towering over the two men at the castle gate. 'She's an army in herself.'

'Not against a man with an axe. I want you out of my house, my lady.'

'That's not very friendly,' she reproached. '*I am right glad when ye will go And sory when ye will come*, is that it?'

He coloured up. 'Once this is done wi you'll be a welcome guest if you choose, but right now it's not safe. Lady Kate, I beg you, will you go back to Rottenrow?'

'Aye, when I know the bairns are safe.'

'Send Andy to me when you get back down the brae,' said Morison. 'I'll gie him his orders. If you'd just let him have a bit coin out the small kist in the counting-house – I'll gie you the key. Ursel can show you where it is.' He patted his doublet, and drew a key on a chain from inside it.

'He'll come up as soon as he's free.'

'Is there anything he should bring with him?' Alys asked.

Morison shook his head. 'I'm right well treated,' he confessed. 'I think Sir Thomas doesn't believe ill of me. Unless,' he added hopefully, 'Andy brought one of my books.'

'Where are they?' asked Kate, turning the key over. It was warm in her hand.

'They're in my counting-house and all, on the shelf above the desk. Just send any of them, but you'll make sure, Lady Kate, won't you, if it's one that's bound in two-three volumes, that they're all there?'

'No,' said Kate deliberately, 'I'll send you one volume of this and another of that.' He stared at her and laughed uncertainly. 'It adds variety,' she told him, straight-faced, and opened her purse to stow the key safely.

'What have you in mind?' asked Alys as they made their way down the crowded High Street.

'In mind?'

Alys turned to look up at Kate, her quick smile flicker-

163

ing. 'You did not say you would leave Morison's yard,' she observed.

Kate, perched on the back of her mule, answered the smile, but at her other side Babb said, 'Leave? I should think not, my doo! Leave those bairns wi nobody to see them safe but a pack of daft laddies and that bauchle Andy?'

'I'm glad you agree,' said Kate, but Alys said:

'Oh, the bairns! I meant to ask Maister Morison what ails the older one.'

'I asked that Ursel this mornin,' said Babb. 'She said she's been that way a year or more. Seems they'd both had a right dose o the rheum, they got it a year past at St Mungo's tide when the lass that was minding them let them get chilled at the Fair, and the older lassie took a rotten ear wi it, and after that she seemed never to hear what was said to her, says Ursel, except it was her sister. What's her daft-like name, now?'

'They're both daft-like names,' said Kate. 'Wynliane and Ysonde.' And how, she wondered, had such a gentle soul managed to get away with naming his daughters out of the romances, instead of after their grandmothers in the proper way? There was a strong current of determination, she recognized, under the gentleness.

'Aye,' said Babb, striding onwards down the hill. 'Wynliane.'

'There are simples for a rotten ear,' said Alys, clicking her tongue in annoyance. 'And for the rheum, indeed. Poor poppet. So what do you have in mind?' she asked again.

'The house, for one,' said Kate. Alys nodded. 'The yard. Those men will sit about all day playing at dice if they're not put to work.' Alys nodded again. 'The bairns. I asked Jennet this morning and she says there's barely a stitch in their kist that fits them, and little more in the wash.'

'And with the rest of the day?' asked Alys, the smile flickering again.

Kate looked at her, then at Babb, occupied in coaxing the mule past an assertive cockerel on his midden. 'I thought,' she said airily, 'we could ask about a bit, see if we can learn anything about Billy Walker and the man with the axe. Maybe even have a drink in the Hog.'

'Oh, yes!' said Alys.

'Oh, no, my doo!' said Babb. 'Back in that nasty place? Do you want the other pole cut down and all?'

'I'll go without you, then,' said Kate.

'You will not!'

'Indeed aye!' said Ursel, stirring a pot over the fire. 'There's store of linen in one of the presses up the stair, we can easy stitch them shifts.' She paused for thought, her spoon suspended over the kale. 'I've a notion there's a bolt of woad-dyed and all, that would make wee kirtles to them. Better for them running about in than Wynliane's good brocades.'

'Excellent,' said Alys. 'We can cut them out after dinner.'

Kate was only half attending. She had two of Maister Morison's books in her hands, a printed *Bevis of Hampton* and a handwritten collection of long poems, and was leafing through them. The printed book had occasional pencil marks in the margins, which somehow seemed very personal, but the choice of tales in the other book gave her a strange feeling of looking right into the man's mind. She could visualize him, sitting over these books like the reader in Chaucer's poem. How did it go? Here it was, indeed, and the page well-thumbed. *In stede of reste and newe thynges, Thou goost hom to thy hous anoon; . . . thou sittest at another book Tyl fully daswed is thy look.* What else had he copied? The whole of *Sir Tristram* and a portion of *Greysteil* were followed by an extraordinary poem which seemed to be English and involved babies stolen by wild animals, and then by *Lancelot of the Laik*. None of the humorous or bawdy tales which went around in such collections, no sign of *Rauf Colyer* or the *Friars of Berwick*. *But alle is buxumnesse there and bokes, to rede and to lerne.* Morison was clearly a romantic, through and through.

165

And yet a brief glance at the account book lying open on his tall desk had revealed still another side of the man. Details of load after load of goods from Irvine or Dumbarton or Linlithgow, with exotic ladings and amazing prices, showed a trim profit on every barrel.

'Aye, well, mem,' said Jennet from the kitchen doorway. She cast a glance out into the yard, where Babb and several reluctant men were weeding or shifting rubbish, and the two little girls were constructing an elaborate maze out of shards of pottery. 'I washed them both as best I could last night, but they could do wi a bath.' She grimaced. 'And their hair needs a good seeing to, mem, if you tak my meaning. We'll likely need to cut it and all, afore we'll can get a comb through it.'

'It'll take all of us to bath them,' Ursel warned. She put the lid back on the pot and turned away from the fire. 'Wynliane screams till she boaks at the sight of that much water. That's how they've no been washed right for months.'

'Well,' said Alys, 'we must start the bath heating, and then get to work on the house.' She craned to see past Jennet as the yett swung open. 'Who is this? Someone with a horse?'

'Three folk,' said Jennet. 'Is that Maister Gil's Matt? Who's he got there on the crupper?'

'And here's that Mall Anderson,' said Ursel, swelling with indignation. 'The cheek!'

Firm footsteps on the flagstones by the door heralded Matt, who dragged off his bonnet and ducked in a general bow.

'Brought ye a nourice,' he said. 'Name's Nan Thomson. Widow woman. Raised five. Great hand in a house and all.'

His passenger's voice floated in from the yard. 'My, that's a fine building. What's it to be?'

And, after a pause, Ysonde's reply, almost civil by her standards: 'It's the Queen's palace. Can you no see that?'

Anything Mistress Thomson might have said to this was

166

lost in an explosion from Andy as he recognized the third arrival at the yett.

'Mall Anderson, what are you doing in this yard? Get your thievin' shiftless face out of my sight afore I slap it for you!'

'Fetch Mall in here,' said Kate urgently, setting the books aside. 'I want a word with her.'

'I'll get the bairns out of the yard,' said Alys. 'I want to try physicking that ear. Ursel, have you tartar of wine?'

Mall was propelled into the kitchen by a furious Ursel, with Andy exclaiming angrily behind them. Ignoring them both, she stopped in front of Kate, wringing her plump hands in her apron. There were tear stains on her face, and her lip quivered.

'Oh, mem,' she pleaded, 'what's this they're saying about my Billy? Tell me it's no true, mem?'

'Oh, my dear lassie,' said Kate, with a rush of sympathy. 'I'm afraid it is. Billy's dead, Mall. He was slain in the night.'

She was aware of Alys pausing in the doorway on her way out to the children, but all her attention was on the girl in front of her, who had collapsed in a wailing heap, flinging her apron over her head. Amid the racking sobs words could be made out.

'I tellt him no to do it, I begged him to leave it! He wouldny listen to me. Oh, my Billy, my dawtie, my dearie!'

Andy abandoned his indignation, heaved the girl up and set her down beside Kate. Ursel, in grim practicality, dragged away the apron and forced a mouthful of aqua vitae down her throat, which made her choke but stopped the wild sobbing, and Kate took her hands with a sudden recollection of Augie Morison clasping her own hands not an hour earlier, and said earnestly, 'Mall, if you tried to persuade him against it, you did your duty by him. Now tell me all about it. Who put him up to it? It was never his own idea.'

Mall nodded, gulping, and freed one of her hands to scrub at her eyes with her apron.

'Tell me what happened to him, mem,' she begged, sniffling. 'Was it one of the household took him? How did he dee? Tammas constable wouldny tell me, he just said he was found . . .'

Kate bit her lip.

'He was taken redhand in the night,' she said carefully, 'here in the house, breaking into a lockfast kist. We questioned him, but got no sense of him.'

'No, you wouldny,' said Mall, shaking her head. Subdued like this, with the cockiness all gone out of her, she seemed much more reasonable than her lover.

'So we bound him, and shut him in the coalhouse for the rest of the night,' Kate continued. 'Now, Mall, he was man alive when Andy here shut him in.'

'And cursing,' put in Andy.

'He can curse like a mariner,' agreed Mall, and her lip quivered.

'But when Andy went to fetch him out this morning, to see if he'd tell us any more before we sent for the serjeant, he was lying dead.'

'How?' the girl whispered.

'It looked as if someone wi an axe went at him,' said Andy bluntly. Mall stared up at him, open-mouthed. The high colour receded from her face, leaving two patches of red flaring on her round cheeks; then she put up her hands to cover her mouth. A thin high wail escaped from behind them, and she began to rock back and forward.

'Some more usquebae, I think, Ursel,' said Kate.

'It's no usquebae,' said Ursel, pouring out another small measure. 'It's the good stuff, come from the Low Countries.'

She pulled Mall's hands from her mouth and administered the dose with efficiency. Mall choked on it, hiccuped a couple of times, and began to weep again, but when Kate said, 'What can you tell us about the man with

168

the axe, lassie?' she shook her head and said coherently enough through the sobs:

'Aye, it must ha been him. It must ha been him. I never heard his name, mistress. Billy said he cam from Stirling, or Edinburgh, or one of those places. He speaks strange-like.'

'How, strange?' asked Kate. 'Is he maybe no a Scot? Could he be foreign?'

Mall sniffled. 'He might be. I never heard anyone foreign speaking.'

'Mistress Mason's French,' said Andy.

The girl considered this briefly, and shook her head again. 'No, I canny tell. He doesny sound like Mistress Mason, but that's all I ken.' She scrubbed at her eyes with her sleeve. 'Oh, my dear, my Billy. Oh, if he'd never met that man.'

'When did he meet him?' Kate asked gently.

'Yesterday.' Mall stopped to think. 'After the noon bite.'

'What did he tell you about him?'

'Oh, he'd no need of telling me. I heard it all.'

With careful questioning, she produced an account of how, after the household had eaten, she had slipped away for a tryst with Billy. Ursel exchanged a glance with Andy at this, but neither said anything. Waiting for her sweet-heart in the hayloft of the stable, down at the end of Morison's property next to the mill-burn, Mall had heard voices on the path beyond the fence.

'So I keeked out,' she said, 'at the eaves where the swallas fly in, and I seen Billy out on the path by the burn, talkin wi this big ugly man. A grim-lookin' chiel.'

The man had been all dressed in black, with a long-hafted axe, and a silly wee bit beard. He had told Billy that some task was not yet finished; Billy had claimed he was paid only to open the yett, and had done more than that already.

'What yett?' demanded Ursel. 'This yett here?'

'He never said. No here, I dinna think, no this one. But

Billy said, if he'd kent what he'd have to do he'd never ha taken the chiel's money.'

The man with the axe had pressed Billy to complete the work, threatening to tell his master what he had done already.

'He didny want to,' Mall assured Kate, wiping her eyes again. 'He tellt me after, it didny seem right. But I think he was feart what the man wi the axe would do to him, no just for him telling the maister. The man said he cheated him, and he never did.'

'What was he to do?'

He had been instructed to tell the Provost at the quest that afternoon that he and the other men had been got out of the way when the barrel was opened. Kate, listening, decided the two must have been talking for some time before Mall heard them; the stranger already seemed to know a great deal about Billy's part in the day. Billy had objected, saying it would get his master arrested, and the man with the axe had laughed.

'It fair made my spine creep,' said Mall, remembering. 'Then he said, That was the point, to get the maister out the road, and Billy was to get the key to his kist and all. So after,' she closed her eyes, and tears leaked under her lashes, 'he tellt me to get the key. And if Andy hadny sent him off −' Andy snorted at this − 'it would ha been easy, and he'd never been taken, and never . . .' She scrubbed at her eyes with her sleeve. 'Where is he? Can I see him?'

'The serjeant took him away,' said Kate gently. 'There has to be a quest on him.'

'Up at the castle?'

'He was mighty cut about,' warned Andy. 'You'd maybe no want to see it.'

'I want to say farewell to him,' said the girl. 'And when I think just yesterday . . .' Her face crumpled again.

'What else did Billy and this man say?' Kate asked. 'Did they say what Billy had done already? Did you hear anything about what the man wanted him to find?'

'Just the rest of the treasure,' said Mall, 'that he said was in the barrel.'

'There was no –' began Andy.

Kate shook her head at him. 'The rest of it?'

'Aye. He kept on about that, and Billy kept telling him he kenned naught about it. He said, he said,' Mall shut her eyes to think better, *'You tellt us it was in the barrel already. You can find the rest of it, wee man.* Then he laughed.' She shivered. 'Made my skin creep, so he did,' she admitted again, and dabbed her eyes with her apron.

'That's why Billy was so certain there should be another bag hid in the house,' said Kate thoughtfully. 'And you never learned his name, or anything about him? He never mentioned any other names?'

Mall shut her eyes again, thinking.

'No,' she said after a moment. 'No that I recall. I canny mind clear.' She sniffed, and managed a watery smile. 'Oh, aye. There was one orra thing. He was saying the Baptizer wanted his goods and gear back, and Maidie would help him. Was that no a strange thing to say?'

'The Baptizer?' Kate repeated. 'St John Baptist, did he mean? Was it a joke, maybe? Was he talking about the man whose head was in the barrel?'

'Maybe he was.'

'And who might Maidie be?' said Andy.

'Oh, his strumpet, for certain,' said Ursel grimly.

Mall shook her head. 'I wouldny ken.'

'Have you kin in Glasgow, Mall?' said Alys from the doorway to the stairs.

The girl looked at her, while the question sank in. 'My sister dwells in Greyfriars Wynd,' she said drearily. 'I lay there last night.'

'I think you should go to her now. Andy, may one of the men take her there?'

'No need to disturb the men, when they're working,' said Ursel grimly. 'I can leave the dinner for now, mistress. I'll see her to her sister's door.' She untied her apron and took her plaid down from its nail on the back of the door, saying with rough sympathy, 'Come, lass. You'll be best wi your kin the now.'

'And Mall,' said Kate urgently, 'don't say aught about the man with the axe.' Mall, halfway across the kitchen, turned to stare at her. 'Not to your sister, nor anyone else, unless the Provost himself.'

Mall's pale eyes grew round again. Her hand went up to cover her mouth, and she nodded emphatically as Ursel drew her from the kitchen.

'Well!' said Andy.

'Well!' said Alys.

'How much did you hear?' asked Kate.

'From the hayloft onwards.' Alys came forward, her smile flickering, and sat down beside Kate on the settle. 'She may have more to mind Billy by than she bargains for, poor lass, if they trysted in a hayloft.'

'And what's this daft stuff about the Baptizer?' said Andy. 'What's he mean by that?'

'The Axeman's maister, surely,' said Kate. 'Some kind of by-name, I suppose. Could it be a priest? Someone who baptizes people? Is he from Perth, maybe, or is there a church of St John hereabouts?'

'Could it be the Knights of St John?' suggested Alys.

'You mean, the Axeman is from Torphichen?' Kate frowned. 'There was no cross on his cloak. And would the Knights kill, in secret like that?'

'They would kill,' said Alys, 'but not like that. Either more secret, so that nobody knew how or who, or else quite openly.'

Kate eyed the younger girl speculatively, but said nothing. Andy said, 'And was that Matt Hamilton in the yard, my leddy?'

'It was, with a nurse for the bairns.'

'A good woman, too,' said Alys approvingly. 'She held Wynliane for me to wash her ears and put drops in them – oh, they were bad, I've never seen such a crust on a bairn's ears – and she paid no attention when the little one was rude. I left her just now singing to them.'

She turned her head as footsteps clopped on the stairs, and Ysonde appeared round the curve of the spiral and stepped into the kitchen with her sister and their new nurse behind her. Seeing Kate, Ysonde made her way directly towards her and announced gruffly, 'This is Nan. She's come from Dumbrattan – Dumbarton,' she corrected herself, 'to mind us for a bit. She kens stories.'

Nan Thomson bobbed a brief curtsy and smiled at Kate.

'You're Matt's Lady Kate, mem, aren't ye no?' she said. 'He's tellt me about you.'

She was a bulky, black-browed woman in a widow's headdress and a worn homespun gown, but she had a comfortable bosom and capable hands, one of which was curved round Wynliane's shoulder at the moment.

'I can see there's plenty for me to be doing,' she added.

'Has Matt explained?' asked Kate.

The linen headdress nodded. 'We'll see how we all get on, mem,' Nan said firmly.

Introduced to Ursel and Andy, she gave them both a friendly smile, and then gathered up Ysonde's hand and announced, 'We'll see you all later. These two good lassies are going to show me their chamber where they sleep, aren't you, my poppets?'

Ysonde stuck out her lower lip and nodded; Wynliane peeped up at her and turned obediently back to the stair.

'She looks a good worker,' said Ursel once the footsteps had died away into the hall.

Alys's eyes danced. 'Matt got a very hearty buss when he left. I think they know one another well.'

'Andy,' said Kate, 'tell me again how you found Billy.'

Nothing loth, he sat down on a stool and launched into what was clearly becoming a well-practised recital.

'I went to the coalhouse, like you tellt me, my leddy, to fetch him in to see if he'd changed his story at all, afore we called the serjeant. And the first thing I noticed, the bar wasny on the door.'

'Where was it?' Kate asked.

He halted, clearly not having considered this before. 'Laid on the ground at the side of the door,' he said after a moment, gesturing with his left hand. 'And I thocht to mysel, I thocht, Oh, our man's away, he's got out while we was all sleeping. The next I noticed was the marks on the door, like someone's hand. So I opened the door, and what I saw –' He stopped abruptly. 'I've been on a battlefield, my leddy. I've seen the kind o thing afore. But this was, this was – and a man doesny expect to meet it in his own yard.'

'No,' agreed Kate, since something was obviously expected of her.

'It wasny –' He stopped again, and swallowed. 'It wasny a clean kill. He'd tried to get away, poor loon. That's why I wanted to stop the lassie going to see him. Thievin' wretch she may be, but he was her leman. Hacked into pieces, he was, and blood all over the coalheap.'

'We must wash that,' said Alys immediately, 'before it sets any further.'

'Likely you could sell the whole load o coals to Mattha Hog just as they are,' said Andy darkly. 'If I ken my maister he'll no want to burn them, that's for sure, washed or no. Our Lady be praised, we've enough broken barrels and that on the woodheap to burn till we can order up more.'

'Aye, we could sell it and be rid of it, if the serjeant has seen all he needs to,' said Kate.

'He's seen it,' said Andy. 'He looked at the coalhouse, and the blood everywhere, and he looked at me and the men, no what ye'd call clean since they're good workers but none o us wi blood on his shoes or his clothes, except my boots from when I found him, and he said it wasny any of us, it must ha been another intruder, maybe Billy's accomplice, and lucky we were no to have been cut up oursels. And for once in his life,' he added drily, 'I think John Anderson's right.'

'I want a look at these marks on the door,' said Alys.

'And I,' said Kate, and reached for her crutches.

The coalhouse was part of the stone structure containing the kitchen, the laundry and several other storehouses. Each of these had a stout door of broad planks, the storehouse doors secured by a wooden bar lodged in slots in the stone jambs. The coalhouse was nearest to the kitchen; Kate, approaching it, looked back along the length of the house and saw that the kitchen building was not so deep as the timber-framed hall and chambers, so that its doors were set some way back compared to the house windows. Besides, the windows of the room where she and Babb had slept, with difficulty, after the excitements of the midnight had been firmly shuttered. Small wonder that she had heard nothing.

The men at their weeding and tidying glanced sideways at them, but carefully paid no more attention. Babb, restacking huge yellow pots on a rack near the gate, straightened up to see if her mistress required her, then went back to her task.

'There ye are,' said Andy, gesturing at the coalhouse. 'That's about how I found it, my leddy.'

The door was standing shut, the bar lying on the ground beside it. There was a single large handprint, slightly smudged and now quite dry, showing dark against the bleached wood, as if someone had set his hand against the door to push it to. Kate, balanced on her crutches, put her own hand up without touching the mark.

'A bigger hand than mine,' she said, 'and someone taller than me.' She remembered the big man she had seen in the Hog, the flat, ugly face with its wisp of beard, and shivered.

'His left hand,' observed Alys. 'And the bar laid down this side. I wonder if the man is left-handed?'

'He went by on my right,' contributed Kate, 'and hacked at this pole.'

Alys nodded. 'May we open the door?'

'You don't need to open the door,' said Andy roughly. 'I've tellt you what's inside.'

'I want to see,' said Alys. Kate moved aside, and Andy opened the door with reluctance. Kate peered inside, and swallowed. She had not been prepared for the way the heap of coal betrayed Billy's last moments so clearly, the pits and hollows where he had trampled about trying to escape his executioner, and the blood smeared among the coal-dust halfway up the walls as well as caked among the loose coal. She thought of the man in the Hog, and the long reach and swing of a Lochaber axe. With that great bulk blocking the doorway, there would have been no escape.

Beside her Alys stared dispassionately, but her hand crept out and closed over Kate's where it gripped the crutch.

'We must certainly have this out of here,' she said, her voice trembling slightly. 'And the walls scrubbed down before you order a new load of coals.'

'Christ and Our Lady have compassion on him,' said Kate, and crossed herself. 'It is still extraordinary,' she added, 'that none of us heard anything. Surely he had time to cry out?'

'Perhaps he was t-too busy trying to get out of reach,' said Alys, her hand still tight over Kate's.

'Seen enough?' said Andy, and shut the door without waiting for an answer. 'What now, my leddy?'

'I want to look at the back gate,' said Kate, 'where he likely got in, and then the men must have their noon bite, and someone must take those books to Maister Morison, and then . . .'

She looked at Alys.

'What are you planning, Lady Kate?' asked Andy suspiciously.

'That's just it,' she said. 'I think now it might not be so clever.'

Alys nodded ruefully.

'What's no so clever?' Andy looked from one to the other of them. 'Oh, no. No back to the Hog. I'll take your

176

mule up to Rottenrow my ain sel' first, to keep you from going out.'

'No need,' said Kate, setting off towards the back of the yard. 'I can see for myself that sitting in the tavern asking openly about this man that slips into places to kill by night is no the best way to carry on the enquiry.'

'Just the same,' said Alys. Kate paused, and looked at her again. 'What if . . .' she began. 'What if someone went down to the Hog – don't worry, Andy, we could send one of the men – to offer Mattha the chance to purchase these coals.' She paused. 'Perhaps he could take money,' she continued, thinking aloud, 'to buy Billy's friends a drink.'

'The whole of the Hog would turn out to be his drinking-fellows,' objected Andy.

'So they would. Then how can we learn more?'

'What are ye after?'

'Anyone who overheard him yesterday,' said Kate. 'Anything we can learn about the man with the axe and what he and Billy said to one another.'

'But without the man with the axe learning we are seeking for him,' supplied Alys.

Andy gnawed at his lip. 'A tall order,' he commented. 'Jamesie and William might manage it. If we gied them some drinksilver after their dinner, and the message for Mattha right enough, they could sit a while and see what they might hear.' He glanced over his shoulder at the industrious men, and grinned suddenly. 'I've a notion they'd like it better than shifting broken crocks. I'll have to let them all have the evening off.'

The back of the yard, beyond the barn and the cart-shed, was defined by a tall fence of split palings, well maintained, though the whitewash had worn off it. Kate commented on this, and Andy grunted.

'I've kept the palings tied on,' he said, 'for it keeps the hens out the yard mostly, but we've no had the time for whiting things for a while. See, while we were at Linlithgow last week,' he explained, dragging the gate open,

'William and our John stayed here to mind the yard, but the other two fellows had the other cart to Irvine wi three great pipes for Ireland, laden wi crocks and St Mungo kens all-what gear. They brought back a couple of tuns of wine and some small stuff for Clem Walkinshaw and a few others, and they'd ha been out again the morn with another load if this hadny happened. He's been driving us and himself, ever since – well, for the last couple of years.'

Beyond the gate the rest of the property sloped down towards the mill-burn, ending in another, lower fence with a gate in it, and the stable where Mall had waited for her sweetheart. Kate stood at the top of the slope, looking about her. The kale-yard nearest the fence, where the chickens were pecking, was obviously being worked, and was well tended, but beyond it to one side was a small pleasance whose formal shapes were outlined by un-trimmed box hedges and full of weeds. There was a bench, disappearing under a rampant honeysuckle, and two strips of standing hay which were probably intended to be grassy paths, Kate thought.

'The mistress sat there often,' said Andy, seeing the direction of her glance.

Kate nodded. She remembered Agnes Cowan, a round-faced girl with brown curls, a ready laugh and a significant tocher. What, she wondered, had brought her down so far that she drowned herself, leaving her two little girls motherless?

Alys bent to look at the neat plots of vegetables.

'I would like some seed off these turnips,' she said. 'They are different from mine. Who minds the garden?'

'Our John,' said Andy.

'He would make a gardener,' said Alys. 'Kate, have you seen all you want?'

'Aye. Not hard to get in by the fence down yonder,' she said, 'and this gate can be opened from either side. He'd have had no trouble getting into the yard.'

As they turned to go in, one of the men threaded his

way between the buildings with a word for Andy, glancing sideways at Kate and Alys as he delivered it. Andy nodded, and sent him back.

'That's one of the constables at the yett, Jamesie says,' he reported. 'We're all summoned to the quest on Billy. They want it for the morn, after Terce, to get it out the way afore the King gets here.'

'I have never seen such a quest,' remarked Alys.

'I've seen one too many,' said Andy sourly. 'You can come along if you will, mistress. I've no doubt Lady Kate'd be glad o yir company.'

Chapter Nine

They were clearing the table away after the midday bite when the gate thumped. Andy, gathering his workforce together as the women carried out the empty dishes, turned to peer out of the hall window.

'St Mungo's banes,' he said, staring. 'Is this no your uncle, my leddy?'

'My uncle?' Kate swung herself towards the window. Out in the yard, severe in his long black gown and acorn-shaped hat, Canon Cunningham was gazing about him with the air of one surveying a battlefield. Beside him Matt was looking hopefully at the house. 'Indeed it is. What's brought him down here?'

'I hope nothing is wrong!' Alys joined her with an armful of folded linen. 'No, he does not look as if he brings bad news.'

'That's good lassies,' said Nan, handing a wooden platter to each of the little girls. 'Take those down to Ursel, now, just like Jennet did, and then we'll go out in the yard.'

'Likely he's come to see what you're about, the two of you,' surmised Babb from across the room. 'Let him in and bid him sit down, my doo, since we've made oursels at home.'

'Yes, indeed.' Alys moved to stow the linen in the great press, and paused. 'I wonder, has he eaten? Do you suppose Ursel . . .'

'No, no,' said Canon Cunningham when she asked him the same question. 'I've eaten well, my lassie. You ken the kitchen Maggie keeps. Thank you for asking,' he added. Seating himself on one of Maister Morison's backstools he looked closely at his niece. 'Well, Kate.'

'Well, sir,' she responded, seated opposite him and wondering why she felt as if she had been caught in mischief.

'Tell me, what are you at here? What about all these tales reaching the Chanonry?'

'What tales are those, sir?'

'You had a thief in the house last night, did you no? And a murder this morning.' The Official looked round him at the gloomy hall. 'Was it just the one murder, or was it half the household as Maggie swears that Agnes Dow tellt her?'

'Just the one, sir,' Kate assured him, her mouth quirking in spite of herself.

'So it's true, then?' Her uncle raised one eyebrow. 'Who?'

'The thief, Christ assoil him. Babb and I took him redhand at his master's kist, and we shut him in the coalhouse till morning. Then when Andy Paterson went to fetch him out, he was dead, slain by another inbreaker.'

'I don't know, it's fair coming to it when a decent young woman canny sleep safe in her bed at night. Are you sure you've taken no hurt, lassie?'

'I'm not hurt, sir.'

David Cunningham tut-tutted, shaking his head.

'It's the fault o that brother o yours,' he said. 'I'm sure we never had the half of these killings before he started looking into them. And your father just encourages him,' he added severely to Alys. Her elusive smile flickered, but she made no answer. 'What was a thief doing in the house anyway? And then another ill-doer in the yard. And what were you doing sending a man up for your spare poles? What came to the good set?'

They explained, as clearly as they might, and he listened intently, asking the occasional penetrating question. When they had done he sat silent, sipping at the tiny cup of

Dutch spirit which Babb had quietly brought in while they talked.

'So who is this man with the axe working for?' he said at length. 'It seems to me you need to find that out.'

'We thought,' said Alys, 'to send two of the men down to the Hog after dinner, to see what they might learn.'

'Aye,' he said thoughtfully. 'It would need to be done wi care, but it might pay you.' *You*, thought Kate, and exchanged a glance with Alys. 'You got a sight of him, did you say, Kate?'

'I did, sir,' she agreed. 'I'd ken him again – even if he shaved his wee beard. But there was no badge on his cloak that I could see.'

'I never seen one neither, Maister David,' said Babb from behind Kate's chair. 'And I got a right look at him as he cam out of that nasty tavern.'

'And what did the servant lassie say about him? Do you think you can believe her?'

'She thought he was a stranger to Glasgow,' supplied Alys, 'with an accent from Stirling or Edinburgh or some such place.' She grimaced. 'I confess I would not hear the difference. He pressed Billy to complete some task, and Billy said he was paid only to open the yett. She thought they did not mean this yett. Then the man ordered him to get his master arrested for murder, and to steal the key to the kist.'

'The Axeman seemed certain there should be more treasure,' added Kate. 'Oh, and there was that odd thing he said about his own master.'

'He did not say it was his master,' objected Alys scrupulously.

'True. He said – Mall told us he said, *The Baptizer wanted his goods and gear back*. We assumed he meant his master.'

'I think we can believe the girl,' Alys said judiciously. 'She was in such great distress, I do not think she was lying, and the rest of her story knits well with what we know already.'

Canon Cunningham nodded, and took another sip of the Dutch spirit, rolling it thoughtfully on his palate.

'Juniper,' he said enigmatically. 'Aye, Alys, she had reason to be distressed, I suppose.'

'It makes no sense,' said Kate. 'There was a strange man's head and a bag of coin and jewels in a barrel brought home from Blackness, and now another stranger running about Glasgow, persuading Billy there should be more of the coin and jewels still hid in this house, and killing him when he can't find it.'

'And chopping your oxter-pole in two and all, my doo,' said Babb.

'Maybe Gil has learned something more,' said Alys.

'Aye, Gilbert,' said Canon Cunningham. 'Where did you say he was gone?' he asked casually. The two girls looked at each other.

'He was going to Stirling,' said Alys. 'He left with four of Sir Thomas's men, I thought.'

'Aye, and Rob and Tam from my household and all,' agreed the Official. 'I ken he went to Stirling. I'm just wondering where he would go after that.'

'Linlithgow,' said Alys positively. 'My father left this morning, to go by Kilsyth and then meet him in Linlithgow. He would not change his plans without letting us know.'

'Why do you ask, sir?' said Kate.

'No reason,' said her uncle. He drew his spectacles from his sleeve, unfolded them and fitted them carefully on his nose. 'I had a word from Robert Blacader,' he went on, feeling in his sleeve again. 'He writes that he saw your brother yestreen, and had the tale of the treasure and the quest from him. And,' he glanced at Alys, 'that he has bidden Gilbert report to him.'

'Oh!' said Alys, and her eyes shone.

'Quite so,' agreed the Official. He located the piece of paper, drew it from his sleeve and unfolded it. 'Where are we now? Aye, and also that Will Knollys had a long word wi Gilbert after he spoke wi the King, and *I am tellt he was avysit to carry his search intil Ayrshire.*'

'Oh, no,' said Alys positively. 'He was certainly to meet my father after he was in Stirling. To go to Ayrshire he must come back through Glasgow, not? Linlithgow is the other way, I think.'

'I doubt whether your father would let him go into Ayrshire alone,' Kate contributed.

'Aye, I've no doubt you're right,' agreed her uncle. 'We needny worry about Gilbert. He's a man grown, after all.'

'I never worry about him,' said Kate.

Her uncle threw her a sharp look, and Alys said, 'I know very little about Treasurer Knollys, sir. Do you know him?'

'I do,' said David Cunningham without expression. Alys waited hopefully.

'Isn't he one of the Knights of Rhodes?' Kate asked.

Canon Cunningham snorted. 'He contrived to be made Preceptor here in Scotland of the Knights of Jerusalem and Rhodes, the Order of St John, though he isny in minor Orders, let alone one of the Knights. He pays the Preceptory's taxes,' he added fairly, 'as he can well afford to do, between the income he has from the Order and his own trading along the English coast. He's been Treasurer of Scotland since the commencement of this reign, if I mind right, and spends a lot of his time bickering wi Robert Lyle about where the late King's hoard went to and trying to lay his hands on what's still to be found. He'd be overjoyed to see that bagful your brother found.'

'Would he so?' said Kate. 'And to see it brought before the King like that?'

'Oh, aye,' said the Official, with the same absence of expression.

'How did he serve the late King?' Kate asked.

Her uncle threw her an approving look. 'He was one of the custumars,' he recalled, 'and made a fair profit on the customs of Leith. I think he served for the King in that sorry business wi my lord of Albany's treason, ten or more year ago, and I've no doubt the Preceptory held some of

184

this same hoard for the King in '88, when it was clear what way things were going.'

'So why should he not know where the treasure is now?' asked Alys.

'The late King planted boxes of it all up and down the east side of Scotland before the rebellion,' said Kate, 'like a squirrel in autumn. Quite likely he'd not have recalled all of it himself, even had he lived, from all I've heard, let alone the rest of us guess where it might have gone.'

'No to mention,' added David Cunningham, suddenly abandoning legal discretion, 'my lord St John of Jerusalem changing sides just afore the rising.'

'Is that his title?' said Alys, round-eyed. 'Kate!'

'Of course!' said Kate. 'The Baptizer!'

They exchanged glances all three.

'It fits,' agreed her uncle slowly. 'It fits what I know of the man. But we have no proof.'

'Proof is easy,' said Alys sweepingly. 'It is merely a matter of evidence.'

'I like the "merely",' said Kate.

'No, but wait. What do we know? The man with the axe had paid Billy to open a gate somewhere, and he was sure there should be more treasure here in the house.' She paused. 'There was Billy's tale of a thief in the yard at Linlithgow. What if the treasure had been held there, and the man with the axe was the thief?'

'Billy said the thief ran off,' objected Kate.

'He said there was a fight,' Alys reminded her, 'so there must have been more than one man. He also said the thief was nowhere near the cart, but patently somebody was. If he lied in that, he may well have lied in other things.'

'I wonder if Mall heard any more?'

'We can hardly ask her just now, poor lass.' Alys clasped her hands and gazed down at them. 'If the treasure was hidden in the yard, and this man of Knollys's came to fetch it, and something went wrong – I suppose it means that Knollys has known where this part of the treasure has been, and perhaps intended to keep it to himself for some reason.'

'Will Knollys would need no reason to hold on to money,' said David Cunningham. 'It's what makes him a good man for Treasurer. Your conjecture is no bad, Alys my lassie, but it could as well be Noll Sinclair.'

'Sinclair?' said Kate. 'I mind him. We stayed at Roslin one time, my mother and sisters and me, when I was a wee thing. They were kind to me. Do you mind, Babb?'

'No doubt,' said her uncle, over Babb's agreement, 'but he holds land in Linlithgow, and I'm certain he's let some part of it to a cooper. If the coin was hidden in the yard, it was hidden on Sinclair's land.'

'Is that likely, sir?' Kate asked.

'Oh, aye. Sinclair was aye a good friend to the Crown.'

'But the man with the axe did not mention Sinclair,' objected Alys.

'You need more information,' said Canon Cunningham firmly. Kate noted the *you* again. 'But for now, lassies, what are the two of you to do? I suppose you must go home from time to time,' he said to Alys, who smiled quickly. 'But you, Kate, are you to stay here? I hardly think it safe.'

'Maister Morison said the same,' said Kate. 'But I don't like to leave the bairns. There should be someone in the house to take charge.'

'Bairns?'

'They're in the yard,' said Alys, 'with Matt's friend Mistress Thomson.' The Official craned to see out of the window. His thin cheeks creased in a rare smile as he saw the little girls, who were industriously sweeping a small patch of ground with two very large brooms, while Matt and Mistress Thomson lifted broken crocks. 'Kate is right, sir, there should be someone in control. There are only the two women in the house, and one of my lassies on loan, and though Andy has his master's trust, he also has his hands

186

full with the men and the yard. He can't see to two bairns as well.'

And for how long? Kate wondered, biting her lip. What will come to their father? Imprisoned, however kindly, kept from his trade and his household –

'What will happen to Maister Morison, sir?' said Alys.

The Official abandoned the view of the children and sat back, looking from Alys to Kate.

'That depends,' he said. 'He needs to show clearly he had no knowledge of the barrel, which is no an easy thing. This matter of his man breaking in and then being murdered, while he himself was held secure, should go in his favour.' He paused to consider, eyeing Kate carefully. 'Aye, I suppose you had best stay here the now, Kate. If it comes to a trial, no doubt the law will put someone in place, but the Justice Ayre won't reach Glasgow for weeks.' His thought was clear to Kate: At least it gives the lassie something to think about. She lifted her chin and eyed him back, and after a moment he gave her another of those rare smiles. 'My, Kate. Times I see your father in you. Does it matter to you, what happens to Amphibal Morison's boy?'

Kate opened her mouth to deny the imputation, closed it again, and looked down. Behind her Babb said, with a warmth equalling the sudden warmth of Kate's face, 'Who'd want to see a man brought to his end by a spiteful creature like Billy Walker? No wonder she's taking an interest, Maister David!'

'Aye,' said Kate. 'Babb's right, sir.'

'Aye,' said her uncle, with that legal lack of expression, and rose. 'Well, I had best be up the road. I have a case to look over for the morn. Gang warily, my lassies,' he added, looking from one to the other. 'You'll keep me informed, won't you?'

'We'll report to you, sir,' agreed Kate. His mouth twitched, but he only raised his hand for the blessing.

*　　*　　*

187

By the time the two men selected by Andy for the task came home from their expedition to the Hog, the house was relatively quiet. The hall, swept and polished, bright with fire and candlelight, was strewn with cut pieces of linen, and more was stretched out on the great board which had been set on its trestles for the purpose. Round it, under the branches of light, the women were sewing, with the support of small cups of a reviving herbal cordial which Ursel had produced from her stillroom. When Andy stepped into the house with the two cheerful men behind him, he looked round approvingly.

'Where's the new one?' he asked. 'The nourice?'

'She didny want to leave them,' said Ursel. 'Wynliane's no right yet. Here, Jennet, that's a sleeve to that shift, and I think Babb has the other.'

'Aye, well, I tellt you how it would be,' said Andy.

Kate grimaced, and Alys nodded. 'You did indeed, Andy,' she agreed, 'but we had to try to bath them. I wonder if there is a better way to approach it,' she said thoughtfully. 'Perhaps if an adult got in with them?'

'We'd be better to wash the bairn standing in a basin,' said Kate. 'It can't be good for her, upsetting her so she screams like that.' She looked past Andy. 'Jamesie, William. What did you learn?'

They came forward, dispensing fumes of ale and the greasy cooking smells which clung to their clothes. Ursel sniffed, and primmed up her mouth.

'No a lot, my leddy.' This was Jamesie, lanky and dark-haired, turning his bonnet in his hands. 'Mattha Hog says he'd be right glad to take the coals off our hands, my leddy, but I never discussed the price, since you never tellt me to.' Kate nodded approvingly. 'And then we sat down, like Andy tellt us, and took a stoup of ale, and listened a bit, and talked a bit. They were wanting to hear how Billy dee'd.'

'What did you say?' asked Alys.

'What we saw,' said William. 'How he was cut to pieces like wi an axe.' He looked at his colleague. 'I thought one or two folk looked sideways at that. As if maybe they were feart the fellow wi the axe was in the place the night.'

'Aye, but he wasny,' said Jamesie.

'Naw. So then,' pursued William, 'one fellow asked what Billy was after when we took him redhand last night, so we tellt them what he said about the maister's kist, and how a'body kens the maister keeps his coin up at the castle. And we tellt them how it was you and Babb that catched him,' he added, 'and how Babb wanted to put skelfs under his fingernails and set light to them –'

'That wasny me, it was Jamesie that wanted to set light to them!' said Babb indignantly, needle poised over a scrap of linen.

'I never!' said Jamesie, equally indignant. 'It was your brother Ecky, William Soutar.'

'Whoever it was,' said Kate, 'we never took up the idea. What did the Hog have to say to that?'

'Well, I think they'll no come calling uninvited,' said Jamesie, grinning.

'It was so you,' muttered William.

'Did you learn anything more?' said Kate, seeing the way the discussion was heading.

'No in the Hog, no,' admitted Jamesie. 'But when we left –'

'Calling me a liar –'

'This fellow came out after us, casual-like, and had a wee word as we cam along the Gallowgait.'

'What fellow was this?' asked Alys.

Jamesie shrugged. 'He never said his name. What he did say was, he'd heard Billy and this fellow wi the axe talking in the Hog yestreen. Afore you were there yourself, my leddy.'

'Yes?' said Kate.

'Our Ecky never said such a thing in his life.'

'He said there was something about a barrel, and a yett, and a key. And he said the fellow said Billy had cheated him.'

'It was a' havers,' said William, suddenly abandoning

189

his brother's reputation. 'You don't need a key to seal a barrel.'

'Did Billy seal the barrel?' asked Alys hopefully.

Jamesie shrugged again. 'He never said. He said Billy was feart for the Axeman.'

'We kenned that,' said Andy. 'Is this all you've got, you pair of useless loons?'

'Naw,' said William unexpectedly. 'Other thing he said, he'd seen the fellow wi the axe in the Hog afore. Wi two other men.'

'Men? Not a girl?' said Alys. 'We still need to look for this Maidie.'

William shook his head. 'He just said men.'

'When?' Kate asked. 'Did he know the other men? Or describe them?'

'He didny ken them, for we asked him that. He said one had a hat wi a feather in it.'

'Like half the householders in Glasgow,' said Andy in disgust. 'You're a useless –'

'When was this?' Kate asked.

'No yesterday but the day afore. Wednesday,' said William, counting on his fingers.

'Did he hear what they were saying?' asked Alys.

'Naw.'

'They stayed in a wee corner, by theirsels,' elucidated Jamesie.

'But,' said William, 'he reckoned Mattha Hog knew them, for they got the good ale without asking for it.'

'A pity they never got the fellow's name,' said Kate, once the men had been thanked and sent out to the bothy.

'I said the man with the axe was not acting alone,' said Alys. 'But why was he in Glasgow on Wednesday? That was before the cart ever came home with the barrel on it.'

'Maybe they'd missed it on the road,' suggested Babb, running her thread across the beeswax.

'It still makes little sense,' said Alys, and frowned down at her seam.

'I think we only have half the picture,' said Kate. 'We've no more than we can learn here in Glasgow. Gil may have the other half.'

'True,' agreed Alys, and sighed. 'I wonder when he will be home?'

And when he comes home, thought Kate, will he set Augie Morison free?

The inquest on Billy Walker was an altogether more expeditious affair than the one on the unknown head in the barrel. This probably had something to do with the imminent arrival of the King and half the court; most of the supporting column had already arrived and the outer yard was full of men shouting over laden mules and oxcarts full of cushions, folding furniture and half of the Master Cook's *batterie de cuisine*. French curses floated over the chaos; as Kate was hoisted by Babb up the fore-stair into Sir Thomas's own lodging she heard Alys giggle.

The corpse lay on a hurdle propped on trestles in the midst of the hall. In deference to Mall's feelings, and possibly those of the other women present, someone had spread a length of canvas over it. Mall herself was stationed near the bier, dry-eyed and apprehensive, her beads in her hand and a clean apron over her worn blue gown. The woman beside her was so like her she could only be the sister from Greyfriars Wynd.

'He's done better wi the assizers this time,' muttered Andy as one of the men-at-arms set a chair for Kate. 'There's Mattha Hog again, but the rest's no so close wi him as Thursday's lot was. Just the same, I should ha sent our men to find some of our own friends. And you stand here, Ecky Soutar, where I can keep my eye on you.'

The serjeant bore in the burgh mace, and Sir Thomas made an entrance, took his seat on the dais and dealt briskly with the business of choosing the assizers, ignoring any suggested names of which he did not approve and ending with a group of sheepish citizens being sworn in by the clerk in batches of five.

'Right, neighbours,' said the Provost when this was complete. 'We've the body of a man here, and this court is convened to establish who he is, how he died and if we can tell who was responsible.'

'If ye dare,' said someone from behind Kate.

Alys twisted round to look, and Sir Thomas stretched himself up, glaring. 'Who said that? Andro, see who it was. Another word and you're out of this chamber, whoever you are.'

'Jemmy Walker, was it no, maister?' muttered Ecky Soutar to Andy, who gave him a look that silenced him. Sir Thomas was speaking again.

'Now, neighbours, the first thing is to determine who the dead man is. Has any of you looked on him?'

With some shuffling of feet, the assize admitted that the most of their number had keeked under the canvas, and that those who had done so were agreed that the corp was Billy Walker, that had been carter to Maister Augustine Morison of Morison's yard in the High Street. Sir Thomas nodded, and his clerk wrote the name down.

'And who found him dead?' he asked.

'That was me,' said Andy with reluctance.

After her recent experience of questioning witnesses, Kate admired the economy with which Sir Thomas extracted what Andy had seen when he opened the coalhouse door, and had it confirmed by the serjeant, who was more subdued than Kate had seen him. Then it was her turn; Sir Thomas very courteously bade her stay where she was, and came down into the hall to take her evidence, followed by his clerk. The assize were let out of their pen to come closer, so that they could hear her, and she described how Billy had broken into the house, how she and Babb had trapped him, and how they had questioned him and shut him in the coalhouse.

'We thought he'd be safe there till the morning,' she said, and was surprised to find her voice shaking.

Alys, beside her, put a hand on her shoulder, and Sir Thomas said gruffly, 'There, now, you wereny to ken. Is there any questions?' he demanded fiercely of the assize.

'Aye,' said someone. 'Ask the leddy what Billy Walker was after, breaking in like that.'

'He said he was looking for treasure,' said Kate. They keep coming back to that, she thought. We can't deny it forever.

'Which is daft,' said Andy at her other side. 'When it's well kent my maister keeps his coin up here wi you, Provost, and there's never been treasure in Morison's yard.'

'And what was the leddy doing in Morison's yard anyway?' said another voice. 'It's nane o your house, is it?'

'I'm there to keep an eye on the bairns,' said Kate, raising her chin.

'Oh, aye,' said the serjeant. 'These bairns I never saw. I didny see them yesterday either.'

'They're six and four year old, a bit big to miss. Maister Morison fetched a barrel of spectacles last week to the pothecary's,' said Kate rather tartly. 'Maybe you should go and try some, serjeant.'

There was laughter, and Serjeant Anderson scowled. Sir Thomas looked round.

'Is there any more questions for Lady Kate?' he demanded. 'Right. Thank you, my leddy. Now who was it heard a noise in the yard?'

Ecky Soutar stood forward and admitted to having heard a noise, thought it was a cat knocking something down, and gone back to sleep.

'Hmph,' said the Provost. 'I'll wager your master's steward had a word to say about that.' Ecky's eyes slid sideways to Andy, and he gave a shamefaced nod. 'Well, and what time was this?'

'I don't know, maister,' said Ecky. 'It was still dark, that's all I can say, sir.'

193

With some evidence from the serjeant about the amount of blood on the coal, at which Mattha Hog looked smug and Mall looked as if she might faint, and about the absence of blood on any of Morison's household, Sir Thomas wound up the questioning. The assize was led off to the refreshment presumably waiting in an inner chamber, and Sir Thomas stepped down from the dais again and came to speak to Kate.

'A bad business, my lady,' he said. 'It must have been a shock to you.'

'A shock to the whole household,' said Kate. 'Andy, here, found him, as he just tellt you, sir, and the other men were working wi him the day before.'

'And why were you in the house, anyway?' Sir Thomas went on in a low voice.

'As I said,' said Kate, 'I'm there to mind the bairns till we sort out this charge against their faither. He's an old friend, sir, and a friend of my brother's. I knew his wife, I've known Maister Morison since I was the age his bairns are.'

'Oh, I see.' Sir Thomas nodded. 'You're acting for your brother, are you?'

'What about the man wi the axe?' said a voice behind Sir Thomas before she had to answer this. The Provost turned sharply, and Mall came into Kate's view, dry-eyed and pinched with grief, her sister beside her. 'You never mentioned him,' she went on, looking at Kate, 'you never named the weapon that killed my Billy. Is he to get off wi it?'

'Speak respectful to my leddy, you,' said Babb over Kate's shoulder.

'What's this? What's this?' demanded Sir Thomas.

'It's Billy's sweetheart, Mall Anderson,' said Kate. 'Mall, did you not speak to the Provost before?'

'I tried,' she said, 'but my uncle wouldny let me.' She jerked her head towards Serjeant Anderson, who had just reappeared leading the assize from the inner room.

194

'Oh, he wouldny?' said Sir Thomas a little grimly. 'What's this about a man with an axe, lassie? Tell me quick.'

'There was a m-man wi an axe at the back yett to our yard,' said Mall, stumbling over her words, 'I heard him talking to my Billy, and he threatened him to d-do what he wanted, to break into his maister's house and steal for him, and it must ha been him that slew him, sir, and is he to get off free?'

'It's no right, maister,' said her sister at her elbow.

'Do you ken this man's name, lassie?' asked the Provost severely. Mall stared at him, and shook her head. 'If we canny name him, we canny put him to the horn. Still I wish it had come out afore this, for someone in the room might ken him.' He turned as the men of the assize were herded behind their rope again. 'Aye, neighbours,' he said, making for his chair on the dais. 'Have you reached a verdict, then? And are you minded o the penalties for a false assize?'

'At least they brought it in murder,' said Alys, as Kate settled herself on her saddle.

'That wasn't enough for Mall,' said Kate, who had seen the girl's face as the verdict had been announced. 'I think she feels if the weapon had been named, the man might somehow be taken for the killing.'

'Hah!' said Babb beside her, taking up Wallace's reins. 'She expects justice for a common wee thief, that got his own master put in prison unjustly?'

'It's different when it's one of your own that's affected,' said Alys.

Kate said nothing; she was thinking of the conversation she had just had with the prisoner, fetched down to the yard to speak with her while Alys snatched a quick word with a harassed Lady Stewart.

'Andy tells me they questioned you about you being in my house,' he had said in embarrassment. 'Lady Kate,

195

there's no end to the trials you're undergoing on my account.'

'I'll survive,' she had said lightly. 'It's a different kind of trial, maister. Makes a change from wondering how to get up a stair. Mattha Hog tried the same questions, when I spoke to him this morning, but I dealt with him and all.'

'Hog?' he said, startled. 'How so? What kind of a word?'

'I sold him the tainted coals,' she said. 'From the coal-house where Billy was killed.'

'Andy was saying something about them. I never took it in. You bargained with Mattha Hog? What did you get off him?'

She told him, and he gave her an admiring look.

'That's as much as I paid for the whole load, my lady. It's not many can get the better of Mattha Hog.'

'You've never heard my mother selling horseflesh, maister,' said Kate, with her wry smile.

Morison smiled in answer, and then bit his lip, and put his hand out to touch hers. 'D'you know, I mind carrying you up our fore-stair in Hamilton one time.'

'You'd not find it so easy now.'

'And those days, Lady Kate,' he said, and hesitated. She looked up, and met his blue gaze. 'You used to call me by my name. My own name – my given name.'

'So did you,' she said after a moment. 'We're old friends, Augie.'

'Aye, Kate. We are that.'

'So we'll hear less about what I'm undergoing on your account.' He seemed about to reply, but Alys arrived beside them. 'You'll scarce know your bairns when you join us again,' she went on. 'We've clipped their hair short, the better to wash it, and we've been making wee gowns for them, that they can run about the yard in.'

'There's been precious little sewing done in the house this while,' he said. 'But I thought you were to send Andy up to me, for orders to take the bairns to Bothwell.'

'You'd hardly have sent them to their uncle with the

clothes they had in their kist,' said Kate briskly. 'We'd to get those gowns finished.'

Morison's mouth twitched in a reluctant smile.

'They had the first ones on this morning,' said Alys, 'of blue linen, and they looked like two little flowers.'

'Aye, they would,' he said, and covered his eyes. Kate, in her turn, put a hand over his other one.

'They're well,' she said. 'They're safe, and we've found a good nourice to them. You've no need to concern yourself about them for now, Augie.'

'Aye,' he said again. He lowered his hand and looked at her with that blue gaze. For a moment he seemed about to say more, but at length he managed only, 'My thanks, Kate.'

By the time the dinner was ready, both Kate and Alys felt some sense of achievement. With Babb and Jennet they had made a more thorough attack on the hall, swept, dusted and polished again, taken the hangings outside and beaten them with sticks and rehung them, and done the same for everything in the chamber where Kate and Babb had slept except the great bed. Kate had wiped and oiled the heap of neglected instruments and cleaned candlesticks, Mistress Thomson had beaten cushions, and polishing the stools, with a rag each and a pot of Ursel's sweet-smelling bees-wax and lavender polish, occupied the children spasmodically for most of the afternoon. However now the army of cleaners had reached the door of Maister Morison's counting-house at the other end of the hall.

Here they met a predictable obstacle.

'That's my da's chamber,' said Ysonde, lower lip stuck out, a smear of polish on her nose. 'Not to go in there.'

'Now, poppet,' began Jennet.

'What does your father keep there?' asked Alys. 'Is it all his order-books and counting-books?'

Ysonde looked hard at her, and nodded. 'And all his books with poetry in, no-to-touch-wi-sticky-fingers.

197

Wynliane's in a poetry book,' she announced proudly, 'and so'm I. But you're not to go in.' Beside her, Wynliane shook her head and her mouth framed a silent *No.*

'We only want to sweep and dust,' said Jennet.

'There's a good lassie, taking heed to what her da said,' announced Nan. 'You come wi me now, poppets, and we'll see what there is for your dinner.'

'No,' said Ysonde. Wynliane shook her head again. Nan was just holding out her hand when there were hasty steps at the house door, and Andy's nephew John appeared in the hall. Behind him Kate heard distant shouting, and the tuck of a drum, and then a fanfare.

'Here's a great procession coming down the High Street!' John said in excitement. 'There's horses, and trumpets, and folk in velvet and satin, and fancy livery. Come and watch!'

'My!' said Nan. 'A procession! I've not seen a good Glasgow procession in years. We don't get them the same in Dumbarton,' she confided. 'Will you come and help me watch the procession?'

'No,' said Ysonde.

Kate, seated on a newly brushed tapestry backstool, reached for her crutches and said, 'We'll all go and watch the procession. Every one of us.'

John, hovering in the doorway, took in the situation and added his mite: 'They're saying it's the King. Come and see!'

By the time they reached the gate the outriders had already passed, drum and trumpet briefly silent. They were followed by what seemed like an endless, clattering, richly dressed cavalcade, silks and velvets glowing in the afternoon sunshine, jewels glinting on hats and gowns, the horses draped in dyed leather and turkey-work. The inhabitants of Glasgow, drawn by the fanfares, watched and commented, dogs and small boys ran alongside in excitement. The outriders raised their instruments and put up another resonant blast, but from further up the street over the noise Kate could hear cheering and shouts of,

'Guid bless the King! Jamie Stewart! Guid save the King's grace!'

The trumpeters had reached the Tolbooth and were blowing another fanfare as the King drew abreast of Morison's yard. Kate, who had seen the late King and had also, as a little girl, been presented to Margaret of Denmark, had no difficulty in recognizing the young man at the centre of the group, and Alys, used to the comings and goings through the town, identified some of the others for her.

'That's the Archbishop, you can see his ring, and that's my lord of Angus –'

'I ken him.'

'Those two are Boyds, I think, are they your cousins?'

'Sandy and Archie, that's right.'

'That is my lord Hume, and there is Maister Forman.' Alys paused to curtsy as the King drew level, and the men around them pulled off hats and bonnets and flourished them in the air. Ysonde clapped her hands in excitement on Andy's shoulders, and even Wynliane, held up in Babb's arms, smiled and waved.

'I think,' Alys continued, 'that may be the Abbot of Cambuskenneth. And Kate, could that be my lord Treasurer? With that badge it must be, surely!'

'Aye,' said Kate, looking at the blue-jowled, smiling man with the eight-pointed cross on his cloak. 'I think it must be.'

The procession clattered onwards, and was greeted further down the street by another blast of the trumpets. The outriders had rounded the Mercat Cross and were working their way back up the High Street. The denizens of the lower town were to get two opportunities to hail their King and his government.

By the time the King had passed the gates the second time, Kate had had enough. The day had begun early, she had had two broken nights in succession and a third in a strange bed, and she was extremely tired.

'Time for dinner,' she said.

'I want to *see*!' objected Ysonde.

'Let her see the last of it,' said Andy tolerantly.

'What's going on up-by?' asked Babb, staring up the street past the child in her arms. 'They've stopped by the Greyfriars Vennel.'

'Someone's spoke to the King, I think,' said one of the men.

Babb narrowed her eyes, peering over the heads. 'You're right,' she said. 'It's that Mall Anderson again.'

'What's she up to?' demanded Andy.

'Stepped into the procession and caught hold of the King's stirrup,' reported Babb.

As the riders round the King halted, those behind them caught up and also halted in a trampling, disorderly crowd. Someone's horse backed in a circle and onlookers shouted as an apprentice narrowly avoided being stepped on. Other voices, from up the street, were commenting adversely on the delay. Beside Morison's yard a rat-faced cleric on a piebald horse said sourly, 'What's holding us up now?'

'Some lassie wanting justice,' pronounced a rider from nearer the King. A name was called. 'Here, William, you're wanted.'

'Oh, aye,' said the rat-faced man. 'No doubt of that. All the tiresome tasks for William Dunbar. Gie me room, there.' He spurred his horse forward through the crowd, with some difficulty, and by the time the procession set off again Mall was perched on his saddlebow.

'Well!' said Babb.

'My, the effrontery!' said Ursel at Kate's elbow. 'And what will it gain her?'

'Trouble,' said Andy.

'After this morning,' said Kate, 'she likely thinks it's her only hope of justice.'

'She's in it as deep as he was,' objected Andy.

'She may not realize that,' said Alys. 'Now, I believe it is dinnertime. Then we may do a little more cleaning, and after that surely the water will be hot enough.'

Kate turned herself, to go back into the yard. Beside her Babb straightened up from setting Wynliane on the ground, and met her mistress's eye.

'It may no be for Mall Hamilton,' she said grimly, 'but there's trouble in that for somebody, my leddy, or I'm Kate Bairdie's coo.'

Chapter Ten

This attack was rather more professional.

They were making good speed round the flank of the Pentlands, with Edinburgh town under its pall of coal-smoke on their left, the castle at one end and Arthur's Seat outlined against the hills of Fife at the other. In the fields below them, the hay had been cut, and in places was still being turned; here and there was a field of wheat, sheared and stooked and waiting to be carried home, and every-where the barley stood golden and rustling in the August afternoon like the grain they had seen by Linlithgow.

Gil was ruminating on what they had learned so far, but at his side, Maistre Pierre rode watchful, and the Hospital-ler sergeant brought up the rear with his hand on the hilt of his sword. Socrates was ranging on either side of the track again, alarming the rabbits.

'I've kin in Edinburgh,' remarked Luke. 'My sister's man has a cousin that's a journeyman saddler on the High Street. Or so he claims,' he added darkly.

'There's a mony saddlers,' began Rob. His voice cut off, and he choked.

Johan shouted, and Gil turned in the saddle to see his man clutching at his throat, bright blood spurting between his fingers.

'Rob!' he exclaimed, and made out the cold blue end of a crossbow quarrel in the midst of the blood. He kneed his horse about, looking for the source of the bolt. Luke had already drawn his whinger, and Tam was reaching left-handed for his cudgel, staring at his colleague with a bemused expression.

'*Da!*' said Johan. He was pointing with his sword to the hillside above where a flock of sheep scattered bleating. A big man in black was leaping down across the rough grass, his long-hafted axe whirling in a double loop before him, and after him one, two, three other men rose from the ditch where they had hidden and rushed downwards, long swords gleaming in the light over their heads.

The party on the road had just time to group, the three trained swordsmen to the fore with Johan in the centre, Luke behind them with the two injured men, before the axeman reached them. His rush had carried him well in front of his fellows, but this did not seem to deter him. Gil knotted his reins on the saddlebow and drew his own sword and dagger. Well aware both of what such a weapon could do if it made contact and of the fact that this very knowledge was the axeman's greatest strength, he tried to ignore the bubbling, choking sounds Rob was making, and concentrate on the feel of his sword in his hand and the likelihood of controlling this horse in a pitched fight. He had to admit it was not good.

As Socrates reached them and took up position snarling under the belly of Gil's horse, the axeman leapt on to the earth dyke at the side of the road, checked his rush, and grinned at them past the blue steel axehead. It was longer and wider than his flat big-featured face, the hooked point at the back of the blade the same shape as the scrap of beard on his chin.

'Come on, then,' he taunted, and growled back at the dog. 'Are ye up for it? Who's first? Or will ye just lay down yir weapons the now and gie us yir packs? Grrh!'

'Vot does he say?' asked Johan. Maistre Pierre beyond him, watching the axeman, translated absently into a mixture of French and High Dutch, and the sergeant shook his head.

'Vy ve should do zis?' he asked.

'Because there's four of us,' said the big man, grinning

203

again, 'and only three of you can fight. Because Maidie here,' he kissed the axeblade, 'says ye should.' The three swordsmen jumped on to the dyke beside him. 'Because we're coming to get yez!' he shouted, and sprang forward at Johan, who deflected the swing of the axe with a sweeping blow of his long blade, following it by a kick to the man's shoulder. He slid away from it, and Gil had time to think, He has fought mounted men before, and then he was dealing with two swordsmen at once, his horse squealing as a parried stroke caught it a glancing blow on the shoulder. Below it Socrates leapt growling for the nearest man's thigh.

It was all very hectic for several minutes. The man on Gil's left was hampered by the dog, and by his own crossbow slung on his back. He was further discouraged by a boot and a backhanded dagger-blow, and Luke contrived to urge his horse forward and strike him down, leaving Gil to manage his own horse and parry the attack on his right. This man was good, and had also fought mounted men before, but Socrates was now slashing with sharp teeth at his thighs and codpiece. Moreover, the grizzled warrior who had taught Gil and his brothers swordplay had been at least as good, and Gil had not wasted his free time when he was in France. Standing in the stirrups as his mount trampled screaming in circles, he blocked the swordsman's attack, aware on the edge of vision of Johan's horse reared on its haunches and punching with iron-shod hooves at the axeman while its rider's sword beat the axe aside. More blacksmithing noises beyond them suggested that the mason was well engaged.

Then, as Gil seized his chance and disarmed his opponent in a move old Drew would have approved of, the axe flew sideways, its haft split in two, and with an agonized cry the axeman fell, first to his knees and then, when Johan's sword descended on his helm, into the dust and gravel of the track.

'Run, Baldy!' shouted Maistre Pierre's opponent, leapt

away from his attack and set off downhill in the general direction of Edinburgh. Gil's opponent, leaving his weapon in the dust, dived between Gil's horse and Luke's and over the dyke, and followed him. Socrates soared after them and set off in pursuit. As Gil whistled furiously for his dog the mason turned his horse as if to join the chase, looked at his companions, looked again at the fleeing men, reined back and sheathed his sword.

'*Mon Dieu!*' he said. 'They are persistent.'

'But alvays run avay,' said Johan. He had already dismounted, and now kicked the axeman accurately in the fork, nodded approvingly when there was no reaction, and knelt beside Rob, who had fallen from his horse some time since. Tam, unable to kneel, was standing over him, holding his bonnet with its St Christopher medal, tears running down his face.

'He's away, sir,' he said. 'Dead and gone. I showed him my St Christopher, but it never held him back.'

'He looked on it earlier,' said Luke, 'for I seen him. Maybe he's no gone yet.'

Johan stripped off his heavy gloves and touched Rob's face with gentle fingers. Gil dismounted and dropped to one knee opposite him, taking up one of the limp, bloody hands. Socrates returned, to sit down at his master's side panting and nudging his long nose under Gil's other elbow. Gil patted him, but his attention was on his servant.

'Rob?' he said. Rob's eyes opened, staring unseeing at the sky. His lips moved, but only a faint bubbling sound emerged. Now Johan was asking the urgent, familiar questions about repentance and salvation, taking the answers for granted, almost as if he was a priest. The hand in Gil's was growing colder. It gripped his, briefly; the bubbling stopped; Johan sketched a cross on Rob's brow and muttered, '*Dominus deus te absolvet,*' and Gil crossed himself, not sure if Rob had heard the words or not. He would hear nothing more, that was certain, though he still stared unseeing at the white clouds above him until Johan closed his eyes with that gentle touch.

Tam crossed himself stiffly, flinching as his bruised elbow twinged. Luke and Maistre Pierre were standing by, holding the reins of the horses. Gil stayed where he was, holding Rob's slack hand and looking down at the empty face, at the bright blood caking on his throat and on the neckband of his shirt. A Lanarkshire man, he thought. Born in the Monklands, ten years or so older than I am, fought as a mercenary alongside Matt in the wars in Germany, travelled to Rome so he told me once, and came home safe. And here he is, killed by robbers on a hillside in the Lothians. *And in a twincling of an eye Hoere soules weren forloren.* Why?

'*Nur Gott weisst,*' said Johan, gripping his shoulder briefly, and he realized he had spoken aloud.

'This one's deid, maister,' said Luke, pointing to the man they had taken down between them. 'I never killt him, I think one of the horses tramped him.'

'Zis vun not.' Johan stepped over to the axeman and kicked him again. This time he elicited a groan. 'Ve take.'

It was some time before they were back on the road. Luke, it turned out, had a slash on the arm, and Gil's horse was now drooping and shivering while the cut on its shoulder dripped into the dust. These had to be dealt with, by Maistre Pierre and Johan acting once again in committee. Gil stepped away from the group, leaving Tam still standing over his colleague's body, and stared out at Edinburgh. Socrates leaned hard against his knee.

Someone has died, he thought, caressing the dog's soft grey ears, because of an action I took. If I had never set out for Roslin, he would be alive now. Despite Johan's efforts, Rob had died without confession, unshriven. Gil had his own views on the importance of that, preferring to trust in the all-merciful justice which Rob now faced, but to the man's kin and friends that would matter.

'What kin had he?' he asked, turning to Tam.

The man wiped his eyes with his sleeve. 'He's an auntie in the Monklands, near to my folks, for he mentioned her more than once, but I've no more notion than that, Maister

Gil.' He managed a shaky grin. 'It comes to us all, soon or late, maister. He'd ha wanted to go quick like that.'

Gil nodded. But maybe that was too quick, he thought.

They stripped the dead thief of his effects. Boots, sword, crossbow, all went into the Hospitaller's pack along with the remains of the axe; the Order could make use of them. Rob's body was wrapped in his own cloak and tied on his horse, but the other was left by the roadside. Someone might come out from Roslin to bring him in for burial, or might not. Maistre Pierre stood by him for a few minutes with head bent, fingering his beads. The axeman, coming back to full, blasphemous consciousness, found his arms bound and a rope about his neck, its other end tied to Johan's saddle.

'Where's Maidie?' he demanded, staring round. 'Where's – where's ma axe?'

'Never mind zat. You vok!' said Johan, prodding the man with the point of his long sword.

'Aye, think yoursels clever,' said the man, and spat at the sergeant. 'You'll get what's coming to you afore long, so you will.' He leered at Gil. 'And how's Blacader's new man? And yir bonny sister, how's she walking now?'

Gil stared at him open-mouthed, silenced by the flare of rage that rose in his throat at the words. The man was bound, one could not –

'Vot you say?' demanded Johan, prodding again.

'What do you know about my sister?' said Gil, finding his voice.

'Go to Glasgow and find out,' said the axeman savagely. 'Aye, that's got you worried, hasn't it no? As for that clever wee lassie you're ettling to marry –'

'Yes?' said Maistre Pierre, turning away from the dead thief. 'What of my daughter?'

'Away and find out,' repeated the axeman, and spat again. Johan's sword arm jerked. 'Christ's bollocks, man, leave me alane wi that wee dirk o yours.'

'You vok,' repeated Johan, nodding along the track towards Roslin.

'What's he mean about the mistress?' asked Luke anxiously.

'And Lady Kate,' said Tam.

Gil moved forward. 'Tell us,' he said. 'What do you mean? What are you saying?'

'Aye, ye'd like to hear it,' said the axeman.

'We will hear it,' said Maistre Pierre. He exchanged a glance with Johan, who nodded, and untied the end of the rope about the prisoner's neck from his saddle. 'Any man can be made to talk, given time.'

The axeman gave him a wolfish leer.

'Your lassies didny find that,' he said. 'They done their best, I'll say they did,' he licked his lips suggestively, 'but they never got a word of what they wanted to know.'

Someone was shouting in Gil's ear. His hands were about something, the dog barked once, and again. Socrates never barks, he thought. As his vision cleared, he found himself staring into the empurpled face of the prisoner while Maistre Pierre's big hands tried vainly to slacken his grip on the man's throat. Socrates leapt around them, desperate to defend his master, unwilling to attack a friend, and compromising by pawing at their arms and baying, huge deep sounds like a great bell.

'Let go, Gilbert,' repeated the mason. 'We may kill him after he has told us –'

Gil loosened his hands and stepped back, shaking, unable to answer. Johan eyed him respectfully, and the axeman sucked in a long breath, glaring with furious popping eyes, and also took a step backwards to the limit of the rope. Socrates, silent, pawed eagerly at his master.

'Now tok!' commanded Johan.

The man threw him a surly look and shook his head. 'Canny talk – like this,' he gasped hoarsely.

'Let us get down to Roslin,' said Maistre Pierre in disgust. 'Someone there will assist us, surely. Sinclair himself may be in the place by now.'

They mounted up; Johan prodded the prisoner before him, the rope about his neck tied once more to the saddle-bow, and they went on, silent at first, round the final angle of the Pentlands and down toward the distant wooded valley of the North Esk.

Gil, leading his own horse and Luke's, was grappling with a turmoil of emotions such as he had not felt since boyhood. There was grief at Rob's death, mingled with a furious anger with himself and with whoever was behind the repeated attacks on their group, as the cause of his death, and – yes, he admitted, with whichever horse had kicked in the head of the man carrying the crossbow. Revenge for his servant would have been good.

And what had the axeman meant by his unpleasant remarks about the girls in Glasgow? Had they somehow become involved in this? He was aware of painful anxiety for Kate, his favourite among his three younger sisters, and burning through everything a fierce apprehension for Alys. Curiously, he was unconcerned about the insinuation the man had made, though it had triggered his attack on him. It was so far from what he knew of either Alys or his sister that he simply did not believe it.

As for his own behaviour – exploring his heart, he had to admit that he felt neither remorse nor embarrassment about his attempt to strangle a bound man. He knew both would be appropriate, but he could only find a sort of amazement at himself for giving way to his rage and a faint regret that Maistre Pierre had stopped him. It would be much more sensible to question the man and then hang him for theft, but it would be by far less satisfactory.

'Do we cross that river?' asked Maistre Pierre.

'No,' said Johan. Gil looked about him, and discovered they were well down off the hillside and nearing the Esk. 'Roslin that vay.'

'And the castle is beyond the town, in the gorge,' Gil supplied.

Maistre Pierre glanced at him, and nodded. 'You are with us again, are you?' he said. 'You have been cheerful company these three miles. Tell me, is this where there is the wonderful church of St Matthew building? I have the right place?'

'Yes,' said Gil, 'though I believe building stopped east of the crossing when the old lord died. They're putting the roof on what's there, my uncle said.'

'Ah. The builder is dead, is he? I have heard much of it. I shall try to visit.'

The inn was large, prosperous, and conveniently placed for Maistre Pierre's purpose, right beside the scaffolding-shrouded mass of the church. A board with a painting of a man holding a book swung from its ale-stake: the St Matthew Inn. The evangelist had a squint. Inside, the taproom was crowded, but the service was quick. Spooning down fish stew while the dog dealt with yesterday's ham bones under the bench, Gil realized that it was nearly Compline and they had not eaten since Bathgate.

'Ve stop here?' asked Johan, wiping his spoon on his sleeve.

'I think we must,' said Gil. 'One night at least. We need to find one man in the place, possibly two, maybe more.' Maistre Pierre frowned at this, obviously reckoning in his head. 'I wish Sinclair had been at home.'

'Perhaps he will return this evening,' suggested the mason.

Sir Oliver's sub-steward, a plump and self-consequential individual, had received them with ale and small cakes and a worried frown which grew deeper when he set eyes on their prisoner. No, no, he told them anxiously, Sir Oliver was from home, he could not say when he was expected. If they had really seen him in Linlithgow that morning, perhaps he had gone by the Edinburgh house. Yes, he could house the prisoner, there was a cell empty. At this the prisoner cursed hoarsely, but was silenced by Johan's still-vigilant blade. No, he couldny question the prisoner till Sir Oliver came home. They would have to make depositions on oath about the charges, he would have to fetch the notary –

'I can set it down,' said Gil.

That had taken an hour. A point-blank enquiry for Barty Fletcher or Nicol Riddoch had been met with another worried frown: were these names the steward should know? Did Maister Cunningham want to stop in Roslin, if he was to meet someone? Maister Preston could give them a token would warrant them a room and a welcome at the St Matthew.

This had proved to be true. Moreover, Rob's body had been laid, curled as he had stiffened over the saddle, on a board in a space just off the scullery, sworn to be rat-free and patrolled by the St Matthew's terrier. In the morning he could be washed, shrouded, and buried in the kirkyard of the little parish church on the other side of the town. The terrier herself, after making sure that Socrates knew who was in charge here, had bustled off on her rounds.

'Are we to ask after that musician here and all?' Luke asked his master.

'I've asked,' said Gil. 'I asked the fellow at the tap.'

This time the question had met with understanding; the tapster knew Barty Fletcher. He just couldny say if he was in the town the now.

'Bide you there wi your jug of our good ale, maister, and I'll ask about for ye,' the man offered, wiping the inside of another jug with his apron. 'My brother's marriet on Alice Fletcher, he can likely find out.'

'I'd be grateful.' Gil indicated his gratitude with a coin on account, which vanished inside the tapster's doublet. Since then he had been aware of quiet questions going about the room, of the odd curious glance in his direction. Someone came in, spoke to the tapster, went out again. What have I set in motion? he wondered.

'But who else do we look for?' asked Maistre Pierre now.

'The dog should go out,' said Gil. 'Let us walk him.'

'I kom viz you,' pronounced Johan.

'Johan,' said Gil, 'I sink ve could lose ze accent.'

'Accent?'

'I heard you shriving Rob,' said Gil, and bit back another tide of mixed emotion. After a moment he went on, 'Your Scots is near as good as Pierre's, here.' The sergeant met his challenging look, and then shrugged and smiled wryly. 'Have we said anything useful?'

'No,' the other man admitted. 'But it vos – was worth the try.'

'Can you tell me why the Preceptory is interested?'

'No.'

'Fair enough,' said Gil, 'but if you won't, then why should I help you? You don't kom viz us.'

'Fair enough,' echoed the Hospitaller, shrugging again.

Accompanied by a well-fed dog, Gil and Maistre Pierre strolled outside and gravitated naturally into the building site next door. In the evening light, piles of timber and slates lay under tarred canvas, but the stone-cutter's lodge stood empty. Work had stopped for the day, and the masons had all gone home to the houses which the chapel's founder had built for them, more than doubling the size of the castle's little town.

'*Ah, mon Dieu!*' said Maistre Pierre, soft-voiced. 'Look at those lines. The proportions.'

'I can't see past the scaffolding,' said Gil with regret.

'So who do we look for?' asked Maistre Pierre.

'The musician,' said Gil quietly. The mason nodded agreement. 'The cooper's boy. The dead man's kin, very possibly.'

'Why should those be here?'

'Because Riddoch's yard lies at the back of the Engrailed Cross tavern. Those were Sinclair's men I saw in the street before the tavern, and Sinclair's men were collecting the barrels of salt herring when we arrived. I saw one going into the barn where we found the empty barrel. I'll wager Sinclair owns the whole of that toft and has let the back-lands to Riddoch for his house and his yard. Riddoch is Sinclair's man.'

'Ah,' said Maistre Pierre. 'As well as –' He stopped

short, staring into the distance. Gil made no comment, and the mason went on, 'So is Sinclair behind all this?'

'I'd say he is involved,' said Gil. 'He asked me, when I saw him in Stirling, whether our friend in the barrel was a thief or a fighting man. And I think he has our books.' He kicked at the scraps of wood and slate underfoot. 'But I don't think he is behind these repeated attacks, any more than the Preceptory.'

'Heaven forbid,' said Maistre Pierre involuntarily.

'I think St Johns is involved.' He looked at his friend in the evening light. 'If they send this fellow with us, an experienced fighting man who is also a priest, though priests aren't supposed to bear arms –'

'No,' said Maistre Pierre, distracted. 'He is probably not priested. I have not asked him,' he admitted, 'but I have seen this before, where they will confess and absolve a companion *in extremis*, where no priest is present.'

Socrates, ranging round them, paused in his inspection of a stack of timber and stared at the gate of the site. Gil looked round, to see a familiar, elegant figure picking its way across the trampled ground. Clad in a worn leather doublet and patched hose, the man still had all the presence of a performer. He halted in front of them and bowed, waving his feathered hat in the elaborate French style.

'Balthasar of Liège at your service, gentlemen,' he said. 'I'm told you were asking for me.'

He straightened up and looked from one to the other. Even in the dwindling light, the colour of his eyes was obvious: one blue, one brown.

'I'm very glad to see you alive, man,' said Gil. 'Do you mind me? Gil Cunningham, from Glasgow.'

'I do, sir,' said the musician. 'You were a good friend to the McIans a few months back, were you no?'

'And still am, I hope,' said Gil.

'So what can I do for you, maisters?'

'We may have sad news for you,' said Maistre Pierre. Balthasar raised his eyebrows. 'Have you any kin with your eye colour?'

'What, odd eyes? It runs in the family. I've a sister has one ee green and one grey.'

'No, but have you male kin,' said Gil, 'with one blue and one brown?'

The musician looked at him. 'This is serious, isn't it?' he said, and scratched his jaw. 'I wonder, maisters, have you found my cousin Nelkin? We'd looked for him back afore this.'

'Ah,' said Gil. 'Where had he been?'

Balthasar shrugged. 'We heard word he'd gone on a pilgrimage,' he said, 'to Tain or some such. It didny seem like our Nelkin,' he added.

'And who had you heard this from?'

'From himself.' Balthasar jerked his head in the general direction of the castle. 'From Sinclair. He's been one of Sir Oliver's men-at-arms these ten years.'

'Ah!' said Maistre Pierre.

Gil glanced at him, and said, 'Noll Sinclair told you he'd gone on a pilgrimage?'

'Well, no,' admitted the musician. 'That fool Preston told his sister, but he said it as if the word came from himself – from Sinclair.'

'Is that all the word you've had?'

'I think so. What's this about, maister? Have you found him? You're saying he's deid, and canny answer for himself, are you no?'

'It seems very like it,' said Maistre Pierre. 'I am sorry. Was he close to you?'

'He was kin,' said the musician tensely. 'What came to him? What have you found?'

'We found,' said Gil carefully, 'a man's head. Short dark hair, one ear pierced, odd coloured een. Oh, and the remains of a blued ee.' He touched his cheekbone. 'He'd been headed, and the head put in a barrel of brine along wi a bag of coin and jewels from the old King's hoard.'

Balthasar bent his head and crossed himself.

'It sounds like,' he said. 'The blued ee sounds like our Nelkin. Ah, weel, I feart as much. When the laddie –'

214

'What laddie?' asked Gil.

'Oh, just – just one o his kin.'

'Nicol Riddoch, would that be, the cooper's boy?' guessed Gil. Balthasar's head came up sharply. 'What kin is he to you?'

'None o mine. His stepmother's some kind o kin by marriage to Nelkin's brother.' The musician crossed himself again. 'Would you excuse me, maisters? I'll need to break it –'

'I could do with a word with Nicol Riddoch,' said Gil. 'What did he say? I take it he didn't see your kinsman killed, but did he bring the other bag of coin here?'

Balthasar stared at Gil in the failing light.

'You ken the maist o it already, sir,' he said. 'Why are you asking me?'

'I never heard what it was,' said Nicol. 'Just it was worth a good bit.'

He stood uneasily before them, a spare youngster at the hands and feet stage, with a strong resemblance to his father the cooper. He had emerged reluctantly from the inner chamber of the house to which Balthasar had delivered them, and was taking some persuasion to fill in the gaps in Gil's account of what had happened. Socrates, lying at Gil's feet, watched him carefully.

'It was part of the rent, you see,' he added. 'We owe his lordship duty of carriage, and he turned up two week since, said to my faither he was calling in the duty for the year.'

'So you and Nelkin were set to fetch this great load of coin,' Gil prompted, 'and not told what you were carrying.'

'Just the two of them!' expostulated the householder, whose name seemed to be Robison. He had big scarred hands and a round, weatherbeaten face; Gil had lost his place in the reckoning but thought the man was a cousin of the late Nelkin's sister-in-law. 'Two men, to bring home a load like that.'

'It does not seem enough,' agreed Maistre Pierre, shifting on the bench beside Gil. The cushion slid with him, jolting Gil sideways.

'Aye, but nobody else kent what it was neither,' said Nicol. 'Except maybe Nelkin.'

'And you fetched it from one of Sinclair's other properties by Stirling,' Gil said.

The boy nodded. 'Garden-Sinclair,' he agreed. 'It was well hid. The man that holds the place never kenned it was there neither, so Nelkin tellt me.'

'But how did you carry it?' demanded Robison.

'In two bags on the old horse's packsaddle, under that load o withies,' said the boy. Robison sat back in his great chair, frowning.

'And when you got to your father's yard,' said Gil, 'thinking you were home and safe, you were attacked. Did you expect the gate to be open?'

'No,' admitted Nicol. 'I was to sclim ower and unbar it,' he grinned wryly. 'I've done it a few times. But here it was open, standing just on the jar. So we pushed it open, and there was naught stirring, so in we went, thinking nothing of it, and we'd no more than got the first o the saddlebags off and put it in a barrel as Nelkin said he'd arranged wi his lordship, when these three men came at us, all quiet in a rush.' He shivered. 'I seen the axe, and the swords, and then Nelkin shouted to me to run, and I grabbed the reins and louped on the old horse wiout thinking, all on top o the withies, and ran for it, and I – and I –' He swallowed. 'Did you say he was heidit, maister?'

Gil nodded, and the boy crossed himself.

'I feared it,' he whispered. 'When he never followed me here, I feared it. I should never ha left him.'

'Just as well you did, laddie,' said Robison. 'You'd ha gone the same way, unarmed against a chiel wi a great axe.'

'Aye, but . . .' said the boy, and shook his head. 'He was our good friend, and Jess's kin. I should never ha left him.'

'If he ordered you to run,' said Maistre Pierre, 'and you obeyed, you did right.'

'And then you came here?' said Gil.

'Turned up at first light,' supplied Robison, 'chapping the shutters there and gied us the fright o our lives. The auld horse just about foundered, half the withies snapped and hanging off the pack, and him half-dead wi fright. And nae wonder. What Nelkin was about, taking a laddie wi him on a duty like that –'

'It was for the horse,' said Nicol. 'He wanted me to lead the horse. Old Pyot'll do anything for me, so he will.'

'Well,' said Gil. 'And you say you never kent what you were carrying?'

'Well,' said the boy, and looked at Robison.

'No, he never,' said the householder. 'And no more do I.'

'No till you looked once he got it here,' suggested Gil.

'I wouldny do such a thing!'

Socrates raised his head to look at the man, and Gil said deliberately, 'Then you're more of a fool than I took you for.'

Maistre Pierre's eyebrows went up, and Robison bridled.

'Well, maybe I took a wee look,' he conceded.

'And?'

'More coin. All coin, it was, by the feel of it, in three great purses, all sealed,' said Robison regretfully. 'Two wi the Spitallers' seal and one wi the old King's.'

'Ah!' said Gil. He heard an echo at his side, and the bench-cushion shifted again. Not looking at his friend, he went on, 'So where is it now?'

'Now that I canny tell you, sir.'

'Do you mean you don't know?' Gil asked. 'Who took it? Why was it not put safe?'

'I mean I canny tell you,' repeated Robison.

'You may tell me,' said Maistre Pierre, and his big hands stirred on his knee. 'As a fellow craftsman.' That's the second time today he has used that expression, Gil thought. What does he mean? 'Are you working on the church, Maister Robison? I've heard there are two great

217

pillars at its heart. A pity the builder is dead, for the complete building would have astonished the world.'

Robison stared at him, his scarred fingers also moving. The dog had sat up, and was looking intently at the shuttered window. Gil stroked his head.

'Aye,' said Robison. 'I'm working on the roof, wi square and level and plumb, but I still canny tell you, sir, for I'm no the master in charge.'

'Uncle,' said the boy quietly. Robison turned to look at him. 'Would his lordship –?'

'He's from home,' said Gil.

'He cam back an hour since,' said Robison. 'I saw him ride in off the Edinburgh road.'

'He's here,' said Balthasar of Liège, stepping in at the door, Oliver Sinclair behind him.

'Oh, indeed there's more of it,' said Sinclair. Seated in Robison's great chair, large, fair and handsome in a big-sleeved gown of blue wool, he dominated the room. 'I have the half-load the laddie here brought on Monday night, which I take to be the other half of the shipment that turned up in Glasgow in your barrel. It's safe enough here. If you want it, you'll have to convince me you've a right to it, Gil Cunningham.'

'I've no right to any of it, sir,' said Gil politely. 'But we've a sergeant of the Hospitallers with us, looking for their portion, and I feel the treasury would like to see the late King's hoard again.'

'I've no doubt they would,' said Sinclair, with irony. 'And so would this fellow you brought in as prisoner. Who the deil is he? D'you think he's a treasury man?'

'Not a treasury man, no,' said Gil. Sinclair's eyebrows went up at the emphasis. 'Have you asked him yourself?'

'I have not. He's got away. That fool Preston never chained him, and he struck down the guard and ran.' Gil and Maistre Pierre looked at one another in dismay. 'But Will Knollys can whistle for the treasury portion. It's safer in my care.' He grinned at Gil. 'And I'll deny saying that, on oath.'

'And there are our books,' added Gil.

Sinclair's expression changed, and the sapphires on his hat caught the light as he pushed it forward. 'Oh, aye, those books. Quite a surprise, that was, when we unstitched the canvas just now and found *Knowe well to Dye* in black velvet, rather than a wee box of coin. D'ye ken what else is in the batch?'

'I've got Halyburton's docket,' said Gil. 'Have you unpacked any more?'

'Not yet. If there's anything good, I might make you an offer.'

'Fair enough, but I want the *Morte Darthur.*'

Maistre Pierre stirred on the bench beside Gil. 'This treasure. Some of it was, I take it,' he said, picking his words with care, 'a loan from the Hospitallers to the late King?' An interesting assumption, thought Gil. 'I think they want it back.'

'Seems likely,' agreed Sinclair.

'I also think,' continued the mason, 'if it is hid in the obvious place, that we need to get it out before work begins in the morning.'

Sinclair gave him a sharp look, then nodded. 'Also likely. I'd need proof the Order's looking for it, of course.'

'I think Johan can give you that,' interposed Gil.

Sinclair looked round the room, and rose to his feet.

'Right, then,' he said. 'We'll go and find this Johan, will we? Where is he, in the Skelly Matt?'

The sky was still greenish to the west, but overhead it was dark, and the moon had not yet risen. The torches made little difference, and the shadows of the pine-scented timber stacks around the church jumped distractingly.

'We do better without,' said Johan, tramping his out underfoot. 'Now where?'

'The roof,' said Sinclair.

219

The Hospitaller looked upwards, into the web of poles. 'You mean we go up the scaffolding?'

'There's a ladder in the lodge,' said Robison, 'and another within the kirk.'

Behind him the musician eyed the towering bulk of the building in its cloak of timbers, and turned away.

'Which part of the roof?' asked Maistre Pierre. 'Above the vault?'

'No,' said Sinclair. He grinned, in the leaping light of the torch in Robison's grasp. 'I'll tell you no more. It's well protected. If you're the craftsman I think you are, you'll find it, and if you can find it, you can take the St Johns share. But mind, the rest's to stay where it is, till it suits me to gie it ower.'

'We'll need lanterns,' said Gil, 'rather than torches.'

'You come too?' said Maistre Pierre doubtfully. 'I cannot take two who are new to scaffolding.'

'I'll be careful,' said Gil. 'My brothers and I climbed every tree from Glassford to Carscallan.'

'I also,' said Johan.

Balthasar returned across the building site with three lanterns in his arms.

'From the Skelly Matt,' he said, distributing these. 'Your dog's fair creating, maister. Your man says he's no sure how long he can hold him.'

'Well,' said Maistre Pierre, lighting the candle from his lantern at Robison's torch. He fitted it back on to the spike and closed the trap. 'Let us go, then, and solve this puzzle we are set.'

Chapter Eleven

The door of the church opened quietly when Gil lifted the latch. They stepped in, and it swung shut behind them with a boom which reverberated in what seemed like a vast, draughty space smelling of incense and pine resin. The floor was flagged; when Gil held his lantern up the vault of the aisle where they stood glowed in the dim light, but beyond the pillars the nave vanished upward into darkness, with a faint, distant hint of high scaffolding. How do the poles stay up there? wondered Gil.

'*Mon Dieu*, the carving!' exclaimed Maistre Pierre. He held his own lantern high and turned, staring up at the walls. Pillar, vault, arch and architrave, capital and springer were carved into elaborate designs in high relief which seemed to move as the light passed over them.

'Here is a ladder,' said Johan. Gil craned to see where he was pointing. At the top of the wall-pillar beside the door was a complex scene: the crucified Christ surrounded by many figures. There was something which might be a ladder at one side.

'That is a Descent from the Cross,' said the mason authoritatively from behind Gil. 'It will not reveal where we must ascend. But I think you are right, my friend, we look at the carvings. One of these moral jewels will tell us what we need to know.'

'How many weeks do we have?' asked Gil, looking round. 'There must be thousands.'

'We start here,' said the mason, 'and keep looking.'

They moved slowly eastward, pausing to identify each

of the carvings so far as possible. Some were obvious, versions of the familiar scenes to be found in any church; others were more enigmatic. There were angels enough to fill seven heavens, Gil thought, and Green Men to match them, but what was an elephant doing here?

'Here is a Dance of Death,' said Maistre Pierre, gazing upwards at an elaborately worked arch. 'Very handsome drafting. Look how it fills the spaces.'

'There Death takes a man with a spade,' said Johan, pointing again. 'Is the money perhaps buried beneath here?'

'Sinclair said it was in the roof,' said Gil.

Apart from their voices and footsteps, the church was quiet, but he found himself looking uneasily over his shoulder. Perhaps it was the eyes of all the Green Men, leering out of their foliage in the lantern-light, that made him feel threatened.

'What ever does this signify?' he asked, pausing before the Lady Altar. 'A falling angel, bound with a rope?'

The rope, by this light, looked as if one could lift it and knot the ends.

'I cannot say,' said Maistre Pierre at his shoulder.

'The pillars,' said Johan. They turned round, to see him staring to right and left. 'Are these the pillars? I have heard much of them.'

'*Ah, mon Dieu,*' said Maistre Pierre again. He moved forward as if drawn by a cord, and bent to the southern pillar, holding his lantern close to the ornament and muttering incoherently. 'Dragons – and the vines – ah, the detail! This stone, it shapes like butter, it must be a dream to work!'

'What's that beyond the pillar?' Gil asked. 'Is it stairs?'

'They go down, not up,' said Johan.

'Then so shall we,' said the mason, dragging himself reluctantly away from the pillar. 'Oh, and see, there is a sacrifice of Isaac on the capital. Now what is down here?'

The flight went down steeply, into darkness only slightly relieved by Maistre Pierre's lantern. Gil found himself hesitating at the top of the stairs, his uneasy feeling increasing. He opened the horn window of his own lantern and held it up, looking about him, but its light went no more than a few feet.

'You feel it too?' said Johan beside him.

'Come and look,' said Maistre Pierre. 'It is the drawing-loft.'

'Loft?' questioned Gil, setting foot on the stair. 'Down here?'

'How else should I call it?'

The chamber at the bottom of the stairs was at least half the size of the nave. It was much plainer, with only one or two carvings visible, and seemed to suffer from a lack of certainty about its purpose, since it boasted an altar with piscina and aumbry and also a fireplace. As Johan followed Gil off the awkward steps and into the chamber, the mason looked round from his intent scrutiny of the north wall.

'See, it is the working drawings.' He gestured at the curves and counter-curves scratched into the whitewashed surface. 'That,' he stabbed with one big forefinger, 'is the profile for the east window tracery, I noticed it in particular. And here is the outline for that wall-pillar, the one that has the Descent on its capital.'

'I'll take your word for it,' said Gil. 'What else is there?'

'It is many drawings, one on top of another,' observed Johan. Maistre Pierre, his nose inches from the wall, did not reply. Gil set off round the room, finding one or two more drawings which would have been better obliterated before the church was handed over, and paused in front of the two carvings by the altar.

'Ah,' said Maistre Pierre at last. 'I see. It is a space at the foot of the vault.'

'What is?' Gil came over to look.

'This sketch here.' The forefinger stabbed again. 'You see, here the vault, here the wall-head, and this is the string-course – the ornamental band along the wall-head. And *here*, in this other drawing, we have a space behind the string-course.'

'Do we?' said Gil, peering at the scratches. 'I can't read it, Pierre.'

'I can,' said Johan unexpectedly, 'but where is it? There is a lot of that string-course. It goes right round the church, does it not?'

'Now there I might be able to help,' said Gil. He returned to the altar. 'See this? The arms of the founder – old Sinclair, this lord's father –'

'The engrailed cross. Yes, it is everywhere up above,' agreed Maistre Pierre. 'But what is that heart doing there? That is Douglas, surely?'

'That's right. Sir William's first wife was a Douglas lady, I believe. Aye, it's a heart. *Ubi thesaurus– Where your treasure is, there will your heart be also,*' Gil quoted, and suddenly recalled the harper saying the same thing. Could this be what McIan meant, he wondered, rather than some cryptic observation about my marriage? 'If we can find a heart up above too, maybe the treasure will be close by. I've seen none so far, but perhaps in the south aisle?'

'It is worth the try,' said Johan after a moment.

Maistre Pierre looked back at the scratches on the wall. 'There is no other hint,' he admitted, 'and this one comes from St Matthew's evangel. If we find no heart, we must seek all about the string-course. Assuming it is all within reach of the scaffolding.'

At the top of the stairs, the darkness receded unwillingly from their lanterns. Gil stretched his ears, wondering if he had heard something move elsewhere in the building, or imagined it. Maistre Pierre held the light to the window arch, and shook his head.

'I never saw plants like that,' he said. 'And yet the carving is good, as if it is a true portrait. What are they meant for, do you think?'

'Who knows?' Gil stared at the carved leaves flopping back around what seemed to be fat heads of grain, then looked around. A bagpiper. An inscribed quotation from – from – the book of Esdras, his memory supplied. What seemed to be the seven virtuous actions, though something was out of key about them. He moved on. On the other side of the virtues, appropriately enough, the seven deadly sins, and in the window –

'Ah!'

'You found?' asked Johan, and joined him. '*Ach, ja*, is a heart.'

'An angel holding a heart,' said Maistre Pierre. 'So the treasure must be aloft, on angel wings.' He shone his lantern on the other corner of the window-embrasure. 'And here we have Moses, if I do not mistake, with the tablets of the commandments, and on his head the horns of enlightenment. It fits. It fits well.'

'Is here?' Johan looked doubtfully at the vault of the aisle above them.

'No,' said Maistre Pierre, 'in the roof of the nave, and next to the rib above this one.'

'And how do we get to it?' asked Gil. 'Fly into the rafters, like St Christina the Astonishing?'

'It is a vault, not rafters. Maister Robison spoke of a ladder.'

They found the ladder at the west end of the building, propped against the lowest levels of a tower of scaffolding which rose up into the dark. Maistre Pierre looked at it with disapproval, and clicked his tongue.

'I took him for a better craftsman,' he said. 'One does not leave the ladder like this to tempt the idle.'

'This rises up here, at this end,' said Johan. 'We wish to be yonder.' He waved his free hand eastward.

The mason gestured into the roof, just as airily. 'The church is in use. They do not wish to fill it with Eastland logs. This tower section is only to go up by – you can see from outside that further along, the poles come in at the clerestory and cross above the nave. There are no poles at floor level, so the clerks may make processions when they need to.' He was testing all the bindings on the structure within his reach as he spoke. 'Now, we climb up. I go first, you follow, my friend, and then Gilbert. Follow me closely,' he said, very seriously, 'and watch where I put my feet and my hands. And leave the lantern,' he added as an afterthought, 'if you cannot climb with it.'

He set off up the ladder with surprising nimbleness for such a big man, with one hand on the rungs, carrying the lantern in the other. Johan put one foot on the bottom rung, paused, put the lantern on the ground, and followed him cautiously. Gil gave him time to get to the first of the creaking wattle platforms, eight feet off the ground, then stripped off his short gown and dropped it by the foot of the ladder, thinking its folds would impede his movements, laid his sword on top of it and climbed up in his turn, taking his own lantern. As he found his footing on the platform at the top, Maistre Pierre spoke from the other side of the building.

'Three more to go. The next ladder is over here.'

Gil could see it, lit by the mason's lantern, rising into the dark.

'I –' said Johan.

'What is it?' asked Gil. The man was rigid beside him, his arms held away from his sides. 'Is it too high?'

'N-no,' said Johan with difficulty. 'I – I –'

'You must go back,' said Maistre Pierre, striding across the hurdles. The whole structure bounced resonantly. Gil braced his feet and swayed with the movement, but Johan cried out and dropped to his knees. 'I have seen this before. It is the balance,' the mason said to Gil, and bent over the kneeling Hospitaller. 'Some cannot take it. Like seasickness. Come, man. The ladder is here. Not far.'

Johan was persuaded on to the ladder, where he clung for a moment.

'I am sorry!' he gasped, and scrambled downwards. At the foot he stepped on to the flagstones and stood with one hand to his head, clinging to the ladder with the other.

'You must stay here,' said Maistre Pierre, bending to look at him over the edge of the wicker panels, 'sword in hand, to defend us from attack. Can you do that, brother?'

'I can,' said Johan, releasing his grip of the ladder. He

nodded, gasping a little, the lantern-light gleaming on the pale skin of his brow. 'I can.'

Maistre Pierre watched him for a moment, then nodded and returned to the next ladder, Gil following him.

'Maybe you go first, Gilbert,' he said. 'If I fall on you, we neither of us survive.'

They climbed up, and up again, and then again. It was strange climbing into the dark. The small light from the lanterns illumined the wooden rungs and glimmered faintly on the scaffolding poles and their rope lashings, but beyond them it struggled to touch anything in the void. Maistre Pierre came off the fourth ladder, looked about him, and set off with a confident, careful step along the hurdles. Gil followed him trustfully, walking in the small patch of wickerwork visible around his lantern, aware that if he missed his step there was a long flight in the dark to the same judgement which Rob now faced.

At this level they were above the heads of the tall clerestory window-spaces, with the cool night air around them. The vaulted roof bent over them, patterned with stars, and then beyond the next vault-rib with roses.

'Be handsome when they paint this,' said Maistre Pierre. 'Blue, I expect, and the stars gold. Two – three – four. It should be here. And it is. Well thought, Gilbert.' He leaned sideways, clinging to the nearest upright, and Gil realized there was a significant gap between the hurdle they stood on and the head of the wall. '*Peste!* Gil, can you shine your lantern here?'

The string-course was at hip-height, carved with flowers in roundels and crenellated with little upstanding tabs on its upper edge. Gil, studying this briefly, decided it was typical of the whole building that the two patterns, the roundels and the tabs, were differently spaced. He raised his lantern and held it near the curve of the roof and there, next to the vault-rib, behind the tabs of the string-course, was a dark shadow.

'You have the longer reach, I think,' said the mason. 'Set

227

down your lantern, and feel what may be there. I will brace you.'

This is too easy, thought Gil. Not that it was easy, precisely, but – after the hunt, the long pursuit of the dead man's identity, the attacks on their party, this seemed too simple. His wrist clamped in the mason's firm grasp, he leaned out to reach over the string-course with the other hand, and found a hollow space, almost a small aumbry. There were shapes in it, hard objects.

'Boxes,' he said. 'Two – no, three. Two are of wood. Kists, really.'

'How big? Can you lift them, or is it too awkward? We need the one with the St Johns money in it.'

'I can lift them, but it will need two hands. Can you hold me?'

'I wish we had a rope.'

'There's a rope here,' reported Gil, feeling further round the embrasure. He drew out the coil of hemp, and passed it back to his companion. 'I suppose whoever placed these here will have used it, and left it against their removal. Pierre, there is something embossed on the metal box. A shield, with – with –' He shut his eyes, all sensation in his fingertips. 'Ah! An animal of some sort, with a bordure flory counterflory.'

'The arms of Scotland.'

'I think it must be. So we can leave that one. I've no wish to make an enemy of Sinclair.'

'Can you reach the others? Come back, and I will rope you.'

With several passes of the hank, Maistre Pierre contrived a harness of sorts, and belayed the long tails round the nearest upright.

'You had better not slip,' he said, 'unless your codpiece is well padded. Alys will not thank me for gelding you before you are wedded.'

'I've no intention of slipping.' Gil checked the loops of rope himself, hitched at the two strands to which his

228

friend referred, and braced himself to lean out over the dark again.

He took the smaller of the two wooden kists first. It was not large, perhaps the length of his forearm, half as wide, a little less deep, but it was not an easy matter to turn it within the dark space so that he could grasp the rope handles at each end, lever it over the string-course, tilt it so that it would clear the carved tabs of stone. Maistre Pierre, tensely watchful at his back, heaved on the knotted ropes of his makeshift harness and drew him upright, and he set the kist on the wattle between them.

'It is very dirty,' he said. 'This has been hidden, here or elsewhere, for a long while.'

'I do not think it is what we seek,' agreed the mason. 'Does it open? Should we make sure?'

There was no lock, only a length of tape tied in a dusty loop to keep the lid fastened. Gil slipped it free and raised the lid, and brought his lantern closer.

'Paper?' said Maistre Pierre.

'One parchment.' Gil lifted it and unrolled the beginning one-handed. 'Sweet St Giles! It seems to be a map, but of what? I have never seen such a coast.' The mason took the other end, and they spread the parchment out. 'Ah – there is the northern sea, and I suppose Norway, and Iceland. But what lies beyond?'

'*Grunland*,' said Maistre Pierre. He peered closer. 'And *Estotilanda*.'

'Where? I've heard those names somewhere.' Gil relinquished his grasp of the curling skin and turned to the open kist. 'What have we here? A broken sword, very old, and a little box with –' He held it to the light, the contents rustling under his gentle touch. 'Look, Pierre, it is some kind of grain, long dried. I never saw grain with leaves like that. Could this be some of the plants on the window below us?'

'It could,' said Maistre Pierre cautiously. He let the map roll up, and stared into the box. 'It could, but I never saw grain like that either. Wherever is it from?'

'I think I could guess,' said Gil, in growing amazement. 'But that would mean the stories about Earl Henry are true.' He reached out to the kist again. 'And if those are true, what else may be? What might be in that bag –'

Maistre Pierre put his hand over Gil's.

'No.' They looked at each other in the lantern-light. 'No, Gil. Not for us, I think.'

Gil dropped his gaze to the bag in the bottom of the kist. Worn embroidery gleamed dully in the light, rich silk brocade visible between the stitched saints. A bag for a relic. A very rich bag, for a very important relic, the relic guarded by the Sinclairs with their canting arms, the cross engrailed which appeared here and there all over this rich little building. Whatever the brocade bag held would, he knew, be wrapped in more silk and brocade, to keep it from harm, but its shape, smaller than one would have expected, was just discernible under the padding. There would be a slip of parchment in the wrappings, with an inscription saying what was inside them. In what language, he wondered. What alphabet, even. As for the thing inside – to hold it – to touch it – even to look at it –

'No,' he said after a moment, and crossed himself. 'We are not worthy. But how I wish I was. And to be this close to it . . .'

'*Et moi, je le veux aussi*,' said the mason fervently.

And how, Gil wondered, packing the little box of exotic grain and the rolled parchment back into the kist, how does Pierre know what might be under that brocade? He knows a surprising amount about what we are doing.

The other wooden box was the right one. Once the first one, with its strange cargo, had been restored to its place in the shadows and the other lay on the wattle at their feet, Maistre Pierre hauled Gil in, and he stood letting the darkness settle round him while the mason bent to study their booty.

'Three sacks of coin inside it,' he reported. 'And there are seals, the eight-point cross. This is what we seek.'

'Robison mentioned two with the St Johns seal,' Gil recalled, 'and one with the old King's.'

'I suppose Sinclair restowed them,' speculated his friend. 'The King's purse will be in the other kist, the metal one, by now.'

'How do we get them down?' Gil asked. 'Three sacks will make quite a burden, and we can't take the box down between us. I wish I hadn't taken off my gown. It would have made a sling of sorts.'

'And the rope is not –' Maistre Pierre put up a hand. 'Listen.' They both listened, and heard the scaffolding creak. Wattle squeaked. '*Merde, alors,*' said the mason. 'It must be Johan. He has tried again. He will assuredly turn to stone on the next level. Gilbert, it is best if I go down and stop him, before he gets any further. Can you stay here alone?'

He snatched up his lantern and set off without waiting for an answer, leaving Gil isolated in his own little patch of light. Moving cautiously, he disengaged himself from the coils of rope, and wound it into a hank. Another Green Man grinned at him without humour from one of the knots of vegetation on the vault-rib. Outside the moon had risen, and there were great pale bars across the flagstones far below. The wicker sang and crackled as Maistre Pierre made his way to the flight of ladders, the poles creaked and hummed as he descended first one ladder, then the next. Gil heard his voice, speaking reassuringly, and recognized the change in the movement of the scaffolding as he stepped on to the third ladder, climbed down it, set off across the lowest level of hurdles.

'Johan?' floated up through the darkness. 'Johan, *wo sind Sie?*' Johan's voice answered. And then, sharply, Maistre Pierre: 'You?' and louder, in real alarm, 'Gil, have a care!'

Gil tensed, staring as if he could see through the wattle he stood on. The scaffolding spoke shrilly of hasty movement, in which there were grunting noises, a gasp, an exclamation which rang in the curve of the roof. Something fell, someone shouted. There was what seemed a very long pause, with more gasping movement in it.

'Pierre?' he called.

There was another pause, then the pine logs creaked again. Ears stretched, he tried to locate the sound. There was someone on one of the ladders, but was it more than one person? More than one ladder?

'Pierre?' he called again. The creaking stopped, and there was a breathless silence. Not Pierre, then. But if not Pierre, who?

'Guard yourself!' said a hoarse voice from the dark depths. 'He goes free.'

That was Johan, whom they had left at the foot of the ladder. Pine sang again. What had Sinclair said? *That fool Preston never chained him, and he struck down the guard and ran.* Could this be the axeman? Quietly, Gil opened the horn panel of his lantern, licked his fingers, pinched out the flame of the candle. Darkness covered him, in which the scaffolding began to creak again.

'Cunningham?'

Below, on the floor of the church, there was shuffling movement across the bars of moonlight. Voices rose outside. The door boomed. Up here in the darkness among the echoes, with the night air stirring, there was the crack and rustle of wickerwork, and as the echoes died a whispered question.

'Where are you, Cunningham?'

Turning his head, he tried to place the sound. His pursuer must be westward, where the ladders were, but the whisper rattled in the vault, and came at him from all sides. The wicker hurdles flexed like a corach he had sailed in. Did the fellow have a weapon? he wondered, and was assailed by the sharp recollection of his sword, on top of his short gown, conveniently placed by the foot of the first ladder. And what had come to Pierre? And Johan?

Johan's voice rose on the cue from the barred floor of the church.

'Maister Cunningham! Are you safe? Are you hurt?'

232

The echoes shot his name round the roof. I dare not answer, he thought, not with an enemy hunting me in the dark. He already knows where I was when I put the light out.

'Cunningham?' The whisper again, surrounding him. '*I* ken you're no hurt. No yet.'

There was a patch of light growing in the corner of his eye. He turned his head and saw a silvery glow, as if someone to the east of his perch had another lantern. A hand appeared, and beckoned in silence. He lifted the coil of rope and moved cautiously towards it, leaving the box with its three sacks where they were. There was just enough light to make out the walkway in front of him, not enough to see who held the lantern, but he was sure the whisperer on the ladders was more of a threat.

There was a ladder here. He descended, cautiously, pausing to listen. Down here away from the vault, level with the huge empty windows, it was easier to determine direction, and the creaking was coming closer.

'Where are you hiding?' Again the whisper, from the same place as the creaking. 'Where have you hid the gold?'

The light beside him still did not illuminate its bearer. The hand pointed to the window-space. He moved out, into moonlight, and found himself stepping from one pole to another among a forest of flying buttresses and pin-nacles, the thin soles of his riding-boots gripping the bark, more poles at head height offering support. The mesh of scaffolding, mounted on the roof of the south aisle of the chapel, was like the biggest tree he had ever climbed. Below him strange cavities and hollows showed blackly where the vaults of the south aisle roof had not yet been covered. He had swung on tree-branches out over the Linn pool whose depths had never been drawn. These dark cavities did not alarm him.

'Cunningham!'

It was the axeman, right enough. He appeared further along the tangled structure, stepping like Gil out through an empty window-space, white face and hands floating in the pale light until he clambered out and his black-clad body was outlined against a lit pinnacle. Gil ducked behind a buttress. The man appeared to have a weapon; he thought it was an axe rather than a sword. Neither would be good news, since he only had his dagger.

'Come here, you scabby clerk. I swear by the Magdalen's tits I'll pay you for the trouble you've cost me. I've an axe here for you, 'ull trim your pen no bother. It's no Maidie, God rest her soul, but it's sharp enough for the job. Come and face me. Where have you put the gold?'

Gil looked about, gauging his chances of tackling his opponent. Not good. Then the lantern-lit hand appeared at another window – how had its owner got there so silently? – and beckoned. Gil moved, lightly and rapidly, and pulled himself in on to the scaffolding again. The wickerwork creaked as he stepped on it, and his pursuer shouted.

'I hear you! I'll get you!'

The axe glinted as its bearer scrambled for the next window, swung himself in on to the walkway, rushed forward. Gil slipped back out into the moonlight, working his way between the pinnacles, while the axeman blundered along the wicker platform just inside the wall.

Gil had no very clear plan, just a conviction that if he kept the other man moving, sooner or later he would make a mistake. Always supposing I don't make one first, he thought, sliding between two buttresses. Inadvertently he looked down.

For a long moment he clung, staring down past the stonework to the silvered grass at the wall's foot, while his grip tightened on the stonework and the depths seemed to reach for him. He could feel himself beginning to topple outwards.

There was movement at the edge of his vision. With difficulty, he dragged his gaze from the dazzling depths of air and turned it towards the dark windows. Round a pinnacle a moonlit hand appeared, stretched towards him, just out of his grasp. He fixed his eyes on it, took one hand from the gritty stone, stretched out for the bleached fingers. The hand drew back, and he leaned inwards, still straining towards it. Then suddenly his weight was all inside the wallhead, inside the web of wooden poles. He was safe.

He gasped his thanks and clung to the pole at shoulder height, his eyes closed in relief. By the time he opened them the other had gone, but the man with the axe was still snarling blasphemously at the far end of the building.

Holding tightly now to the scaffolding, Gil worked his way westward, reasoning that if he climbed in at the furthest window he would be close to the ladder and might get down before the axeman realized where he was. And then what? he wondered. Where is Pierre? He must have been hurt, if he hasn't joined the hunt.

'I see ye, traitor! Gallows-cheat!'

The hurdles within the gaping windows crackled and sang as the man trampled along them, his wild movements making the whole wooden structure buck, inside the church and out, like a corach in a high wind. Gil froze by the window, clinging tightly to the pine-logs, fearing he would be thrown off into the half-completed vault of the aisle below him. The man arrived at the aperture hefting the axe, braced himself and swung at Gil's hand grasping the pole beside his head.

It seemed to happen very slowly. The axe swung, shedding moonlight into the dark air. Gil released his grip, but could not seem to move his hand. The man's expression changed, little by little, from triumphant fury to amazement and then to horror. Gil's eye was drawn down, and he saw, very clearly, a pale hand thrusting the axeman's back foot backwards. Back over the edge of the wicker hurdle. Off into the fathomless dark of the church. The leg followed it, the other foot slid, the body contorted trying to save itself. A hand dragged at the edge of the hurdle, but the other still held the axe, and only succeeded in cutting splinters from the wickerwork. The man fell, vanishing downward like the roped angel.

There was an unpleasant sound from below, and a clat-

235

ter as the axe hit the flagstones, followed by some shouting, and running feet.

A face appeared in the space the axeman had vacated. The lantern-light, or moonlight, robbed the man's eyes of colour, but Gil could see that one eye was pale and one was dark.

'Thanks, friend,' he said shakily. 'I owe you for that.'

The other grinned at Gil, shook his head. A pale hand came up in a salute, then the face turned away. Gil leaned against the nearest piece of stonework and closed his eyes. *For there is not so much joy in holding high office*, he thought, *as there is grief in falling from a high place*. Who wrote that? Something about the Order of Knighthood, was it?

After a while he pulled himself together. There was no sign of the man with the lantern. Moving carefully, he made his way back to the eastward ladder, which was now moonlit, and groped his way along the topmost level to his own lantern and the sacks of coin. He lit the lantern with the flint and tinder in his purse, and laboriously but with more confidence contrived to shift the sacks one at a time, along the scaffolding, down the ladders. He became aware of movements below him, of urgent voices, but ignored them until, as he reached the foot of the second ladder, helpful hands took the sack he was carrying.

'Are you hurt?' asked Balthasar of Liège. 'Come this way, man. That was well done – I'd not go higher than this for a great fortune.'

'No,' he said. 'I'm no hurt. You ken that.' He took in what the musician had said. 'What do you mean? You were up there –'

'No me.' Balthasar set the sack down at the top of the lowest ladder. 'Can you get down alone?'

He could. The flagstones felt hard under his feet, and he stood for a moment, wondering why he felt so surprised to be there.

'Pierre,' he said.

'Out here. It was touch-and-go for a bit, but he's safe now.'

'You must go back to Glasgow,' said Maistre Pierre, enthroned against the pillows of Maister Robison's best bed.

'I don't like to leave you.' Gil eyed his friend. There was a bandage on his head, and a thicker one on his arm, which reposed on another pillow.

'He'll be looked after,' said Sir Oliver robustly from Robison's great chair. 'No need to worry about him, Cunningham.'

'Mistress Robison will tend me. I agree, I am not fit to ride until maybe tomorrow, but we must take home what we have learned, and also Alys will be concerned.'

Gil nodded, preserving his own counsel about when Maistre Pierre would be fit to travel. He was very much aware that it was two days since he had seen Alys, the longest period they had spent apart since their betrothal, but he also had to admit to himself that he did not look forward to telling her that her father was injured.

He eased his right foot from under the dog. After being reunited with his master in the midnight, and checking him carefully to make sure no harm had come to him, Socrates had gone off with the St Matthew's terrier, who had apparently spent the rest of the night teaching him to rat. The innkeeper had taken a groat off the bill in his gratitude for the pile of corpses left neatly in the yard, and Socrates had slept all morning.

'So Johan got you outside,' he said. 'Did you fall off the scaffolding?'

'No, I praise God and Our Lady.' Maistre Pierre crossed himself left-handed. 'I must, I suppose, have fallen near the edge of the hurdle, and Johan climbed up and dragged me to the ladder. It was an act of great courage,' he said. The Hospitaller, silent in the corner of the room, shrugged. 'It was, my friend. Then I managed the ladder somehow, and we went outside, and . . .' His voice trailed away.

'They came staggering out the kirk,' said Sinclair, 'knee to knee and hand over back, either holding the other up, and him trailing blood. A sight to fright the weans.'

'I thought him spent,' said Johan. 'It was a close thing. If the lutenist had not those spare strings with him, he had bled to death by the cut of the axe.' He rubbed his own upper arm, and grimaced.

'And the lutenist was out in the kirkyard that whole time,' said Gil.

Johan nodded. 'Indeed. He held the strings, and tightened them while the bleeding stopped. It was only when we heard a fall, and Maister Robison went to look and came out to say the man with the axe was lying there dead, that he left us and went to find you. We have tried to call you before that,' Johan said earnestly, 'but I suppose you could not answer.'

'The axeman must have been on the scaffolding when we went up,' said Gil, and shivered. 'Waiting in the dark, till we found the treasure for him.' And who else was up there? he wondered. *Hold the hye wey, and lat thy gost thee lede.* Who helped me escape, who pushed the axeman out into the shadows, if it wasn't the lutenist?

'A merry thought,' said Maistre Pierre.

'And what now?' said Gil.

'You go back to Glasgow, as you're bid,' said Sinclair. 'From what you tell me, you've business there. You know who killed Nelkin Fletcher, you can report that to Robert Blacader's man, and we'll get the rest of your books repacked and loaded on a mule for you.'

'And the coin?'

'I take that,' said Johan. 'It goes back to the Preceptory, since it is St Johns money.'

'Does it?' said Gil. Johan and Maistre Pierre exchanged glances.

'I think it does,' said Maistre Pierre. Johan nodded. 'Now it is known to be in the hands of the Preceptory, it becomes an internal matter.'

'Not entirely,' said Gil. They both looked at him, and

Sinclair leaned back in the chair as if awaiting entertainment. I must be careful here, he thought. 'I assume,' he said delicately, 'the money was a loan from the Preceptory to the late King.' He looked at Johan, who gave him back that enigmatic stare. 'Clearly, since it is still packed and sealed as it left the Preceptory, the King never had the chance to spend it. Indeed, I wonder if he ever got his hands on it, if it didn't rather stay with – someone, who stood between the King and the Preceptory.' Still that enigmatic stare. He looked at Sinclair: still waiting to be entertained. 'That person I think gave it to you, sir, to keep safe. He's been a good man up to now to have owing you a favour, which I suppose is reason enough to oblige him.' Sinclair's eyebrows went up at this, but he gave no other sign. 'And since he gave you a portion of the late King's hoard along with it, I suppose it was around the time of the troubles of '88. Perhaps he had that direct from the King, perhaps he came by it otherwise. That hardly matters.'

Sinclair still gave no sign, but Johan nodded. Assenting to what?

'The Preceptory wants its loan back,' Gil said baldly. 'It's now over four years since it was lent out, so this is no wonder. I suppose, sir, the person who gave it you for safe keeping must have asked you for the Preceptory money he had lodged with you, and you decided to move the King's hoard as well, all at once. That makes sense – if the hiding place was compromised, it would be better cleared.' Sinclair raised his eyebrows again. 'Maybe in two instalments,' Gil speculated, 'since we saw more up there than Nelkin Fletcher brought away with him. Did you shift the other load, sir?'

'Did I?'

Gil waited a moment, but the handsome face was still studiously blank. He went on.

'The second instalment, which we're dealing with, got as far as Riddoch's yard, and should have gone onward hidden in a barrel as part of Riddoch's rent, but the two carrying it were attacked. Some of the load was already in the barrel, the attackers threw Nelkin's head in after it to hide his death, filled it with brine, put it on a cart – though why for Glasgow?' he wondered. 'These same people, I take it, have been pursuing us all across this side of Scotland, hoping we had either found the rest of the load of coin or would lead them to it. They evidently had some idea of how much there should be. Do you agree, sir?'

'How should I agree or no?' Sinclair had relaxed slightly, and his tone was slightly friendlier than the words. 'Are you going to spread these ideas about Scotland?'

'Not widely, sir. And you can be sure,' said Gil, meeting his eye again, 'that we took nothing else from the place we found.'

'Oh, I ken that,' said Sinclair. 'You got down safe, after all.'

'What puzzles me,' said Gil, 'is who the axeman and his friends were working for.'

'Someone who knew the money was being moved,' said Maistre Pierre after a moment. Both the other men looked sharply at him.

'Aye,' said Gil. 'Of those, I think we can leave out the Preceptory itself, and you, sir.'

Sinclair bowed ironically. 'Narrows it down very little,' he observed.

'Precisely,' said Gil. 'I'm still involved in Nelkin Fletcher's death. It seems more than likely it was the axeman killed him, and I've no doubt the Provost of Glasgow would be happy enough to bring it in as murder by a stranger when I take home what I've found so far, but Augie Morison's been suspected and the only way to clear him completely is to get a name for the man behind the axeman. With proof.'

'Proof might be harder to come by,' said Sinclair absently. 'And we never got a name for the fellow himself, either. I wish my fool of a steward hadny let him get away.'

'So do I,' said Gil. 'Was it foolishness, or something else, sir?'

Sinclair's eyebrows went up at this. 'That's for me to deal wi, d'you not think? And I will, you may believe it.'

'Oh, I do,' Gil agreed, meeting the other's eye. 'Anyway, I think the axeman's name may be Carson. And he has certainly learned the grief of falling from a high place.'

Sinclair's mouth quirked as he too recognized the quotation. He considered Gil for a moment, but did not comment.

'I wonder where the two who ran went to?' said Johan.

Chapter Twelve

'Are ye for Rottenrow, Maister Gil,' asked Tam as they picked their way along the Gallowgait, 'or are ye going straight to your sweetheart?'

The warm dusk was deepening fast. Gil had paid off Sinclair's escort outside the gates; they could command a lodging at a house Sinclair owned near the crumbling Little St Mungo's chapel. He and Tam had only got into Glasgow after a brisk and personal discussion between Tam and the gate-wards, who were just about to go off duty and were reluctant to unseat the great bar which held the gate shut. Most of the houses they passed were quiet, the fires smoored so that only a trickle of smoke floated from chimney or thatch, the shutters firmly latched against the night air. Taverns here and there spilled lamplight and laughter, and some of their patrons were ambling homewards, forming a shifting hazard to horse traffic. Gil's horse was too tired to resent this, but the pack-mule seemed to be looking for an opportunity to kick.

'I ought to go to Rottenrow,' he said now, in answer to Tam's question. 'They need to know about Rob.'

'But the lassie needs to ken what's come to her da,' the man said. 'I'll take the mule on to our house, maister, and break it to them there. Will I take your beast and all? And the dog?'

'The dog will stay wi me.' Gil looked down at the animal, wedged snoring across his saddlebow. 'Tam, I'm grateful. Ask Maggie not to bar the door yet.'

At the mason's house there was candlelight in the hall

windows. Crossing the shadowy courtyard, Gil wondered where Alys would be waiting. On the settle by the empty fireplace, with a stand of candles and a book? Upstairs, in her father's panelled, comfortable closet, with a book or her lute or the monocords, practising some of the keyboard music which arrived occasionally from France? He whistled to Socrates, and rattled at the front door latch.

'Oh, Maister Gil,' said Kittock, opening the door to him. 'The mistress is no here.'

'No here?' he repeated.

'Madam Catherine's in the hall,' she said, bobbing a curtsy. 'Come you in and get a word wi her. Is the maister no wi you, sir?'

In the hall, on the settle by the empty hearth, Alys's aged aristocratic nurse Catherine was seated under a branch of candles, staring at the wall-hangings while her fingers moved automatically with thread and hook. The long strip of lacy stuff twitched across her black skirts as she worked. As Gil stepped into the hall she looked round and set down her work.

'*Bon soir, maistre,*' she said. 'Welcome home. Is our master not with you?'

'I left him in Roslin.' At her invitation Gil sat down opposite her.

'Where? I trust he is well.' She paused to acknowledge Socrates, who had padded forward to nudge her hand with his long nose.

'He has taken some hurt. I left him well looked after,' he assured her. Inevitably this was not enough; he had to detail the mason's injuries and treatment while she listened with a critical frown. Finally he managed to say, 'Where is Alys, madame? She should be told.'

'I regret,' said Catherine disapprovingly in her beautifully enunciated French, 'the demoiselle has not been home today. She spent yesterday with your sister, monsieur. Then she went out early this morning and she is not returned. She sent word a little time ago that she would remain the night with your sister.'

'You mean she's in the Upper Town, madame?' said Gil in some chagrin.

'But no,' replied Catherine, her toothless mouth primming up again. 'The demoiselle and your sister are both at Morison's yard.'

'Whatever are they doing there?' he demanded. 'Did Alys say why she would not be home?'

'I sent one of the girls for her more than an hour ago,' said Catherine in mounting indignation, 'and that was all the word she brought back. What her father would say if he heard of it – though perhaps,' she added, as if she had just thought of it, 'they are still trying to restore matters after the burglary.'

'Burglary?' Gil stared at her. 'Where? What burglary? What are you telling me, madame?'

'A thief broke into Maister Morison's house last night. He took nothing,' she assured him, 'and he was captured. By your sister, I understand, sir.'

'Kate?' said Gil in amazement. 'Sweet St Giles, how did she manage that?'

'I have not heard,' said Catherine resentfully.

'I must go and see what is happening.' Gil looked at the dog, who had flopped on to his side and was already snoring faintly. 'I'll leave Socrates with you, if I may – he's had a hard day, poor beast.'

The sky to the north was still light, but the first stars were pricking above the Tolbooth as he walked the short distance down the High Street. The leaves of Morison's great yett were shut, but one of them yielded to pressure, and he stepped cautiously into the yard. Barn and sheds were dark shapes in the twilight, the racks of Morison's wares were gathering pockets of shadow, and an occasional reflection gleamed on the rim or flank of a glazed pot; but even by this light it seemed to Gil there was less clutter underfoot.

The house door stood open, light spilling on to the steps. The hall was lit, but so also was the kitchen at the end of the range, and beyond it from the door of one of the

244

outhouses came lamplight, voices and steam, a crashing of wooden buckets, and splashing water. Laundry? he thought. At this hour of night?

'Hello,' he called. 'Is anyone home? Alys? Kate?'

'Gil!' It was his sister's voice. Her crutches scraped and thumped, and she appeared at the house door, outlined against the light. 'Gil, Our Lady be praised you're back. Are you safe?'

'Quite safe,' he said, startled. 'Is all well here? What's this Catherine tells me? Where's Alys, anyway,' he demanded, getting to the nub of the matter.

'She's busy,' said Kate. 'She'll be out in a little while. We never thought it would take so long. Come in, Gil. We have – we have something to tell you.'

'What is it?' he asked, alarm gripping his throat. 'Is Alys –'

'Alys is fine,' Kate assured him. 'Come into the house, till I tell you what's been going on here.'

'You are getting more and more like Mother,' he said, setting foot on the house stair. 'Where is Alys? Catherine's anxious, and – and Pierre has been hurt. I need to tell her.'

'Her father hurt? Oh, Gil. And she feels guilty about what happened,' said Kate, turning in the doorway so that he could enter the house, 'but the fault was mine, really it was. You won't be angry at her, will you?'

'Kate, what is this about?' he asked. 'How do I know whether I'll be angry till you tell me what you're on about? Why would I be angry with Alys anyway?'

'The inbreak,' said Kate. 'Not last night, but the night before. Thursday. We had an inbreak. A thief in the house.'

'Catherine told me.'

'Did she tell you there were two?'

'What, two inbreaks?' He stared at her. She turned again on her crutches to look at him, and nodded. Then, along the length of the house, from the vapour-bathed doorway beyond the kitchen, the screaming started.

Gil leapt from the fore-stair and set off running. As he

was drawing his sword it dawned on him that it was not an adult screaming. It was a child, terrified.

Kate's voice followed him: 'Gil! Gil, come back, it's all right!'

He kept running.

'Let me get this straight,' said Gil, without a great deal of hope. 'You had two intruders in the place on Thursday night, you caught the first one opening Augie's plate-kist, the second one chopped the first one into pieces, and you feel you owe me an apology.'

'Not really,' said his sister drily, 'but I thought you might expect one.'

Alys said nothing. Gil gave her an anxious glance. He could not work out whether she was embarrassed, angry, offended or frightened for her father, and his head was still reeling with the sight which had met him earlier.

Reaching the door of the – bathhouse, laundryhouse, whatever it was, he had halted, staring, whinger in hand, unable to see the source of the screams. Amid clouds of lantern-lit vapour and a smell of soap, what seemed like a great number of women appeared and disappeared, sleeves rolled up, muscular forearms wet, around a tent of suspended linen, from which came splashing. Then, as the steam dissipated at one side of the chamber, he recognized Alys standing in a pool of water, her hair knotted up on top of her head, bending over a screaming, dripping child. A second child spoke, happily, inside the tent of linen.

'Maister Gil!' said someone out of the clouds. Alys straightened up with an exclamation, and he realized she was wearing only a very wet shift, in which she might as well have been naked. And she was standing next to a lantern.

He had backed away, stammering an apology, sheathing his sword, but he could not get the image out of his mind, of the fine wet linen clinging to her slender curves, of the way the light shone on shoulder, breast and thigh.

And now Alys, fully dressed, slightly damp and rather pink, was sitting upright and formal on a backstool opposite him. She had failed to respond to his embrace of greeting, and though she had listened anxiously to his account of her father's injuries and accepted his reassurances, she now would not meet his eye. Candlelight gilded her hair and skimmed the blue linen which covered the glories he had glimpsed. Beside him on the long settle his sister surveyed him with a sardonic expression.

'Tell me it from the beginning,' he said, collecting his mind with an effort.

'Two days since,' Kate began. 'St Peter's bones, was it only Thursday? Andy gave Billy Walker his room, but I managed to speak to the man first.'

As her account of the time since he left Glasgow unfolded, he listened in mounting alarm, visualizing the events she described so tersely.

'What a thing for the two of you to get entangled in!' he exclaimed.

'Alys was out of the worst of it,' she assured him, looking from one to the other. Alys stared resolutely at the jug of flowers in the fireplace.

'I wish you had been too,' he said. 'The man with the axe is dead – it must be the same man –'

'Dead?' she exclaimed. 'When? How could he be? He was in Glasgow yesterday morning.'

'He was in Roslin last night. If he left Glasgow when the gates opened,' Gil calculated, 'he could have got to Linlithgow in time to gather his friends and follow us from there. He likely got ahead of us,' he speculated, sidetracked, 'when we were up the hillside about the dead pig. But Kate, even so, Augie's right, you should be out of this house –'

'Not till the bairns are safe,' she stated. 'Andy's been too taigled here at the yard to go up for orders the way Maister Morison wished –'

'What, since yesterday morning? And whose doing was that?' Gil asked shrewdly. She gave him another wry smile.

'And Kate, how is it keeping the bairns safe to wash them –' he checked, glanced at Alys, swallowed, and went on – 'to wash them at this hour, with the bathhouse door open and the yard gate unbarred?'

'And five grown women in the bathhouse along wi them,' she pointed out. 'It would be a bold man who took on Babb and Nan Thomson together. They began in daylight, but it took near an hour to get the older child into the water, poor wee mite. Oh, Nan says she kens you, Gil. Matt brought her in from Dumbarton to mind the bairns.'

'From Dumbarton?' he said, diverted again. 'Oh, I ken who that is. Matt drew her daughter's rotten tooth last May. I think he's been courting her ever since, he'd jump at the chance to get her settled in Glasgow.' He returned to the point. 'Kate, you should all be out of the house. Can you not take the bairns somewhere else till all's settled, if you're troubled for them?'

'Likely I could,' she said dismissively, 'but hardly at this hour of night. Now tell us how the Axeman comes to be dead, Gil. Have you found a name for that poor man in the barrel? What did the King say? How did Maister Mason come to be hurt?'

'I have the King's thanks, and the reward for the hoard money,' he said. 'Augie can discuss that with Andy. And we've a name for the dead man, and I think it was this Axeman killed him. It was certainly him that injured Pierre. But I've still no more than a suspicion of who's behind this.'

There were steps on the fore-stair, and Babb appeared, carrying a linen-swathed child. She crossed the hall to set her burden down at the door to the stair.

'Stand nice now,' she admonished, with a pat to its rear, and turned to speak quietly to her mistress. The child, ignoring the instruction, pattered over to stand directly in front of Gil. It had a cloud of short, fluffy fair curls, and a penetrating grey stare, and with some surprise he recognized Morison's younger daughter.

248

'Why are you in our house again?' she demanded. 'My da's no here.'

'I'm here to talk to the ladies,' he answered her.

'Why?'

'Because I'm going to marry one of them, and the other is my sister.'

She looked speculatively from Alys to Kate, then put a possessive small hand on Kate's knee. 'Can't have this one.'

'She's my sister,' said Gil. 'So I can't marry her.' Kate's face was unreadable. The child nodded, and pointed at Alys with the other hand. Some of her linen wrappings fell away, revealing a thin bare shoulder. Alys smiled at her, but got a scowl in return.

'You can marry that one. She put Wynliane in the bath.'

'That's right,' he agreed. 'That's the one I want. *She is gentle and also wise; of all other she beareth the prize.* And when I've married her, I'll be the most fortunate man in Glasgow.'

'Huh,' said the child, and studied him for a moment with that penetrating stare. 'Can me and Wynliane come to the feast?'

A black-browed woman Gil faintly recalled from a difficult morning in Dumbarton entered the hall with another linen-wrapped child in her arms. She took in the situation and said firmly, 'Come away now, Ysonde!' Finding she was ignored, she set down the little girl she carried. There was a small sound of protest, and a hand emerged from its wrappings and clung to her skirts. 'Come up, poppet, and go to your bed.'

'Can we?' said Ysonde, still staring at Gil.

'If your da says you may,' he said diplomatically.

'Ysonde!' Mistress Thomson came forward to take her hand, trailing the other child, and paused to bob to Gil. 'Good e'en to ye, maister. I hope I see you well. Come up, my lammie. Time you were in your bed.'

'Ask the lady for her blessing,' said Ysonde, pulling away and sticking out her lower lip. Her sister, silent within her cocoon of linen, nodded agreement. Kate, to

Gil's surprise, without hesitation delivered the blessing their mother had used all their lives. Ysonde submitted to being shepherded towards the stairs, and as their new nurse paused at the cupboard by the doorway to light a candle for the ascent peered past her sister and suddenly gave Gil a brilliant smile.

Babb had gone into the other room, and now returned and strode out of the house with a bundle of linen. Kate watched her go, then said, 'The Axeman killed the man in the barrel? So does that mean Augie – Maister Morison's not like to be tried for the murder?'

Alys raised an eyebrow, with a glance at Gil, before she recalled herself and looked away again.

'I hope Augie's in the clear, for we found, or to be exact Socrates found where the man was likely killed, in Linlithgow.' Kate muttered something, closing her eyes, and crossed herself. 'It seems to me Billy was involved in the death, which might be bad for Augie, but Billy's actions since have not suggested they were in it together.'

'So what did you find?' Kate pressed. 'Tell us.'

'Can I not get a drink first?' he parried. 'Is all the household out at the laundry?'

Alys, tight-lipped and blushing darkly, rose and took a candle out to the kitchen. Gil watched her go, and looked anxiously at his sister, who shook her head and shrugged. After a little Alys returned with a tray, and handed cups of ale, not looking at Gil and deftly eluding his attempt to touch her fingers as he took his. She had brought a platter of bannocks and cheese; wary of causing further offence, he took one when she offered it, but when he bit into it found that he was hungry.

'I needed this,' he said. She still did not meet his eye, but her expression lightened a little. He went on eating, and between mouthfuls gave them a description, as terse as Kate's, of the events of his journey, from the musicians in Stirling to Rob's burial in Roslin that morning. Alys listened as intently as his sister, and when he described the fight above Linlithgow her hand went up to her mouth, though she still did not speak. At the mention of de Brinay and his men, Kate clapped her hands together.

'We were right!' she said to Alys. 'The Preceptory is involved! Mall said a strange thing,' she explained to Gil. 'She heard the man with the axe say to Billy that the Baptizer wanted his gear back. At first we wondered if it might mean the Knights of St John. It is the Baptist that's their patron, isn't it, not the Evangelist?'

'It is,' he agreed, through another mouthful of bannock.

'But then the old man said the Treasurer's title is Lord St Johns, so could it be him?'

'The Baptizer,' he repeated. 'Well, the Preceptory is involved, I ken that for certain now. The Baptizer might fit. Listen to the rest of it.'

He went on with the tale. They heard him out, Kate frowning, Alys thoughtful.

'I am truly sorry about Rob,' she said when he had finished. 'He was a good servant, and kind to the horses.'

'Aye,' said Kate. 'He'd been to Rome, had he not, Gil? St Peter bring him to bliss, then.'

'Amen,' said Alys, and they all crossed themselves.

'We have nearly all we need,' Gil said after a moment. 'We've still to find the man Baldy, and the one with the feather in his hat, and find out which side they were working for. Did you say they'd been seen in the Hog?'

'On Wednesday,' Kate nodded. 'It sounds like the same men. And the fellow who saw them thought Mattha Hog knew them. Mind, it's second-hand news, Gil. The two we sent down there last night were tellt this by another.'

'There are more than two sides,' said Alys, 'that is obvious.'

'The cooper is Sinclair's man,' said Kate, counting them off on her fingers. 'So was the man in the barrel, Our Lady defend him. This Johan and the knight were for the Preceptory. The Axeman – I'm right glad to hear he's dead, and so will Babb be – he was against both the others, but were Sinclair and the Preceptory acting together?'

'Not entirely,' Gil admitted. 'However that's sorted now.

And I did think that Treasurer Knollys was very eager that I should go into Ayrshire.' He reached for another bannock, and found the platter empty.

'So the old man said. But surely he's involved anyway,' said Kate, 'both as Treasurer and as Preceptor.'

'The two interests may conflict,' said Alys.

'But then who did the Axeman mean by the Baptizer?' wondered Kate again. 'Who was he working for? The Preceptory, or Knollys, or someone else? And who is his woman? We've had no luck asking about this Maidie.'

'He called his axe Maidie,' recalled Gil.

'His *axe*?'

'He cannot have been from the Preceptory,' said Alys.

'You see that too?' said Gil. Kate looked from one to the other. 'He wasn't with the cooper,' Gil expanded, 'else he would never have had to ask about the carts, and the cooper would never have told me he did ask. But we ken the cooper is with the Preceptory, since he sent Simmie to warn them we were on the road.'

'Um,' said Kate. 'It's far more complicated than I realized. I thought you just went about asking questions till the right answer came out.'

'But how do we get proof?' said Alys, pursuing her own train of thought. 'He will never admit it without some kind of proof.'

'It may be more complicated than that anyway,' suggested Gil. She nodded absently.

'What are you talking about?' said Kate. 'Have I missed part of the conversation?'

'It depends who paid the man Baldy,' said Alys suddenly. 'What a pity you did not catch him too.'

'We lacked forethought there,' he admitted, and she giggled, and then finally met his eye and smiled at him a little sheepishly.

'Could it have been Noll Sinclair who paid him?' said Kate. 'Or the cooper, even, setting a trap for someone with you as the bait?'

'Now I never thought of that,' admitted Gil. 'Though

I thought the trap was for us. I still feel a fool, being decoyed up on to the hillside to look for a dead pig.'

'We know the Axeman killed Sinclair's man in the cooper's yard,' offered Kate.

'Something was killed in the cooper's yard,' corrected Gil. She pulled a face, but nodded agreement.

'And probably the same night,' supplied Alys, 'the barrel of books was taken off Maister Morison's cart and the barrel with the head and the treasure put on it.'

'Why?' said Gil. 'That's the strange thing. Why send the barrel to Glasgow?'

'Accident,' said Alys. She sat up straight. 'I know! Kate, you know we thought the Axeman was left-handed. It is the kind of mistake they make. We had a left-handed kitchen-lassie once and she could never put things in the proper place.'

'So it simply went on the wrong cart!' said Kate.

'That must be it. It should have gone to Leith.'

'Of course,' said Gil. 'The cart for Leith was a big mixed load, so Riddoch said. Far likelier, if it went on that, the exchange could have gone unnoticed till it could be collected.'

They exchanged another look, and Alys nodded agreement.

'And if the Axeman did not enquire at the cooper's until Wednesday, there had been time for him to go to Leith and find his barrel was not there and return to Linlithgow. And then he came straight to Glasgow,' she speculated. 'He must near have worn a groove in the road.'

Gil, rarely aware of her accent, was suddenly, delightfully, distracted by the foreign turn she gave to the Scottish placenames. Concentrating with an effort, he found his sister saying, 'But we still don't know who the Axeman was, or who this Baldy and Feather Hat might be, or whose men they are, or why they are so persistent about it.'

'A fair summary,' said Gil.

'You forgot Sinclair and Knollys,' said Alys.

253

Gil opened his mouth to answer her, and was forestalled by a sudden commotion outside in the dark yard. Shrill voices, a thump as if the gate had been slammed, questions and shouting. Women's voices. Then, through it, a deeper note: 'Friend, I'm a friend. Word for Maister Cunningham. Is that you, Babb? Is Nan no here?'

'Matt?' said Gil. He jumped up and hurried to the house door just as his uncle's man reached the top of the fore-stair. 'Matt, is all well?'

Matt stepped in and pulled off his bonnet, saying drily, 'Aye, Lady Kate. Your watch is waukin.'

'I never expected callers this late,' said Babb from the doorway.

'Watch?' said Gil. 'What watch? Kate, what is going on here? Where are the men, anyway?'

'Sleeping,' she said, 'save for two we sent down the Hog again. The rest of them will watch the second half of the night, we're taking the first half.'

'Kate!'

'You can see for yourself it works,' she pointed out, laughing at him. 'They caught Matt, but they've done him no damage.'

'Kate, this is a fighting man we're seeking. How can a bunch of women –'

'Wi no argument,' said Matt succinctly.

'Aye, well, you came quiet,' said Babb, grinning, before she turned away to go back down the stair into the yard.

'I'll stay here, then,' said Gil.

'You will not,' said his sister, though Alys's expression brightened.

'No,' said Matt. 'You're sent for, Maister Gil. The castle. Robert Blacader wants a word.'

'To the castle?' repeated Gil blankly. 'Whatever does he want?'

'How did he know you were back in Glasgow?' said Alys.

*   *   *

254

The moon, five days past the full, was just rising behind the towers of St Mungo's as Gil made his way by lantern-light up from the Wyndhead towards the castle gatehouse. Noise and bustle floated over the wall; lute music came from the Archbishop's lodging, a more raucous singing from one of the towers, and a smell of new bread suggested the episcopal bakehouse was working through the night.

Gil gave his name to a guard, and after a short wait a sleepy-eyed page in a velvet jerkin appeared and conducted him across two courtyards, past the fore-stair of the Provost's lodging – Sweet St Giles, Gil thought, was it only two days since that we had to climb that in a hurry? – and up a turnpike stair. There were lights at most of the windows, and torches burned beside other doorways.

Robert Blacader had given up his own lodging to his monarch. Beyond the great hall and the entrance to the Archbishop's private chapel, the outer and inner chambers of his suite were crowded, like the string of stuffy chambers at Stirling, with weary members of the court playing cards or dice to music from competing lutenists or discussing the best road to Kilmarnock. Mismatched tapestries hung on the walls, and there seemed to be a shortage of seating. Off the inner chamber, with its ostentatious display of plate set out on the cupboard, the page opened a door and ushered Gil through it.

The closet was panelled, painted and ablaze with light. There were several dozen candles burning round the walls, and more in pricket-stands here and there, flickering in the draught from the window which had been opened to let the heat out. Gil, blinking in the brightness, took in rather slowly that the room was also full of richly dressed people, and that only one of them was wearing a hat.

He snatched off his felt bonnet with an apology, and dropped to one knee.

'Get up, Maister Cunningham,' said James Stewart from the centre of the group, 'and come and tell us how you've progressed since we saw you last.'

The King was seated near the fireplace, a card-table beside him as before, though this time it bore only a jug and some glasses. Tonight he was wearing tawny woollen and black silk, the huge sleeves of his gown decked with amber-coloured ribbons. Gil, thinking of his sister's much-worn gown of the same colour, made a note to tell her about the ribbons. On one side of the table Robert Blacader acknowledged Gil's salute with a wave of his ring; on the other, expansive in gold-coloured satin with wide fur facings, William Knollys smiled affably. Behind the King a cleric was in deep discussion with the Earl of Angus and my lord Hume the Chamberlain; as he turned his head Gil recognized Andrew Forman the apostolic protonotary, whom he knew to be a friend of his uncle's. Beyond him a familiar profile must be his mother's cousin, Angus's brother-in-law Archie Boyd.

'Come, maister,' said the King again. 'Is there a seat for Maister Cunningham? Now tell us, have you put a name to your man in the barrel?'

'He's none of mine, sir,' said Gil hastily. One of the liveried servants brought forward a stool, and he sat down, assembling his thoughts, filtering, sifting. 'I have his name and I think I know who killed him and where,' he added. 'But I've not found the rest of him.'

Choosing his words with caution, passing lightly over any mention of the purpose of moving the treasure, he recounted his visit to the cooper's yard and what he had learned there, the finding of the patch of blood, the empty barrel, the idea that the other barrel had gone on the wrong cart through simple error.

This was not like discussing matters with Alys or his sister. Every step, every word had to be explained, justified, expounded, to one or other of the two plump, blue-jowled faces scrutinizing his account. Blacader's questions betrayed a deep concern for the truth, but Knollys's seemed more directed towards dismantling Gil's theories and suppositions. At times Gil was aware of impatience in James's movements, but he listened carefully to the questions and to Gil's answers, nodding now and then. Behind him the Earl of Angus watched intently.

'But your own suspicions, maister. Surely you suspect more than you've learned?' the King said, when Gil had recounted his conclusions after his interview with the cooper.

'I do, sir,' agreed Gil.

'You've little enough proof for some of your tale, it seems to me,' said Knollys, still wearing his open smile, though the yellow gems in his rings flashed in the light. 'Most of the carter's actions can only be guessed at, for one thing.'

'Quite so, sir,' said Gil, 'but someone opened the gates, someone swept up the shavings, and I think the cooper was telling the truth.' In that, at least, he thought.

'And this man with the axe,' said the King reflectively. 'He fair gets about. Linlithgow, Glasgow, maybe Leith.'

'He got about,' Gil agreed, 'but he'll go no further. He's dead, last night, sir.'

'Dead?' said the Archbishop. Gil was aware of sharp attention from the group. 'How did that come about?'

'Did you question him?' asked Knollys. 'Who was he?'

'We had no chance,' said Gil. Who had relaxed a little? he wondered. It was hard to keep an eye on everyone present, particularly in the leaping candlelight. 'We took him prisoner when he attacked our party, but he died before we could question him.' And I know his name, he thought, but we'll keep that quiet just now.

'And you're saying,' said James, 'this is the same man that slew the carter here on Thursday night? The carter's lassie was before us earlier this night, asking justice for her man. Do we have more than her word to link this axeman to this carter?' He held out his hands, one for each miscreant, and linked the fingers to illustrate his meaning.

'My sister saw them talking in a tavern,' said Gil.

The King's eyebrows went up, and the Treasurer said, laughing indulgently, 'Now, maister, surely not! Your sister would never be in the kind of tavern such a man would drink in!'

Gil, preserving his expression, explained the purpose which had taken Alys and Kate to the tavern. James nodded in approval.

'A clever notion,' he said. 'Very clever. That's a good-thinking lassie you're betrothed to, Maister Cunningham.'

'She's the wisest lassie in Glasgow,' said Gil, and could not keep the warmth out of his voice.

The King grinned at him, a sudden man-to-man look. 'You like them clever, do you, maister?' he said. Before Gil could find an answer to this he went on, 'Well, we've a name for the man in the barrel, but no body, and now we've a body for the man with the axe, but no name. This'll not do, gentlemen. My lord St Johns,' he said formally to Knollys, 'I hope you can write the morn's morn as Sheriff of Linlithgow, and have your depute get a search made up on the hillside for the body that went out those gates.' Knollys bowed his head, and behind him a servant in the St Johns livery drew a set of tablets from his purse and made a note. The men of Linlithgow will love that, thought Gil, just at harvest-time. 'And, my lord Treasurer,' continued the King, 'I hope you're searching already for the place where the treasure was hidden. Where there's some of it, there might be more.'

'Aye, sir, you can be certain,' said Knollys, smiling. Blacader watched him across the table, his face inscrutable.

'And you, Maister Cunningham,' said James, 'can find me the name of the man wi the axe and his confederates. But I'd sooner you stayed in one piece yourself, maister, for Scotland can do with clear thinkers.'

'I'll do my best, sir,' said Gil.

'And now,' said the King, 'shall we have the servant lass and the merchant in, and set all these tales thegither?'

'Is it not ower late for that, sir?' suggested Blacader.

'Havers. It canny be past midnight,' said James. 'Fetch them in.'

Gil, in a moment's hesitation, considered announcing

that his tale was not finished, dismissed the idea, and found he was aware of someone else hesitating in the same way. He looked from one blue-chinned face to the other on either side of the table. Blacader's gaze slid sideways from his towards the door, where a servant was just leaving; Knollys said pleasantly, 'You had a good day for such a long ride, Maister Cunningham. What road did you take to reach Glasgow?'

'It was,' Gil agreed, following this lead. 'Dry, but no too hot. I came direct from Roslin, so I rode through Bathgate and the Monklands, and it was dry all the way.'

'It's been a good week for the harvest,' said James, looking round from a low-voiced conversation with Angus.

By the time Augie Morison and his servant were escorted before their King this topic was being generally explored. It was clear that James had a good understanding of the work of the land and its place at the centre of existence. Gil, who had met scholars older than James who failed to accept this, was favourably impressed.

Someone had evidently taken care of Mall for the evening. Her face and hands were clean, her hair combed out over her shoulders, and though nervous of all the fine people she seemed much calmer than the grief-stricken girl Kate had described from the previous morning. As she knelt before him, the King broke off what he was saying and turned to her.

'And here's this bonnie lass again,' he said. Gil, comparing Mall's plump bosom and round cheeks adversely with Alys's fine-boned person, drew his own conclusion about how the King liked them. 'And Augustine Morison, merchant of Glasgow,' he went on, looking past her. Morison also dropped to his knees. 'We've learned a wee thing or two more about this business, and it's time to go over it all again.'

'Aye, your grace,' said Morison into the pause. He threw an apprehensive look at Gil, who smiled at him as reassuringly as he could, trying not to show the pity he felt. Two nights' confinement, however gentle, had left its mark on the man; he was drawn and anxious, with a haunted look in his eyes. Gil guessed he had spent the time worrying about his children.

'Now, Mall,' James continued, 'you asked us for justice for your man, since he was killed by an intruder in the night. But tell me this, lass. He was a thief himself. What justice does he deserve?'

Mall, hands clamped together before her waist in a pose of prayer which, deliberately or no, made the most of the view down her bodice, bent her head and said, 'Aye, your grace, he was taken thieving from our maister's house.' She ducked her head even further, as if to avoid meeting the master's eye. 'But that never deserved death, your grace, least of all s-such a death –' She bit her lips, and after a moment went on, 'It's just no right, your grace, it's no right at all.'

There was something in one of the old statutes, thought Gil. He could visualize the section of the St Mungo's copy. Which one was it?

'Are you saying that even a thief deserves justice?' said Blacader. She glanced fleetingly at him under her eyebrows and nodded. 'Why not leave it to the Provost? Is there no justice in Glasgow?' Behind her, Morison closed his eyes. Across the card-table, Knollys's eyes seemed like to pop out of his head and down the girl's bodice.

'I'm feart they'll no trouble themselves further,' she whispered. 'They brocht it in as murder by a stranger and I'm feart that'll be the end on it.'

'And is it not murder by a stranger?' asked James.

'I seen the man,' she said desperately. 'Like I tellt your grace, I seen the man. I heard what he said to my Billy. Surely he can be socht and hangit for his death?'

'*Quoniam attachiamenta*,' said Gil, and several of the bystanders nodded. The King raised his eyebrows. 'It provides,' Gil went on, and heard his uncle's voice in his own, 'that where a thief has been killed secretly, without calling the watch or bailies, the thief's kin or the bailies can charge his killer with murder just as if he had not been a thief.'

'Very proper,' said James. 'I'll have justice for all Scots, gentlemen, be certain of that. Mind you,' he added, humour tugging at his long mouth, 'the case is no that straightforward.'

'Why should we believe a word of this?' said Knollys. 'The lassie's lying all through. I can't see why your grace is wasting time on her. She wants the attention, and she's getting it.'

She's getting it, thought Gil, assessing the direction of the Treasurer's popping eyes.

'She's getting it,' agreed James, considering Mall again. 'Surely she wouldn't lie to her King?' Mall shook her head energetically. 'Especially not before the relics. What is it you keep here in the chapel, my lord?'

What was this about? Gil wondered. What did the young King hope to draw from the girl? Or was it simply an excuse to keep Mall and her bodice in view as long as possible?

'We've a fragment of St Bride's veil,' Blacader was saying, as Mall crossed herself, round-eyed and apprehensive, 'and a fingerbone of St Martin. Either of those would do, I should suppose.'

Chapter Thirteen

Dunbar slipped from the room, and after a time returned followed by two acolytes, a candle-bearer, and another priest robed and bearing a reliquary in the shape of a gold hand with a jewelled cuff and several rings. Gil looked at the object and thought of the saint who shared his cloak with a beggar, but slid from his stool to kneel and cross himself when everyone else did. The robed priest intoned a Latin prayer commending St Martin, and the King, seating himself and replacing his hat, said, 'Now, Mall, tell us again here in front of the relics. What happened between your man and this stranger?'

Mall, her eyes on the reliquary in the hands of the priest as if she thought it would turn and point an accusing finger at her, was led back through her story. To Gil's ears it differed little from the account Kate had summarized for him, but the statesmen picked carefully at the details.

'What yett was this?' Blacader asked her sternly. 'Remember, woman, you must tell us the truth.'

'I swear it's the truth, maister,' she said, crossing herself again. 'I swear on that hand and all its jewels. May St Martin himself strike me dead unshriven if it's no the truth. They never said what yett it was, nor what else Billy had done.'

'Surely it was your maister's yett he was to open,' said Knollys, hands in his gold satin sleeves.

'No, sir, for it had never been opened when it shouldny.'

'It was opened on the night the barrels were exchanged,' suggested Knollys. 'You and your limmer let him in and

262

changed the barrels. Or was this fabulous man with the axe your limmer and all?' he persisted avidly.

'No!' protested Mall.

'If you'll tryst with one man in a hayloft, how about another? Tell us the truth, woman.'

'The barrel we were expecting,' said Gil, 'the barrel which should have been on the cart, never left Linlithgow. We found it there. The exchange was made there, no in Glasgow.'

Mall looked fearfully at him, and then at the King. She still had not looked at her master, who was listening with an expression of amazement.

'Billy's my – Billy was my dearie,' she said steadfastly. 'I never loved any man but him, nor I never trysted wi any other man. And we never opened the maister's gates. I never did my maister any harm,' she said, beginning to sniffle, 'till Billy bade me get his key to his big kist, and that was the first either of us did that was a wrang to him.'

'And why did Billy bid you do that?' asked Blacader.

'She admits it openly,' said Knollys. 'Why are we wasting our time with this thieving wee trollop, sir, when there are –'

'I'll decide how I spend my time,' said James. 'Answer your lord, lassie.'

Mall threw a doubtful look at the Archbishop, but said obediently, between sobs, 'The man wi the axe had tellt Billy to get the key, for I heard him. I begged Billy to do no such thing. But he was feart for the axeman telling the maister, and he wouldny hear me when I said the maister would forgive him.' She was weeping openly now. 'The maister's a good man, he'd maybe ha turned us off but he'd ha done no worse.' Behind her Morison nodded, frowning.

'Forgive him what?' asked James. 'What had he done?'

'I never knew! He wouldny let on. It was something about when he opened the yett, but he wouldny tell me.' Mall scrubbed at her eyes with her sleeve.

'This is all nonsense,' said Knollys. He cast his hands in the air in a gesture of exasperation, and his rings glittered in the candlelight.

'Why is she so sure it was the man with the axe killed her man?' asked Angus from behind the King.

'Tell us, lassie,' said the King.

Mall looked up through her tears. 'Who else could it ha been, sir?'

'Any of the household, I should have thought,' said Knollys impatiently.

'None of the other men was marked,' said Gil. 'And whoever it was would certainly have blood on him, from what I have heard.'

Mall covered her face and moaned at the words, but James nodded his understanding.

'And why were you to get the maister's key?' asked Blacader. 'You realize what a sin you are confessing? To conspire to rob your own maister like this?' Mall nodded, and mumbled something into her hands. 'What was that? Answer me openly, Mall.'

The girl kept her head down, but lowered her hands enough to be heard: 'He wanted Billy to seek for the rest of the treasure. He kept on about it, how there should be another bag of it, though Billy kept saying he kenned nothing of any treasure.'

'How did he ken that?' asked Angus. 'This axeman – how did he ken so much?'

I would like to know that too, thought Gil.

'He never said.'

'Is there anything else you should tell us, daughter?' asked the Archbishop.

Mall, slightly reassured by this form of address, raised her head enough to look at him sideways.

'No, maister,' she whispered. 'I dinna think so.'

'Well,' said the King. 'Mall, you have appealed to me for justice for your man, and as it happens, justice has been done.' She stared at him. 'The man with the axe is dead, killed in a fight with Maister Cunningham here.'

264

She turned her head slightly, to glance at Gil, then returned her gaze to her monarch.

'But there must be justice for you too, Mall,' James continued. He looked at her as sternly as Blacader had done. 'And for your maister. You must see that.'

She nodded, and whispered some affirmative. Blacader gestured, and Dunbar, with a resigned expression, came forward to help the girl to her feet. She bobbed a low curtsy to the King, and the rest, and turning to go came finally face-to-face with her master. He looked up at her from where he knelt, with an earnest, pitying smile, and almost automatically she bobbed to him as well. Morison acknowledged the curtsy, and sketched a cross.

'Guid save you, my lassie,' he said. 'Our Lady guard your rest this night.'

She whispered something, and Dunbar led her past him and out of the room.

'Well, Maister Morison,' said the King. Gil, aware of the elderly Blacader shifting on his padded stool, found himself thinking, Christ aid us all, he's indefatigable. 'Come closer, maister, and tell us about Linlithgow.'

Morison, shuffling forward on his knees, stopped and stared open-mouthed at his monarch.

'Linlithgow?' he said blankly. 'I – I mean, what did you wish to hear about it, sir?'

'What passed the last time you were there?'

Morison paused, casting his mind back, and glanced at Gil.

'Well, we – we took my goods off Thomas Tod's vessel at Blackness,' he said, 'and took the cart back to Linlithgow. It was ower late to set out by then, we'd never have made Kilsyth in daylight, so we ran the cart into William Riddoch's barn, by the arrangement we've for three year now, and Billy Walker, Christ assoil him, slept under the cart and the rest of us lay at the Black Bitch by the West Port.'

'The rest of us?' questioned Blacader. 'Who was that?'

'Me myself, and Andy Paterson my servant, and Jamesie Aitken my journeyman.'

'And how did you lie that night?' asked the King.

'Well enough,' said Morison wryly. 'Since I'd no notion what was waiting for me. Oh,' he said, grasping what was meant. 'We lay in the one bed, the three of us. I was at the wall, and Jamesie next me, and Andy at the outside, since he's up and down in the night.' Several of his older hearers nodded in sympathy at this.

'May I ask something, sir?' said Gil. The King gestured in reply. 'Augie, tell me, when was Billy alone in Linlithgow? Had you lain there the night before?'

'Aye, we had,' Morison nodded. 'He'd plenty time alone in the burgh. I let them be to drink or talk as they liked, I knew they'd not get ower fu or into bad company . . .' His voice trailed off and he smiled ruefully. 'Aye. While I went about to get a word with one or two friends I have in the place.'

'And did you see him at all while you went about the town?'

'I caught sight of all three of them now and then.'

'Was he talking to a big man in a black cloak?'

'Linlithgow's full of men in black cloaks,' said Angus, grinning over the King's shoulder.

William Knollys inflated himself and stretched his neck like a cockerel about to crow, the light gleaming on his gold satin plumage. 'Are you implying, my lord, that the Knights of St John are involved in this? That one of our brother knights slips about by night slaying unlawfully?'

'Not the knights,' said Gil, almost to himself. James glanced briefly at him.

'Not me,' said Angus, still grinning. 'It was you said it, my lord St Johns, not me. I'm saying Linlithgow's full of men in black cloaks, no more than that.'

'I never saw Billy talking to such a one,' said Morison to Gil. Knollys subsided, glaring at Angus. 'Maybe Andy or Jamesie saw, you could ask them.'

Gil nodded.

'This man Billy,' said the King, 'that the lassie wants justice for. Why did you keep him? Had he been a good servant?'

'Not a bad servant, sir, anyways,' said Morison, considering the matter. 'He was pert, but they can all be pert. A good enough worker, a good carter, understood the old mare well. Understood barrels and all, with his father being a cooper.'

Out in the High Street it was raining, though the gibbous moon sailed in broken cloud above the Dow Hill. The torchbearers in the escort the King had ordered for them made a great difference, Gil found, striding down the hill behind them with a bewildered Augie Morison at his side. Two other sturdy fellows in helm and breastplate followed, keeping a watchful eye on the shadows.

There had been little more of use said after Augie's revelation about Billy's parentage. The Treasurer had shown signs of wishing to interrogate him further about Linlithgow, but the King, yawning ostentatiously, had announced, 'Well, gentlemen, as you said a while since, it's ower late. We'll have this cleared away the now.' A wave of relief swept round the crowded little room, and he smiled slightly. 'We'll be up early for Mass, after all. In the chapel here, my lord?' Blacader nodded. 'And after it,' he said thoughtfully, 'I want a game of caich before we ride. Maister Cunningham, you look like a fit man. Do you play caich?'

'I do, sir,' Gil had said, slightly apprehensive. The quarry must feel that way, he thought now, when a twig cracks in the undergrowth.

'You'll gie me a game? Good! In the caichpele off the Drygate here – you ken?'

Gil knew it. It belonged to one of the canons, who found the steady supply of pence from the tennis-players and spectators of the town made a valuable income. He had played there a few times, but he and his opponents among

the poverty-stricken songmen generally used an impro-
vised court in Vicars' Alley, with two sloping roofs to be
the pents and chalked marks on St Mungo's north wall,
renewed every time it rained, for lunettes. The scorer had
to have sharp eyes.

'Good,' said James, and rose. Gil and the two elderly
statesmen rose too, perforce. 'I'll meet you after Mass, say
about Terce. And now we'll have you seen home, maister.
Where do you lie the night?'

'David Cunningham's house – the Cadzow manse in
Rottenrow,' supplied Blacader.

Gil shook his head. 'I'm bound for Maister Morison's
house in the High Street,' he said. 'My sister is there, and
maybe Mistress Mason, keeping an eye on the bairns.'

Morison, still kneeling at his feet, put one hand over his
eyes. William Knollys looked round sharply, with the
arrested expression of the stag who hears the hounds.

'What does the lady there?' he demanded. 'Surely
Maister Morison has servants of his own?'

'My sister was concerned for the bairns,' said Gil again.
Knollys grunted, and turned casually away to speak to a
man with the eight-pointed Cross of St John on the breast
of his velvet doublet.

'Find Davie Wilkie,' he began in a low voice. The King
spoke across him, directing someone to deal with Gil's
escort, someone else to take word to the Provost that his
prisoner had been released at the King's command.

'Released?' repeated Morison incredulously. 'You mean
– your grace means – I can go free? I can go home?'

'Aye, maister. Thanks to your friend here.'

Blacader nodded approval; Angus was standing back,
watching enigmatically. Knollys was still speaking to his
servant in a confidential mutter. Gil thought he had caught
another name: 'Bid him and John Carson . . .' He had heard
these names before, in the same muttered tone. And why,
he wondered, should getting a message to them be important enough to discuss before the King?

A velvet-clad servant with the King's badge on his chest

appeared at his elbow, the King dismissed them, and they were both spirited out into the wet night where the gate-guards peered from under the vault of the gatehouse like deer in a forest. Morison seemed dumbstruck, floating along at Gil's side staring at the torches, the people, the castle walls, as if he had never seen such things before.

Why, Gil thought now, striding down the High Street, does my mind keep running on hunting? Is it because I am being followed? He turned his head from side to side, trying to see over his shoulders, but although the shadows beyond the pool of wet torchlight in which they moved were black and jumpy he could not focus any of his unease in them.

'Nobody will try anything on six men, maister,' said one of the two at his back, 'and four of them in the King's livery.'

'That's a true word,' agreed the left-hand torchbearer.

As he spoke, a group emerged from a vennel just ahead of them. Gil, bracing himself, was aware of sudden tension round him. Morison stared apprehensively. Four men with a lantern which gleamed on a selection of ill-fitting armour stared back at them in alarm; then one of them took a better grip on his cudgel and said firmly, 'Who goes there, in the name of the King?'

'It's the Watch,' said Gil in relief.

The right-hand torchbearer was already answering: 'The King's men, about the King's business.'

The man with the lantern came closer, with his fellows straggling after him as if they would rather not be left in the dark. Gil could not recognize the men in this light, but felt it to be unlikely that any of them was a burgess. Most people sent a servant or other substitute when their turn to guard the burgh through the night came round. The lantern dwindled against the torchlight, which clearly showed the royal badge on cloak and velvet surcoat. Two of the Watch nodded.

'Aye, Geordie, that's the King's badge,' said one of them. 'They're likely from the castle.'

'They'll be seeing these fellows to their doors,' said another. 'And I hope neither of their women's lying awake for them, for they'll get a warm welcome, coming in at this hour o the night.'

'Wheesht, Jaik!' said the fourth man in a hissing whisper. 'That's Maister Morison. Him that found a heidit man in a barrel.'

'Oh, aye, so it is,' agreed Jaik in the same tone. 'They must ha let him off wi it.'

'On ye go, then, King's men,' said the one who had challenged them. 'And a peaceful night to ye, maisters.'

'And the same to yersels, neighbour,' said the torch-bearer, and they moved on. The Watch plodded past them and on up the hill. After a little Gil found the feeling of being followed had dissipated, though he still felt on edge, as if the hunt was only on the next hillside.

At the gate to Morison's yard he halted. Beside him Morison reached out and touched the heavy planks caressingly.

'This is the place,' Gil said to their escort.

'We'll see you through the gate, maisters,' said the left-hand torchbearer in a strong Stirling accent. 'Is it barred, maybe? Will you need to rouse the house?'

Gil leaned on a leaf of the gate, and it swung easily, as before. Bait? he wondered. Or has there been trouble?

He peered inside, but there was no movement in the yard. There was light at the house windows, and his sister's voice came faintly, making Morison turn his head to listen. The moon slid out from behind a cloud and lit the open expanse between gate and door, silvering the wet edge of the fore-stair. Nothing there. Why do I still feel I'm being watched?

'All quiet?' said the torchbearer.

'I think so,' Gil said, a little reluctantly, and reached for his purse. 'Thanks for your time, fellows. You can get up the road and into the dry.'

The group, suitably rewarded, stepped back and waited while he drew Morison in and barred the gate. He heard them tramp off up the High Street and turned towards the house. The door was open, though nobody was visible. The back of his neck prickled. Drawing his whinger, catching his plaid round the other arm, he took Morison's elbow and moved forward through the moonlit rain, two steps, three.

The creak of the gate warned him, in the same moment as a quiet voice from the house said, 'Behind you.'

Heart thumping, he straightened his left arm, pushing the unarmed Morison sharply towards the house, and sidestepped, sword at the ready, turning towards the rush of footsteps.

One figure was approaching from the gate, another leaping down from it as he looked. The nearest had a weapon raised against the dark sky, which he knocked spinning across the yard with a sweeping blow. Wood clattered on the flagstones, and there was time to think, This has happened before, and also, This is quite ridiculous.

The other man seemed at first to have huge black wings, but as Gil ducked away, shouting, they turned into great folds of cloth which brushed across his arm. He dodged sideways and snatched out his dagger, then braced himself, the two blades poised to attack, and several more figures emerged from the shadows as if in answer.

'Aye, Maister Gil!' said one of them in Andy's voice, and bent to seize the cudgel as it rolled across the yard. The man who had wielded it tripped over his stooping form, knocking him flat, stumbled over him and ran cursing for the gate, closely pursued by two more of the shadowy figures. The other assailant was struggling with someone, but a dark shape which could only be Babb loomed over the conflict and pounced; there was a startled yelp, and in the same moment a thump and rattle from next to the gate, an outcry, and then a long-drawn-out sliding, slithering crash.

Someone groaned.

'Well done!' said Kate from the house door. The whole thing had taken only a few heartbeats.

271

'Christ and his saints preserve us!' said Andy's voice. Gil, peering round, placed the small man, just climbing to his feet. 'Have we got them, then?'

'Well, that was a welcome,' said Morison from the darkness, sounding more alert than he had for the past hour.

'Maister?' said Andy, and started forward.

'Augie?' said Kate from the door. Morison turned and moved towards her.

'What the deil's name's goin on out there?' bellowed a voice from overhead. Gil looked up, and saw Maister Morison's neighbour leaning out of an upper window, his linen nightcap pale in a brief gleam of moonlight. 'Is it more thieves in the yard there?'

'Aye, Maister Hamilton, it's thieves,' answered Andy. From under the thatch of Morison's house came a child's wail.

'Ye'll need to put up a sign for them,' said Maister Hamilton in disgust, 'then they can just come in quiet-like. Call the Watch, man, and let's us get our sleep.'

'We've got this one,' said Babb, shaking her catch.

'We have this one also,' said Alys from the shadows by the gate, 'but I think he is hurt.'

'Alys!' said Gil. 'Alys, what are you –?'

He sheathed his blades and hurried over. She was bending over two shapes, which as the moon came out again resolved into a kneeling man with a knife at the throat of a recumbent one. The light slid on the glazed rims of countless tumbled pots and dishes which surrounded them. The recumbent man groaned again. Under the roof the child was still wailing.

'The rack fell,' Alys said. 'All these crocks landed on him. Gil, was that Maister Morison?'

'Come on, man,' said the one kneeling. 'Get on your feet.'

'I canny,' said the recumbent man with difficulty. 'I'm hurt. I'm hurt bad.'

'Let's get him in the house,' Gil said, 'and the other one, and see how bad it is. Andy, is there a hurdle we can put him on?'

'Aye, do that,' shouted Maister Hamilton, 'and be quiet about it!'

'What's to do?' demanded another voice, from somewhere across the street.

'Thieves at Augie's yard,' responded Hamilton. A dog started barking, and another answered it. 'They should call the Watch, and let the rest of the town get some sleep.'

'I'm right sorry, Andro,' began Morison, from the fore-stair.

'Augie! Is that you let loose, man? Did they let you off, then?'

To an accompaniment of mixed congratulation and heckling from neighbours and dogs, the injured man was heaved groaning on to a wicker hurdle and carried indoors. Morison issued a general invitation for the morning and went in, Babb's prisoner was dragged in after him, and for a precious moment, as windows slammed shut to one side and another, Gil was alone in the yard with his betrothed.

'Alys, are you all right?' he said in soft French, and reached out to her. She came willingly to his embrace, and he drew her close, relishing the feel under his hands of the warm curves he had glimpsed earlier.

'Of course,' she replied. 'Why should I not be? That was exciting.'

He stared down at the pale outline of her face in the moonlight, struck yet again by her power to astonish him.

'Perhaps I should teach you to use a sword,' he said, and kissed her.

'I should like that,' she said hopefully after a moment, leaning against him. 'We ought to go in, Gil. These men must be questioned. And was that really Maister Morison? Is he free?'

'Soon,' he said, and kissed her again. 'Oh, I have missed you. *Nas never pyke wallowed in galantyne As I in love am wallowed and ywounde.*'

'And I have missed you, *trewe Tristram the secounde,*' she said, capping the quotation, and kissed him back.

When they finally went into the brightly lit hall, Kate was seated rather stiffly in Morison's great chair, Morison himself on his knees beside her with his arms full of two small girls. Gil looked at his sister's expression and found his mind going back to an older poem than the Chaucer he had just quoted to Alys: *Yern he biheld hir, and sche him eke, Ac noither to other a word no speke.* The two captives were before them in the centre of the hall. Babb still had a punishing grasp of the man in the cloak, but it was evident that the other was unlikely to run far. Alys went forward and knelt beside him, and he opened his eyes.

'A priest,' he moaned. 'I need a priest.'

'You'll tell us what you were after in this house first,' said Andy fiercely.

'I'm deein!'

'Is he?' asked Kate.

'Probably not,' said Alys judiciously, 'but there are broken bones. Several ribs at the least.' The prisoner yelped as she felt carefully at his chest. The hurdle creaked under him, and Gil caught his breath, transported for a moment to the moonlit pinnacles of Roslin. 'And maybe some bruising to his insides also,' Alys finished. She passed her hands cautiously round the man's black felt coif, without eliciting a reaction, and rose to her feet.

Gil studied the man. He was wearing a sturdy leather jack, and there was a sheath at his belt for the whinger which Andy had brought in from the yard. His hair showed under the edges of the coif, dark round the collar of the jack, a white tuft sticking sweatily to his brow.

'I'm deein, I tell ye,' croaked the prisoner. 'Fetch me a priest.'

'But what was going on?' asked Morison. 'Why were these fellows in our yard?' He looked down at his daughters. 'My poppets, you must go back to your bed now. Da will still be here in the morning.' Ysonde, her hands clamped on the facings of his gown, said something muffled into his shoulder. 'What's that, my honey?'

'She said you'd get your head cut off.'

'Well, I haveny. See, it's still fastened on.'

'She said the man wi the axe would cut it off.'

'The man with the axe is dead,' said Gil firmly. The man Babb held looked round quickly, dismay in his expression, but the other prisoner closed his eyes again and the crease deepened between his brows.

'Who said that to you, Ysonde?' Morison asked in concern.

'I'll wager it was Mall,' said Kate, breaking a long silence. 'She said a few things I'd like to skelp her for, before she left. Wynliane, Ysonde, you must go back to bed now. Da will be here in the morning.'

'No,' said Wynliane. Morison looked quickly down at her, then at Kate, his eyes wide. She nodded, smiling slightly, and he swallowed and turned back to the children.

'I have to talk, down here, poppets,' he said. 'I'll come up to you once you're in your bed.'

'No,' said Wynliane.

Ysonde's grip tightened on her father's gown. Gil thought Morison's clasp on the girls tightened in response. His sister must have seen it too, for she said, 'Oh, let them stay, Augie. Nan, their father will bring them up when he can.' Nan, waiting quietly in the stair doorway, bobbed to the company and withdrew. Kate looked at Morison again. 'Our Lady guard you, man, sit down properly, then Gil and Alys can sit down too. Andy, bring the settle forward for him – no, there.'

Andy obeyed, and Morison rose, slightly impeded by his satellites, and sat down opposite Kate. Settling the children on either side of him, he stared round the room and said, 'Were you looking for these fellows, Andy? Were you expecting an inbreak?'

'Aye, we were,' said Babb happily. 'We were looking for them to come for this treasure that's never been here. And we were right.'

'You set the watch as you intended, then?' said Gil.

'Not quite,' admitted Kate.

'Watch?' said Morison. 'I thought it was all over. What need of a watch?'

'You can see what need. It's not over yet,' Kate pointed out.

Gil, seating Alys on a backstool, said, 'Are you saying these are the two who were seen in the Hog earlier this week? Let that one go, Babb, so he can answer our questions.'

'Aye, that's right,' agreed the man who had helped Alys. 'And I'd a word wi them the night and all. Tellt them all about how the maister keeps a locked kist at the foot o the great bed in the chaumer there.' He grinned. 'I never tellt them about the watch in the yard, did I, you gangrel thieves.'

'That's very interesting,' said Gil, looking closely from one to the other. 'I last saw these two on the Pentlands yesterday sometime after noon, pelting downhill with Socrates on their heels. And before that there was a matter of a dead pig above Linlithgow. The biter's been bit,' he said agreeably. Most of his hearers looked blank, but the man on the hurdle closed his eyes and groaned.

'I never!' said the standing prisoner. 'It wasny me. I've been in Glasgow the whole time. So's he.' He jerked his head at the man on the hurdle.

'A pity Socrates is not here,' said Alys. 'Where did you leave him? We could see if he knows them.'

'Ye've no need to set a great hound on us,' said the standing prisoner apprehensively. Gil raised an eyebrow, and the man swallowed, realizing what he had given away. 'It wasny us,' he repeated.

'He cutted the pig's head off wi his sword,' said a small voice from within Morison's gown. He lifted his arm and looked down; Ysonde blinked back at him.

'You were dreaming, my poppet,' he said indulgently. 'Go back to sleep. The man hasn't got a sword.'

'Does too. He had a sword this morning.' She pointed at the standing prisoner. 'When he looked in our gate, but Nan and me told him to go away and he went.'

'You see!' said Babb's prisoner. 'The bairn kens! We've been here the whole time.'

'So you were poking round here earlier, were you?' demanded Andy, and the man swallowed again.

'Which of you is John Carson?' Gil asked. Alys looked round at him. The recumbent man opened his eyes, but the other one made no move. 'So you must be Davie Wilkie,' he went on. The man still did not move, but Gil saw the faint stirring of his cloak as his shoulders tensed. 'You had a hat with a feather in it yesterday,' he said conversationally. 'I suppose it must have fallen off, somewhere between the Pentlands and here.'

'It could be out in the yard,' said Morison, still trying to follow the exchange.

Gil nodded. 'It could. And Carson there gets called Baldy,' he went on.

'He's no bald,' said the man nearest the hurdle. 'See, he's got more hair than Andy there. It's all sticking out the back o his coif.'

'You stay out o this, Ecky Soutar,' growled Andy.

'It's sticking out the brow of his coif too,' said Gil. 'Take it off for him, Ecky, will you.'

Ecky obliged, despite the injured man's feeble attempts to push his hands away. The coif came away, revealing damp hair flattened to the man's skull, dark in the candle-light except for the sharp-edged streak of white hair which grew forward over his forehead.

'And that,' said Gil, 'is why he's called Baldy, like a horse. Not because he's called Archibald, and not because he's bald, but because he's got a white blaze.'

'What does that mean?' asked Morison.

'It means we've made the two ends of the circle join up,' said Gil. 'Would you send someone to call the Watch, Augie? These fellows should be put somewhere safe for the night, what's left of it.'

Only a royal summons would have got Gil out of his own

bed in the attic in Rottenrow before Nones. As it was, despite a cold wash, a shave and a meal of bannocks still warm from the girdle, he felt as if he would rather sleep for another week than plod down to the caichpele with the long spoon-shaped racket over his shoulder to play tennis with his monarch.

It had been more than an hour after the Watch were summoned, before he could leave the lower town and head for home. He had had to explain to the Watch why these dangerous miscreants should be held in the Tolbooth rather than the castle, without letting them suspect that in the castle he feared Wilkie, at least, would find himself free as the Axeman had. Then, once the reluctant procession had left, supplemented by two of Augie's fellows to keep the Watch safe as far as the Tolbooth, he had attempted to persuade Alys and his sister to go home.

'Catherine will long since have had the door barred,' said Alys. 'No, no, I can very well share a bed with Kate and Babb.'

'But Kate will go back to Rottenrow, surely,' he said.

'Not me,' said Kate firmly. 'I'll not leave without saying farewell to those bairns.' Her eyes rose to the ceiling, where Morison's voice could be heard quietly from the floor above. Alys gave Gil another of her significant glances, and shook her head.

'Leave them,' said Morison, when he had persuaded his daughters to sleep. 'I'll be glad of the company, Gil, to tell truth.'

'Do you want someone else to watch?' Gil asked quickly, but Morison shook his head.

'No, no. That's no the difficulty. I just – I just – it's good to have friends round me,' he achieved, 'and you have to go back up the hill, if you're to be at the caichpele betimes. And if Mistress Mason's to stay and all,' he added, 'then all's decent. The two of them and Babb will be down here in the chamber yonder,' he nodded at the inner door from the hall, 'where they can bar the door for privacy, and the men are out in the bothy, and I'm above-stairs within call.' He glanced at the ceiling-boards, as Kate had done.

'I've no doubt of that,' said Gil, who had not thought about it. 'I just thought it might be imposing on the household.'

'Considering what she's – they've done for me,' said Morison, 'I'd say the imposing goes all the other way. Leave them here. They're more than welcome.'

Now, before Terce, the first beasts of the baggage-train were already making their way down the High Street to cross the river and head south for Kilmarnock. Behind them, arguments, bustle and French curses floated over the castle walls. Across the Wyndhead and into the Drygate, Gil turned up the pend which led to the high wooden walls of the caichpele. There was obviously a game in progress already: he could hear the irregular thud of the ball against the planks, and the occasional spatter of applause.

The door was guarded by two men in royal livery, who let him pass when he gave his name. Within, the near gallery was crowded. Another royal servant greeted him, ushered him into the other gallery, where only two men stood at the far end, their heads together: Angus and his brother-in-law, Boyd of Naristoun. They looked up and nodded to him as he entered, acknowledged his brief bow, went back to their conversation. Gil leaned on the window, watching the play. The young King was serving, his back to them, and Archie Boyd's brother Sandy was at the hazard end.

'Still don't like it,' said Sandy's kinsman emphatically at the far end of the gallery.

'Archie, it might no happen,' soothed Angus. 'They'll maybe no take to one another. She's got every chance to turn him down.'

'What, turn down her –'

'Wheesht, Archie!'

'And what does that do to us all,' Boyd went on, soft but still indignant, 'if he pursues her and she sends him off?'

279

'We find another one,' said Angus. 'I'd fly my own Marion at him, but she's handfasted wi Kilmaurs. Your lassie's the only other in the close kin that's the right age for him, but we can try one of the older lassies if we have to.'

Well, well, thought Gil. The players had changed ends, and Sandy Boyd served, putting a spin on the ball that dropped it off the other wall on to the smooth-packed floor before the King could get to it. The scorer called numbers.

'It might no work.'

Angus made an impatient noise. 'Christ save us, he's a Stewart. Ye have to feed his appetites. He'd lose the Honours of Scotland at the cards, or any other game ye name, gin he were left to play unwatched, and as for the other, he's quite old enough to slip out and pass himself off as second sackbut in the burgh band, only to get closer to some trollop he's taken a notion to. We have to set him on to a lassie we can trust, for his first. And we have to distract him, Archie. He's taking altogether too much interest in the business of running the country, and he doesny understand it all yet. You saw him last night.'

'Mind you,' said Naristoun thoughtfully, 'that might pay off.'

'Wheesht, Archie.'

Sandy Boyd served again, and this time the King was ready for him, or perhaps Sandy put the ball where the King would be ready. There was a chase, the ball bandied back and forth across the net, which ended in a point for the King, and applause from the other gallery under the pent as the two players shook hands. His grace had won the set and, it seemed, the match.

Acknowledging the applause, James stripped off his doublet and threw it to a ready servant, accepted a wet towel from another and a goblet from a third. A clerk approached him with some documents, another with a quiet message, and he looked about.

'Maister Cunningham?' he called. 'What about that game you promised me? Aye, Sandy, a good match. You're

280

a strong player, sir. Give me five minutes, maister, to deal with these papers, and we'll have a fresh ball and begin.'

Gil, stripping off gown and doublet in his turn, stepped out on to the court and bowed to his opponent.

It was an excellent game. The King, as he had seen while watching from the gallery, was a vigorous player with a sound grasp of the strategies. He was also in good practice. Gil, willing to play with tact, found he had no need to do so. He was faster, and had a longer reach; the King had a stronger stroke, and the ball they were chasing was from his own box. Set by set, the match went the full eleven, and by the time the King took the final point both men were stripped to the waist, shining with sweat, hair plastered to their faces.

'And the match point!' called the scorekeeper, with what sounded to Gil like relief. 'The King's grace takes the match.'

There was another patter of applause. Gil lowered his racket and found himself grinning at his opponent, the involuntary response to a rewarding game.

'St James's staff and shells!' said the King. He met Gil's grin with one of his own, and threw his racket to yet another servant. 'What a chase, that last set. Maister Cunningham, we'll ha another game the next time I come through Glasgow, or my name's no James Stewart.' He offered Gil his hand, and used the clasp to draw him under the net to his side. 'I thought you looked like a good player, man. Come and wash.'

He led him towards the service gallery, where Angus and the Boyds still watched. The blue-liveried servants came forward with wet towels, a folding table, goblets, a tray of biscuits, and retired again. James handed Gil a towel, mopped happily at his neck and chest, then said, with another grin, 'Dicht my back for me, Maister Cunningham, and then I'll do yours.'

'Yes, sir,' said Gil inadequately, trying to conceal amazement. James turned, peering into the shade of the gallery. His back was lean, well muscled, decorated here and there

281

with spots. The chain belt showed at his waist above the top of his hose. Gil wadded his own towel and wiped hesitantly at the royal hide.

'Harder, man,' commanded the King. 'You'll never shift the salt playing pat-a-cake like that. Aye, that's better. Now, while we're not to be interrupted,' he said, staring direct at the three men in the gallery, 'tell me what you didn't tell me yestreen.'

Gil froze for a moment, then continued rubbing at the King's shoulders.

'How much of it, sir? There's a fair bit.'

'Let's have the kernel of it. Some of my late father's hoard,' he crossed himself, and his other hand strayed involuntarily to the iron chain at his waist, 'was being moved about the country, and it seemed to me someone was trying to thieve it on its way. Am I right?'

'Yes, sir,' said Gil again. 'There was also some part of what may have been a loan from the Knights of St John. It was still in the sacks, with the seals on. I would say his late grace never saw it.'

'And if my father never kent it was there,' said James, leaning back against Gil's ministrations, 'and it could be stolen away, whoever got it could write it down sheer profit.'

'I think so, sir.'

'Who?'

'I would say you've guessed, sir.'

'Aye, but guesses are no proof. Have you proof, maister? Let's hear it.'

'I have,' said Gil. He gave as compressed a summary as he might of the successive attempts to intercept the search for the identity of the dead man and the remainder of his load. The King listened intently; halfway through, without interrupting, he turned, gestured to Gil to turn his back, and twisting his own towel into a rope began rubbing Gil down as if he were a horse. The three watchers in the gallery never stirred.

'And these two you took last night,' said the King when

Gil finished his tale, 'that the Watch have put in the Tol-booth for you, are the same as attacked you along with the axeman on the Pentlands, and have been seen with him in Glasgow.' Gil nodded. 'Body of Christ, the road from here to Edinburgh must be smoking by now. Even at this time of year with the long days, it's a hard ride across Scotland. And how much have they admitted, maister?'

'Unless the Watch got anything from them,' said Gil, 'not even their names, though I know what those are, and the injured man at least is linked to –'

'Ah!' said the King, and paused. 'I suppose he could still deny it.'

'No matter, sir,' said Angus from the shadows. 'If we tell him they're taken –'

'Aye, and ask for his seals. We'll have both off him, my lord Angus, before we leave Glasgow. The Treasurer's seal and the Comptroller's both.'

'And gladly, sir,' said Angus emphatically. 'Bring them to you, will I?'

'Aye, for we'll need to discuss who gets them next. But first,' said James, as a thought struck him, 'I want enough coin off him for two–three days. Including,' he slapped Gil on the shoulder quite as if he were a horse, 'there you are, maister, you're done, including two, no, three purses for this morning. You know the sort of thing, my lord.'

Chapter Fourteen

'This curst litter is full of boulders,' complained Maistre Pierre.

'We're nearly at Glasgow now,' said Gil, hiding a grin. 'You'll be home in an hour or two, and then you can lie in your own bed.'

He looked over his shoulder at the small cavalcade of their baggage and the escort Sinclair had provided. It had taken them two days to travel from Roslin, and Maistre Pierre had grumbled most of the way, about the horse he was expected to ride, about the litter which he did not need, about not having found a barber in Roslin, or about any other subject which came to mind. Clearly, the ten or twelve days he had spent being nursed by Mistress Robison had done little for his temper.

'Why should I wish to lie in any bed?'

'I've sent Luke on ahead,' Gil said, ignoring this, 'to warn the two households. I thought my uncle and Kate should know we're near home, as well as Alys.'

'And what if they don't wish to know?'

'And I need to get a word with Augie,' Gil added. 'He was wanting to speak to me the day I left, but Robert Blacader was back in Glasgow and sent for me, and there was no time.'

'Tell me again what his lordship said.'

'I'm attached to his retinue,' said Gil. 'It's a formal appointment, with the title of Quaestor, and a benefice attached.' He grinned. 'Somewhere in Argyll. Not one of the fat ones, of course, no manse in the Chanonry or seat in Chapter, but still it's a benefice, with enough to pay a vicar and still have a bit income.'

'And the duties of this appointment?'

'I've to do more or less what we've been doing. Look into any case of secret murder within the diocese, or maybe the entire Archdiocese, I wasn't quite sure which he meant. Go where his lordship sends me, I suppose. Report to him, find justice for the dead.'

'A wide remit,' said Maistre Pierre doubtfully. 'And when you are not so employed?'

Gil shrugged, and steered his horse round a pothole in the road. 'I'll have to wait and see if Blacader wants me at his side or not. If not, then I can live in Glasgow and set up as a notary, fetch in a little more money.'

'So we may set a date for your marriage.'

'Yes,' said Gil with satisfaction. *I long for the wedding*, he thought. The lute tune sprang into his head, and with it the image of the three lutenists in Stirling bent together over their instruments, passing not that melody but its companion from one to another, runs and trills and doubling passages thickening the texture, while McIan sat in his great chair clasping his harp and listening intently. *All will be well*, he had said, and it was.

'Does Alys know?'

'I took the time to go by the house and tell her before I left Glasgow. When I came away she was considering the dry stores. She seemed to feel there were not enough almonds in Glasgow for her purpose.'

'More than likely. I suppose she will want a second fine gown to be married in,' said her father, with spurious resignation. 'Black brocade is likely too sombre.'

They went on in silence for a while, past Garrowhill and Springboig. Maistre Pierre lay back among the cushions which supported him, staring at the swaying roof of the litter. The escort started an argument about a battle a few of them had been in, which someone tried to settle by singing a ballad in High Dutch. Gil thought of Rob, and then of Johan.

'Will you stay in Scotland now?' he asked.

Maistre Pierre turned his head to meet his eyes. 'Why ever not?'

'I wondered,' said Gil deliberately, 'if your task was now over.'

The mason considered him for a short time, then grinned without humour.

'Well, I liked you for Alys because your mind is at least as good as hers, so I should not be surprised. No, my task is not over, Gilbert. That was only a part of it.'

'So you remain in Scotland.'

'I do.'

'Good,' said Gil lightly.

'What brought it to your notice? I suppose I have been clumsy.'

'I've been in the church at Brinay. While I was in Paris I had a friend came from near there.'

'Now that I would never have expected. I have not, as you may have guessed.'

'I wondered,' said Gil. 'My friend took me down to his father's home for a week's hunting one spring, and we went over to look at the church.'

'Ah,' said Maistre Pierre.

'It's a tiny building, with a truly astonishing set of wall-paintings,' Gil went on, 'well worth the ride over there, but not a pillar to its name.'

'So naturally you began to pay attention to such remarks.'

'The more so as de Brinay himself didn't correct you.'

The litter swayed on. Behind them, the escort had moved on to drinking songs. Their repertoire seemed to be considerable.

'I am able to tell you very little,' said Maistre Pierre at length. 'The facts are not mine to reveal.'

'That doesn't concern me,' said Gil. 'You wouldn't reveal the inmost secrets of the mason's craft either.' They looked at each other again. A small smile flickered in the depths of the mason's untrimmed beard, the first time Gil had ever seen that trait of Alys's in him. 'No, what I would like is an assurance that you do not act to the detriment of my country.'

The litter lurched as one of the horses put its foot in a rut. Its passenger exclaimed sharply. Gil put a quick hand to the roof of the structure, but the animal recovered, and the litter swayed on.

'At present,' said Maistre Pierre after a little, 'I am not acting, nor am I asked to act, to the detriment or danger of Scotland. France is an ally of Scotland,' he pointed out.

'But you aren't acting for France,' said Gil.

'I am not acting against your country, Gilbert. I will swear it on anything you choose.'

'Your word will do me.' Gil studied his friend a moment longer, then reached down, and they shook hands. 'What does it do to Alys's status?'

'Nothing. I was lawfully wedded to her mother, Christ assoil her, and can you doubt that she is my daughter?'

'No,' admitted Gil, and grinned again, thinking of the strong resemblance between the two. 'Not that it would trouble me,' he added, 'but there are legal considerations.' He looked about him. 'Have we passed Carntyne already? We must be less than two miles from home.'

Kate Cunningham, sitting in the arbour in her uncle's garden where it seemed to her it had all begun, stared out over the lower town and thought bleakly of her future.

There was really, she thought, very little about it that was positive. Less than three weeks since, on the morning after her failed petition to St Mungo, Alys had said to her, *What has changed?* and she had said, *All my hopes are away.* In taking brief charge of Augie Morison's house and children, she had found first distraction and then, like green shoots in the snow, a new hope. But the buds, it seemed, were frost-bitten and would not flower. What a literary metaphor, she thought bitterly. Worthy of Augie Morison himself. Better with Chaucer: *Love hath my name ystrike out of his sclat.*

The last good moment she could think of had been when the King's procession paused outside Morison's yard, on its way out of Glasgow on the Sunday morning, the day after Augie – after Maister Morison had been freed. Alerted by a servant in blue velvet, the entire household had been out at the gate, herself and Alys on either side of Morison, the men around them, Nan and Babb with the little girls at the back of the group. The King, glowing in blue satin and black velvet, his chestnut hair combed down over his shoulders, a gold chain with a sapphire jewel gleaming on his chest, had halted his dappled horse as everyone round Kate bent the knee.

'Maister Morison,' he had said. 'I hope you found all in order when you got home.'

'Y-yes, sir,' managed Morison, straightening up, and he stepped forward in response to the King's beckoning hand.

'You lie, maister, you lie,' said James in great good humour. 'You mind, I've had a game of caich with Maister Cunningham this morning. I've heard about last night's inbreak, just as you got to your own gates. Two of my lord St Johns' men,' he said, audible to all the neighbours, 'taken in the act of housebreaking by the women of the household. I've thanked Maister Cunningham already, and I thank you now, maister, for your help in righting more than one great wrong these last few days.'

Morison bowed and stammered inarticulately. James drew the gold chain with its sapphire over his head and leaned gracefully down from the saddle. He must have practised that, thought Kate, watching.

'A small token,' said the King, setting the chain about Morison's neck. As Augie, extinguished with amazement, backed away, James looked beyond him and called Kate and Alys forward.

Kate could hardly remember what he had said first, except for a teasing remark about Alys's wisdom which had sent the younger girl's chin up. There had been an exchange of sorts, and then the King had said seriously, 'Scotland needs folk wi courage and a love of justice, ladies, and if the women of Scotland have such attributes as well as her men, we'll breed sturdier sons to defend this realm. I'm proud to have such as you among my subjects.'

Rhetoric, thought Kate, is a royal study.

'Now, I hope you'll divide this among the folk of the household,' he tossed a fat purse to Morison, who caught it at the last moment as his men grinned hopefully, 'and here's another wee token for the two of you ladies and all.'

Then there had been a heavy purse of red velvet in her hands, she had bowed her head, Alys was curtsying to the ground with another such purse clasped in the crook of her arm. The King's voice above her head bade them *Good day*, his horse wheeled and set off down the High Street, and the procession clattered after it.

There was a hundred merks in the red velvet purse. Apart from the heap of coin which Morison and Maister Mason had counted on the majolica plate across the grass here, it was more money than Kate had seen together since her father's death. If she had ever had any prospects of marriage, it would make a tocher, she thought. Or maybe she could buy a bit of land with it, rent it out, get some income that way. What point was there? she thought wearily.

'Are you ready, my doo?' said Babb now at her elbow.

'Ready?'

'We're to go down the hill. Maister Mason cam home yesternight −'

'I know that,' she said impatiently.

'And we're all bidden to his house the day. Maister Gil told you yestreen, for I heard him.'

'So he did,' she said. He had also told her, grinning like an ape, that he would be able to set a date for his wedding. She had heard the news from Alys already, and listened to her for three days while he was away thinking aloud about

289

her plans; she had smiled, at both of them, and said the right things.

'Come on, lassie, Maister David's waiting,' said Babb, with rough tenderness. 'Do you good to get out. Mistress Mason's company's no that bad. Come on,' she coaxed.

'I saw Mistress Mason yesterday,' said Kate. But she allowed Babb to hoist her upright, accepted her crutches, and clumped into the stable-yard where her mule waited for her. He turned as he heard her approach, and whuffled at her, nuzzling hopefully at her hand when she stroked his face.

'Aye, Kate,' said her uncle, stepping out at the house door as Babb led the mule round from the stable-yard. 'Are we to get the whole tale of what happened now, do you suppose? Now that you and your brother and Peter Mason can each tell us a chapter?'

'I never thought of that,' she admitted. 'There's not been the time to fit it together, has there, what with Gil taking Alys to Roslin last week to see how her father did, and then going back this week to fetch him home. Aye, you could be right, sir.'

'Good,' said Canon Cunningham, striding out beside her towards the Wyndhead. 'For I canny make sense of the half of it I've heard.'

Away down the High Street, dismounting before the mason's house, Kate tried hard not to glance at the gates of Morison's yard four doors away. Babb was less inhibited.

'They've painted that yett, I see,' she said as Wallace was led away. 'Matt was saying they were working on the yard. So I should hope, the work we put in to redd it up. Matt tells me they've been building and all,' she added, in the face of her mistress's indifference. 'He's put new glass windows into hall and chambers, so he says, and sent all the hangings to be cleaned, and hired two new lassies that Matt says'll no last long what wi Ursel and Nan wanting them to work harder than they like.'

'It aye surprises me,' said Kate acidly, 'how much Matt

290

can tell you of other folk's business, considering how little he ever says.'

'Aye but,' said Babb cheerfully, following her into the pend and missing the point of her remark, 'he's Maister David's man. He's bound to take an interest in other folk's business. And those bairns are doing well wi Nan, he says.'

'He would say that,' said Kate, making her way across the courtyard between the bright tubs of flowers.

'Aye, likely. Mind you the wee one's as wild as ever, but the dumb one's chattering away now, it seems, and their faither's trying to learn them a wee poem. Did you ever hear the like? Can you do that stair the day, do you think, or will I lift you, my doo?'

Canon Cunningham was already within doors, seated beside Catherine near the hearth with its bowl of flowers and congratulating Maistre Pierre on his return home. He looked round as Kate found her balance, took her crutches from Babb and thumped into the hall from the fore-stair. Socrates paced over to greet her, his claws clicking on the polished boards.

'Aye, here's my niece. Our friend looks well, doesn't he, Kate, for someone whose life was saved by a lute-string?'

'We have prayed for him,' said Catherine in French. Kate caught sight of Alys, beyond her father's chair, biting her lip and crossing herself.

'We won't think about that now, sir,' she suggested, and came forward when Maistre Pierre waved her to a seat. Socrates sat down with his chin on her knee, and she stroked his head. 'Did you ever get a look at the church at Roslin by daylight, Maister Mason? It was still building when I visited there, and they would never let me look close at it.'

'Indeed aye,' exclaimed her uncle, accepting a glass of Alys's cowslip wine. 'I've seen it once, but that was a good while since. Is that right they've stopped the building at the crossing? What kind of a roof have they put on it?'

Alys flinched again. Kate took the proffered glass and drew the other girl down on the settle beside her.

'Let them talk,' she advised. 'No good ever came of making them bite their tongues.' Alys nodded, pulling a face of resignation. 'Where has my brother got to?'

'He was here earlier, but he went out,' said Alys vaguely. 'He had an errand of some sort in the town.'

'How is your father? He looks well enough.'

'Tired from the journey. He may not dine with us, if I can persuade him –'

'Small chance, I would say.'

'Likely. But the wound is well mended.' She shivered. 'I've always feared a fall from scaffolding for him – I never thought of him meeting a man with an axe up there.'

'It was the Axeman that fell,' said Kate firmly, 'and my brother that pushed him down.'

'He said it was not,' said Alys, her expression softening as she thought of Gil.

Save us from young lovers, thought Kate, but hid her exasperation. 'He confronted Gil, and he fell,' she said. 'So put the Axeman out your head, he's gone now. And falling to his death in a church like that,' she added, 'is a certain judgement.'

'So Catherine says,' admitted Alys. 'I am less convinced.'

'Oh, there's no doubt at all, mistress,' said Babb stoutly from behind Kate. 'A clear judgement on him, for slaying folk behind barred doors and chopping folk's oxter-poles in two.' The door opened, and Socrates scrambled to his feet and hurried forward, his tail wagging furiously. 'Aye, Maister Gil,' added Babb.

Alys jumped up and went to meet Gil. He took her hands and kissed them quickly, and a significant look passed between them before he turned to bow to his uncle, greet Kate, draw a backstool into the circle and sit down.

'Well, you've cast down more than this fellow with the axe, it seems, Gilbert,' pronounced Canon Cunningham. 'Oh, certainly I'll have more of your wine, lassie. I've a letter this morning from Robert Blacader with the details of your appointment, and he tells me my lord St Johns is in some difficulties.'

'He was removed with great suddenness, by what Gil tells me,' said the mason. 'I suppose he had not time to tidy matters as he might have wished.'

'He has certainly been up to some joukery-pokery,' said the Official. 'I wish I could understand his part in what happened his last few days in office.'

'Simple enough, sir,' said Gil. Maistre Pierre rolled his eyes at him. 'Well,' he admitted, 'perhaps not that simple. I think,' he said with care, 'we were pursuing two lots of coin, which were being moved about together. One was part of the old King's hoard, as we thought, and the other was a loan from the Order of St John of Jerusalem to James Third, which I suspect that James never saw. It seems as if Knollys gave both to Sinclair for safe keeping, without telling him what it was, about the time of Stirling field. They were both friends of the old King, after all, it would be natural enough.'

'Ah,' said David Cunningham. 'Instead of using either sum to the King's benefit.'

'Aye. But it seems word has come to the Preceptory from abroad to get the loan money back. Knollys asked Sinclair for it, and Sinclair realized what he held and rather than give it back he decided to move the whole lot, the St Johns money and the King's hoard both, to . . .' Gil hesitated. A strange look crossed his face. Where has he been, Kate wondered, and what has he seen? 'To a place where it would be well protected,' he continued. 'By his account, he wanted to find out more about who was now responsible for the two sums of money. But Knollys, learning it was on the move, decided to seize it anonymously, so to speak.'

'I see,' said the Official. 'If it was thought to be stolen, he might not have to repay it, and in any case he would be able to use the King's jewels to pay the Hospital.'

'Indeed,' agreed Gil. 'Since he could hardly use them as currency anywhere in Scotland. So Wilkie and Carson, and Carson's brother with the axe, attacked the cooper's yard after persuading Billy Walker to leave the gate open for them. But their raid went wrong. The coin was to go in a barrel, to be covered by salt herring, and sent onward to Sinclair's land disguised as part of the quarter's rent. Half the coin had gone into the barrel, the other half was still on the horse, and Knollys's men attacked too soon.'

'How did they know when to attack?' asked Alys.

'Knollys's net was both wide and fine, so I have heard,' said Canon Cunningham.

'In this case,' said Gil, nodding agreement, 'he likely had intelligence from Sinclair's own household. They're looking for a new sub-steward at Roslin, so Pierre tells me.'

'It seems the previous man fell down a stair,' expanded Maistre Pierre.

'So,' Gil returned to his narrative, 'though it was no part of their plan, Carson's brother, who we've seen was very ready to use his axe, killed Nelkin Fletcher.' He hesitated, staring at nothing. Kate wondered what he could see. 'The boy bolted with the horse and the other saddlebag. Wilkie and the two Carsons put the head in the barrel to conceal Nelkin's death, in on top of what they thought was the whole of the treasure –'

'Ah!' said David Cunningham again.

Gil glanced at him, and nodded. 'Then they filled it up with the brine from the vat standing ready, and Billy Walker was induced to seal the barrel for them, being a cooper's son and understanding the craft.'

'And that was what woke the cooper's wife,' said Maistre Pierre. 'No, *ma mie*, no more wine for now.'

'It must have been. Then I think the Axeman simply put the barrel on the wrong cart. His brother has now told us he was left-handed.'

'I knew it!' said Alys triumphantly, and Gil smiled at her where she stood with the flask of cowslip wine.

'Mistress Riddoch looked out just in time to see one of them carrying Nelkin's headless body out of the yard, and I suppose it's still somewhere on the hillside, since there's been no word yet from Linlithgow to say it's been found.'

'As simple as that,' said Canon Cunningham.

'And that was why they were so sure we had the rest of the money,' said Kate.

'They were certainly very persistent,' said Maistre Pierre, 'both here in Glasgow, I gather, and also in the Lothians.'

'Knollys must have been desperate to have the money found,' agreed Gil.

'Quite so. It seems,' David Cunningham reported without expression, accepting more wine from Alys, 'as if there was maybe a wee bit confusion between his own account rolls and the treasury's. He's already posted a string of cases to be heard at Edinburgh about sums owing to him personally, and Robert Blacader thinks there's like to be at least one brought against him by the new Treasurer.'

'*For there is not so much joy in holding high office as there is grief in falling from a high place.* I wonder,' said Gil thoughtfully, 'whether the Preceptory will be involved in those?'

'Probably not,' said his uncle. Maistre Pierre leaned back against the cushions in his great chair and closed his eyes. 'There was a bit of legal bickering a few years since, and its connection was mostly straightened out then. And the loan, of course, is a separate matter and now concluded.'

'And you got your own barrel back,' said Kate.

Gil grinned. 'We did. And there was some rare print in it. I told you that. Another *Blanchflour and Eglantyne*, a very bonny Virgil, the *Sons of Aymon*, a marvellous book on hunting. And –' he exchanged a complicit smile with Alys – 'a betrothal gift.'

'It will come home from the bookbinder's next week,' Alys said. 'Two volumes in red leather, each with our initials on the cover and *Le Morte Darthur* on the spine.'

'And that will be the pair of you,' said Kate, keeping the acid from her voice with difficulty, 'jugged in your books like James the Gentle till you have to emerge for the wedding.'

'Aye, you're well suited,' said Canon Cunningham. 'But we are tiring our friend.'

'No, no,' said the mason, opening his eyes again. 'Far

from it. What were we saying? Are we about to set a date for the marriage?'

'Ah!' said the Official, and Catherine's attention sharpened. Kate hid her hands in her skirts and clenched them tightly, pinning a smile on her face.

'Next week?' said Gil hopefully.

'I thought late November,' said Alys, setting down the flask of wine.

'*November*?'

'It's barely three months hence,' she pointed out, her smile flickering. 'It will take me near that long to order up the dry stores we'll need. We'll want to hold the feast before Advent begins, and by then the Martinmas killing will be past, and there will be fresh meat in plenty. And your sisters will be able to attend.'

'Hmm.'

'Indeed,' said Catherine in her elegant French. 'I understand your next sister is about to become a mother again.'

'Aye,' said Babb, catching the drift of this. 'Margaret, out at Bothwell. She's due in a few weeks, so the word is, and it's her third, it's no likely to be late.'

'So she should be able to travel by then,' Alys said hopefully. 'And if we give Dorothea plenty of notice, she should be able to find an errand for the convent to bring her over on this side of Scotland about the right time.'

And Kate and Tibby will be able to attend any time, thought Kate. No ties, no responsibilities, nobody else to consult.

Gil was laughing. 'You have it all thought out, haven't you? Well, if it can't be next week, it might as well be November.' He reached out and drew Alys close, and she looked down at him. The expression on her face dug to Kate's heart. 'But how I'll last till then, sweetheart, I don't know.'

'There is a deal to be done before then,' said Maistre Pierre. 'If you are to live in the lodgings we picked out over the courtyard yonder, there will be decisions to make,

and work to be commissioned. We have the rooms panelled for you, I think.'

'Well, well,' said the Official. 'So you'll be leaving my
house in late November, then, Gilbert?'

'He's near left it already,' said Kate, and managed to
keep the tart tone out of her voice. 'He's barely been home
all the time I've been staying with you, sir.'

'You must tell me as soon as you've the dates settled,'
went on David Cunningham, acknowledging this with a
quirk of his mouth, 'and I'll bid Fleming keep them clear
of cases. I'd not wish to be tied up in the Consistory tower
while the dancing went on down here.'

'And we must write to your mother with all the news,'
said Alys.

'I shall be glad to renew my acquaintance with *madame
mère*,' said Catherine.

'Which reminds me,' said Canon Cunningham. He
fished in his sleeve for his spectacles. 'I wrote to my good-
sister a few days since, to tell her about the appointment
Robert our Archbishop had offered you, Gilbert, and she
has replied.' He produced a folded sheet from the other
sleeve. 'She's well pleased, sends good wishes now the
marriage can go forward, says she'll write direct to you,
Peter. But here's a thing.' He peered at the tightly written
page. 'She sends that she's heard from her kinswoman
Elizabeth Boyd at Kilmarnock. Angus's countess,' he elucidated. 'It seems the King is still at Kilmarnock too, and like
to be so for some while, for he spends his time with
Elizabeth's niece Marion. Which one's Marion, Gilbert?'

'Archie's older daughter,' Kate supplied. 'I mind her. A
wee plump thing, a bit younger than me. I suppose she's
nineteen by now.'

'She would be,' muttered Gil. What did he mean by
that? Kate wondered.

'Aye. Seems the King's much taken wi her, spends night
and day in her company. Night and day,' he repeated with
relish, 'and can think of naught else.'

'Well, he is a young man,' said Maistre Pierre tolerantly.

297

'So it worked,' said Gil, but did not explain.

'That's the Boyds back in favour,' said Kate. Her voice came out harshly. 'If they've supplied his first mistress, the King'll no forget them.' And even Marion Boyd, plump and giggling, from a family which had seriously offended James Third and suffered for it, would achieve something Kate would not. Whatever else she provided for the King, she had already given him enough to ensure herself a handsome tocher, a good marriage.

'No wonder Robert our Archbishop's fixed at Stirling the now,' mused the Official. 'The Lords in Council can get on with running the country, with no interference from the King's grace.'

'Aye,' said Gil, very drily. He sounds just like the old man, thought Kate.

There was a knocking at the house door. Maistre Pierre turned his head, frowning.

'Who might that be?'

'Are we expecting anyone else?' Alys looked towards the door as one of the maidservants made her way up from the kitchen. 'Who is it, Kittock?'

'I don't just know, mem,' said Kittock, but Kate could hear a laugh in her voice. 'Seeing it's no the season for guizers. Will I let them in?'

Hardly waiting for Alys's consent, she swung the great door open, exclaiming, 'Oh, my, who can this be come visiting?'

Children, then, thought Kate, and unaccountably her heart leapt under her ribs.

Small bare feet pattered on the polished floorboards of the hall. Socrates tensed at Gil's side, growling faintly, and was hushed. Two little winged figures came round the end of the settle into the circle, and paused, gazing in confusion at the number of people present. They wore smocks of white linen, embellished with white ribbons and little knots of daisies; crowns of ribbons and daisies were fastened among their short curls, and each one carried a posy of flowers. The smaller one's wings were on crooked. The dog stared intently at them, the hackles standing up along his narrow back.

Our Lady preserve us, thought Kate, trying her best not to laugh, are they angels or cupids?

'Who is this?' asked Alys.

The smaller figure scowled at her. 'That's not what you say. You've to say,' it struck a pose of amazement, 'Who-are-these-finged-wigures?'

The men laughed, but Kate covered her mouth, straightened her face, and said, 'Who are these winged figures?'

The children looked at each other, visibly counted to three, and recited together, beating time with their posies, *'Nobles, gentles, tender friends, we are here to make amends.'*

'I am Liking,' said the older one in the thread of a voice, while her sister mouthed the words with her.

'I am Love.'

'We are sent by heaven above,' the two little voices went on, *'to bring you thanks for all you've done, and promise heaven's blessing.'*

'And to hope that the sun,' continued the younger one uncertainly, *'will shine on your wedding.'*

'Maybe not in November,' muttered Gil.

They seemed to have come to the end of their verse. Canon Cunningham began to applaud, but Love stamped her bare foot at him.

'Not yet. There's more.'

'Do we have to say anything else?' Kate asked. He must have spent days teaching them that, she thought. He's had this planned for a while.

'*She* has to say Thank you for the blessing,' said Love emphatically. 'And then you get a poetry.'

Alys complied, and Gil echoed her, receiving another scowl for his pains. The two winged figures turned to Kate, counted to three again, and announced:

'Flowers for the bonniest may, wi een of brown and hair of grey –' Behind them Gil snorted with suppressed laughter, and Alys shook her head sternly at him. *'Take these flowers we here presentis, and the heart of him that sent us.'*

They stopped in triumph, and simultaneously held their knots of daisies out to Kate. Canon Cunningham applauded, more confidently, and the mason joined in. Before Kate could take the posies, Love pushed her sister aside.

'No! You can give the other one flowers. I'm giving flowers to our one!'

'No!' said Liking indignantly, showing more spirit than Kate had yet seen in her. 'I'm giving them!'

Between laughing and weeping, Kate covered her eyes with her hand. *And the heart of him that sent us.* Oh, my dear man, she thought. In front of friends and family like this –

'She's greeting,' said Ysonde. Her posy fell to the polished floorboards, and she fled round the end of the settle. 'Da! Da, it's not working. She's greeting!'

Wynliane's flowers joined her sister's, and Wynliane herself leaned against Kate's knee. Her small hand reached urgently to draw Kate's down, and as Morison's heavier tread came forward to join the group she said, almost inaudible, 'Do you no want the flowers? They're bonny.'

'Yes,' said Kate, and smiled into the blue eyes looking up at her. 'I'll take the flowers.'

'I want to give her the flowers!' said Ysonde, hurling herself forward from her father's side.

'No, I will!' Wynliane bent to snatch at the nearest posy. Her sister pushed her aside, shrieking inarticulately. Morison stooped to separate them, making chiding noises.

'I've a better idea,' said Kate over Wynliane's response. They stopped squabbling to look at her. She looked from one to the other, and then up at their father, watching her anxiously over their heads. He was wearing the King's chain. 'Both of you can give one posy to Mistress Mason, because you said her blessing very nicely, and then both of you can give the other posy to me, because I liked the poem you said for me.'

'Did you?' said Morison, as the children picked up one of the posies and advanced on Alys. 'It's no very good poetry.'

She looked down, and used her fingers to ease the tears from her eyes.

'It's the best I ever heard,' she said.

Behind her, Babb blew her nose resoundingly on her sleeve.

'I thought that too,' she said. *'The heart of him that sent us*, it's fair lovely. Will you take him, my doo?'

'Babb!' said Kate indignantly. 'I don't need your help to accept him!'

'I just want to make sure,' said Babb. 'It's the only chance you're like to get, I don't want you to waste it.'

'Are you sure you want me?' said Kate, her head on Morison's shoulder.

It was much later. Love and Liking had been fed little cakes and milk and eventually removed screaming by Nan and Babb. Maistre Pierre, just as weary, had been persuaded to retire after dinner, and Canon Cunningham had gone reluctantly back to his duties at St Mungo's after arranging to meet Morison and his nephew in the morning to discuss Kate's marriage contract. But Catherine still sat upright on the cushioned settle nearest the bowl of flowers in the hearth, her handwork trailing across her black skirts, while on one side of the hall Alys and Gil said almost nothing with their heads together and on the other, now, Augie Morison looked fondly at Kate within the circle of his arm and said, 'I'm very sure.'

'I've a sharp tongue,' she warned him, 'and no tocher but the King's purse.'

'The King's purse is yours, my lass. I'll advise you if you want to venture it, but I'll not lay a finger on it.'

'Oh, I see,' she said. 'You don't want me at all, it's the thought of venturing the King's hundred merks you're taken wi.'

He laughed at that. He's getting the idea of my jokes, she thought.

'Kate, my bonnie Kate, I tell you, *ye ben of my lyf and deth the quene*. It's your sharp tongue and your sharp mind and

301

your sharp courage I want. Wi those for your tocher, I'd take you barefoot in your shift.'

She tilted her head back to look at him, with a sudden recollection of the dream which had seemed like the end of all her hopes. Barefoot in her shift, she had stepped forward when the saint led her. Forward to an unseen, unknown bridegroom. I should have had more trust in him, she thought. He has sent me a miracle.

'You nearly had to,' she said. Morison's mouth quivered, and he turned on the bench beside her and put both arms about her.

'Stop talking,' he said, and bent his head to kiss her. She held him off a moment.

'Don't let me forget, Augie,' she said. 'I owe St Mungo a pound of wax.'

His grip tightened.

'We'll make it five pounds,' he said. 'It's no every day you get a wife wi a King's purse to her tocher.'